Something vaguely familiar about the slim blonde woman struck Joachim.

Catherine! She looks like Catherine! My God! It's a trap! They think they've arrested Catherine.

But they had arrested this woman instead. Who was she? Why was she pretending to be Catherine? Question after question buzzed through Joachim's mind. He unconsciously pressed Catherine's face more deeply into his chest, almost smothering her.

One of the secret policeman pushed the woman into the back seat of the black sedan. The two uniformed men then climbed in back with her, while the plain-clothes man got in front, and the Mercedes gunned its engine as it swiftly made a U-turn heading back towards them. When the car swerved out to avoid the old grey mare and the cart, Catherine twisted her head in time to see what Joachim was watching. Instantly she saw the blonde woman sitting between the two SD officers in the back seat, and when the Mercedes wheeled back close to the curb, she could clearly see her face. Catherine's world exploded.

"*MARLA*!!" The scream tore from her throat as she impulsively reached out to grab her.

To Jack -
Hope you find this novel a good read. Best wishes always. Bonnie

Treason & Triumph

BONNIE TOEWS

Whistler House
TORONTO

Other than using historical events and figures to serve the plot, all circumstances and characters are completely invented. Any names or links to actual persons, either living or dead, are purely accidental or the result of fertile speculation.

Canadian Cataloguing in Publication Data

Toews, Bonnie, 1941-
Treason & triumph

ISBN 0-9697967-1-4

I. Title II. Title: Treason and triumph

PS8589.06346T73 1997 C813'.54 C97-932243-X
PR9199.3.T63T73 1997

First Edition: Printed and bound in Canada.

Cover Design: Eli Vranesic
Editing and Typesetting: Whistler House
Printing and Binding: Webcom Ltd.

WHISTLER HOUSE
16 Innismore Crescent
Scarborough, Ontario
M1R 1C7

OTABIND Otabind (Ota-bind). This book has been bound using the patented Otabind process. You can open this book at any page, gently run your finger down the spine and the pages will lie flat.

Author's Tribute

In life, people come and go. Many times they are unaware of the impressions they leave behind.

Two people I've never forgotten were my music teachers. Before I met them, Robert Unwin was a church organist in Germany, while Mme. Hendrikse was an opera coach in Amsterdam, Holland. These sensitive artists taught me that true talent is not only a gift from God. It is a responsibility. Out of discipline, commitment and personal sacrifice springs an all-consuming passion for greatness. Nazi jackboots goosestepping across Europe denied these two musicians the fulfilment of their dreams. But rather than wallow in fear and despair, these gentle souls slipped into the shadows of the secret war and, with the same dedication they gave to their music, risked death to fight Hitler's tyranny.

Though this novel is not about them, my characters are filled with the substance of their beings, with their quiet bravery, steadfast faith and fierce tenacity.

I doubt I would have finished this book without the encouragement of my friends and family. The first person, whose inspiration and indispensable criticism I want to acknowledge, is Violeta Rostas. The next is Jeanine McCreight. And for very special help, I acknowledge Eli and Inge Vranesic, Dietmar Arff, Jane Rotering, Dena Brooker, Sid Cassel, Christine Pletch, Jean Moore, Eleanor Fitzgerald, Pearl Cassel and Brian and Claire Mills.

But most of all, for just being there every step of the way and for faithfully recharging my belief in myself when I became disheartened, I have saved my greatest gratitude for my beloved Wally. To Dad, my daughter, Trish, and my brother, Chris, who impatiently waited for this book to be published, here it is at last!

BONNIE TOEWS

"We live in a time of economic
insecurity and social change:
fertile ground for hate to grow,
for scapegoating.
We can't
remain silent.
We need to be
active and alert."

**Jesse Hordes, Washington Director
of the Anti-Defamation League**
SEPTEMBER 1995

Chapter One

Monday, April 26th, 1937

ANNOYING STATIC scratched through the radio speaker. Then, despite the background crackling, the listeners could hear a woman's voice—her words barely intelligible:

At four o'clock this afternoon, a lone Heinkel 51 bomber began the bloodiest day of the Spanish Civil War… In a surprise attack on Guernica, he hit the town square, the Julian Hotel and the rail station where it's been reported over 200 people, who were on the platform waiting for the next train, have been killed. For the following two hours, Guernica rocked under six air strikes by Germany's Condor Legion, yet neither its one munitions plant nor the strategic Renteria Bridge was hit.

Historically, this small town in the hills of Northern Spain has been the cultural and religious center of the Basque people. Churches, convents and mona-steries abide here, not military targets. But now, the Monastery of Augustine Fathers is gone. Today's bombings razed it to the ground.

After awhile, seeing so much death numbs you, until you come across a small boy lying dead in a street littered with bodies of children. He stands out because he's still clutching his fishing pole. All around him are the mangled faces of the dead—their brains, guts and limbs strewn over the jagged craters where once buildings stood. I escaped Guernica. Many didn't. Tonight, Guernica burns.

What kind of monster kills and mutilates hundreds and hundreds of unarmed civilians? Some observers believe the Basques, an especially willful and proud people, are General Franco's test case. The Fascist theory is, if the Basques surrender to these terror tactics, all of Spain will surrender, and the rules of war can be rewritten.

On April 26th, 1937, history will record Guernica suffered the heaviest air attack ever launched against a civilian population. But the bombings have not crushed the Basques' spirit as expected. Instead, a common hatred is uniting them. Manuel Ortuz, the leader of the Basque resistance fighters, says this hatred is forging an iron will amongst the Basques to keep fighting or to die fighting but never to give up to the Fascists.

"Nobody but God can deprive us of freedom and the right to our homeland," he said just moments ago. The rules of war are being rewritten, but not by the Fascists alone...I'm Marla Franklin reporting ON THE SPOT for the London Times."

The three men grouped around the fireplace in the host's library sat with their eyes glued to the radio as the regular news program resumed broadcasting. One analyst after another was interviewed for their opinions on the day's event. Finally, in disgust, Sir Isaac Malcolm rose from his seat and switched off the radio. A big Scotsman, he unconsciously licked the shaggy tips of the red bush drooping over his upper lip before he spoke.

"The fools still don't see it," he noted grimly. "Hitler's tipping his hand. He's testing his *total war* strategy on the Basques."

"How are we going to get Chamberlain to recognize Hitler's preparing to invade Europe?" asked Lord James Rushmore. The softly featured middle-aged man directed his question to the paunchy figure hunched down in the Queen Anne chair.

Winston Churchill concentrated on the curl of smoke spiraling upwards from the chewed-down cigar he held in his pudgy hand. Then, he jammed it into his mouth and growled: "Hitler's words of peace blind everyone to our gravest concern. Einstein says the Third Reich is capable of developing an atomic bomb. All that is holding them back is learning how to moderate the chain reaction once they split the atom. Gentlemen, if Hitler develops an atomic bomb before we do, I fear all free nations are doomed."

"The pacifists can't continue to wear blinkers with reports like Marla Franklin's blasting the airwaves," predicted Lord James. "My bet is you'll be prime minister by year end, Winston."

Churchill shook his head emphatically. "No, James," he said. "It will take a major reversal to unseat Chamberlain."

Sir Isaac agreed. “Everything hinges on what Hitler does next. That is what will decide when we can assume the leadership of the country is Churchill’s.”

Lord James accepted Sir Isaac’s assessment over Churchill’s. Had the knighted Scotsman remained a private citizen in Aberdeen, Scotland, he might have been an extraordinary entrepreneur earning fortunes with the same skills he now used to organize their secret project.

From another part of the house the sudden interruption of piano music seemed to accent Churchill’s pensiveness. He cocked his head and jutted out his chin as he listened. “Tschaikowsky’s *Concerto in B-Flat Minor*,” he said, identifying the piece. Suddenly he frowned. “Do I hear two pianos?”

“Yes, Winston, you do.” Lord James acknowledged Churchill’s astute ear. Churchill’s eyes narrowed, signaling he expected an explanation.

“My daughter is practising her entry for the Belvedere Festival in Vienna,” Lord James told him. “My wife is playing her orchestral accompaniment.”

“I have no doubt Lady Catherine will win. No doubt,” Churchill repeated himself as his chin sunk into his chest. He closed his eyes, dismissing further conversation, as he let the music carry him away from his immediate political concerns.

MARLA FRANKLIN didn’t hear what the leader of the Basques was saying. She was still staring at her sketch of Guernica. It had been such a peaceful refuge. She relived the sights and sounds captured on the page in front of her. She had been so intent on her sketching that she had failed to notice the relentless droning of a plane approaching from the other side of the mountain. Far across the horizon, all she saw was the peak of *Monte San Miguel* arching its old woolly brow above the river that wound its way along the valley floor beyond Guernica . . .

Periodically, she shook her head to ward off the stiffness creeping into her neck. She was going to have to work fast if she hoped to capture the spectacular scenery of Northern Spain, so rich in color and song, unfolding before her. She continued drawing with swift bold strokes.

Now the aircraft's low-pitched thrum, purling down the windward bluffs, blended with the sound of the cicadas, a cricket-like creature that dwelled in the trees, clicking their castanets. The melodious murmurings of the countryside comforted her. Marla turned the page of her sketching pad and switched to a different view of the vineyards and orchards laden with spring blossoms embroidering the mountain slopes. Nearby, the fresh scent of newly plowed fields mingled with whiffs of bread baking in wood-burning stoves inside Basque cottages. The smells reminded her she hadn't eaten yet. But, once she settled on the three wooden crosses overlooking Guernica, the play of light between them so fascinated her she forgot her twinges of hunger. Before her, the lengthening shadows of the crosses welded together in a moving silhouette like an advancing Roman legion, dark and ominous.

She gripped the charcoal pencil and tightly squeezed her eyes, trying to will the disturbing picture away. Instead, a too familiar sense of loss lingered. Heaving a long weary sigh, Marla resumed drawing and shaded in the outline of the crosses' joint shapes jig-sawing across the western slopes.

Just as she finished her sketch, the unoffending droning suddenly rumbled like angry thunder over the valley. Startled, she look up and scanned the sky for the intruder. Barely skimming the northern mountain ridge was a lone bi-plane. She squinted, trying to identify it: Six horned vents spewed out from a rigid lip running down the side of its nose.

Oh God! Her spine shivered. *A Heinkel 51!*

Leaning forward, as if the motion would bring her closer to the plane, she followed its direction intently. On a seemingly single track passing from the right to the left up the river, it never veered from its heading, and as the plane flew on, it cast an eerie cross that rippled along the valley floor and shimmered over the tree tops.

Maybe he's lost, Marla thought. *A straggler looking to regroup with his squadron.*

From her position on the mountainside, it felt as if he were flying at eye level. All of a sudden he banked and headed straight for her. Instinctively she ducked, cowering under the Heinkel's roaring blast as it made a screaming climb overhead and vanished beyond the towering peaks behind her.

She stood dumbfounded. He had whizzed out of sight so quickly she couldn't believe her eyes. Did she imagine them, or did she see four blimp-shaped darts pinned in racks underside his lower wings? If so, the bloody bastard was carrying bombs! Where was he headed? North? North-west? Of course! Cripple the seaport, then the airport. He was on his way to bomb Bilbao's airport.

She had to get to a phone. Marla jammed her sketching pad and pencil into her shoulder bag. As she scrambled down the steep hillside, she tripped and sprawled on all fours. Cursing, she smoothed her skirt under herself and slid down the rest of the slope to the bicycle she had dropped by the roadside. No sooner had she yanked the bike upright than she heard the warning rumble again. She squinted into the sun, tracing the sky in the direction of the sound. There it was! The same bi-plane following the same route up the *Rio Mundaca* at about four thousand feet.

Fear buttoned her stomach. Then she remembered the munitions plant in Guernica. *Oh God! Toby's there! That damned kraut! I'll kill him!* she swore, sucking in a sob, as she began running the bike down the road before mounting it and peddling away. At the S-turn, she misjudged the sharp angles and nearly lost her balance, barely saving herself as the bike skidded on the left rim of the front wheel before she righted it, precariously wobbled for a split second and carried on downhill at breakneck speed. *Not Toby!* her panicked mind begged whatever invisible force controls the universe. *Not until I've had a chance to question him first!*

Oblivious to her own danger careening from side to side down the mountain road, Marla madly raced to beat the bomber. She had to hope Toby had already left the munitions plant. It would be his only chance. And hers.

BANG! BOOM!

Like banshees pitching their strident warnings over the mountain pass, steeple bells rang the same instant thundering bombs hammered the valley. One, two, thud after thud rocked the countryside. Their continual poundings burst inside Marla's head. Fires spread. The smell of their burning snaked through the air. A shroud of black smoke, draping death and destruction, its puffy entrails spilling over the town, choked the sunlight.

Recklessly jamming on her brakes, Marla locked the wheels of the bike and almost flew over the handle bars as she jumped off the peddles, using her feet like drags to bring the bike to a standstill. She stared aghast at the black clouds now spiraling skywards from Guernica's core. *What the hell!* There was no munitions plant in the center of town. Only the railway station and the hotel.

Oh my God! In horror, her fingers squeezed the handle bars so tightly they bled with her sweat as the purring bomber slid out of sight over the far horizon. Marla trembled. A sudden shrieking from the valley wrung her soul. *The pain. Their pain.* She stood transfixed, too numb with shock and disbelief to move. Then a fit of rage took hold, and she remounted the bike, panically peddling as she resumed her way down the mountain road to reach the carnage below. As she crossed the Renteria Bridge heading towards the belching smoke trails, curtains of debris collapsed over the marketplace. She tried to steer through the mounds of rubble littering the streets but gave up and continued pushing the bike on foot.

Everything she found in the town square was in shambles. The front of the Julian Hotel was sliced away, its four stories as bare as the back of a doll's house. Across from it, the Station Plaza lay flattened. Marla wandered amongst the desperate people madly scrambling for some sign of a loved one still alive. She would never forget their ear-splitting screams and their grief-torn shapes veiled behind murky sheers of red dust settling over the gutted square. The stench from disemboweled corpses fusing with the burning smells nearly suffocated her.

Dazed by the slaughter surrounding her, Marla was unaware she let go of the bike as she stumbled over it and hastily backed away from the square onto the *Calle de la Estacion*. Under the late afternoon sun, she saw gruesome shadows shifting in broken patterns.They shed a desolate darkness over the horror, but through the midst of it, patches of sunlight checkered the changing and growing gloom. In such a pool of brightness, she found the children. First, the body of a boy, no more than nine or ten years old. Two more corpses of children lay beside him on the street. Beyond them stretched lines of bodies and parts of bodies baked by the blast and pasted with a reddish loam, but it was the boy and his bent fishing pole that grabbed her. Even in death, he refused to let go.

Memories churned…little children in Madrid, made homeless by relentless Fascist bombings—hungry ones, bleeding ones, silent ones, hardly more than babies reaching out to her, begging to be fed, held and comforted, to be relieved of their endless nightmare. These were the children she had left behind. Unable to wipe away their tears and heartsick with the realization there was nothing she could do except report what was happening, she clung to the hope that somehow, soon, someone would care and do something to stop this ungodly struggle of Spaniards fighting each other. But, for the moment, this boy's death crushed her hope. No one cared. She had failed them. Guilt gnawed at her.

By some fluke, the side effect of the bomb's impact had left the boy's body intact yet partly undressed, vaguely tinted in inky browns. His mouth still gaped open like the beak of a baby bird starving. A fly landed on the dried dribblings caking his swollen lips and, with frenzied little hops and skips, jumped onto his protruding tongue, never pausing in its quest for food. Marla's own loathing for bugs fixed on that one single fly crawling inside the boy's mouth, probing with its sharp feelers for his most succulent blood. She imagined she could feel the fly's feathery feet brushing her own skin, and with growing hysteria, she batted at the air, against invisible buzzings beginning their torment, before an eerie screeching that made no sound pierced her very being. She froze, frightened. It seemed to come from deep within the boy's mouth—a silent scream, a voiceless protest against his own extinction howling into nothingness. Caught in eternal agony, the silent echo of the boy's anguish shattered her.

Her last awareness was of his gums and lips, in their bruised browns and blues, merging into one petrified scream like a carving in wood of his protest. The image engraved itself on Marla's mind forever, and she had crumpled in sobs beside the boy's body.

The leader of the Basques repeated himself, forcing Marla back to the present.

"When the Republican government in Madrid granted us home rule," he told her, "we knew they did it because they needed us to fight with them against the Fascists. Because we knew this, we did nothing. We did not fight them. But Franco's pigs have attacked us. This is our land, our country. They attack, so now we will fight them. We will fight anyone who tries to take away our independence and our land." His eyes blazed with hatred.

As his words sank in, Marla took real note of Manuel Ortuz. The old Basque's knotty fist gripped his iron walking stick. The Basques called it a *makhila*. If it were grabbed by its leather tong and swung around like a gaucho's bolo, it could also double as a defensive weapon to ward off attackers. Then she noticed the small black beret, a *boina*, proudly angled over his straw white hair, which capped his remarkable face. Weathered lines seemed chiseled into his leathery skin, yet, in anger, his eyes were a sharp youthful blue. *The Basques are so proud*, she thought. *Hitler wants to strip them of all dignity.*

"Could you satisfy a reporter's curiosity?" she asked him. "I can speak some Spanish, but I haven't been able to recognize any words in the dialect I hear you Basques speak. Is my ear that bad?"

The old Basque laughed, coarse noisy booms bursting from wells of glee. "Your ear is good. We do not speak a Spanish dialect."

"You don't?"

He shook his head emphatically. "No, no."

"What do you speak then?"

"Our own language. Even the name, Basque, is not from our tongue. It comes from French and Spanish roots. There is no language like ours."

"If you do not call yourselves Basques, what do you call yourselves?"

"*Eskualdunak*. It simply means those who speak the *Eskuara*, and *Eskuak-Herria* is the land of those who speak the *Eskuara*."

"*Eskuara...Eskualdunak...*" Marla repeated slowly, trying to remember the pronunciations as well as trying to picture the strange words of his tongue in her mind.

"And *Eskuak-Herria*," he said for her again when she couldn't remember it.

He cranked the field phone Marla had just used for her broadcast. It sat on a small card table placed in front of a bank of field radios inside the operations hut of a camp a band of freedom fighters had built into the highlands above Guernica. He listened, cranked it again, muttered a terse message, listened, answered gruffly, then dropped the receiver in place.

"We couldn't clear all the interference, but your broadcast did get through."

"Thank you for setting up the phone lines to connect with London. It would have been easier to air from Bilbao, but I just couldn't bring myself to leave here."

"But you must. You must leave here and tell everyone what is happening." A deeper sadness filled his eyes.

"The oak tree," he began to explain to her, "is the Basque's symbol of independence. If the oak tree blooms late, it is a bad omen. This year, in Guernica, the oak tree did bloom late. The omen is true. Do you see? It is not just an omen for us. It is an omen for the world."

Marla looked down at the sketch in her hand to prevent him from seeing the tears blinding her eyes.

"Marla!"

Christopher Tobin poked his head through the flap draped across the hut's doorway. "Thank God, I've finally found you. We have to fly back to London at once."

Seeing anger charge Marla's eyes, the old Basque discreetly excused himself.

"There's no need, Toby. I've already filed my story with London."

"Fantastic. By now your story will be crossing the air waves to the world. How did you do it?"

Marla's cold anger greeted his question, stilling his

excitement. Tobin peered into her face more closely and was jarred by the gaunt sorrow he saw there. Black soot streaked her brow and cheek, like a broken shadow running across her cameo features. The profound blueness of her large wide-set eyes had turned a deep violet, and her dust-caked hair fell like a matted mane down her shoulders. The way her eyes snapped and her nostrils flared reminded him of a long-legged filly ready to race. He sensed he was in for a wire-to-wire battle, but he had no idea why.

She picked up her shoulder bag from the table and, with methodical deliberation, slowly opened it. He watched with growing curiosity. She pulled out her drawing of Guernica and a file folder. More puzzled, he watched her open it and lay the file flat on the table. Then she picked up the brown envelope lying inside and drew out four photographs, one after the other.

"How did you get this photo of Franco's letter to Hitler? And these?" she demanded. "Pictures of forged passports the German military are using to smuggle in troops and the Luftwaffe into Spain as tourists?"

"I told you..."

Marla cut him off. "You told me Hitler's strategists believed the toughest people to beat in Spain are the Basques. Defeating them, you said, could shatter Republican morale in Madrid. Go to the heart of the war, you said. Go to Guernica."

She paused, looking bleakly into his face. "I'm a woman, and I dare to break into the brotherhood of war correspondents with my *On The Spot* column. But, I am *not* twice as smart as the next journalist because I am a woman, *nor* am I twice as lucky. I want you to tell me how you knew Guernica was going to be attacked."

Tobin shifted from one foot to the other. "Let's go outside."

Marla refused to budge.

"Please!"

Reluctantly, Marla gathered up the pictures, put them into the envelope and dropped the folder back into her shoulder bag before she followed him outside.

As he led her to a poplar tree beyond the hearing range of the freedom fighters' camp, frothy pink streamers wreathed the twilight sun hanging over the mountains like a pharaoh's headdress bent over in prayer. Its sinking light glazed the grassy belt and shivering leafage with a copper glow. Blazing crimsons melted over the western sky.

Tobin stopped at the poplar tree and rested his back against the trunk. A tall man who was regal looking even in casual dress, he spoke with a barely detectable Irish accent. "We've come far enough."

Bunched on a bulging rise of ground over the tree's thick taproot was a patch of wild mushrooms. Marla bent down and picked one.

"Eat that," said Tobin, "and it will be your last meal."

Marla scoffed. "Are you kidding? I'm starved."

"Eat it, and see if I'm kidding."

Marla hesitated. "How do you know it's poisonous?"

"See the white markings on the pale yellow coloring of the caps?"

"In this light, it's almost impossible to pick them out," she said.

"Nevertheless, an important distinction, Marla. See where these mushrooms are growing."

She nodded. "On top of a taproot."

"Your next clue. These mushrooms are the death

caps from a fungi group called *amanita*," he explained. "There is no known antidote for the amanita's deadly poison."

Marla shuddered, visibly shaken. "I would never have known."

"It's lucky I was with you," said Tobin, putting a comforting arm around her shoulder. "I wouldn't want our new partnership split up by a mushroom."

"What new partnership?" Marla asked, suddenly suspicious again.

"I'm your new boss."

Marla broke away. "What in hell are you talking about?"

"The *London Times* has sold your column to a private syndicate operating out of London. From now on your column is going to be distributed worldwide, and the agency has hired me to be your bureau chief."

Marla couldn't resist the sarcasm she felt. "You don't say! And why would you do that?"

"You're a damned good journalist, Marla."

"And you're a damned good liar, Toby! For two weeks you've been courting me, leading me on. If it was to get my news column, you and this syndicate of yours just wasted your money. I quit!"

"Why, for God's sake? What have we done? You get a wider reach and a chance to boost your career. I think you should be grateful."

"What have you *done*?" In utter frustration, Marla's hands clenched into fists. "You've *interfered*! That's what you've done. You know things before they happen. Dammit! You've placed me at stories before they've even happened."

"Would the news have been any different if you had

not been there?"

Marla stared him down with an icy glare, then thawed as she saw the truth in his question. "Okay. I've seen the inside of stories I wouldn't have been able to see otherwise."

"Isn't that what's really important?"

"It still doesn't change the fact you're lying to me, Toby. No news agency has access to the top secret photos you've handed me." She searched his eyes.

"I've been doing some of my own snooping, you know. You are not listed as an employee of the Foreign Office." Then, with jaw set, she added, "Obviously, Christopher Tobin is not your real name either."

In sudden disappointment, she turned away from him, facing the tree.

"Look," Tobin admitted. "Meeting you hasn't been all cold cunning. Your friendship has become absolutely essential."

Marla squared her shoulders, resisting the genuine regret she heard in his voice.

"Marla, please turn around and look at me."

She shook her head.

He sucked in a breath, seeking patience. *She is so unlike her mother*, he mused. Freya Shalimov, whose plays lauded Marxist ideology and defended social justice, was an enigma. She flaunted exotic fashions with the carelessness of an arrogant peacock. It was as if—even though she touched the common person's most common needs with her words—she wanted to reject their common touch.

But her daughter! No. Marla dressed with complete disregard for her natural sensuality, even to the sensible low-heeled shoes she wore. There was nothing pretentious about Marla Franklin, except perhaps her name. She had completely divorced herself from her mother, from her reputation and her Russian past, and from the father who had abandoned her, and had instead embraced everything American. She was so proud to be an American that, before she began university, she legally changed her last name of Shalimov to the first name of President Roosevelt—Franklin.

A salty musk, seeping out from Marla's soft glistening skin, filled his nostrils with its teasing scent until his tongue could taste it, arousing forbidden sensations. The past fortnight had been an endurance trial. A flame was eating away his insides. The more it consumed him, the greater the temptation.

"Damn it, Marla! Don't make it harder than it is." He grabbed her and turned her around to face him. Tears brimmed her eyes. She looked so defenseless with the loose locks of her thick dark hair tumbling down her shoulders. Her unbuttoned cardigan had parted revealing the fullness of her breasts. Under her blouse, they rose up and down in rhythm with her breathing. On impulse, he folded her into his arms and held her.

"Toby," she whispered, and turned inside the circle of his arms to look up at him with her magnificent eyes. Their pools upon pools of iridescent colors so like lingering embers began to smolder. "I want to feel your life inside me, Toby," she pleaded softly, pressing against him. "I need you so much."

He stiffened then, resisting her.

Her finger tips glided in ever-growing ripples up his chest and around his neck, toying with his ear lobes, and continued traveling up the back of his neck into his thick hair. She twirled his tight burgundy waves and gently squeezed them like a kitten kneading its mother's belly with all the joyful pleasure aroused by its nursing.

"Please, Toby." Her velvet lips caressed the chest hair peeking out of his open collar. The tip of her tongue tickled his skin, then she tweaked individual hairs between her teeth. Their tender tugs sent electric charges down his spine, like lightning bolts that suddenly came to ground in his groin. He groaned.

Taking his utterance for consent, she closed her lips around his mouth and crushed his hair between her fingers as her tongue darted between his teeth—probing, exploring, then tasting and licking every sensual surface her tongue could reach inside his mouth. She hungrily searched for life, savoring the juices that flowed like honey between them. For a fleeting second, he felt selfish. He wanted to yield to her consuming fire, to revel in all the awakened sensations surging through him, then a swift sense of guilt flooded him with remorse.

"Stop it, Marla."

"What's wrong?" she asked playfully. "Do I smell so terrible you can't bear to touch me?"

"Good Lord, woman!" Tobin growled. "You are humiliating yourself."

The sting of his voice slapped her brutally. Marla's senses reeled. "You son of a bitch!" She tore herself away from him. "Always unpredictable, just like the damned weather. One minute, warm. The next, cold. Now you want me. Now you don't. I'm sick of it!"

Tobin's features stilled, and he withdrew to a part of himself she could not reach. Yet, she still tried. "For God's sake, what is your problem?"

"Leave it alone, Marla."

"Leave *it* alone! *IT!*"

Just then, jagged glints of light from the last rays of the sinking sun struck his pant legs and scuffed shoes in a bile yellow. Marla stared at the sickly glow covering his feet. Disgust with herself burrowed into her soul. "So be *it*. I have to get back to London. I can't say *it's* been a real treat knowing you, Tobin."

"Don't quit on me, Marla. You have to listen. Guernica changes everything."

She couldn't turn away from what she had seen. "How?" she relented.

"Guernica is a preview of Hitler's vision of war. The barbaric Huns in all their terror have risen again. It will take extraordinary imagination and relentless commitment to combat Hitler's intention to unite Europe under the Nazi Swastika. His *total war* scheme depends on coordinating radio communications effectively from air to ground and sea and between assault forces. Such a massive system is susceptible to mistakes and mechanical failures. Hitler is vulnerable. Intelligence—astute, finely tuned, analytical, resourceful, aggressive intelligence—could confuse and defeat him in the war games to come. That's what matters to me. Our victory."

Marla's adrenaline stirred.

"You're wrong about one thing. My real name is Christopher Tobin, but you are quite right. I work with the British Secret Service, and we need your column for two reasons: first, and foremost, you have broken into the *brotherhood of war correspondents*, as you put it. Funnily enough, men read what you have to say even if they don't want to admit it. They read you because they believe you. That leads me to the second reason. We need to make the public aware of Hitler's real threat to the free world. Your column can deliver that message at the same time as it provides me with a cover for a secret mission into Europe."

"How can my *ON THE SPOT* report give you cover?"

"As your bureau chief, I can be seen talking to all kinds of people in all sorts of places, all in the name of research for your stories."

"And me? What's my part?" Marla asked.

"Just what you've been doing."

"And...?"

Pain jabbed Tobin's eyes. "You don't want to get more involved."

"Don't be a horse's ass! I'm already involved. I can't walk away from what I've seen here, at Bilbao and in Madrid. Do you want me to pretend it didn't happen? Well, I can't. Hitler must be stopped. If not here, then somewhere else, or before we know it, he'll be banging down our door next."

Then she stopped herself and admitted softly, "You didn't have to set me up, you know."

"That's what the spy game is, Marla. One set up after another. We agents are pawns. We never see the whole chess board. We simply do the job we're assigned and hope that it makes a difference."

His jaw tightened. He looked down at his feet, bent from the waist and plucked a blade of grass. He twisted it between his fingers as he pulled himself upright.

"According to your dossier, you are a Russian-born American. Your mother is Freya Shalimov, an American-based playwright, and...a Jew. Even though your father was an agnostic Gentile, in the eyes of the Nazis, you are also a Jew. We can lessen the risk by deleting your Jewish background from your file, but either as a spy or as a Jew, if you are caught, the consequences will be terrible."

"I know," Marla said with stoic resignation.

"And then there's your reputation to deal with."

"My *reputation!?*"

Tobin cleared his throat and avoided her eyes again. "It seems the men you've slept with you've never loved."

Marla chilled. A private part of herself felt shredded. "How dare you!"

Embarrassed, Tobin answered stiffly. "I'm sorry, Marla. We have to dig into everything. I wouldn't have brought it up except…it's necessary to know…"

He sighed from deep inside. "Shit! I hate this! You are a beautiful woman and…" He stumbled and finished lamely, "It may be necessary to use that beauty to attract the beasts."

"Patriotic prostitution, you mean," she corrected him coldly.

"Can you do it?" Tobin asked gruffly.

A haunting sadness clouded Marla's eyes. "Yes, damn it. I can do it."

Chapter Two

Saturday, September 25th, 1937

THE DATE was forged in Lady Catherine Rushmore's mind. She was about to give her first public performance in Vienna, the last contestant to compete for the coveted gold medal. As she gazed around the gallery of royal boxes, each scarlet booth cradled in Baroque splendor, a sea of faces swirled from balcony to balcony. Row upon row of scarlet seats stretched around the lower levels of the Vienna State Opera House while down below, directly in front of the footlights, sat rows of visiting Nazi officers. Peering down on them from her position on stage was like staring down the throat of a colossal whale. All the scarlet colors inside the massive theater ringed an arch over the pit of black and silver uniforms, and Catherine felt momentarily trapped inside a formidable monster.

The conductor tapped the podium, commanding all attention on him. His brows tweaked in silent question.

She smiled nervously in answer and leaned more forward, pulling up on her pelvis.

He paused...drilling his compelling eyes into hers;

then his gaze moved over the whole orchestra, boring into each member until he was satisfied they were united as one mind under his baton before he swung into the opening bars of the piano concerto.

A powerful electric current jumped from point to point. His eyebrows arced, his head twitched, and the ivory keys beneath Catherine's fingers sprang to life.

The composer cried through her fingertips. As she played, Catherine felt herself running through black forests. Diamond droplets pricked her face, and stormy winds whipped her body. She reveled in the pain. She was alive! Alive because she could feel the pain. And she was free! Free as only the music could free her.

Suddenly, in a fury, frenzied cadenzas peaked in glorious orgasms of piano and orchestra exploding together, until the last strains held and quivered into nothingness.

A brief moment of astonished silence paralyzed the Vienna State Opera House before excited cries of "*Bravo! Bravo!*" pealed through the tumultuous applause.

Spent and shaking from the rapturous intensity, Catherine sat dazed, too overwhelmed by the thunderous clapping to move. Never had she felt so consumed. Like a terrible tugging, almost as if her spirit were being ripped from her body, she felt the world struggling to claim her. It frightened her. Inwardly, she fought her panic.

It wasn't like this when Decency won, she thought. There had been a dignified ovation for her horse. A humble tribute. Peers courting greatness amongst their own kind. Not this tug-of-war, this dreadful demand to possess her wholly. She felt violated and remained frozen to the piano bench.

When she ignored the conductor's tiny flick of his baton, he quickly stepped down from the podium and extended his right hand. She stared at it, desperately, like a drowning person, before she clasped it and clung. He pulled her to her feet and stood beside her, holding her up by her waist as she deeply bowed. The applause swelled again.

"You have won Vienna's heart," he whispered to her.

"Oh..." Catherine's lower lip trembled.

Simply clad in a sailor middy blouse and navy jumper, she reminded him of a bewildered Alice in the midst of the Mad Hatter's tea party.

He had seen it before. After years spent in isolated study, the sudden exposure to public approval could be overwhelming. For some, the first clamorous adoration is like an aphrodisiac reaction: they hunger for more and will do anything to hear it repeated. For the chosen few, the waves of noise rebounding in louder and louder swells become like spikes hammering the echo chambers of the mind: they learn to tolerate the pain that is their due. For those who possess this God-given humility, he mused, it seems to drop anchor in the unsheltered harbor of the fragile soul, yet once moored in such quiet waters outrides the toughest storms, unharmed and uncorrupted. The conductor believed Lady Catherine was such a soul.

"Grip my hand and smile, my dear," he directed.

The seasons of the sky dancing in the blue pools of his eyes warmed and cooled in magical rhythms that drew Catherine into their deepest reflections, soothing her. She did as he directed. The waves of applause swelled higher.

"If not now, WHEN?" he softly quoted to her.

Distracted by the strange words, she searched his face with puzzled interest. "*If not now, WHEN?*" she repeated in wonder.

Dr. Otto Kantor was not the Belvedere Festival's regular conductor. He was a music professor from Budapest, Hungary, but she noticed then that he was wearing the traditional navy blue blazer with the embroidered Belvedere crest. His unruly mop of steel wool hair, if plopped on any other receding hairline, would have appeared clownish, but not on his. It crowned a high noble forehead and a lovable face.

With his strong Hungarian accent, he whispered into Catherine's ear. "This moment is yours. No? Relax. Enjoy. You gave from the soul. Now you receive."

The tips of his thick eyebrows unfurled in merry curls, almost like a cartoonist's embellishment of his perfectly sculpted features. He gave her an encouraging smile.

She relaxed. Finally, the clapping dribbled away.

Catherine almost tripped up the side stairs back stage that led to the first gallery where the other contestants and their families were sitting in the front row. As she sank down in the empty seat beside her mother, Princess Isabelle clasped Catherine's chilly hands in her own.

"It was a remarkable performance, the best you've ever played, dear," she whispered, barely able to contain her proud delight.

Lord James leaned across Princess Isabelle's lap. "Good show," he said, and then motioned for her to sit back and relax.

She continued to cling to her mother's hand as the

minutes waiting for the judges' selection dragged on. Her mind was still with the experience. She had endured her first public baptism and surrendered nothing of herself. She was the same person she was before she performed. Yet something was different, something deep inside her. Like a river once damned up, she felt a tremendous release. Peace flowed within, and she relaxed. Her mother felt the easing of her tension and patted her hand. They exchanged a quiet smile.

Suddenly, she remembered Dr. Kantor. "Mommy, the conductor..."

"Not now, Catherine," her mother said. "I think they're going to make the announcement. See! The curtains are moving."

Princess Isabelle's excitement touched Catherine. She had forgotten her mother had sacrificed a concert career to marry Lord James. Theirs was a romantic story. But, for the first time, Catherine realized the Gold Medal meant as much to her mother as it did to her. Her years of patient teaching and the many long hours they spent together practicing flashed to mind.

While preparing for the festival, her mother played the orchestra's part and made Catherine stretch every musical instinct, every technique to her utmost. Catherine had become a superb pianist but only because her mother was a greater one. If Catherine won the medal, it was as much for her mother as it was for herself. She gently squeezed her mother's hand with fresher understanding. They were about to share the moment of truth. How good was she?

The audience restlessly buzzed with chatter.

Dr. Kantor appeared first and positioned himself beside the first violinist. Emerging from stage left, the leader of the festival's panel of seven judges followed. A portly man, he strode with measured dignity towards center stage. In his pudgy hands, asparkle with rings, he carried a small velvet-covered box. Turning to the audience, he paused and smiled up at Catherine, a pompous smile that unsettled her. The whites of his eyes bulged like beads of greasy sweat. Unconsciously, she recoiled and comforted herself by fixing her attention on Dr. Kantor. His searching eyes found her doelike gaze peering down on him from the gallery. He winked. She couldn't resist the clownish sweetness in his face and grinned in response.

The adjudicator then stepped down to the footlights and looked out over the audience. A reedy rumble rolled in his throat. At once, a hush smothered the excited din. She nervously edged forward on her seat.

"Now I know how the Empress Maria-Theresa felt when she heard Mozart play the first time at six years of age. Such musical brilliance is thrilling," he began in a surprisingly resonant voice.

Another ripple of applause rumbled. He raised the flats of his hands to repress it.

"Since 1820," he continued, "the Hapsburg family has recognized outstanding young pianists in an annual competition that has become an international event. This year our panel of judges has unanimously decided our winner is from England, and it gives me great pleasure to present this gold replica of the medal the empress awarded to Mozart in 1762 to Lady Catherine Rushmore."

Pandemonium erupted.

The orchestra, flanking the adjudicator, rose in one fluid motion, their eyes raised to the gallery where

Catherine sat. Next, the spotlight swung and bathed her in blinding light. Still rooted to her seat, she squinted. Now that she had won she couldn't believe it.

"Catherine," her mother urged, "he wants you on stage to receive the presentation. Go on, dear."

Catherine shakingly rose to her feet. Suddenly, she knew how a fish felt flapping around in a catcher's net. She looked down at her mother's radiant face. Beside her, her father beamed. As if in a dream, she let go of her mother's hand and made her way down the row, past the other contestants' sporting congratulations.

As she stepped out from the wings, a deafening applause greeted her. Instantly, her field of vision narrowed to a startlingly selective range, like disassociated segments of a picture looming larger than life: Dr. Kantor's reassuring eyes drawing her forward as he escorted her to center stage; the adjudicator, stepping back, like a broad canvas swinging away to reveal a fuller view of the audience…waxen bobbing images pinned under the great white light; then, like a giant wave, he rolled in again, hemming her to the edge of the stage, and ceremoniously kissed her on each cheek. Catherine had to overcome a violent urge to wipe off the glistening imprint his wet lips left.

All at once, intense blue eyes piercing through the footlights like diamonds cutting glass engaged her attention. Peering through the hazy brilliance, hoping to catch a glimpse of the face that belonged to the magnificent eyes, she was stunned when she tracked them to a young Nazi officer in the front row. Fascinated, she couldn't turn away. His striking perfection totally absorbed her.

The portly adjudicator's opening the small velvet

box intruded on her strange spell. She watched him pull out the precious medal on a long gold chain. While he slipped the chain over her head, she stood reverently, momentarily in awe of the great honor she was receiving. Even the vast audience grew subdued until he stood back to let them see the beautiful medal fastened around her neck.

"Ladies and Gentlemen," he announced with grand flourish, "I give you Lady Catherine Rushmore of England, the Belvedere winner for 1937!"

She humbly bowed and, in gratitude, stretched out one hand to include Dr. Kantor. He declined sharing her victory, choosing instead to step back into the inconspicuous shadows of the orchestra. She stood alone; then she raised her eyes to the gallery and blew a kiss of tribute to Princess Isabelle. For one instant, she thought the long reach of the great spotlight caught tears glistening on her mother's cheeks.

Earsplitting applause followed. From beneath her lowered lids, she yielded to the desire to snatch one last look at the handsome German officer. His magnetic gaze caught her, and in that breathless moment, their souls linked. Never in her life had she experienced such elation, and as difficult as it had been to mount the stage before the concert, now she didn't want to leave.

The din of the clapping and cheering dissipated. The curtain dropped. The finality of the curtain falling severed their connection. It was as if someone had turned off the tap. She felt empty. Would she ever see the German officer again? Not likely, she realized. Her feelings didn't make sense. She had worked long and hard to win this medal. Why didn't it matter? What was wrong with her?

The clang of metal music stands being folded and piled pried her thoughts away from the German to Dr. Kantor. The orchestra members were packing their instruments and preparing to leave. Where was he? She had to find him and thank him properly.

"Dr. Kantor! Wait!" she called when she spotted him pulling on his coat and gloves in front of the musicians' cloak room. He smiled wanly as she ran to catch up to him. Away from his compelling conducting, he seemed more stooped, more aged. Instant concern gripped Catherine.

"Dr. Kantor, please don't go. I'd like you to meet my parents." She anxiously scanned over the heads of the visitors milling backstage, hoping to see them. "They will want to thank you for helping me," she insisted.

"That's not necessary, my dear."

For the second time tonight, his eyes mesmerized her. What's happening to me? she wondered. Why am I feeling so drawn to this conductor and the blonde offic...? She had observed the color of his hair after all, she realized with sudden cheer. It gave flesh to the image locked in her mind.

Dr. Kantor's attention darted to the shadows behind the dressing rooms. Catherine sensed his instant tension and wished she could relieve his anxiety the way he had helped her. "Please, Dr. Kantor, join my parents and me. There is so much we can talk about."

He smiled with gentle amusement. "You are so like fine crystal…brilliant and delicate yet as solid as rock. Being a star will never go to your head."

"That line you quoted to me—*if not now, WHEN?*—is that what you meant? That now is my time for recognition?"

"Is that what you think it meant?"

"I honestly don't know."

"It's not as complicated as you think," Dr. Kantor said. "There will come a time when you will say these words to someone else because they will seem to fit the occasion as they did tonight."

"Can I find the line in a play or poem?" Catherine persisted.

Sorrow veiled his eyes. "It is from a verse by the Hebrew philosopher Hillel." Then he glanced over her shoulder and grew fidgety. "Forgive me, but I must excuse myself, Lady Catherine. I'm expected back in Budapest at once."

He took her right hand and cupped it inside both of his. His gentleness so touched her that she wanted to wrap her arms around him, but she knew that whatever was troubling him would make his inner resources crumble if she succumbed to the impulse. Her heart flooded her eyes.

"Thank you." Like cracked china, the rich timbre of his voice broke. "I'll always remember your magnificent performance, my dear, and your loving kindness."

And then he was gone.

"Dr. Kantor…?" she cried.

Suddenly, out of the dressing room shadows, two men in dark suits roughly brushed Catherine aside and hurried out the stage door after him. She stood confused.

"Oh, there you are, Catherine," Princess Isabelle called as she dodged stagehands dismantling the symphony platform. "You must show me your gold medal. I've been dying to see it! Your father is arranging a concert tour for you this very minute. Catherine?" Her chatter instantly switched off when she saw how upset her daughter was. "Catherine? What's wrong, dear?"

"Dr. Kantor…I think he's in danger."

"Why would you think that?"

"He was very afraid of something or someone, and two men just rushed out the stage door after him."

"They did? Did you see them chasing him?"

"No."

"Then it's nothing more than a coincidence. Your imagination is running away with itself."

"I do hope you're right, mother."

Catherine seldom called Princess Isabelle *mother* in that tone. She looked more thoughtfully at her daughter and placed a comforting arm around her shoulders.

"He was so sweet. For a moment I lost my composure, and he…" The rest of the sentence foundered over the lump in her throat. She wanted to crawl inside her mother's arms and leave the terrible misery there.

"You were wonderful. We are so proud of you."

"This should be the happiest day of my life, but I don't think I have ever felt so miserable."

"You're just tired," Princess Isabelle assured her. "You've worked very hard. This feeling will pass, and all you will remember will be your great triumph."

But she wasn't tired. She was miserable for another reason she couldn't tell. Privately lodged in her heart was the memory of the golden-haired German in the formidable Nazi uniform. For one crazy instant, they touched some intimate portion of their lives that would never be the same again. "I feel as if he's a part of me, mummy. Why?"

Thinking she meant Dr. Kantor, her mother tightened her arm around her shoulders. "Everything we do...everyone we meet becomes a part of us, Catherine. Almost like scattered parts of our soul coming home to roost. For a moment, everything fits, and we belong...to that moment...or to that person," she finished wistfully, as if she had not yet gathered all the missing parts to her own soul.

Chapter Three

Wednesday, November 9th, 1938

BARON JOACHIM KONSTANTIN VON DAREN, a colonel in Hitler's elite police and military organization, the SS, drove in his canvas-topped roadster along the autobahn to Berlin. The car was snug and warm despite the chill outside. At the end of a five-day furlough, he was returning to duty and could barely resist the impulse to press more weight to the accelerator, except that he wanted nothing, particularly an accident, to prevent the evening ahead. His thoughts drifted from the uneventful drive.

Joachim's home, located at the tip of a triangle between Sieburg, Cologne and Dusseldorf, was a grand four-story villa built of stone. Unlike the steepled castles studding the magnificent hills throughout the Rhineland, his estate's rustic simplicity was like a needlepoint tapestry stitched into the countryside. In winter, it became a snowy wonderland. His favorite memories were of the mares and weanlings taking turns joyfully rolling on their backs in the snowbeds spread over the oak-fenced paddocks. Thick forests with their boughs swaddled in white lace flanked the family house and towering fir trees stood like stiff sentries guarding the hilly pasture lands all blanketed with snow. Further upland, his father's hunting lodge sent up welcome smoke signals that were more like cotton curls wafting up from its chimney into the clear blue sky. This pastoral harmony was far removed from Joachim's rigid military life, and he longed for the day when he could return to it, free of any patriotic obligation.

From landed nobility, Joachim felt the heavy responsibility of being the only one left in his family to pass on his aristocratic heritage. He should have been proud that his mother's ancestors traced back to the *Junker* knights, to the *Uradel* title predating the 13th Century, but he was more proud of the less prestigious barons from his father's side of the family. He could more comfortably relate to their love of farming.

Since 1723, a string of only sons had inherited the von Daren's 100-acre wooded estate. Originally, the von Daren family had produced the finest mixed fruits in the Rhineland, until the 1890s, when Joachim's grandfather became fascinated with horses and established his own racing stable. By 1936, Joachim's father was offering yearlings for sale by the great 1929 Hambletonian winner, *Walter Dear*, and his patronage of the spectacular world champion entrenched the von Daren name as first class breeders of European trotters. But, just before Hitler reoccupied the Rhineland, a sudden stroke felled Joachim's father, and Joachim, as the next only son, had inherited his father's title and estate.

From the moment the Wehrmacht's troops marched in, Joachim expected the Rhinelanders to resent their military presence, but instead, they seemed pleased with

Hitler's daring maneuver. Certainly, his mother hated the Wehrmacht's occupation of *her* land. With bitter disgust, she told Joachim that even the Catholic priests, who had complained earlier of Nazi persecution of the church, met the soldiers at the Rhine bridges and blessed them. She couldn't believe her eyes.

Thereafter, when the local air waves echoed with Nazi dogma, Joachim's mother accused the Rhinelanders of heresy, but she was shrewd enough to voice her feelings only in private to him. In those moments together, she would recall the Great War. If it were not for their horses, she told Joachim over and over again, the von Darens would have lost all their wealth, as other aristocrats had after Germany's defeat. She warned him of the shadow of war that she sensed threatened the von Daren's peaceful fields and forests, for she was convinced Hitler's rearmament was inviting a terrible disaster on the German people.

Worse than that, she feared her son's allegiance to the *Schutzstaffel*—Hitler's SS—the black-coated elite guard, once the Nazi Party's paramilitary arm but now more powerful than the secret police. What was left to bind a son to his mother if all his devotion and duty were to the Fuhrer and the fatherland, she would ask him. He couldn't give her an answer that satisfied her, and soon after his father's funeral, Joachim observed her mounting despair. Not even her love of the horses comforted her. Soon, she had lost all desire to eat, until eventually, heartbroken, she had passed away in her sleep.

Joachim understood she died of worry for him. Now, more than ever, he regretted he could not have relieved her lonely turmoil or offered her peace of mind. But, he dared not confide in anyone, not even to his mother whom he adored, not even to prevent her death. And, as the dark days of guilt and grief passed, he had come to believe she was better off dead. A cold, harsh reflection, yet from the cruel things he was seeing, perhaps a more humanitarian sentiment.

The farm, always his haven from the radical propaganda consuming the cities, seemed so empty this trip. Mingling with his prize trotters in the paddock and watching them jog on the farm's training track failed to lift his spirits. More and more, he found himself turning to the piano for solace.

As he played treasured pieces he had learned as a boy, the young English girl's face crowded his thoughts. Mere infatuation paled in comparison to the magnetic obsession that gripped him whenever he recalled Lady Catherine's performance in Vienna. He had never heard the piano played so brilliantly, and when their eyes had locked, their souls had merged. No matter what he did to forget her, she lingered in his mind like a shadow that popped into his consciousness whenever he was either the most vulnerable or the most relaxed, comforting his increased revulsion at the insensitive role he must play while teasing his senses with her ghostlike realness. So sharply was her image etched in his memory that sometimes she seemed close enough to touch.

How Joachim ached to hold her, to smell her scent, to fondle her hair, to trace the contours of her face with his lips, to feel her bodily warmth against him. The wanting was unendurable torture. He needed her in the flesh. And so, sometimes, to relieve the torment, he took other women to bed. While pretending he was really making love to her, he released his pent up passions with them. Willing substitutes were easy to find. Women craved to be seduced by the irresistible blonde SS colonel, but he was only aroused by sleek, honey-haired, fragile, Aryan beauties, not by the voluptuous country maidens the Fuhrer approved of for his elite SS studs. And the women Joachim found never forgot his masterful loving. They hungered for more, but he never returned to the same woman twice. He was too loyal to Catherine's memory to let go of his fantasy.

With time, however, he had resigned himself to the futility of thinking about her. He recognized how harmful his distraction was becoming. Too many lives depended on him. They were ready to do their part when the time came. And so must he, though he hoped it would never come to that.

Before he had taken his leave, he had received new orders. He was being transferred from the Propaganda Ministry to the *Sicherheitsdienst*, the SD, Reinhard Heydrich's Security Service, to a specialized department investigating nuclear fission under SS General Walther Schellenberg. It was the assignment he had prepared himself for in England, where he had studied nuclear physics at Cambridge. Being in England during the rise of Hitler's power had given him a different perspective of the new Germany but rather than desert his homeland to a politics he had grown to hate, he knew he could neither abandon his family nor the life in the Rhineland he loved so much. That's what attracted Sir Isaac Malcolm. The two met once, and when Joachim returned to Germany after he graduated in 1934, he used the influence of his father's high brow customers—the horse owners and race fans who were in Hitler's inner circle—to join the SS. Both his parents died feeling their son had betrayed their values, but, in truth, Joachim had gone home with a secret mission to save everything they loved.

In Berlin, he quickly learned the Nazis were experimenting with the possibilities of atomic energy. If they could find a practical way to split the atom, he estimated they could increase their energy yield by as much as 50%, or maybe even by a hundredfold. Joachim believed whoever unearthed the atom's secret of power first owned a tremendous advantage over his enemy. The job Sir Isaac had trained him to do was to monitor the Germans' progress and, if necessary, prevent them from succeeding ahead of the Allies. To that end, Joachim needed to gain a trusted position with Schellenberg. He had finally achieved that, but the accomplishment had seemed hollow until today.

Joachim had used gossip that Schellenberg found Hitler's fascination with British royalty an irritating breach of security to gain the general's favor. He volunteered to host the exiled King Edward and his American wife, Wallis Simpson, during their visit to Germany, thus making it easier for Schellenberg's men to monitor their movements and conversations. But, in Hitler's eagerness to demonstrate his power, he ignored Schellenberg's security plan and took the couple through some of his secret war-building industries. Now, the Fuhrer seemed mesmerized with the ex-king's cousin, Lady Catherine Rushmore. After her Berlin concert, the newspapers ran pictures of Hitler rising in tribute to her magnificent performance. They claimed he laid Berlin at her feet.

Joachim wished he could have seen it. Tonight was going to make up for that. Schellenberg had assigned him to be Catherine's watchdog at a reception the International Press was holding for her. The irony of their paths crossing again awed Joachim. One day's difference and he would have missed her. Tomorrow, he was on his way to Copenhagen to begin his covert duties as Dr. Sven Holbak's liaison with the German Scientific Institute in Berlin. That's what the nuclear scientist would believe, but Schellenberg was instituting a plan for his agents to monitor all major technical experiments developing in countries the Fuhrer intended to occupy, particularly in atomic energy and in rocket engine design. Schellenberg was Sir Isaac's counterpart, and the set up allowed Joachim to work for them both, for now. Holbak was the most advanced in his research, and if he succeeded in finding the moderator to control atomic energy, Joachim's subversive role would take over. The Nazis must not have the formula to make an atomic bomb before the Allies.

Joachim took the Potsdamerstrasse exit off the autobahn that led to an outer station of the electric rail that ringed Berlin and followed a streetcar route into the heart of the city. Berlin had the most sophisticated transit system in the world. It resembled spokes in a wheel. Underneath the city, a subway network spread out from its hub to meet the intermittent train stations located on the outer rim above ground. Streetcars ran on alternate routes over the surface to the subways below.

He chose the Kurfurstendamm, a grand avenue in the west end, so he could drive past the showplace of *haute couture* shops, designer boutiques and antique stores. In front of each shop stood open glass display cases imbedded in square concrete legs. Their loose assortment of richly colored silk scarves and expensive trinkets invited fingering, but no one in the Nazi capital ever thought to steal the unguarded items. Above many of the window boxes that characterized most of these stylish stores hung small crude signs painted in yellow: *Juden sind hier nicht erwunscht*—Jews are not wanted here.

From habit, Joachim ignored the disturbing signs in the windows. Driving past the inviting Café Kranzler, a sidewalk café breaking up a continuous row of fashion houses on the Kurfurstendamm, he continued on to the outskirts of the Tiergarten. It was a park with nude statues of exaggerated male physiques, mostly Nazi-approved works by Thorak and Breker, decking its grounds. Near one of the gates, a small brass band played lively waltz tunes. It switched into a tune that the crowd of spirited singers gathering around the players could sing.

Du, du, liegst mir im Herzen,
Du, du, liegst mir im Sinn;
Ja, Ja,
Ja, Ja,
Weiss nicht wie gut ich dir bin.

Joachim drove on humming the song to himself. Through the linden trees in the park, he could see young riders on handsome roans cantering along the riding paths. They were keeping pace with his car. Suddenly, he jammed on his brakes.

Marching columns of brown shirted Hitler Youth forced him to pull over as they entered the boulevard at the cross street. They came, one proud company after another. To Joachim, their precision goose-stepping, galvanized bodies and glazed eyes made them look like golden-haired parodies of a comic opera. Their strident voices, singing in unison—*We follow not Christ but Horst Wessel, we are children of Hitler*—pierced Berlin's pristine air.

To pass the time, Joachim watched a group of boisterous children boarding the merry-go-round at the entrance to the Tiergarten zoo. They jostled each other over the most roguish-looking rocking horse on the carousel. One small boy scrambled on top and clung to its head pole. The merry-go-round started up. Faster and faster it whirled. The children shrieked with excitement. Remembering the fun of his youth, he mentally rode with them until the abrupt bong of steeple bells redirected his attention to the time. He didn't want to miss a second of Catherine's reception.

Finally, the tree-lined boulevard was clear of marching youth, and he proceeded up Budapesterstrasse, where foreign correspondents had taken over an abandoned library and turned it into their press club away from home.

The splendor of the library's Baroque architecture enchanted even the most cynical journalist. The main courtroom just off the entranceway reached up through two stories to an arched ceiling covered in renaissance paintings. This area, which had previously been the receiving area for books on loan, had been converted into a comfortable reception area filled with deep-cushioned leather chairs and sofas. Branching out from the upper level of the two-story atrium were cozy chamber rooms—each lined with walls of mahogany bookshelves surrounding a fireplace that provided a much needed refuge for thinking, reading and writing. A private bar and kitchen occupied the small wing, which was originally the music room adjoining the reception area. From here, the grand piano had been moved to the center of the lounge to encourage sing songs and gatherings around the piano. It was amazing how many journalists were either hobby pianists or enjoyed the company of those who were. It substituted a sense of family, something most correspondents missed. Later, Catherine would perform on this piano.

The Press Club filled in two waves every day, either before five o'clock or after midnight, depending on deadlines. Journalists at the Press Club were accustomed to talking to Joachim at the Propaganda Ministry. They often sought him to translate the German text of Hitler's speeches, and though he easily got along with them, he didn't kid himself. They despised his uniform and didn't trust him, so they rarely talked freely in front of him. As he hung up his great coat in the cloak room, he could hear blustery voices arguing in the anteroom and paused to listen.

"Look, Hitler hasn't shed the blood of one soldier, yet in two years he's walked in and taken over *all* the Rhineland, Austria and now the Sudetenland." Joachim wasn't sure if the speaker came from the mid-west or a southern state, but there was no mistaking his American drawl. Joachim guessed he must be the bureau chief for United Press. He knew he was a southerner.

"Tell me he's not outwittin' the western powers every step of the way," continued the voice, rising in frustration. "In the west, the French army outnumbers the German army ten to one. *All* the French have to do is overtake the Ruhr, and Hitler's arms industry is finished. So what does England and France do? They hand over the Sudetenland to Hitler because they're afraid the Luftwaffe will wipe 'em out. In God's name, what is your Chamberlain usin' for brains? London is beyond the German bombers' range."

"I agree." Joachim recognized the woman's voice. It was Marla Franklin. Occasionally, she broadcast her *ON THE SPOT* reports to England from Germany. She continued, "Hitler won't be satisfied with just the Sudetenland. He wants all Czechoslovakia. It's just the way Churchill said it would be. He told Chamberlain: *Hitler gave you a choice between war and dishonor. You chose dishonor, and you WILL have war.*"

"Old Churchill's right about that," drawled the deep southern voice in disgust. "And once Hitler knows how feeble-minded the Western powers really are, he will pick his own time and take over the whole cotton-pickin' country of Czechoslovakia."

"What's worse," commented a softer yet richer voice, which Joachim knew at once was the Columbia Broadcasting System's European broadcaster, Wilson Meredith, "he's convinced the German people he's invincible."

"Why not?" It was the southerner again. "He's delivered three bloodless victories. He's so puffed up with his own power, he believes he can get away with anythin'. You can blame that dimwit Lindbergh for makin' it so easy too."

"Come on, Kramer. You're getting nasty," Marla told him. So the southern voice does belong to the United Press chief, thought Joachim.

"Fred's right," interjected another voice. "Charles Lindbergh is one helluva pilot, but he knows nothing about military planes. Why you Americans sent over such a gullible bloke to scout out the Luftwaffe is an even bigger mystery. The Germans convinced him the

Luftwaffe is superior to the combined air fleets of Britain, France, Czechoslovakia and Russia. After the Condor Legion's performance in Spain, he really believes the German airforce is capable of wiping out the biggest cities of Europe. He in turn convinced the British, the French and the Americans that Hitler's bluff is true when, in fact, the Luftwaffe can't reach England from their present bases."

"Both you and Kramer have said London is beyond the Luftwaffe's reach," broke in Marla. "What proof do you have to support that, Tobin?"

"The range of a bomber carrying a thousand-pound bombload is 430 miles. For fighter planes, it's even less. So, the maximum range any German plane can fly has to be the same, 400 miles at best. The Luftwaffe has to get to England from German bases and back without refueling. That's a round trip of 800 miles. Anyone who can figure out simple arithmetic knows it's impossible."

Joachim chose this moment to break in on the small group gathered around a card table, drinking schnapps and conversing, but as soon as the correspondents spotted Joachim, they visibly closed ranks and fell quiet. Fred Kramer, looking as if he hadn't slept in days, rearranged his hand of cards. "Whose turn is it?" he asked.

Joachim, hoping to put them at ease, approached with his most congenial smile. "Am I too early for Lady Catherine's reception?" he asked them.

"You certainly are," spoke up Marla Franklin first. "That's not for another two hours." She was plainly dressed, almost dowdy, which surprised Joachim, but when she looked up at him, her startling blue eyes reflected an inviting sharpness. He admired her articles.

Despite German censorship, she managed to convey subtle descriptions of the truth through the layers of lies. The man beside her he immediately recognized was her bureau chief, Christopher Tobin. The table of journalists, he noted, were all well-known and respected.

"Then would you join me for a good meal and some friendly conversation?"

"The meal is no problem, but...," Marla looked directly at him, "we may have some trouble with the friendly conversation."

"Ah, my uniform. You do not like it. If I removed my jacket and tie, would you like me better?"

They looked questioningly at one another. In public, SS officers were expected to remain in full uniform. His unusual gesture tweaked their curiosity. He could see silent agreement pass around the table. Wilson Meredith said, "Just your cap will do."

"Thank you very much," Joachim said as he removed his cap and slung it under his arm. "What game are you playing?"

"Poker," answered Kramer with a straight face.

"I don't know it. Do you mind if I watch?"

"You said you were here for a good meal and some social conversation," Tobin said folding up his cards. "Anything you order on the menu is excellent." He motioned to the bartender. "Do you mind setting the table beside the fireplace?" he asked. "Our friend here is joining us for dinner."

The burly bartender glanced warily at Joachim, then nodded to Tobin and folded up the card table. The journalists picked up their drinks and moved to the round cushioned booth by the fireplace. Joachim quickly decided on a rouladen dish and wine. Marla ordered veal while the three men chose spaghetti—"as good here as any Italian restaurant and a nice change from German cooking"—and more schnapps.

They enjoyed a hearty meal, and to Joachim's credit, their conversation was quite relaxed. "Well, gentlemen," said Marla at last. "Lady Catherine's appearance is only an hour away. I have to change. May I remind you grubbies that you are expected to show up in penguin suits."

Joachim looked as confused as he felt. "Penguin suits?"

Kramer answered, "You know, bib and tux." When he saw Joachim's puzzlement deepen, he took pity and explained further, "It's slang for evening dress."

"Ah," said Joachim. "American slang I have yet to learn. You mean formal wear. The men wear tuxedos and the women wear gowns."

"That's it, Colonel. And Marla's right. If we want to see this brilliant pianist from England tonight, we need to shave and change, so please excuse us."

"Of course." Joachim rose as the journalists stood and left the table.

Another hour of waiting. He felt like a schoolboy experiencing his first crush. Every second until Catherine's arrival became endlessly long. To steady the excited fluttering inside his stomach, he decided to keep himself busy. He handed in his cap to the cloakroom attendant, who stacked it on the shelf over his coat. Next, he spent time browsing through the multitude of books lining the library hall. From there, he could watch the incoming guests without drawing notice to himself.

Soon the main lounge filled with foreign dignitaries and staff officers from the German High Command. Most of the Nazi officers and their wives Joachim had met through his contact with them at the Propaganda Ministry. How often had he been subjected to their tiresome bragging? If the Berliners weren't gloating over the popular works of German composers, especially Hitler's favorite Richard Wagner, they would prattle on about their film star idols, fancy night spots and elegant restaurants—all safe, non-political topics except for their constant praise of the great prosperity *der Fuhrer* had brought them in just five years. He often felt the crown of one-upmanship should go to the one who could gossip with the most intimate details about Hermann Goring's lavish banquets. Only foreign dignitaries and the party elite, the same gathering that was here for Catherine's reception, were invited to Goring's Karinhall estate, the home of the dual Reichstag president and Luftwaffe chief that was in the Schorfheide forests north-east of Berlin.

One face he recognized, but had not yet met, intrigued him—the Gestapo's new section head for Berlin, Colonel Friedrich Streicher. His silken-textured hair, which was the color of honey and was perfectly groomed back from his smooth forehead, framed the chiseled features of a highly disciplined man. His obviously expensive suit fitted into this room of exquisitely dressed people, but the correctness of his neatness unmasked a deeper need for absolute control. He moved through the gathering like a shark swishing between swimmers treading water. Those he brushed by held their breath until he passed out of range. At one point, he stopped and turned towards Joachim. Their eyes held a curious scrutiny of each other.

Sensing immediate danger, Joachim's core temperature dropped. His survival instincts kicked in, and the blood vessels of his extremities constricted to increase the flow to his heart. In effect, he wrapped himself in a non-conductive shell. The physiological trick dulled his skin tone and dimmed the brightness of his eyes. The mutation completed his master race impression. He acknowledged the Gestapo officer with a curt nod. Streicher's mouth twisted into the thin smile of a fellow conspirator, before his attention shifted back to circling the room for suspicious prey.

From what Joachim had already learned, little was known about Streicher. That didn't surprise Joachim. He well knew SS Reichsfuhrer Heinrich Himmler, who looked like an owl-faced schoolmaster, believed the less people knew about his agents the more intimidating the SS and Gestapo became. Though many believed Himmler was Hitler's closest advisor, Himmler's second-in-command, Reinhard Heydrich, threatened his favor. As far as Joachim was concerned, Hitler played the rivalry between his two intelligence chiefs with such finesse neither trusted the other. It kept the three-tiered organization—SS, Gestapo and SD—unbalanced and cemented the loyalty of the two henchmen to him. Actually, it was a clever strategy that earned Joachim's respect for Hitler.

According to Joachim's growing information, Himmler, like the Fuhrer, had no tolerance for intellectuals. Neither did Streicher, it seemed. He had already gained a reputation for bullying his suspects and torturing his prisoners. Heydrich, on the other hand, was called Himmler's brain behind the Gestapo chief's back. He did respect the academic ego and scholarly mind, with the tolerance of one who understood individual differences. He took pride in seducing his suspects to find out what he wanted to know before executing them. Joachim guessed Hitler's fascination with Heydrich stemmed more from his fear of being outsmarted than from true admiration. If given a choice between the two departments, Joachim definitely preferred working for Schellenberg under Heydrich than for Streicher under Himmler.

Suddenly, the chatter quieted, and all eyes turned to the entrance hall. Joachim could just see Catherine's head wrapped in a fur hood. With her was Sir Isaac Malcolm. His thick red mustache quivered as he laughed at something the Press Club host said. They briefly disappeared in the checkroom with the reception committee.

The respite gave Joachim a moment to regain his composure from the double-barreled jolt of seeing Catherine and Sir Isaac together. If the fleeting glimpse of Catherine felt overwhelming—she had matured into a graceful beauty—the sight of Sir Isaac was utterly unsettling. Yet, the timing of the spymaster's unexpected appearance set Joachim to thinking. He did have information he needed to pass on to London. How he managed it would now depend on Catherine's performance, whether it would be conducted like a concert recital or whether it would be more informal with people comfortably seated around her at the grand piano.

Sir Isaac and he had set up a very intricate method of transmitting messages in an emergency. This might be the opening to test it, in the face of some of Germany's highest ranking generals and the Gestapo's shark-eyed Colonel Streicher. Joachim's sudden thrust into danger quickened another adrenaline rush. He tucked in his stomach, breathed in deeply and strolled into the main lounge just as Marla descended the stairs. Her dramatic transformation astounded him.

A glittering necklace collared her neck, and full-length satin sheathed her body. She had gathered her lustrous dark hair to the back of her head in a smooth French roll. The understated elegance captured her sensual grace and suggestive eyes that strangely reflected the green of her gown instead of the marvelous blue Joachim remembered. This night was evolving into a series of the unexpected, he mused. Earlier, he hadn't grasped what an incredible beauty Marla was. Now, she was drawing the eyes of every man and the envy of most of the women in the hall.

All at once, it struck him. She was stealing center stage from Catherine. Only someone very vain and self-absorbed would do that, he fumed. As Marla came face-to-face with him at the bottom of the stairs, he left her feeling foolishly rejected as he ignored her outstretched hand and walked toward Catherine, who was being led into the center of the main hall by a committee from the Reich Cultural Society and a bevy of reporters.

While walking over to the piano, Catherine caught sight of Joachim amongst the bystanders and paused, openly staring. Her eyes lit up as if she knew him.

What's happening here? Joachim wondered. Acutely aware of Colonel Streicher's sudden interest in their shared attraction, he recovered his senses first and began clapping to divert Catherine's attention. The room suddenly filled with welcoming applause. He thought he detected her blush. She dropped her eyes modestly, and his heart hammered against his chest as she carried on walking toward the piano.

What was he to do? It would be worse, he decided, if he pretended they hadn't experienced a mutual magnetism. The normal reaction would be to let the flirtation run its course. That was the answer then, and it would be his secret pleasure.

And so he let himself be caught up in her breathtaking loveliness and extraordinary music for all to see. He drank in every detail; from the dainty diamond tiara that encircled her crown of honey curls to the swells of creamy skin peeking out from her heart-shaped neckline to the rich teal gown that emphasized her tiny waist and small pointed breasts; from her repertoire of Bach, Brahms and Beethoven—with powerful cadences and frolicking scales of romantic arrangements she surrendered to immortality—to the final lilting passages of the *Moonlight Sonata*, which she shaped with the skill of a *bel canto* singer.

It was a performance of art and spirit blissfully intertwined. The applause did not want to die, but eventually her audience let her rest.

Joachim threaded through the devotees draping the piano and stood at the edge until Catherine became aware of him. Again their eyes linked and the world about them closed in to just the two of them.

"I've heard you play before," he said.

"I know," she said. "In Vienna."

He was amazed. "You saw me?"

She nodded a little shyly. Fate must be drawing them together, he decided. Now was his chance. "Do you know what would really please me?"

"I can't imagine," she said.

"If you would play a duet with me."

She looked genuinely surprised. "I don't know any

duets, Colonel…?"

"Forgive my bad manners, Lady Catherine. I am Baron von Daren."

"But in the uniform of an SS colonel. You must be very influential."

For the moment he resented his uniform and his duty. "Not influential enough, it seems, to persuade you to play with me."

"*If not now, WHEN*?"

She was flirting with him, but was she crazy to quote from a verse written by a Jewish philosopher? Before she could become carried away in some discourse on the line, he moved to the piano bench and sat down beside her. He began to play the opening passages of Debussy's *Clair de Lune*. "Do you know it?" he asked.

She nodded.

"You play. I'll improvise," he told her.

At first she stared at him, as if she couldn't believe what he had just said, and then she placed her hands on the keys and began playing. Joachim introduced a jazz counterpoint to Catherine's classical treatment of the melody. His harmony contained fragments of a prearranged code based on notes and patterns only Sir Isaac could recognize with his perfect pitch. At least, he hoped only Sir Isaac would identify and understand his disguised code. Through the music, he told him of his new assignment with Schellenberg to monitor Dr. Holbak in Copenhagen. He dared not look to see if Sir Isaac was catching on.

As they played together, Catherine became enraptured with his harmony, and her eyes reflected her immediate admiration. They easily blended and extended each other's music. When they finally came to the end of the piece, the gathering around the piano broke into raves and clapped fervently. To show her own respect for von Daren's brilliant playing, she joined in their ovation.

"I would never have believed it was possible," she told him.

"Nor I," he said. "Nor I. But what fun, yes!"

She laughed. "What other surprises do you have?"

"Only one a performance," he said.

She looked disappointed. He understood that he was cutting their connection short. "Would you have time to join me for a drink before you are whisked away?"

"Oh, yes, I would like that."

He escorted her to the only free booth in the anteroom. It happened to be next to Marla Franklin and Christopher Tobin. There was significant silence between the two tables. "I think this occasion deserves champagne. Wait here for me," he instructed her.

Soft chamber music played on the radio behind the bar as he waited for the bartender to bring him a bottle of champagne. He took the bottle and two champagne glasses back to their table. When he was seated again, he poured one glass for her and one for himself, and then raised his glass in toast to her. "To the most wonderful moment in my life...playing Debussy with the woman I most admire."

Catherine blushed at the flattery. He waited until she tipped her glass to his. As they sipped the champagne, their eyes locked. Neither one wanted to drop contact first. Catherine nodded toward the table next to them. "Is that Marla Franklin beside us? Oh!" she caught herself. "How could you know her? She writes for the *London Times*."

He acknowledged her assumption with a smile. "I do read your English papers..."

Suddenly, Joseph Goebbel's high-pitched effeminate voice screeched from the radio behind the bar. "*The murderer has confessed!*"

Immediately alert, Joachim ordered the bartender to turn up the volume on the radio. A hush fell over the reception. Everyone's ears were pinned to the radio. Goebbel's shrill voice continued ranting over the air, denouncing the Jews with a story of a German diplomat's assassination in Paris.

"The murderer has *confessed*!" he screeched again. "Herschel Grynszpan, a 17-year-old boy, a Polish *Jew*, has admitted to killing Ernst vom Rath, the Third Secretary in our Paris Embassy. Let every *Jew* in Germany be identified tonight with this unspeakable crime against the German people. NO *Jewish* business, NO *Jewish* home, and NO *Jewish* body will enjoy Reich protection from German citizens revenging their slain brother. We will rid Germany of these *UNTERMENSCHEN*! The German people are entitled to their time of vengeance!"

His voice shrilled on, out of control. "And the time is NOW! Destroy the miserable *Jews* before they ravage our youth in their prime! Seek out every one and make him pay...PAY...*PAY* for this public assault on an esteemed Reich representative of the German people! Let no mark of *Jewish* life continue to exist in Germany!"

His frenetic pitch cut off sharply, and the *Funeral March* from Beethoven's Third Symphony broke in. Several moments later the radio screamed again with Goebbel's ravings. "No German is safe from the miserable *Jews* until they are all gone!"

"My God!" Catherine cried out in disbelief.

"He's ordering the massacre of the Jews!"

"Hush! Someone might hear you," Joachim implored her. The whites of her eyes bulged, partly in shock, partly in anger. The journalists and the Nazi officers in the Club began rising from their tables. Outside, loud speakers at every corner were blaring Goebbel's news. The streets reverberated with the madness of his caterwaul.

Suddenly, a brown raincoated storm trooper burst through the entrance doors waving copies of *Der Volkische Beobachter* and threw one newspaper down on every table. "Read!" he ordered. "READ!"

Joachim stared at the ugly heavy-set black headlines, sick at heart, until he grew aware of Catherine staring at him.Her gaze fell on the black color of his SS uniform, the silver trim and finally on the three-leaf oak pins, one clipped to each lapel. At last, fear and disgust registered in her eyes.

"No, Catherine..."

Fred Kramer of the United Press came up to him and spat, "This is one story you pigs can't squash!"

The other correspondents joined him and stormed out of the building. As Marla rose to follow, Colonel Streicher stepped in front of her, solidly blocking her path. Across from Joachim, Catherine helplessly watched their confrontation.

Streicher hissed, "I can have you and your press friends deported."

"Just try," she shot back.

He sneered. "Today the Jews. Tomorrow the Catholics. And the day after that *all* journalists."

He stood there in front of her smirking. Marla's chin jutted out in defiance, and as she swept by him, her shoulders seemed to broaden. Streicher glared after her. When his attention turned back to Joachim, he arched one eyebrow explicitly. Joachim stilled every emotion that might betray him and stiffly nodded. In response, Streicher's lips split into a twisted smile of smug satisfaction. He slapped his leather gloves against his thighs, swung around and cut his way through the stunned onlookers to the foyer, leaving in his wake absolute terror.

"Please," Catherine pleaded, "how do we get out of here?"

He led her to the checkroom. The attendants had fled. One officer had taken control and was passing out the coats as the people called out their check numbers.

"Where's Sir Isaac?" Catherine suddenly asked in alarm. "He has my coat check."

Joachim looked around. "I can't see him. Don't worry. No harm will come to you tonight. Not while I'm with you."

A mixture of emotions filled her eyes. Joachim pushed through to the coat rack, retrieved his military cap and tapped it on his head, then found her hooded fur cape. He wrapped it around her shoulders and rushed her outside. Beyond the horizon, a funnel of fire shot into the night sky. Its eerie glow formed an evil halo.

A hushed voice near them whispered, "They are burning the great synagogue on *Fasanenstrasse*." But the presence of Joachim's SS uniform quelled any more remarks. Joachim felt disgraced and helpless.

"Lady Catherine, I could not let you speak your mind inside. I'm sorry. Germany has lost all dignity and decency," he whispered disconsolately. He lifted his cap and shaved his fingers through his close cropped hair as he stared at the torched skyline. Black ribbons of smoke drifted closer as acrid smells from the mixture of kerosene and smoke burned his throat. Tears blistered his eyes. From the distance, a jumble of sounds riddled his ears: jeering shouts, painful shrieks, glass shattering and jackboots thundering. He gritted his teeth and resolutely set his cap with the Death's Head emblem over his brow correctly.

"It's murder!" Catherine angrily hissed at him. "*Full scale murder*! What kind of people *are* you?"

In anguish, Joachim searched to give her an answer. "We are not all Nazis, Catherine. *They* have the power. *They* can destroy any of us at will."

"But there are more of you than there are of them! How can you let them do this to innocent people? There must be something we can do to stop them!" she cried, looking around in desperation for some sign of help, but the people hanging out their windows or filling the nearby streets gawked in silence. One old man shook his head and pulled his wife back inside their upper floor flat. He closed the window and pulled the curtains.

Just then, a black cab pulled up to the curb. Marla jumped out and ran up to Catherine. "I don't have time to explain who I am, but Sir Isaac says you have to come with me, Catherine."

Catherine hesitated.

"NOW!" insisted Marla.

"*If not now, WHEN?*" Joachim quoted to Catherine. Her eyes reflected her confusion and disillusionment. He took her by the elbow and ushered her toward the waiting taxi. "Take good care of her, Marla," he said, helping them slide into the back seat.

As he started to close the door, Catherine's sad eyes pleaded with him.

He paused. "This is my homeland, right or wrong," he told her. "Lock your doors," he instructed, finally banging the door shut. He saluted to them and rapped the hood of the trunk to signal the driver to get moving. As the motorcar pulled away, he could see Catherine's face peering back at him through the rear window. Before the limousine cleared the corner, he thought he saw tears running down her cheeks.

Chapter Four

MARLA GLANCED at the young English girl who had not spoken since she had climbed into the back seat with her. Catherine's expression was set, her eyes, sadly troubled. *Such a lovely face*, Marla thought. *So young yet so old.*

Something had clicked between the king's cousin and the handsome Nazi colonel long before tonight. She was sure this was not their first encounter. During dinner, Marla had sensed the SS officer's interest in her. She had planned to use his attraction to gain more introductions to Hitler's inner circle, but von Daren's abrupt rebuff of her in front of so many of the Nazi Party's elite baffled as well as insulted her. Was she so obvious or was he so sharp to see what she was up to? It was only when she observed the magnetic charge between Lady Catherine and him that she suspected he assumed Marla was stealing attention away from Catherine's performance. Well, she had to admit, that was part of the game she played with herself—the challenge of winning against a "stacked deck." But this SS officer's reaction, no matter what the cause, intrigued her. Was he just gallant in romance or did he act protective towards Catherine for another reason?

Three blocks south of the Press Club, Catherine spoke first. "Where are we going?"

"I'm sorry. I should have introduced…"

"I know who you are. I read the papers." The young pianist looked at Marla with amazing calm. "I just want to know where we are going?"

"The American Embassy."

"Why not the British Embassy?"

"Sir Isaac is at the American Embassy," Marla told her.

"I see," Catherine replied and resumed looking out the window at the fashionable 16th and 17th century villas lining both sides of the street. Each three-story mansion had been divided into luxury flats nestled behind tidy little courtyards.

As they neared the Kaiser Wilhelm Memorial Church, a fire truck blocked the cab's entrance at the intersecting streets. To the west, billowing flames roared out of control. The cab driver kept the taxi's engine idling. "What do you want me to do?" he asked Marla.

Catherine swiveled around in her seat and quietly considered Marla. "I don't know what Sir Isaac's orders are, but I assure you I don't need to be coddled. This is a once-in-a-lifetime story. Do what you would do if I weren't here."

"Right. Thanks," Marla said. "Can you get on the Kurfurstendamm from another street?" she asked the driver.

"The Kurfurstendamm runs west," he said. "We have to go east to the American Embassy. We would be going in the wrong direction."

"Do it." Marla rolled down her window slightly as

he backed up the taxi and wheeled down another back street of elegant Renaissance homes. Despite the blazing sky and insistent clanging of fire bells, the shutters on each home remained shut to the madness storming Berlin.

They heard the yelling and cursing before they saw the flickering reflections of myriad torches lighting the side walls of the buildings on the next block. The driver slowed the cab down almost to a complete stop.

"Roll up your window," he said.

Marla quickly followed his instruction as a roving gang of youngsters rounded the corner. These were the scavengers pillaging the stores. They carried trophies of lamps, fur coats, clothing, shoes, hats, paintings, artifacts...anything they could grab without hauling a cart. Some hoisted plaque cards on broom handles with hand-painted lettering: *"Juden! Verrecken!* Jews die!" Driven by their excitement, a few banged into the cab as they pushed by and peered in at Marla and Catherine in the back seat. A storm trooper tapped the driver's window.

"Where did you pick up these people?" he asked once the driver lowered it.

"The Press Club."

"Where are you going?"

"The American Embassy."

With cold detachment, the storm trooper studied the occupants in the back seat and noted their aristocratic appearance—one flawlessly Aryan and delicate, the other worldly and elegant. "Show me your papers, please."

The driver handed him his papers.

"Your passengers too."

Both women rummaged inside their evening purses,

pulled out their passports and passed them over the back of the driver to the storm trooper. He studied them intensely. A few times he checked the photos against their faces before he handed them back.

"You should not be in this area tonight," he said disapprovingly. "Take Tiergartenstrasse to Wilhelmstrasse. The shopping plazas in the west and southwest districts and along the Kurfurstendamm are off limits. If you do take them, you do so at your own risk." He clicked his heels and saluted. "Heil, Hitler!"

Marla and Catherine nodded solemnly. The driver rolled up his window again and pressed the accelerator cautiously. He steered the cab through the thinning mob at crawl speed, but as he cornered the next block, they were overcome by another, more frightening pack of hardened young Nazis. Marla pointed to the military boots gleaming beneath their pant legs. Catherine's expression became more alarmed as she too realized their ruthless plunder had to be orchestrated by the SS. They carried lead pipes, ax handles and crowbars. The sheer pressure of their frenzied bodies rubbing against the cab rocked it.

Marla clasped Catherine's hand. "Don't show your fear." she whispered. "They'll think we're Jews."

Noisy hooting ruptured the air. "Over here!" someone called. "Another Jew house." The horde wildly cheered and rushed toward the new object of their vindictive fury. "*Tor auf!* Open the gate," they chanted. The first few scrambled over the railing gate with iron letters scrolled across the top that spelled, *Singer Haus*. The gate led to a late Renaissance villa on the west side of the block. The hinges of the gate creaked under their collective weight. Some of the civilian-dressed storm troopers chipped at the lock with their crowbars until the gate gave way for the rest to flood the proudly groomed courtyard beyond. They raced up the front steps of the grand portico two at a time and hammered on the front door.

At this point, Marla could have directed the driver to move on, but she didn't. Instead, she drew out her sketching pad and pencil from her shoulder bag. Catherine watched in amazement. "What are you doing?" she asked.

"Some reporters take pictures," Marla replied. "I draw." As she swiftly flipped the pages to a clean sheet, she instructed the driver, "Keep the engine running."

"*Judenschweine!*" yelled the maddened throng. "*Verrecken!* Jewish pigs! Die!" The pillars supporting the portico trembled with their taunts. "We know you're there!"

Marla's quick strokes became a camera, freezing each act of terror on paper.

Shouting and cursing, the disguised SS beat the front door with ax handles and lead pipes. Some removed large rocks from pockets or back packs and hurled them, pummeling the windows on the first floor with diamond-sharp blows. The panes of glass shattered like fireworks bursting into a thousand pieces of glittering crystals, falling and crashing in a jagged maze on the cobblestone below. A cheer rose after each hit.

"They're all mad dogs!" muttered Marla, drawing furiously to keep up to the hysteria propelling the mob. In no time, they broke down the main door, and the youth, savage in their manic zeal, stormed inside the house. One by one, the lights came on. Shapes behind the curtains bobbed up and down and around like puppets. The drapes were pulled, and one window after the next, on every floor, was smashed from inside. The sound of glass breaking against the side of the house and on the stone courtyard below chimed in tune with the blood curdling screams from within.

Marla was so immersed in catching every detail that the focus of her mental energy had completely detached her from the horrors she was witnessing. When she glanced at Catherine's devastated disbelief, she experienced fleeting guilt, but then the momentum of the story drove her on, and she drew with increasing swiftness. Her drawings erupted into desolate pictures of inhuman breadth.

From the second floor balcony, one rioter after another tossed books and furniture to the ground. Three men shoved a Bechstein piano between the French doors of the balcony. Another younger man hauled the stool over, sat down and began pounding out a German polka on its keys. Down at the front entrance, two uniformed troopers dragged out a man and woman in night dress. The woman clutched a small bundle to her breast. Other families from the apartments inside were herded out and made to stand in their bare feet on the shattered glass. Their prized possessions were heaved out the windows onto the ground. The polka played on in a crazed parody of the humiliating drama. Laughing, the torch bearers set fire to the growing pile while others used their lead pipes to push and prod the victims to dance around the smoking fire on the jagged shards covering the courtyard. Their pitiful cries from the pain of the cuts to their feet and their trail of blood incensed the most vicious of the rabid Nazis. He snatched the bundle from the woman's arms.

"Who wants a Jew baby?" he yelled. A great swelling of laughter rose skyward with the hungry flames. While the beat of the polka pounded faster and faster, the light from the fire and the shimmering heat illuminated the infant he held. The mother looked on in dreadful apprehension as he raised her baby with one hand above his head and hurled it like a rugby ball to a teammate, who caught it and threw it to another. These men and boys lost all touch with reality as they yelled and cheered tossing the baby about. The edges of the blanket wrapping the infant fell open and its little legs flapped loosely as the mother desperately raced back and forth from one to the other, begging them to put her baby down. At last, the one who had seized it from her leered, "So you want your baby back. Here. Catch!"

He wrapped his big hand around its tiny feet and pitched it to her headfirst. She reached out in pitiful hope, but it dropped short of her grasp in a lifeless heap at her bleeding feet. She fell wailing to the ground and carefully gathered up its broken body in her arms. With inconsolable grief, she clutched the baby to her breast and crooned, while rocking on her knees in rhythm with the pounding piano.

Marla had never seen anything so fiendish. Bombing civilians and innocent children was one level of perversion, but this…this monstrous disregard for life was quite another. Flinging the baby to death was so inconceivable, she didn't want to believe what she had just seen. Cold shivers possessed her. She clenched her fists until her nails dug into the palms. A part of her wanted to grieve with the mother, but the journalist in her took up her pencil and drew the terrible anguish of the woman clasping her dead baby to her breast. Once she remembered Catherine and looked at her with concern. She was sitting white-faced and white-knuckled.

But it was not over. More torchbearing youths encircled the piano. One by one, each lanced the piano top with the tip of his torch until little clefts of fire cracked and spread, bursting into one sheet of flame. Barbs from the bunch now drunk on their own power dared the pianist to keep on playing. He lasted until the keys became too hot to touch and the heat scorched his hair. Charcoal crisps twirled above his head. The drapes framing the French doors suddenly caught fire, and he fell back coughing.

"*Dumbkauf!*" fumed the driver. "They could have saved the piano. Who would have known it belonged to a Jew!"

His remark finally penetrated Marla's tunneled detachment. She connected with such helpless rage, the urge to choke him consumed her. Only professional conditioning held her back from betraying her true revulsion.

"Have you seen enough?" he asked, eyeing both women in his rear view mirror. Marla nodded stonily and stashed her sketch pad in her bag. Beside her, Catherine strangled on a sob.

"Catherine...?"

"Why?" she gasped. Catherine's stricken plea twisted Marla's heart. She didn't know the reason for the horrors they were witnessing, only that Hitler's fanaticism was poisoning the mind and morals of a whole nation. Undisciplined passions had become fodder for his twisted concept of Puritanism. He had banned

Berlin's racy nightlife and splashy street sales of sex and dope and channeled the people's lust for sexual pleasures into a demonic orgy with the fatherland. The absolute submissiveness of the true Nazi to Hitler today was as if he had been spawned by the devil himself, and not of man at all.

"Why?" Catherine repeated. "Why?"

Marla reached for her hand and held it. "Easy, Catherine. You must hold on. Can you do that?"

Catherine nodded in quick jerks and released a shaky sigh.

"Go," Marla ordered the driver.

The cab rolled forward just as a large open truck screeched to a halt behind them. The sound frightened Catherine who instinctively ducked and cradled her head between her hands. Marla snapped her neck around to see out the rear-view window. A squad of SS soldiers jumped down from the truck, cocked their rifles and aimed them at the Jews in the courtyard. Most dragged from their apartments were clad only in nightclothes. At the edge of the bon fire, the bedraggled lot huddled together listening to the babel of orders squawking from a loudspeaker on top of the truck. When their tormentors began pushing them into lines to board the truck, the cab pulled away. Above the apartment house, Marla saw burnt orange and crimson flames feathering the sky.

Following the streets through the cosmopolitan area in western Berlin—past homes once gracious but now desecrated, past shops and sidewalk cafés that once strutted with character and charm but were now stripped of all dignity, past spires of flames licking the sky where synagogues burned in disgrace—their cab crunched over the crushed glass that stretched as far as the eye could see. Down every route, they saw stores raided and splintered glass cases with more jagged shards of glass strewn over the sidewalks in front. Mobs running wild through the streets sought Jews they could rob and beat. They looted and ransacked the buildings already plundered by the more organized bands. The local police ignored the victims' cries for help and mercy, and the fire trucks only hosed down Aryan stores and houses threatened by fires next to them.

The smell of kerosene and charred wreckage glutting the air stung the girls' eyes. Even with the car windows closed, black smoke penetrated the cab, burning their throats and sinuses, and filled their lungs until they wretched in spasms of coughing. Marla reached into her purse and extracted a hanky. She motioned to Catherine to do the same as she covered her nose and mouth. Catherine nodded she understood.

The cab finally turned east and escaped the nightmare that had already spread beyond Berlin. They sped along the tree-lined boulevard that bordered the Tiergarten, made a jog south on the Bellevue Allee, then east on Leipzigerstrasse to Wilhelmstrasse. Near the American Embassy, the streets again clogged with people rushing the American gates seeking refuge from the holocaust, and the driver could only thread the cab through the desperate crowd inch by inch until he made his way to a side lane that accessed the rear driveway.

Tobin was watching for them, and as the cab pulled up to the back door, he rushed out to pay the cabbie and quickly ushered them inside.

"What took you so long?" he demanded of Marla. "We've got a U.S. cargo plane on stand by at the Tempelhof airfield to fly you out."

"Toby, do you know what's going on out there?"

"Only what we hear. It's been bedlam since I arrived. The phones are ringing constantly. We've heard Jews are being arrested and put on trains for concentration camps, specifically Buchenwald and Dachau."

Marla nodded. "I saw people loaded on trucks. The SS and the Hitler Youth are dressed up like ordinary Germans, and they're plundering everything and anything that belongs to a Jew. The ones they catch..." she looked down and fought a sob lobbing in her throat, "...they're killing, wounding and maiming. I don't know if there will be any synagogues left standing in the morning. The Nazis are letting them burn themselves out. And you should see the streets, Toby. They're covered in broken glass from all the windows and display cases they've smashed."

Tobin looked grim. "So that's why German reports are calling it *Kristallnacht*."

"The Night of Broken Glass," Marla interpreted. "How apt! Whatever you've heard can't begin to describe how terrible it really is. Where's Sir Isaac?"

"He's still briefing the American ambassador," Toby answered.

"Did you get our suitcases from the Adlon Hotel?"

He pointed to them by the doorway.

"Good. Where can Catherine and I change?"

"In the staff room."

"We'll leave our ball gowns and most of our luggage. The embassy can send them along later. Change into slacks and your thickest sweaters, Catherine. You'll need boots to keep your feet warm. Cargo planes..." Marla clicked her fingers in front of Catherine's eyes. "Did you hear me?"

Catherine stood dazed, still rooted in the world

of horrors, incognizant of her surroundings. "How could they hate them so much? What have the Jews done? A little baby. Just a little baby. Why? The poor mother. What will happen to her? Marla, we should have done something. We didn't do anything! Oh God! We didn't do anything. We just watched."

Tears streamed down her face. Marla understood how time had stopped for Catherine. From her own experience she knew that being a witness deepens one's sense of powerlessness. Marla's reporting at least involved her enough that she could feel she was doing something, even if it failed. Catherine didn't have that leverage. Marla tried to reason with her.

"What could we do? We might have made everything worse for them. Or we could have been taken with them. How would that help? No one would know what happened to them. No one would know what happened to us. But we're still here, Catherine. We can tell what we saw. And we will talk about it and talk about it until we can gather the right forces to do something about it…to do something to make it stop. Do you hear me, Catherine?"

A dim light sparked in Catherine's eyes. "We will never forget."

"It's a pain locked in a corner of your heart forever," Marla admitted.

Catherine's full attention locked on Marla. "I've read the pain in your articles, but I never fully understood. Not until tonight. Oh, Marla, I'm so sorry."

New tears spilled down Catherine's cheeks. Marla, fighting her own emotionalism, gathered Catherine to her and held her. "It's not your fault. None of this is your fault." When Catherine had calmed, she let her go. "We have to change quickly and get back to London."

Catherine nodded. "You can count on me."

Marla smiled for the first time. "I know I can."

Tobin picked up their bags and led them to the staff's quarters. Inside the room, they never exchanged another word as they pulled out the clothes they needed for the flight and switched into them. In five minutes, they were ready and returned to the servants' entrance of the embassy where Tobin and Sir Isaac were waiting. At the sight of Sir Isaac's familiar face, Catherine forgot herself and rushed into his arms. His big hulk engulfed her. Then he firmly gripped her shoulders and stood back. "We must get on with it, Lass," he said. "No more tears." She bit her lip and nodded obediently.

"Sir," Marla interrupted, "I would rather stay here with Tobin."

Sir Isaac's craggy brows pinched together. "No story's worth dying for, Marla. I need you back in London."

His set expression squashed the objection forming on her lips. "That's an order," he added.

"Yes sir," she sighed and turned to Tobin. "Be careful," she said, offering her hand.

He covered it with both of his hands. Relief and regret mingled in his eyes. "You write from London. I'll call in the copy." After a pause, he added, "I'll miss you."

A tell-tale nerve twitched in Marla's jaw. "I'll be back. This war against the Jews has become personal."

Chapter Five

Thursday, March 30th, 1939

THE *LONDON TIMES* NEWSPAPER still lay on the coffee table. It was dated March 15, 1939. The headline boldly read: "PEACE IN OUR TIME A HOAX!"

The front page editorial condemned Prime Minister Neville Chamberlain for his part in the Munich Pact, the agreement between Britain and Nazi Germany that sold out the Sudetenland to Hitler. "That act of appeasement," stated the paper, "paved the way for today's betrayal."

More headlines in block letters shouted the news: "GERMAN TROOPS ENTER PRAGUE AFTER THE CZECHOSLOVAKIAN GOVERNMENT CAPITULATES... HITLER DECLARES TO THE WORLD THAT CZECHOSLOVAKIA HAS CEASED TO EXIST."

Fifteen days later, Lord James was leaving the newspaper story in full view as a deliberate reminder to the circle of influential financiers he was gathering regularly at Rushmore House. Every time Catherine saw it her stomach lurched. She remembered Berlin.

After she and Marla returned from Germany, the correspondent had stayed at Rushmore House for a month. That time became an important bridge back to a safe world for them both, and Catherine had someone to share the pain she was carrying in her heart. Marla helped her see that England's lethargy—actually the western allies' unacceptance of Germany's ominous threat to the free world—was understandable. Unless people had been personally exposed to Hitler's charisma and Germany's underlying fanaticism, as the two of them had been, it was quite possible they might find it difficult to be touched by things happening somewhere else or to imagine it affecting them directly.

That was on the good days, when reason prevailed. And then there were the bad days when the haunting memories of the atrocities they had seen seemed too much to bear. Though Marla and Catherine looked like a strange pair to be kindred spirits—the one so nurtured and the other so neglected in her upbringing—something beyond their mutual pain drew them together. A voiceless calling, there but not there, yet full of need, begging to be answered. A knowing and a coming together in an immortal quest for full acceptance and absolute deliverance. What their hearts sought in solitude, their souls found in unison.

Catherine's mother was the first to realize that all that really separated the two women was Marla's more seasoned worldliness. She told Lord James they were like apple blossoms from the same follicle, with Catherine's unfurling loveliness a shade behind Marla's full bloom. That startled him, but as he watched them grow to know each other, he saw other affinities that crossed their stark differences: They were loners, without friends their own age, and they were both dedicated to their careers. The more time they spent together, the more their friendship flourished. By the time Marla persuaded Sir Isaac to let her go back to Spain, they had shared all their private feelings and were closer than blood sisters.

On this particular day, Catherine felt lost. She especially missed their talks. Marla understood Catherine's restlessness. Nothing could ever be the same after the inhuman cruelty they witnessed. Catherine found it more difficult to memorize the long works for her new concert series. She even doubted her own faith. Now pondering the newspaper on the coffee table, she remembered one of their spirited discussions.

Marla had asked her what was her favorite city in Europe. "Vienna," she had answered.

"Vienna?" Marla repeated. She punched up one of the throw pillows from the deep sofa and wrapped her arms around it. "Why?" she asked.

Catherine could feel herself blushing. "That's where I saw Joachim von Daren for the first time. I really believe he's a very decent man."

"Sure," Marla said sarcastically, tossing her thick mane of hair over one ear. "Don't let romance blind you. He's a German. Worse, he's SS."

The reality tugged at Catherine's heart. "True," she said downcast.

"Is he the only reason Vienna is your favorite city?"

"Oh no. I won the Belvedere medal there, and I met Dr. Kantor. He conducted the orchestra."

"Are there still Jewish conductors left in Europe?"

"Maybe not now," Catherine acknowledged, "but

he's Hungarian. The Nazi influence doesn't seem as strong in Hungary, although I've often suspected he was followed by the Gestapo."

Catherine told her about the two men hiding in the shadows who had followed him outside. "He quoted a line from Hillel that has intrigued me. I've since looked up the verse: *If I am not for myself, who will be for me? If I am for myself only, what am I? If not now, WHEN?* What do you make of that, Marla?"

"Uh..uh, kiddo. You're not roping me into explaining it to you. I'm more interested in what you think it means."

"Well," Catherine said, framing her hands in the form of a church steeple, "*If I am not for myself, who will be for me?* sounds like another way of saying, *to thine own self be true*, and others will be true to you."

"You're a poet," Marla said, "and you don't even know it."

"Are you interested in what I think Hillel means or not?"

"I'm interested. Go on."

"*If I am for myself only, what am I?* is a paradox. If everything I do is for self-gain only, then I have no self-worth."

"If you're right," Marla mused, "you're saying the Nazis have no self-esteem."

"It's true," Catherine said. "I didn't realize it until you said it, but it's true."

"Evil is evil. There is no excuse for it, but if we follow your logic, not mine, the ultimate end for your kind of thinking is self-sacrifice."

"I disagree, Marla. It's fulfillment."

Marla rolled her eyes. "How old are you again?"

"Eighteen next summer."

"You're still a puppy. What do you know?"

"I know that you carry a pain deeper than the war," said Catherine.

Marla's twinkle shriveled. She looked deeply into Catherine's gentle blue eyes. "I think Horace Walpole was right in his *LETTER TO SIR HORACE MANN: this world is a comedy to those who think, a tragedy to those who feel.*"

"You're making fun of me."

"No, I'm not, Catherine. These are the lessons I've learned in life. No. 1: Nothing lasts forever. Things change. People change. Take nothing and no one for granted. No. 2: Never depend on anyone else but yourself. No. 3: Never love someone too much because it hurts too much to lose them."

Catherine found what she intended to say dying on her lips. It was more important to tell her, "I'm going to risk trusting and loving you, Marla. You're worth it."

It was at that point that Marla had told Catherine she was going back to cover the civil war in Spain. And Catherine understood why Marla had to do it even though she never told her. Marla simply couldn't admit how much she cared for all the people who couldn't speak for themselves. By telling about their plight to the world, she hoped to achieve help and support for them. She wasn't just a thinker after all, Catherine mused.

"Catherine!" her mother called. "Come to the library. The BBC has just announced Marla is making a special report on the wireless from Madrid."

Catherine raced up the stairs to the library on the second floor just as her father turned up the volume.

A high-pitched whistle squealed from the radio before Marla's faint words could be made out. *It's March 30th, 1939, and I'm Marla Franklin reporting ON THE SPOT from Madrid, Spain.*

Suddenly, the air waves cleared, and her voice burst into the room.

> *The war on Madrid is finally over. The last pockets of Republican resistance have been snuffed out. It was reported to General Francisco Franco just a few moments ago that his troops have taken complete command of the city...and indeed of the country.*
>
> *So many folks back home have not been able to understand why young sons and daughters have marched off to this land that is not their own and willingly sacrificed their lives to its cause. It makes sense when you are here. This human struggle against anti-democratic forces should be everyone's concern, but North America especially has been too far removed from the guns, tanks and diving planes that rain death everywhere to grasp the significance of what has really happened here.*
>
> *Franco's victory today has smashed Spain's chance to remain a free nation. Only the Soviet Union sent troops and arms to help the Republicans fight their fight and to save this small bud of democracy for future generations. The western allies' reluctance to intervene in this civil war, except for their gifts of relief, may draw them even deeper into the very war they have so carefully avoided, for the Nazi and Fascist bullies have gone un-*

punished one more time. This war was the one to stop Hitler from attacking some other vulnerable neighbor in Europe, but Great Britain, the U.S. and France have failed to recognize their opportunity. It is inevitable that the boys—Hitler and Mussolini, puffed up from their successes in Spain—will strike again soon.

The Nazis return home to Germany more skilled at spreading terror. Their experimental strafing tactics and high explosive fire bombs have worked out too well. They are triumphant. But, in making murder a means to their glory, they have actually lost their power. They do not see that once the oppressed have everything taken away from them that they were afraid of losing, they cease to fear, and a people immune to fear is an unrelenting enemy. If the Civil War in Spain has been our glimpse of the Armageddon to come, then the fire that burns in the eyes of Republican survivors is our torch of victory!

I'm Marla Franklin, reporting ON THE SPOT for the London Times in Madrid, Spain.

When Lord James switched off the radio, Catherine asked him, "Does this mean Marla will be coming home?"

"No dear," her father explained. "Sir Isaac mentioned she is being reassigned to Poland. She'll be working with Christopher Tobin again."

"Oh," Catherine said flatly. She abruptly left the library, and a few moments later Lord James and Princess Isabelle could hear her idly tinkling random notes on the piano. Gradually she began playing, at first a soft lamenting melody that swelled and swelled with more and more chords until finally a ringing march of thundering arpeggios broke through. Then, when all the sounds crying out from her soul were spent, she turned to playing Rachmaninoff.

"Catherine's playing the *No. 2 Concerto in C Minor*," Princess Isabelle commented to Lord James. She sat knitting while he read the *London Times*.

"Yes, I know she's upset," he said from behind his newspaper, impassively hiding emotions stirred at the little notice he was reading. Sir Isaac was calling for a secret meeting. *Project Amanita* was ready to go into action.

Chapter Six

Saturday, August 24th, 1940

FIRST LIEUTENANT BARON GUNTHER VON KOENIG-FORSTER was bone tired. He dozed off long enough to lose sight of his Squadron Leader's Heinkel III, which was the only bomber equipped to pick up the *Knickebein* radio signal guiding their bomb run from the French coast to the target—oil storage tanks about twenty miles east of London. As Gunther fell deeper and deeper into a much needed sleep, his plane drifted away from formation, off course. His wing plane followed him.

The two lone Heinkels shivered in the criss-crossing shafts of searchbeams directing a barrage of anti-aircraft fire. Flak thickened around them. Rumbling and rocking through the pocked airspace, the bombers flew on, too high to be seriously hit.

"Can you see mother?" cracked the German voice in Gunther's ear. His wingman's broken radio silence jarred Gunther out of his sleep. He jerked, hastily shook his head and looked around to get his bearings. Ack-ack puffs peppered the veil of clouds slipping under him.

Ahead, no silhouettes of bombers crossed the moon's face. His stomach fluttered nervously. "I've lost visual contact," he reported to his wingman.

Seconds later the air waves burbled again. "We must have missed the run-in. The oil tanks should have blown up by now. See anything?" asked his anxious wingman.

"Negative. How's your fuel?"

"Dropping. Where do you think we are?"

"Depends on how far we've drifted. If we stay on our present course, we can probably strike the secondary target at Rochester. We can't go back with this load."

"Right."

Another short silence passed before more transmissions spluttered between the two bombers. "Did you know today's my birthday?" asked Gunther's wingman.

"No," answered Gunther. Maintaining radio silence was ridiculous, he had decided. The enemy knew where they were.

"It is. I'm twenty-one..." The radio waves broke, slicing his next sentence in half. "Lots of flak down ... pretty in the black of night, doesn't it?"

"Let's drop our loads and head for home while we still have enough fuel to make it," suggested Gunther. He could hear his wingman sliding into a melancholy state of mind, an early warning of stress fatigue. His own fatigue had already cost them the mission. Better to abort now, he decided, and live to fight another day.

Because Goring refused to believe the Luftwaffe's losses were as heavy as they were, he had ordered his flight crews on round-the-clock saturation bombings over England to crush the enemy in time for Hitler's invasion deadline. As a result, Gunther's bomber squadron had been flying across the Channel, pounding England's airfields and ports, zipping back to home base, refuelling, rearming, and heading back out over the Channel. Again and again. The zigzag pace of flying and fighting, repeated over and over with virtually no sleep, was taking its toll on every pilot's accuracy and efficiency. Under such mad conditions, it was impossible to stay alert.

"Do you want us to drop our load here?" the wingman questioned Gunther. "Goring will have us all shot if our bombs strike London accidentally."

Gunther knew the ban on bombing London had come down from the Fuhrer himself. His edict was to be obeyed. He checked with his navigator. "Is there any chance we're over London now?"

"By my calculations, sir, we should be coming up on the secondary target ... NOW."

Gunther switched over from the intercom to the radio. "My navigator says we are over the secondary target. Does this check?"

"My compass has screwed up. I don't know where we are."

"I'm jettisoning my bombs then," said Gunther. "Are you with me?"

"I'm with you."

"Good," Gunther acknowledged. "Bomb doors open."

"Bomb doors open."

"Bombs away!"

"Bombs away!" echoed his wingman.

"I'm setting a course for home," said Gunther. "Follow me."

Both Luftwaffe pilots banked and circled their

Heinkel III bombers for a south-east course to Arras, France.

Little did they know that two of the bombs they released razed the oldest church in London's city core, St. Giles, while, in the square next door, the force of their blasts tore the statue of John Milton off his base. The rest of their bombs splayed bodies over the northern and eastern boroughs, killing customers coming out of the local pubs and movie goers on their way home. Only later, when Goring threatened to execute them for disobeying Hitler's order not to bomb London, did they hear about the havoc their navigational error caused.

In the meantime, it was the mistake Churchill needed to justify retaliation. Immediately he instructed RAF Bomber Command to raid Berlin: the first group it ordered to load up with bombs for the Nazi capital was a wing of Hampden medium-range bombers stationed in Norfolk on England's east coast. Then, it scrambled the 150 Squadron, which flew longer-range Wellingtons out of RAF Newton. Churchill not only wanted to make a fool of Goring, who had promised the German people that Allied bombs would never fall on Berlin, he wanted to panic the Berliners. So, night after night, British bombs riddled the German people's belief in their impregnable city and invincible leaders until Hitler was provoked into a rage seeking revenge.

Saturday, September 7th, 1940

HITLER'S FIRST TARGETS were the East Londoners.

German incendiary bombs, relentlessly falling on miles and miles of inland docks, straddled the Thames

River in a hellish siege. Like tinder boxes, the seedy mesh of old rundown factories, mills, assembly plants, hastily converted war works and rows of warehouses, which stretched down the river banks for as far as the eye could see, erupted into a lane of monstrous fires. They spread quickly. Vented lethal fumes, leaping ahead of the blazing columns, trapped fleeing workers within their tendrils of gagging death. Shooting sparks caught squalid company houses huddled around the industrial area. In no time at all, hungry flames licked the flimsy dwellings to the ground. Their homeless victims fled to whatever shelters they could find ... inside school basements, inside railway tunnels, any place that offered protection from the horrendous nightmare caving in on top of them.

"Those poor devils," muttered Lord James, looking out at the smoked orange crescent rising above the east side of London. Deep sadness doused the perpetual sparkle filling his hazel eyes. A white streak trimming his widow's peak added distinction to his aristocratic features and cultured air. Today he wore casual pants, a tweed jacket and his preferred paisley cravat loosely knotted around his neck inside a buttoned-down collar instead of his uniform. Whenever he could, he avoided starched collars and restrictive ties.

Lord James had never tried to fit into the inner circle of British aristocracy. Lacking impeccable lineage freed him from their uppercrust snobbery. In fact, he enjoyed telling the story of his origin: the first Earl of Cherington was a handsome peasant soldier named William Rushmore. He received his title and parcel of prime freehold land in the Hog's Back between Aldershot and Guildford in Surrey from King Charles II after he agreed to marry the king's illegitimate daughter and remove her troublemaking presence from his royal court.

It wasn't until the third Earl of Cherington, Edwin Rushmore, who married the only daughter of a neighboring landowner, that his family's fortune began to grow. He renamed the joint land Guild Oaks and built a magnificent stable for the Rushmore's first line of champion thoroughbreds. The fifth Earl, Henry Rushmore, favored a political career. Soon after he married the daughter of Queen Victoria's fleet commander, Admiral Woolsley, he moved his new bride into an impressive London mansion in Chelsea along the Thames River and was elected to the House of Parliament. He called their home Cherington Hall, and they hosted many lavish parties for the rich, the noble and the famous. By the time James was born, his father was already a prominent cabinet minister and a lord in the Upper House. For appearance sake, Lord Henry bowed to his father-in-law's wishes and sent his son to the toughest private schools, first at Osborne and then to the Dartmouth Naval Academy. It was a terrible ordeal for the awkward shy James. The admiral's credo still rang in his ears: "Real men serve their country, cowards hide behind it."

Sir Isaac, on the other hand, wasn't the least bit interested in Lord James' background. As he watched the dreadful bombing of East London beside his free-spirited peer, he was more grateful for his loyalty. He not only needed the nobleman's peculiar blend of intuitive yet analytical brilliance, he needed his generosity. Lord James' financial support was integral to the success or failure of *Project Amanita*. Sir Isaac chose this moment to tell him.

"Marla Franklin and Christopher Tobin have turned up in Moscow," he said. "They claim the Russians are after the same atomic scientists we are."

"To make this damned bomb, we not only have to race Hitler, we have to race the Russkies too?!" Lord James responded angrily. "Why am I surprised? We know Stalin can't be trusted. How is Marla?"

"Her nerves are shot. We'll have to recall her."

"And Tobin?"

"He wants to stay in the field."

"That can be arranged," said Lord James.

Unconsciously, Sir Isaac licked the shaggy tips of the red brush drooping over his upper lip. "I suggest you use Marla as your assistant. She and Lady Catherine can have their own show on the BBC."

Lord James stiffened. "I don't see the logic in involving my daughter again."

"Oh, come now, James. You fought against entering Catherine in the Belvedere Festival. She won it and the gold medal. You didn't want to send her on a concert tour of Europe. It was the most gratifying experience of her life."

"Watching that bastard Hitler stand and bow to her did make it worthwhile," Lord James begrudgingly admitted. "But what she saw in Berlin on *Kristallnacht* broke her heart. I won't let her be exposed to anything like that again."

"Our agents are set up inside Hitler's most trusted departments and in place no matter where he invades. We couldn't have done that without Marla and Catherine. They were perfect foils for Tobin and me. Now we have to activate those agents. Again, Marla and Catherine are our perfect cover."

"How?" Lord James demanded.

"A nightly spot on the air," Sir Isaac answered. "With Catherine playing serenades and Marla providing musical commentary. They're both so popular that together they'll draw terrific audience appeal. We simply work in our special codes to Marla's comments and send our deep cover agents orders the Gestapo can't trace."

"I see. Even though the Nazis have banned British broadcasts, even declared they will behead anyone caught listening to the BBC, you think the Gestapo will forgive our plants for listening to a musician Hitler himself publicly recognized."

"We will be airing music," Sir Isaac went on, ignoring Lord James' sarcasm, "not news. We'll broadcast on an approved European frequency. We can do that."

"When?" In resignation, Lord James' voice was barely audible. "When do you want the girls to start?"

"As soon as Marla has returned from Russia and she's recovered."

"I never wanted to involve Catherine in this thing," Lord James said sadly.

"Sorry, old chap. It's the only way."

A wing of Messerschmitt fighters suddenly roared over the grounds. "Damn those bastards. Where are our Spitfires?" Lord James demanded furiously.

Before Sir Isaac could answer, Princess Isabelle, distraught at seeing the waves of German planes flooding the sky, came racing up the stairs to find Lord James. "How can something so horrible look so beautiful?" she asked breathlessly as she rushed into the library.

Her question startled Sir Isaac.The men hadn't been looking at the artistic impression of the bombing, only the damage it was causing. He shook his head and excused himself.

Princess Isabelle slipped up beside Lord James in front of the open French doors of the library. "It's like a brilliant sunset," she whispered, gripping his arm with frightened fingers.

"It is indeed," he agreed tonelessly, moving her inside the protective circle of his arms. He held her head against his chest with one hand while gently massaging the nape of her neck with the other. They stood locked in each other's arms, watching.

"Shouldn't Catherine be home now?" she asked anxiously.

"I'm sure the hospitals will need every volunteer they can muster. No doubt she'll stay on duty until either she collapses or the ward nurses send her home."

"Yes, of course," Princess Isabelle sighed with despair. "Her volunteer work has become more important than her music and her family."

"Belle, Catherine's music career doesn't mean a tinker's dam if London is blown off the face of this earth." He spoke sharply, with an impatience he had never shown to his wife before. Her wonderful elegance had always fascinated him, and as she aged, that elegance had only become more gracious. This selfish, peevish attitude did not sound like the princess he had loved for twenty-five years.

He pressed. "Up until she became a volunteer, you were pushing for more civil support of the war effort." He turned her around so he could see directly into her eyes. "What has happened to your perspective?"

She never wavered as she pulled herself up to her full five-foot-two-inch height. "I didn't mean she should jump into steady wartime service," she declared. "I was talking about what other people should do. Catherine has a higher calling, a special talent to protect and preserve."

"To perform concerts for Hitler when he occupies London?" he scoffed.

"Of course not!" she flared. "You know better than that."

"I know Catherine feels she is doing something very important for her country and that you've been demeaning her sense of satisfaction from doing it."

"How dare you say that to me, James Edwin Rushmore! I've been doing no such thing! I've simply been encouraging her to keep her sense of duty to her country in balance with her own interests."

"Whose interests?" he mocked, seeing a side to his wife he never believed existed.

"If Catherine continues giving concerts, she contributes much more to a greater number of people," Princess Isabelle insisted.

"You mean, while London burns, Catherine's to play some new version of the Fall of Rome?"

"You are deliberately twisting my words to make me sound foolish, James."

"By all means, explain yourself, Belle. I'd like to understand what has happened to your thinking."

"Thank you," she said cuttingly, and carried on with her point. "Every time Catherine performs, she provides an imaginary escape. People need relief from constant danger and turmoil. They need familiar surroundings, soothing music...things that will lift their spirit in the face of death and destruction. I believe this is very important to all of our survival, James. Wherever we hide from the bombs, we need to carry something of our own with us. We need links to the voices and sounds that remind us of the sane times. Think of it, James," she urged.

"I am," he answered, suddenly aware that her idea to have Catherine perform had been neatly planted by Sir Isaac, in case Lord James balked at his plan. *That crafty old fox never misses a trick,* he mused. Since Princess Isabelle didn't know he had already agreed, he wasn't going to let her win so easily.

"There's a ruthless streak in you, Belle. I never would have believed it."

"These are ruthless times. Only the tough will make it through to the final outcome." She turned back to the view from their library's French doors. A scorched haze hollowed out the eastern skyline. "Hitler has finally come to London."

"Lord James?" chirped a female voice from the doorway. "I'm awfully sorry to interrupt you, sir, but an urgent signal for your eyes only has just come in."

"I'll be right there," he assured the young uniformed woman. "Excuse me, my dear. We'll talk about Catherine later."

"Of course, James." She knew with the bombing of London underway it might be days before she saw him again.

Life turns in strange circles, she thought to herself. When she first met her husband, he had been so stiff and shy, clearly uncomfortable in naval uniform. How he had hated Dartmouth, yet here he was in the thick of military activity. Ever since Germany's invasion of Poland, he had grown more secretive. As various West London gentry converted the ground floors of their large homes into interim War Offices for the rapidly expanding defense administrations under Churchill, Lord James handed over all of Rushmore House. She and Catherine had been forced to occupy the groundskeeper's quarters above their garage. He, along with most of their servants, had already joined the armed services. Only their faithful housekeeper, Nellie, and old George, who managed their horse stable at Guild Oaks in the country, remained. Princess Isabelle was finally ready to admit living over the coach house hadn't been as difficult a move as she had imagined it would be.

When the War Ministry took over Rushmore House, Lord James retained the library as his executive office. Princess Isabelle glanced up at the molded cornices protruding over the top of the mahogany book shelves built into the panelled walls. How long had it been since she had spent a quiet moment alone here? Ten months at least. The library had once been her private sanctuary.

She turned around slowly, drinking in the beloved poses of impish Arion sculpted into the four corners ledged under the high swirled ceiling. Each of his cherub faces seemed to wink down at her. His endearing presence in and out of the house had captured her heart when James had brought her here as his bride. When Lord Henry had died and James had inherited his title and all the Cherington land holdings, he had refused to sell this home they both loved so much to move back into Cherington Hall. His mother had remained there until she died. Then he had sold the estate and put the proceedings in a trust fund for Catherine. Her precious daughter would always be comfortably wealthy no matter what happened to James and her, and that in itself was a comforting thought. Gazing at her dear cherubs, she had forgotten the war, until the dreaded droning returned again.

Like strips of a venetian blind rolling down the glass panes, layers and layers of bombers streaked across the eastern sky. She rushed to the French doors and pulled them wide open for a better view.

It was dusk. Bombs rained over the horizon. Defending RAF fighters sliced through the neat Luftwaffe formations, fiercely attacking the enemy raiders. Spinning smoke trails from Dorniers and Heinkels, hit by enraged British squadrons, corkscrewed into the glowing skyline. On impact, fleeting flashes of smoked orange exploded upwards. Fried carcasses of fallen aircraft joined the wreckage burning in the streets. There were too few British fighters too late. The London docks and the Cockney district were utterly demolished by the falling fire bombs in this second assault.

Princess Isabelle could not see the human devastation, the bodies burned under piles of rubble, the charcoal-faced rescue teams, the moaning wounded, nor smell the heavy stench of death, but she could feel their agony. In her imagination, she saw it all as vividly as if she were there, one of them. She stood, shaking and sobbing, too filled with horror to pray. Her need for God was great. She said His name over and over again, until her last tear was drained. Then she became calm inside, and her prayer took form, for everyone—even for the Luftwaffe crews who had perished in the fight-to-the-death air battles. A mad devil was destroying them all, all the good people everywhere, whether friend or foe. She believed it absolutely.

Chapter Seven

Wednesday, September 11th, 1940

MILITARY STAFF CARS circled the Rushmore drive. The grounds hummed with activity as women in volunteer auxiliary uniforms and civilians and military personnel created continual traffic in and out the front entrance. Overhead flew a flight of British Spitfires.

In the coach house apartment over the Rushmore's three-car garage, Princess Isabelle struggled to close the suitcase mounted on top of the four-poster bed. Dressed in a chic suit and hat, she sat perched on the lid, impatiently shimmying her weight back and forth across the top trying to lock the overstuffed suitcase.

Laughing at her from the doorway, Catherine volunteered. "Here! Let me help!" When she heard the lock successfully click, she asked, "Have you told Daddy yet?"

"No," Princess Isabelle admitted, shaking her head as she slid off the suitcase onto the bed. "I left him a message, but I still haven't heard from him. I'm afraid it's going to be up to you to explain everything now."

Catherine hugged her mother. "I will, Mummy. Gladly."

At this precise moment, Lord James appeared in the doorway. When his gaze fell on Princess Isabelle's suitcase, his eagerness to see her switched to anxiety. "Are you off somewhere, Belle?"

She kissed him. Now that the moment had arrived, it wasn't so easy to explain. She looked at him with troubled loving eyes and decided to go straight to the point. "James," she said, "I'm converting Guild Oaks into a temporary home for displaced children."

His eyes rounded in surprise. "You're turning Guild Oaks into an orphanage!?"

"Not entirely. I expect we'll be able to re-unite some of the children with their families."

"My, my!"

"The children are our future. Everything possible must be done to help them through this dreadful war."

"Of course."

"You and Catherine are doing your bit. This is my contribution."

Watching her parents together greatly relieved Catherine. Even though her father only worked next door, he rarely found time for her mother, and Princess Isabelle was growing more restless and feeling more useless. To fill the void, she had begun interfering and reorganizing Catherine's life.

One second after Lord James had assessed all the possibilities of converting Guild Oaks into a home for displaced children, he beamed with enthusiasm. "It's a terrific idea, Belle. Why it's even great for the stable!"

"The stable?" Princess Isabelle blinked. She hadn't considered the horses.

Catherine immediately picked up on her father's point. "That's right, Mummy. With all our grooms and riders joining the army, George has been looking after the stable alone, except when I can help him. It's too much for him, especially at his age. But once the children arrive, he'll have all the help he needs. The older ones can learn to clean out the boxes and exercise the horses while the younger ones can help with feeding and grooming. I would think it would help the children work through the worst of their grief too."

"Belle, whatever funds you need, I'll look after them."

"I never doubted that, James," she said softly, her eyes reflecting the deep love, respect and longing she felt for him as he lovingly traced a gentle cross from side to side over her forehead and up and down her nose. In that moment there was no war separating them. When Lord James reluctantly withdrew his hand, he broke the tender spell between them.

"Catherine," he said somewhat gruffly, turning in the direction of his daughter, "your mother has told me that the BBC has offered you a spot on the wireless."

It was Princess Isabelle's turn to look surprised. Catherine averted her father's probing eyes. "Yes," she said. "It has."

"Actually, Sir Isaac arranged it. His orchestra is included in the program. It's another way of keeping London's musicians employed. It's too dangerous to carry on giving live concerts. Have you responded yet?"

Before Catherine could reply, her mother spoke up. "No, we haven't. Sir Isaac suggested we take some time to think about it. After all, it will take organization and direction to produce the kind of show Catherine would be happy doing."

"Catherine," Lord James said sternly, "I have never asked you to do anything against your will, but this time, there is no discussing the matter. You shall accept Sir Isaac's offer."

Catherine stared at him in disbelief. "You can't mean it, daddy."

Princess Isabelle also stood dumbstruck.

"I do mean it," he said. "Your music can serve England well. Even King George is delighted with the idea and is looking forward to hearing your program."

Princess Isabelle's one eyebrow raised in recognition. She had heard this argument before. It was her point to him. Men! she mentally sighed. He had fought her so hard, yet now he was talking as if the idea were entirely his own. Well, she thought to herself, he has his work cut out for him. Catherine has that stubborn look.

"The king is involved too, I see," said Catherine. "And what happens to my hospital duties?" she challenged her father.

"There is a greater need for you to serve, Catherine, whether you can see it or not. In war, you do not choose your assignment. You accept it and do as you are told. We are at war, and those who command the greater picture know where you will give your country your best service."

"Will you listen to yourself? When did you and Sir Isaac appoint yourselves God? Don't answer that question. When Churchill became prime minister, that's when. Do you think we're daft? That we can't see what's going on?" She squared her shoulders and declared, "I'm as good a soldier as the next man, but I am not leaving my hospital work."

"If you have time from your new duties, you can reschedule your shifts."

"IF!?" Catherine bristled. "Believe me, Father, I'll *make* time. Whether you, the king, or God himself like it, I have patients who depend on me. *No* one controls my life without my consent. NO ONE. *Not even God!!*" She stormed past her father and stomped down the hall.

"James, could you not have handled her more tactfully?" Princess Isabelle asked gently by his side. "She is not used to such treatment, especially from you."

He moved to the window and followed his daughter's raging retreat to the path through the woodlot. His heart ached. *Forgive me, Catherine*, he cried to her silently. *I had to do it. Project Amanita needs you. There's so little time, and you're the best answer we have. Perhaps the only answer*, he sadly acknowledged.

He knew his daughter. She had fine instincts, like a thoroughbred. Once she had time to walk off her anger, she would see what was at stake. She would co-operate. He glanced down at his wife as she nestled up to him. No doubt Belle believed that her arguments had convinced him. Though her points were valid, more than the regular audiences would be affected by their daughter's broadcasts. Hidden lives in Europe were depending on her too. He drew Princess Isabelle even closer to him.

"There's no time, my love, to persuade a prima donna to do what must be done. When Catherine's had time to mull over what I've said, she'll come to her senses. What's more," he added, smiling, "there'll be no further arguments between you two."

"Impossible. We thrive on our disagreements, but

thank you, dear heart." And she tipped an imaginary salute to him.

He kissed her affectionately on the cheek. "Time to go. By the way, Belle, just how many children are we going to lodge at Guild Oaks?"

"One hundred."

"Phew!" he whistled. "That many?"

"That many."

"It's a big undertaking."

"I realize that, dear."

He pressed her hand, then turned to leave. "James...," she stopped him. "Just a moment please."

He hesitated, attentive to the change in her tone. She looked down, searching for the courage to tell him of her other decision. When she looked up at him again, her eyes were moist. "James," she began, "I love you."

He took both of her hands and held them tenderly in his. "I know you do. I love you too."

"I am going to stay at Guild Oaks with the children," she told him softly.

"You mean you're not just going overnight?"

"No, James, I'm not."

His hands covered hers more tightly as the impact of what she was saying gripped him. "When?" Emotion welled in his throat, choking him. "I mean how long do we...?"

Because she'd been physically near whenever he needed to see her, he hadn't thought of her being alone, or lonely. Now it struck him. "Oh Gawd, woman! How I'll miss you!" He enclosed her inside the circle of his arms and embraced her with all his heart.

"I know, I know. I'll miss you too. I miss you now."

They clung together, aching, wanting, needing and

loving each other. "Will you be able to see me off? The train carrying the children is stopping at Kew Gardens Station to pick me up at 1330."

"That soon?" The pain of their parting so suddenly wrenched his insides. "Of course, Belle. Of course, I'll see you off. This bloody war can do without me for awhile."

Then he crushed her to him, holding her tightly, trying to infuse his love while drawing strength from her for the separation to come.

Chapter Eight

ONLY THE CALM PERSUASIVE INTERCESSION of his commander saved Gunther and his wingman from Goring's wrath. The repercussions of their navigational error, the jettisoning of their bombs over central London, had caused the pompous Reichmarshall to lose face before the German people, a deed as unforgivable as treason. If it were not for the daily raids over England causing staggering losses for the Luftwaffe, Gunther and his wingman would have been courtmartialled and executed for their "stupid mistake." Luckily for them, their Luftflotte commander convinced Goring that, if he hoped to bring London to its knees before Hitler's planned invasion date, he needed every available pilot and crew in the air, not in front of a firing squad. The ensuing investigation thus blamed the mishap on mechanical failure and cleared both their names of any responsibility.

On this Wednesday, Gunther loaded up his Heinkel-111 with over 5,000 pounds of high explosive bombs.

At midday, he took off for London with his squadron from the Luftwaffe's base near Lille, France. Over the whitecaps of the English Channel, they were joined by Messerschmitt-110 fighter escorts.

The medium-range Heinkel's twin engines throbbed incessantly, drilling and pressing the headache growing between Gunther's temples. The air crews were still being driven beyond normal endurance. He couldn't remember the last time he had enjoyed a solid four hour's sleep. He seemed to be running on an endless supply of adrenaline. As the wave of bombers and fighters approached Dover, he switched to his intercom and spoke to the crew. "I'm starting a zigzag course for the target now. Keep a sharp eye for British interceptors."

The familiar mouth of the Thames River, like the head of a long slithery snake, appeared in his cockpit's panoramic view of the terrain below. His whole forward area was enclosed in glass, from the Heinkel's nose cone to his flight deck just back and above it. Like a globe, it provided him with marvellous visibility, but its vulnerability to attack was completely unnerving.

Gunther followed the river's twisted course inland to London, to the city's commercial district. The voice of his navigator-bombardier crackled in his ear. "We're on track. The target should be coming up soon."

"Fighters ten o'clock high!" suddenly shouted the waist gunner.

Volleys of tracer bullets slashed his Heinkel's left engine. A second heavy blow bobbled the bomber. Rapid fire burst from the swivelling turret guns. Confusion swarmed. Shots splintered the air left and right. Then a thin line of black smoke streamed past his cockpit.

"I got it! I got it!" cheered the forward gunner. The hurricane attacker with its left wing sheared off tumbled earthward. Popping like a firecracker, it exploded into a red ball of flame. Amazingly, he could see a small white parachute blossom gently above the plunging fireball.

"I have him in my sights," observed the forward gunner.

"No," barked Gunther. "Save your ammunition for battle." The idea of shooting down an unarmed pilot sickened him. Gunther feathered his damaged port engine, trying to keep the Heinkel on its heading.

"Target coming up," instructed the calm voice in Gunther's ear. "Keep her steady, sir."

The navigator-bombardier pressed the release for the bomb bay doors. The red light didn't blink. He pushed the button again. Still no response. He began sweating. "The bomb doors seem to be stuck, sir," he reported.

"Open them manually," Gunther ordered. "We're losing oil. I can't maintain this altitude for long."

"Yes sir," said the navigator-bombardier. He scrambled down into the plane's belly to the bomb bay's hydraulic control and began yanking the lever. It wouldn't budge. Beads of sweat bubbled over his brow. He exerted all his strength. The chords of his neck strained. His veins bulged. The lever dropped a smidgen.

"That last hit must have jammed the gears," he muttered to himself while searching for something strong enough to force the handle down. Suddenly, the

Heinkel lurched, pitching him off balance. As he fell, he banged his head on a metal strut supporting the bomb rack. A bright flash! Dense smoke filled the belly gunner's cage and swallowed up the gunner's horrible scream. Then the bomber groaned, yawed and nose dived. The navigator hurtled forward. Flailing against the force of gravity pinning him down in the hold, he felt invisible powerful pressure crushing his chest. A rush of icy wind whipped at him mercilessly until he lost consciousness.

Up top, Gunther battled the controls. The smell of hot oil filled his nostrils. The needle on the radio-temperature gauge swung right, just nudging the red-alert band, while his altimeter needle pivoted wildly around the dial, churning off the thousands of feet the Heinkel was falling. Balancing the drag of the dead engine with more power from the starboard engine and counteractive pressure of the right rudder pedal, he pushed the control column forward. It went against every instinct of survival to plunge the plane into a deeper dive, but he resisted the urge to pull back on the control to bring the nose up. His only chance to recover the spin was to create more air speed.

The bomber shuddered and growled. At 600 feet it rounded out. Gunther whistled a tremendous sigh of relief as he eased back the control column for straight and level flight.

"Brauchman!" he shouted into the mouthpiece. There was no answer.

"Schulte! Gruber! Mueller!" he called the gunners. "Anybody?" Only the wind whipped in answer.

It was then he noticed the windshield splattered with blood. The control column shook in his hand again.

There was no time to think. He fought to keep the Heinkel steady. As he lifted the blood-splotched canopy back up over his head, fresh air rushed in. He gulped it greedily. Below him, the tree tops skimmed by.

The bomber was so low Gunther could not see the wide loop the Thames River took hugging the inverted tea cup of land beneath him. His plane had drifted far off course in a steady slip to the west. Though the Heinkel's directional controls were damaged, it somehow lumbered on, moving in a wide aimless circle, hanging onto an altitude of 100 feet.

Gunther felt strangely calm and deliberate. He knew he was going to die. No one could survive a crash with 5,000 pounds of incendiaries on board, but if he could just hold his height long enough to avoid plunging into the old stately homes weaving through the checkered tapestry below, he might be able to save them from the resulting inferno. Preserving their fine Victorian elegance gave him a sense of honor only another gentleman of noble birth could understand.

When the altimeter needle started to quiver, the control column in his hand responded sluggishly. He gripped it with both hands and struggled to keep the plane's nose level with the horizon. All at once, a windbreak of dense hawthorn trees, their twisted limbs furled like graceful gymnasts tumbling through the air, leapt up in front of him.

The people standing in the train station took no notice of the sound of the low flying bomber. They were so accustomed to every pitch and rumble of aircraft engines powering their winged warriors through the sky they were not alarmed. The areas being bombed were to the east of Kew Gardens. They cheerfully carried on chatting.

Princess Isabelle stood in front of her coach. Lord James tenderly planted a kiss on her forehead and stepped back to gather in her loving smile. During twenty-five devoted years together, he had never imagined this moment when she would not be there, by his side, gliding smoothly through his life like a comforting wand. He choked and could not say good-bye. Their eyes clung, not wanting to let go. She gently smiled then and turned to climb into the coach car.

Gunther's Heinkel bomber shaved off the tops of the hawthorn treeline. Their dagger tips showered the trim lawn.

Intrigued with the plane's valiant wiggling and waggling to stay aloft, the little children staring out bug-eyed from windows of the train, cheered it on, until they recognized the Nazi insignia. Then, with growing horror, they heard the bomber's motor stutter and choke, and in the sudden quiet their terrified screams pierced the calm.

As with one mind, the people on the platform rushed forward to open the compartment doors. Lord James reached in for Princess Isabelle and never saw the doomed bomber barrelling towards them from the other side of the train.

At the last possible moment, when Gunther realized it was hopeless, he stopped struggling with the controls in time to look up into the youngster's faces plastered against the train's windows. Their soundless terror raced to meet him.

Chapter Nine

THE SUDDEN HALT of the Martin horn's nasal seesaw was the Emergency Unit's only warning. The double doors swung open. While the ambulance attendants scurried to unload the first stretchers, the leader of the rescue squad hustled over to the admitting station. His name was Grimshaw, a plumber by trade.

Most of his rescue team was composed of skilled tradesmen and engineers who knew their way around every London construction and tunnel. They were a tough and persistent lot, digging through rubble hunting for people buried alive, sometimes for days at a time, refusing to abandon even the slimmest hope.

"Kew Garden's bin bombed!" Grimshaw hoarsely informed the senior nursing sister standing behind the desk. "A trainload of kids and most of the people standin' on the platform got it! The worst cases have been assigned here, Sister." The whites of his eyes poked out of his blackened face like bomb flares spiking a charcoal sky.

"Do you have their tag numbers?" she asked him unruffled.

He wearily swept his grimy hand across his brow. "Sister, we've bin too busy diggin' to look."

"How shall we identify the victims?"

"How the hell should I know?!"

"It's against hospital policy to..."

"Fuck hospital policy!" Grimshaw exploded at the starched nursing sister. "Don't you understand? We're bringin' kids who've bin bombed, Sister. And I mean *FIREBOMBED!!*" he spat. "See here."

He stepped aside, giving her full view of the stretchers being wheeled in. "Look for yourself," he said.

She stood mute.

"I've seen some 'orrible sights in this war," he told her shakily, "but nothin' to equal the poor little mites we're bringin' in now."

The nursing sister grimly appraised the hideous lumps of human cargo passing in front of her station.

"Where do you want them, Sister?" asked one of the stretcher bearers steering a gurney laden with a dazed little boy mumbling, "Bad plane... bad plane..."

She snapped immediately, "Line them up along the east corridor outside the examination rooms," and turned to the other shocked nurses beside her. "Sister Mary, get Lady Catherine to call in all off-duty staff. Sister Maureen, call the switchboard. We have a red alert here."

Seconds later the hospital PA system blared through the halls: *All emergency personnel to the East Wing ....REPEAT...All emergency personnel to the East Wing ...Lady Catherine report to Emergency Admissions...REPEAT...Lady Catherine report to*

Emergency Admissions ...

Suddenly, the Emergency Department swarmed with white coats. Nurses and orderlies rushed to take over the ambulance attendants' burdens. Three doctors positioned at Admitting for quick scans of the critical cases and directed the incoming traffic to the medical teams forming up in the examination rooms along the east corridor.

Catherine, in Ward 7, heard her name called and folded the letter she was writing for an injured airman. "Sorry, Collshaw, duty calls. We'll finish this letter later."

The young man sitting up in the bed nodded. His eyes were swathed with gauze bandages. "Right, ma'am. I'm not going anywhere."

Catherine patted his hand. "I'll be back as soon as I can, Collshaw," she assured him before stuffing the unfinished letter inside the writing pad she hastily deposited inside the RAF pilot's night table. She yanked back his privacy curtain and hurried out the ward.

Although she had learned to steel herself for some of the gruesome sights that came into Emergency, nothing could prepare her for the scene that confronted her in the east corridor. Litters of grotesquely scorched and mangled children lined the walls.

A searing pain stung her heart. Somehow her legs willed themselves down this hall of horrors as her body mechanically carried on while her mind floated outside, watching her, observing her confused awe as, in one zap of a second, she switched from such awful revulsion to feeling absolutely nothing. She was even too numb to feel guilty about feeling nothing. Her mind's eye sharpened. Colors became more intense. Shapes, looming larger than life, branding her memory with charred tangles and swollen bits of flesh…strips of fried skin hanging loosely from an arm here, a leg there…monstrous heads so bloated with edema that it was a miracle they didn't burst wide open…thighs that looked like raw meat roasted to medium rare…dismembered bodies…agonized moaning and frightened whimpering …a gaseous reek of gored stomachs, gouged bowels and burnt tissue, muscle and bone…staring, unseeing eyes.

Thus stunned with shock, Catherine managed to reach the Administration Desk without vomiting. "Lady Catherine reporting to Sister Mary," she quietly informed the desk clerk.

She stood very still, trying to compose herself for the work she was expected to do. She could see a man wearing a rescue helmet talking to one of the doctors checking the incoming victims. In between his giving directions to the attendants and examining the severity of wounds, she overheard the doctor ask, "What happened?"

"Jerry crashed into the train standin' in Kew Gardens," Grimshaw told the doctor. "It was filled with orphan kids the Earl of Cherington and his wife were sendin' to their country estate."

"Good God!" muttered the doctor. "How awful! No wonder these kids look like they've come from Dantes' hell."

"My guess is Jerry hadn't dumped his incendiaries before he crashed."

"Ugh," responded the doctor. More talk was disrupted by the next stretcher being wheeled in.

Kew Gardens bombed! Her mother and father. They would have been there! What of them? Catherine rushed over to the rescue worker and tugged at his arm. "What about Lord Ja... the Earl of Cherington and Princess Isabelle?" she asked frantically. "What happened to them?"

"Oh, they were killed in the crash, miss," Grimshaw reported politely.

Catherine stared at him stupidly.

"Did you know them?" he asked her.

She nodded mutely.

"A terrible thing, miss. A terrible thing," Grimshaw repeated, shaking his head. "I helped find lodgings for most of those children in East London when my team was called in to help. The little waifs peppered me with questions 'bout where they were goin', who was gonna look after 'em. They were so scared. To think they survived the damned bombings and now this. I suppose I'll have to help bury most of 'em too," he added morbidly.

Catherine stood paralyzed. Anything else Grimshaw said didn't register. A voiceless scream welled within her. *NO!* it screamed over and over again.

"Lady Catherine?" Sister Mary touched her arm. "LADY Catherine!"

Catherine stared at her blindly.

Mistaking Catherine's reaction, the nursing sister began again. "Lady Catherine, I know these are horrible cases you've seen, but I need you to get on with calling the off-duty staff immediately. We're seriously overloaded."

"You want me to call off-duty staff," Catherine repeated dazed, unable to assimilate the news of her parents' death with any other reality.

"Yes." Now annoyed, Sister Mary said crisply, "There's a war on, you know. Snap to it."

"Yes, ma'am," Catherine replied obediently. Listlessly she followed the nursing sister down the hall.

"That one's drivin' in neutral with 'er brakes on," Grimshaw commented to the doctor about Catherine after observing her exchange with Sister Mary.

"Who?"

Grimshaw inclined his head toward Catherine's direction. The doctor glanced at her retreating figure and recognized her blonde plaited hair rolled in a figure eight at the nape of her neck. "You can't mean Lady Catherine," he told him. "She's one of the best volunteers we have."

"Lady Catherine? Did you say Lady Catherine?"

"I did." The doctor looked at Grimshaw's face more intently. It had paled.

"She's a piano player of some sort, right? The one that Hitler saluted."

The doctor nodded. "He stood in homage. She's a brilliant pianist."

"Isn't she the Earl of Cherington's daughter?"

"Yes," he said.

"Fuck!" Grimshaw exclaimed. "Now I've done it! Me and my big mouth. I just told her that her parents were killed in the crash."

"*WHAT!?*"

"How was I to know who she was?" exclaimed Grimshaw. "She asked me what happened to them, and damn me, I told her."

"Great shot, old man!" the doctor remarked dryly. "Dr. Barrington!" He motioned to a young intern rushing up the hall. "Take over for me," he instructed. "Grimshaw here knows the routine. Send the worst cases to Team Room Four. I'll be back in a jiffy."

He stuffed his stethoscope into his breast pocket as he charged off in pursuit of Sister Mary.

MARLA, just released from a rest and recuperation station in Scotland, heard news of the explosion at the train station right after she arrived at Rushmore House. As soon as Sir Isaac confirmed Catherine's parents were among the casualties, she drove off to the hospital without thinking about what she would find, only hoping to save Catherine from hearing of her parents' death from a stranger. But, when she entered the Emergency Unit, the agonized screaming from the litters of hurt and terrified children lining the corridors flung her back into the horrors she herself was fleeing from.

She had disconnected herself from the emotional impact of what she was witnessing and reporting on so many times that, when the pain finally struck her, the shock of it shattered her carefully crafted blocks and she fell apart. A snapshot, smuggled out by the Polish Resistance to Tobin and her at the American Embassy in Moscow, triggered her breakdown. The photo provided evidence of Nazi genocide being methodically carried out in the backwoods of Poland by a formidable force of combined SS, SD and Gestapo Special Action Groups called the *Einsatzgruppen*. They were official executioners of a secret plan to rid the Third Reich of its "subhumans." These Death Squads were slaughtering Jews in the thousands, machine gunning them down and dumping them into mass graves dug out over the countryside. This photograph, though fuzzy, had somehow been taken during one of these secret "disinfections." No matter what she had seen the Nazis do, despite everything she had heard, this one, soiled, poorly developed snapshot smashed the two things that mobilized her in the morning and kept her going through the day—her hope and her anger. She connected to the victims in the picture, to their forced isolation, to their abandonment and to their loss of control. The life of a Jew had no value. She was a Jew. She had no value. Everything she had tried to do—the writing, the broadcasts, the risks—it all had no value because no one was stopping the Nazis. Every day they grew stronger and would not rest until they destroyed all Jews. Once the tears of despair flowed, the dam within broke, and she could not stop crying, she could not sleep, she could not write. Tobin was forced to send her back to Sir Isaac.

In Scotland, at the sanatorium where he had arranged for a week's rest and recuperation, no one encouraged her to talk, so her underlying self-esteem found no redemption and no forgiveness. Now, in the hallways of the hospital, Marla faced more pain she could do nothing about. She forced herself to look in the treatment rooms for Catherine. The sights there so sickened her that she fled to the nearest washroom where she wrenched and wrenched but only brought up bile. A dreadful trembling chilled her. She shivered and hugged herself in a futile attempt to keep warm. After more straining, she removed her regulation hat and rubbed her forehead against the back of the toilet seat. Completely exhausted, a cold sweat bathed her weakened body. She struggled to her feet, dropped the hat on a hook beside the sink, grabbed for a towel and doused it in tap water. As she patted her face, she stared at the painfully thin and hollow-eyed reflection of herself in the bathroom mirror.

She was wearing the dress uniform of a woman's auxiliary unit, the First Aid Nursing Yeomanry dubbed FANY by the military. The Polish partisans had cropped her gorgeous hair to almost a crew cut when she had become infected with lice while escaping with them from Warsaw after Hitler invaded Poland. Once she rejoined Tobin in Russia, hcr hair grcw back in with a natural curl, and she had decided to keep it short. It was easier to manage while they were constantly on the move organizing their underground contacts for *Project Amanita*. Damp strands fringed her forehead. She ran her fingers through her hair trying to puff it up. She had to hang on for Catherine.

AFTER CATHERINE called the last name on Sister Mary's list, she pushed her chair under the desk and dropped her head on top of her folded arms to rest. Talking to all those people had been an ordeal. She would have preferred retreating into silence, to cling to her pain, to the jolting realization that, while she was phoning, she hadn't thought about her parents. Guilt needled her. How could she forget them so quickly? Then anger seized her. How could they leave her like that? With no good-bye and no special message. There was no one left. She was alone, really alone. Little by little her crushing loss dug deeper and deeper into her soul. A dry sob mounted.

"*OH NO!*" she cried. "*NOOooo... NOooo... NO...*"

She held her face in her hands, desperately wanting to weep, needing to weep, but the tears wouldn't come.

The hurt was too deep and too shattering.

This was how Marla finally found her, mumbling and shaking her head in her hands. Quietly, Marla walked into the office and wrapped her arms around Catherine's inconsolable shoulders. Unaware of who it was, Catherine patted her hand, grateful for the comfort.

"*If not now, WHEN?*" Marla whispered.

Catherine lifted her grief-stricken face and stared ahead, stunned, too afraid to believe her ears.

"Sister Mary explained how you found out about your parents, Catherine. I'm so sorry."

Catherine blinked. "Marla!? *MARLA!?*" She screamed and rose from her chair. "Marla? *Omigawd!* You're alive. You made it." She desperately grasped the journalist to her. "The last we heard you..." She stopped herself. "It doesn't matter now, does it?" Then she felt the bony frame under Marla's uniform and stood back to study her more closely.

In the FANY suit that hung on her body like a pillow case flung over a broom stick, Marla reminded Catherine of a fading foal, all skinny and helplessly spent, too tired to keep on living. Suddenly it struck her. Marla's hair, once so long and thick, had been cropped short. With growing concern, Catherine touched the stubby ends. "What happened over there? What did they do to you?"

Like an abandoned fawn, Marla stood alone, unsure and quivering, fighting for self-control; then, trembling, she lost the battle and pulled Catherine to her. Her breast began to heave and she wept freely, in great spasms.

Catherine awkwardly rocked her. "Marla... Marla... It's all right. I'm here." And she kept on rocking her until the worst of Marla's convulsive crying had eased.

"I'm sorry," Marla finally rasped. "I saw the children… in the hallway…" Her words drifted. "…and when I asked for you … Sister Mary…" She drew in a shaky breath. "Why were your parents at the train station, Catherine? *Why?*"

"Mummy and Daddy were sending a trainload of children from East London to the farm. Guild Oaks is a war orphanage now."

"I'm so sorry, Catherine. Damn Hitler all to hell!" Marla clutched Catherine's hand as if it were her lifeline to sanity.

Chapter Ten

Saturday, September 21st, 1940

ON EITHER SIDE of the two red barns, pin pricks of grass struggled up through the soft dirt paddocks. Behind them rolled lush pastures, and beyond them, woodlets thick with fall colors. As Marla slowly headed down the lane towards the foaling barn, she breathed in deeply, savoring the fresh country air. Midstep she paused, wistfully looking at the hilly pastures as the morning sun bathed her face with soothing warmth. The war seemed far removed from this idyllic retreat.

Marla crossed over to the rail fence and leaned against a post, watching Catherine exercise her champion filly, Decency. Suddenly Catherine stepped up in the stirrups and crouched forward in the saddle. In response, Decency changed gears and together they streaked down the backstretch, a blur of flying blonde hair and red mane, woman and horse, one spirit with wings.

What was it about Catherine that kept drawing Marla to the younger girl even when they were apart?

It was a question that fascinated Marla. They were a strange pair no doubt, Marla mused, yet sharing the loss of Catherine's parents had deepened the bond between them.

Poor Catherine, thought Marla. That part of her that once envied Catherine felt guilty as she watched the younger girl wildly racing her horse around the turf track. Being in the country with Catherine was helping Marla heal as well. At Guild Oaks she finally felt welcomed. Home. A place where she belonged. Here everyone had gathered her into their loving arms without her having to earn their approval. Here she was part of a very big family that included the orphaned children, the nursing sisters who looked after them, the farm manager, his wife who was the Rushmore's housekeeper, as well as Catherine. The thought of leaving Guild Oaks depressed her.

With Lord James' death, major changes were being made at *Project Amanita*. She had been assigned to replace Catherine's father in field training. That was going to be the toughest and the most heartbreaking task of her life, but it gave her hope again. They weren't going to give up until they defeated Hitler, totally. Underlying her new responsibility, however, was the realization that Catherine would have to be involved in their secret operation. Rushmore House was *Project Amanita's* communication center, and Catherine, who had inherited her father's estate, would have to know what was going on in her father's house. As she watched Catherine race around the far turn, she admired her athletic confidence.

The sound of Decency's charging hoofs sent the farm manager rushing out of the barn. Old George shook his fist at Catherine. "Stop it!" he railed. "You'll break both your bloody necks!" The wind mockingly carried off his angry voice.

Before Lord James had hired George to be the manager of Guild Oaks and his racing stable, the trainer had been unknown to the Ascot crowd. Five years later he was the recognized trainer to beat. After Lord James married Princess Isabelle, the devoted George and his wife Nellie naturally became an extension of the Rushmore family, and so, on learning of the tragedy at the train station, they wanted to carry on Princess Isabelle's plan to turn Guild Oaks into a war orphanage. Now, behind George and all through the fields, the air rang with tapping hammers as the local villagers worked to convert the main house of the estate into a dormitory for the children.

Seeing Catherine race Decency so recklessly lined George's face with worry. "When she's through chasing her demons," he muttered to Marla, "tell her I want to see her." And stomped back into the barn.

There's a story behind that man, Marla decided, watching his departing back. *Someday I'm going to find out what it is.* But her heart was with Catherine, and her attention quickly turned away from the trainer to rejoin the rider.

To Marla, it seemed that what disturbed Catherine most was her lack of preparation for her parents' death. She could sympathize with the younger girl's feeling of inadequacy. How could she keep Rushmore House and Guild Oaks running the way her father did? What did Catherine know about business and financial administration? Quality was a given to her, and value, something she never had to negotiate. What she wanted and needed had always been there.

It was wise of Sir Isaac to send them to Guild Oaks before confronting Catherine with the whole complex truth, Marla decided. They both needed this period of adjustment for their lives would never be the same again.

Down the backstretch, Decency suddenly pulled herself up, almost throwing Catherine over her head. Catherine quickly dismounted and stroked the lathered chestnut's neck, while she carefully scrutinized the filly's legs for signs of puffiness. Seeing nothing, she slowly led Decency forward.

George reappeared in the doorway of the barn. His trained ear had picked up the abrupt halt of the galloping feet. "Is Decency limping?"

Marla squinted, watching the chestnut walk beside Catherine. "She doesn't seem to be."

"If that filly's not hurting, Catherine's bloody lucky," he pronounced tersely and disappeared inside the barn again.

Catherine waved at Marla, reassuring her that Decency had survived her wild ride unscathed. Then she turned the filly around and walked her back over the track towards the barn and Marla.

"George says when you're through chasing your demons, he wants to see you," Marla called to Catherine when she was close enough to hear.

Catherine looked sheepish. "He's right to be annoyed. Thank goodness Decency was smart enough to stop on her own. Help me bathe her, and we'll see what George wants."

When they entered the cool barn, mares curiously thrust their heads over the half-doors of their stalls and, one by one, snickered and snorted or playfully curled up their lips in greeting. Catherine petted each velvet muzzle as she led Decency down the shedrow to her stall. Once stroked, the mares bent their heads back over their feed tubs and resumed chewing their oats. Their crunching sounded like soft marimba music, and through the barn, this rhythmic ritual travelled like tranquil waves over the shores of Marla's soul. For the first time in years she felt her inner tensions relax, and a rare sense of silken contentment slipped from the base of her head through her shoulders and down her back.

While Catherine bathed the sweaty chestnut, Marla steadied the filly's head. Sudsy water splashed over the tuft of mane between her ears, rolled over her white diamond star and down her nose to catch in a well above her nostrils. Before sponging off her face, Catherine kissed her dripping muzzle. "Do you forgive me, girl?"

"She was taking care of you. She loves you as much as you love her," Marla observed.

"I know. I'm really quite lucky." Catherine handed Marla a long narrow metal scoop. "Will you help me scrape the water off Decency? We can't towel dry her while she's soaking wet."

Starting behind Decency's ears, Catherine whisked the filly's mane and drenched coat with long swift strokes, then flicked the water collected in the scraper on the ground. On her side, Marla copied Catherine. As they worked together, Catherine talked. "You know, while you were missing in Poland, I prayed for you."

Marla was touched. "Thank you."

When she didn't offer to explain what had happened, Catherine told her, "In my grief for Mummy and Daddy, I forgot the comfort of Psalm 91.

"*Thou shalt not be afraid for the terror by night;*

nor for the arrow that flieth by day; ...For He shall give His angels charge over thee, to keep thee in all thy ways. That promise came to mind when I was walking Decency back to the barn. God's not to blame for what happened to my parents. Neither is the pilot. They say he was trying to avoid the train when his engine gave out."

"A Nazi with scruples! How lovely!"

"You would be surprised how many times I've heard RAF pilots on my ward tell stories about Luftwaffe seaplanes rescuing them from the channel. Between the airmen, it still seems to be a gentleman's war," Catherine told her.

"That won't last long. Believe me."

Catherine caught the bitterness in Marla's tone. She ventured, "Did your boss...what was his name?"

"Christopher Tobin."

"That's it, Christopher Tobin." Catherine traded the water scraper for a towel and began rubbing Decency down. "Did he make it?" she asked as she worked.

Seeing how soaked Catherine's towel got, Marla wrung out her sponge and began wiping the upper part of the filly's body with it first. "He made it," she said.

"I see. And what about you? Are you giving up your *On The Spot* column to become a FANY?"

Marla raised her head and seemed to gaze into Catherine's soul. Something dreadful haunted that look, something dark like black ink leaking from her pupils, leaking and spreading and merging with the blue depths of her eyes. "Don't you approve?"

"Well frankly, the First Aid Nursing Yeomanry doesn't seem quite fitting for you."

"But it's fitting for you?"

Catherine wished she could understand why Marla was putting her on the defensive. "Being a volunteer nurse's aid is the only way I can help the war effort. Reporting the news from the front lines as you have done is the bravest contribution I can think of. I assumed you would want to carry on your work."

"Being a FANY is the only way to get around the red tape."

"What red tape? I don't understand."

"The WRENs and WAAFs cannot participate in field or battle action," Marla replied somewhat shortly. Seeing Catherine frown, she added, "Some antiquated government ruling doesn't allow it. Consequently, there is no military uniform suitable for women serving in military intelligence except FANY. Belonging to it entitles you to a military commission and guaranteed pay, either in the field or at home base."

"You're in military intelligence. So that explains it," Catherine sighed with obvious relief. "I couldn't picture you changing bedpans."

"Is that what you do?"

"Sometimes." She eyed Marla carefully. "Theoretically, since I'm already a FANY, I could transfer into military intelligence too, and no one would be the wiser."

"True." Marla became very still inside. *She knows already.*

Catherine tried probing from another direction. "You never talk about your parents. Are you an orphan?"

Marla laughed. "More like a tumbleweed." Then she picked up a towel and began vigorously rubbing Decency's flanks. Irritated, the filly shook her mane.

"Softly, Marla. Like this."

Marla followed her example. "Look, you come from solid roots, from parents who loved and adored you. I don't. My parents didn't want me." While she was talking, she had stopped towelling the filly. Now she began sponging off the remaining water shedding from Decency's coat with light airy strokes. "All I remember is one boarding school after another," she continued.

"Oh, Marla, I can't believe your parents didn't want you."

"It's true. My mother left my father and me when I was ten. After that, he couldn't stand to look at me because I reminded him of her, so he sent me to private school after private school after private school. I've lived most of my life in one kind of dormitory or another. The last one was at university. I never saw my father again until the day of his funeral. He lay in his coffin...so still and quiet... That's all we ever shared. Silence."

That one plaintive statement summed up a child's life of rejection. Catherine felt terrible for her. "And your mother?" she asked incredulously. "How could she leave you to a life like that?"

"It's not so hard when you are obsessed with a cause the way she is. Having me was an inconvenience, an interruption in her work."

"What on earth does she do?"

"*DO?* By profession she writes plays. By political affiliation she's a Marxist in pursuit of a perfect social order."

Catherine was dumbstruck. "Is your mother Freya Shalimov?"

It was Marla's turn to be surprised. "Yes, she is... to my everlasting shame."

"But she's Russian."

"So am I, Catherine, by birth, and American by choice. That's why I changed my last name to Franklin. Roosevelt represents everything American to me. Personal freedom. The right to pursue my own choices. Democracy—government by the people, of the people and for the people. It's every person's dream. But my mother fights the very land that gave her sanctuary and the freedom to express whatever she believes. Her plays are mere vehicles for Marxist indoctrination."

Disgust stung Marla's words. "She can't distinguish between the reality and the dream. She has never experienced Stalin's cruelty firsthand because my father smuggled us out of Russia in 1917, during the Bolshevik Revolution before the czar and his family were assassinated. She simply refuses to believe how treacherous Stalin is. The Marxism she preaches and believes in is not the Communism that's practised. In Lenin's own words, she is a useful idiot."

Catherine stared at her, looking as if she were going to gather Marla up in her arms. Marla's eyelid twitched.

"Don't waste your pity on me. I don't."

Catherine's gentle eyes fastened on her. "I'm sorry you've been hurt, but you're wrong if you think I pity you. You have too many wonderful qualities to admire for that."

To hide her flustered feelings, Marla crouched down and asked Catherine to show her how to wipe the filly's legs. Clearing her throat, Catherine knelt down beside the chestnut and picked up her foreleg, carefully wiping out the heel of her hoof with the rub cloth. "It's important to get all the moisture out before you cool her out," she explained. "The big danger is exposing her to a draft. She could catch cold."

"How do you do that? Cool her out I mean."

"Usually by covering her with a wool blanket and walking her. For now, we can cover her and turn her loose in her box on a good bed of straw."

As Marla picked up the water pail and let Decency drink a few swallows, Catherine decided to bridge the last gap between them. "Marla, you may not want to hear this, but I am going to tell you anyway. For some reason I can't explain, I feel as if I havc known you all my life, almost as if we have been the missing parts of one soul brought together again. No matter what happens, I want you to know I will always be here for you. Do you understand?"

Marla bit her lip and allowed herself to nod, afraid that she might show her sudden flush of love for the younger girl. She busied herself putting the water pail outside the stall door, and for a second, she stood with her back to Catherine, silently struggling with herself.

"Tell me," she said finally, "do you believe the real influence on Decency's breeding is 75% her dam's?"

"Of course not."

Marla turned around to face Catherine. "Neither do I. But the Jews do. By their rules, I am a Jew."

For an instant, Marla's meaning eluded Catherine. "Are you saying your mother is a Jew as well as a Communist?"

"I am."

Marla's simple admission flabbergasted Catherine. "Good grief! All those years you reported from Germany! What if the Nazis had found out?"

"Well, they didn't. Everyone believes I am an orphan. I have doctored papers to prove it. Only you, Tobin and Sir Isaac know the truth, Catherine."

Catherine stared at her as the significance of the secret Marla revealed about herself sank in. She recognized it was Marla's ultimate act of trust, the greatest gift of friendship she could offer. Tears glassed Catherine's eyes. "Your secret will always be safe with me, Marla."

"I know." The last vestige of the wall between them crumbled, and their souls crossed over the conquered fear of rejection. Slowly Marla smiled. She reached out to Catherine, and spontaneously they embraced.

"Somehow we're going to make it through this bloody war together," Catherine promised. "I know we are."

Chapter Eleven

Monday, March 1st, 1943

THE TIDE WAS IN.

An American Gato Class subamarine slipped up the Thames River in the smoky light of predawn. Approaching Kew Bridge, it submerged below the water level and veered portside, toward the south shore on what would normally be a collision course for the river bank but, at this point, was the correct heading for a manmade underwater channel that led back to a natural basin under the Kew Palace dungeon. When the submarine surfaced inside the hidden cave and slid into its berth, a handful of sailors dressed in black fatigues sprang out of the forward hatch and moored the sub to Project Amanita's quay. The captain appeared on the bridge with two men in woollen caps and arctic parkas. They hunched against the March chill. Their breaths scaled the morning air as they climbed down from the conning tower and threw the gangplank from topside. It landed on the dock with a splat. Two of the black-garbed seamen anchored it to the iron rings fastened to the landing pier.

"Permission to come ashore, sir?" hailed the captain to the imposing figure standing on the wharf. His voice faintly echoed through the cave.

"By all means," acknowledged Sir Isaac. Under the spill of candle flares, his prodigious shape cast a giant shadow across the bow of the submarine. The captain and the two men immediately disembarked.

"I see you enjoyed good fishing in the North Sea," Sir Isaac greeted the captain, nodding briskly to the two civilians beside him.

He chuckled. "You might say we caught a real live pair, sir."

"Good to have you back, Tobin." Sir Isaac shook his hand. "And you, Rorvig." He grasped the other man's large rough hand with his crushing grip. "There's breakfast waiting for you and your crew, Captain. I hope some black coffee will hold you two over," he addressed Tobin and Rorvig separately. "You will have to forego breakfast until after your debriefing."

"Right, sir. If you want to escort the Captain and his men to the mess area, I know my way about this complex. Rorvig and I can meet you in the debriefing room."

"Fine idea, Tobin." Sir Isaac hurriedly ushered the Captain and his sailors through Security with directions to follow him.

"Black coffee? I hate it," grumbled Rorvig as he and Tobin passed through Security.

"Just about everything is rationed, sir... bacon, butter, meat, sugar, milk..."

"You've made your point, soldier," Tobin flatly interrupted the military policeman sitting behind the wicket.

The armed sentry levelled Tobin with a resentful

glare. He instantly categorized him a commando. The secret agents were a different breed. Most were humble and appreciative while these cliquish commandos acted like conquerors of the night. The world owed them something for surviving the hazards of their trade, or that's how he perceived their attitude.

To Rorvig, there seemed to be a maze of concrete corridors intersecting each other after they passed through the security block. A strangc pinging and whistling noise scooting through the tubes that lined the ceiling followed them. Puzzled, he tugged on Tobin's sleeve and pointed above. "What's that infernal racket?" It was the first time Rorvig had ever been inside *Project Amanita*.

Tobin looked up. "Oh, that..." he grinned, "is Amanita's mail service. We send interdepartmental memos and papers in canisters through these tubes. The noise you hear is caused by the compressed air that propels them along. They zip through at 30 miles an hour. You get used to it if you're here long enough."

Rorvig spotted the concealed course of another canister and traced it whistling through the latticework of pipes criss-crossing the ceiling. "Are they all mail tubes?"

"No. We have a large underground complex to service."

"So some are water, air and heat pipes."

"Exactly."

"It's almost as awesome as the Norsk Hydro Plant," Rorvig observed.

"The underground bunkers were constructed out of the special escape routes tunnelled for King George III in 1829," Tobin explained. "He had a labyrinth hollowed out under the Royal Botanic Gardens to the Thames River from Kew Palace. Since the palace is no longer used, its fortress-like tunnels were perfect for our project. Except for a few new passages we've dug out to give us access to Rushmore House at the east end of the Gardens, we've reinforced what was already here with concrete." He turned down a narrow corridor. Rorvig followed.

"How the hell am I suppose to remember where I've been?" Rorvig demanded, confused. "I'm lost now."

"The sections are color-coded," replied Tobin, pointing to a square brown patch painted on the south wall. "It won't take you long to catch on to our system."

"Yeah," answered Rorvig dryly, sticking close to Tobin. "As easy as falling off a log into a whirlpool."

A dampness greased the amber lit walls. Without warning, the narrow hallway ended at a metal door. Its latch was controlled by a combination lock inset into the key panel. As Tobin spun the dial, Rorvig whispered, "I feel as if we're stepping into a vault."

"We are," whispered Tobin back. "A top secret vault."

They heard a click. An orange light flashed in the tiny window above the dial, and the lock's bolt slipped back. The door eased open. "When you've been cleared, you'll be issued this lock's combination number," Tobin told Rorvig as they passed through into the underground communications center.

It was surprisingly large and well lit. Radio sets, arranged back-to-back, covered three rows of long army mess tables. The air rang with all patterns of Morse code stutterings. Young women in khaki and older women in comfortable civilian dress operated the transmitting stations. Those not occupied on the air knitted or read books.

"These are the radio telegraphists, our heartbeats of the air waves." Tobin introduced them to Rorvig as they passed through the hubbub. Rorvig noticed a young fair-haired girl at one of the sets. Something vaguely familiar about her ticked his interest.

Leading off from the main radio room was a series of anterooms. The sound of teletype machines clicking and typewriters clattering came from the other side of a door marked *CIPHER ROOM—TOP SECRET*. Its access was controlled by another built-in combination lock. The color code bar above the dial was red. Further down from it, small meeting rooms and cell-like offices, each headed *Sector Control* over their doorways, enclosed a classroom area.

"Well, here we are," said Tobin who gestured to Rorvig to precede him to a small group of folding chairs set out in a circle.

EVEN WAR could become boring Catherine discovered. As a radio telegraphist, or *pianist* as they were more popularly called, her duties had taken on a sameness that dulled the long nights she monitored radio signals for off-duty operators. Her only comic relief was setting nonsensical codes—*A bore is a cherry with a pin on top* or *Michael Blue with a mop of green green moss*—to tunes that seemed to be spontaneously composed for the loony lyrics on the air. She called them *DITTIES FOR DOTTIES*, and the listeners loved them. She encouraged her radio audiences to submit their own ditties for her to set to catchy melodies on the show. The challenge was in the silliness achieved, and some submissions were so silly they made the disguised codes seem sensible. It was an outlet for Britain to laugh at itself. Sir Isaac was delighted with the show's success. It made it an even more perfect cover for his radio messages to undercover agents inside the Third Reich. Catherine also devoted a portion of her show—*Champagne Serenade*—to a selection of classical music she played for listeners who preferred more soothing and romantic medleys.

When *Project Amanita* was sending a secret code, she would receive the copy by three o'clock that day, giving her time to alter the daily program's scripts to accommodate the message. For almost three years, this had been her routine. Between her evening half-hour broadcasts and eight-hour relief shifts in the communications center, she was continually busy, but it wasn't preventing her growing restlessness.

Catherine was proud that her father's funding helped keep the civilian intelligence agency going. It was listed under the British War Cabinet's Special Operations Executive (SOE) as *Section G: Code Name—Project Amanita*, and the underground honeycomb burrowing beneath the Royal Botanic Gardens employed fifteen hundred people on secret assignments.

It had been Sir Isaac's idea to protect these vital scientists, engineers and agents from falling bombs and prying eyes in the most unexpected place. London. Feverishly, in the safety of the subterranean bunkers built out from the cellars of Kew Palace to the basement of Rushmore House, refugee scientists worked to analyze the experimental findings and papers published by other scientists in the nuclear field. Not only were they trying to unlock all the secrets of the tiny atom, they were also tracking Germany's progress towards developing an atomic bomb. By all the resources at their disposal, they had to sabotage the Nazis' headway. To this end, their best tactic had come from an inventive use of disinformation.

Busy as she was, Catherine also felt very isolated. Even sharing the coach house apartment with Marla didn't relieve the loneliness because they saw so little of each other. Often Marla didn't come home for days. Since her appointment as Chief of Field Training, replacing Catherine's father, she spent most of her time in the underground facility and only surfaced to rest.

This morning, Catherine flung her FANY cap on the sofa and sank exhausted, with legs sprawled and arms splayed, into the Chippendale Wing Chair. She only had two hours to report to Sir Isaac. She couldn't fall asleep, but she could barely contain her excitement. Her orders had finally come through. Sir Isaac was going to let her be a real *god-mother*. She was going to work with her own field operative...sensitive fingers paired together over the air...*pianists*. She had no idea how eager she was for the change until she received her orders this morning. Now she rose from the chair and skipped with joy.

She washed her face in the kitchen sink, applied a light touch of make-up and brushed her hair, pinning it up into a neat French roll. Feeling refreshed, she decided to make herself a cup of tea. Without her favorite raisin biscuits and Nellie's baking, she was missing breakfast. As she crossed the living room floor, racking sobs escaped from Marla's bedroom. Catherine stopped, puzzled. She heard them again. Muffled sobs. She quickly went to Marla's door, turned the knob and peeked inside. Marla was a buried lump under the covers of her bed. Concerned, Catherine softly approached the bedside.

"Marla?"

The crying under the covers drew in and choked.

"Marla. Please. Come out from under those covers and talk to me."

The curled up lump stilled. Catherine peeled back the blanket protecting her. Marla grabbed the covers and pulled them back up to her chin. Her eyes were swollen, and her nose and cheeks were puffy splotches of pink. "I'm okay. Mind your own business."

Catherine sat down on the edge of the bed. "How long have you been crying like this?" When Marla didn't answer, Catherine probed. "Is it Tobin?"

"Tobin, Schmobin..." She sighed and sniffled. "No one's heard from him in nearly three years. Pass me a hanky. Or toilet paper. I don't care which."

"He's here."

"Who's here?"

"Tobin."

Marla's tearful sniffles stopped. She looked up at Catherine with undisguised interest. Clear nasal drip, which she ignored, began trickling down her mouth. Catherine remembered leaving freshly pressed hankies on the night table beside her own bed and went to get one. When she returned, Marla grabbed for the hanky and blew. She sniffed and dabbed at her nose again. "Thanks."

"Better?"

"Yeah."

"Are you going to see him?"

"Who?"

"Tobin, of course."

Marla's shoulders slumped. "No. It's just good to know he's alive."

Catherine studied Marla thoughtfully. Finally she asked what she'd been dying to know. "What happened over there?"

"Nothing. Nothing happened at all."

"Nothing." Catherine was about to challenge Marla when a light popped on in her head. "I see. Nothing," she repeated. "You were crying about nothing."

"Not really...at least not about Tobin. I'd given up thinking about him." Looking into Catherine's sympathetic eyes brought on another tearful downpour. "Oh, Catherine, it's so awful! Please hold me. Somebody hold me!" she wept pathetically.

"Of course." Catherine quickly gathered Marla into her arms and rocked her. She hadn't seen Marla break down since she had returned, frail and haunted, from Russia at the onset of the war. The rocking seemed to soothe her. She quieted down. Eventually Marla pulled herself away.

"I lost control. I'm sorry. I promised myself I would never do that again," she said. "I'm okay now. Thank you."

Catherine sighed and shook her head. "I thought we trusted each other."

"We do."

"Then talk to me...For your own good...Please."

Marla caught her breath. "Okay. It's a nightmare. I keep having the same nightmare over and over again. It won't let me rest, and it's so real, Catherine. I'm standing there..."

"Where?" prompted Catherine.

"On the pit of hell," she said. "There are thousands

of mouths—all open—all crying and screaming—but there's no sound coming out of their lips. Their agony is inside me. I see lips of voiceless screams multiplying down this eternal pit, and they're dragging me...pulling me...down into the pit with them."

She shuddered. "It's so god awful real. At first I dreamed of the dead boy I found in Guernica...I told you about that. His mouth was frozen in a horrible scream. I was too late to help him. In every dream, I feel so helpless. First his mouth, open, silently screaming, tearing me apart—a lost soul I can't touch. I stand there watching his agony. Then more mouths and more mouths until there's a sea of silent screams."

She grabbed Catherine's hands desperately. "Am I going mad?" Searching for answers, her tormented eyes tore at Catherine. "What can it mean? I feel so powerless, so inadequate. I'm here. They're there."

"Who is there?" Catherine asked gently.

"The Jews—the Jews are there—in Poland, in Warsaw. I *saw* them blockaded by the Nazis in a ghetto ...I *saw* them dumped on trains." Her voice faltered. "Crowded together like cattle going to slaughter. Oh, Catherine, they even mooed like cows from inside the freight cars—creepy, awful moos."

"In your dream," Catherine said, not comprehending.

"No. No. That's what Tobin and I *saw* in Poland after it surrendered to Hitler."

"Why didn't you get out when you had the chance?"

"We were gathering proof that the Russians were planning to smuggle out German nuclear scientists to their side. They have a *Project Amanita* too. Can you imagine what would happen if Stalin developed the atomic bomb before us or Hitler? He's as big a monster or worse than Hitler!"

"Good grief!" Catherine muttered under her breath, completely aghast.

"No one believed us." Marla bit her lip. "No one."

"You mean about the Russians."

"No, I mean the *Jews.*" She clenched her fists and drummed them on her knees pulled up under the covers to her chin. "The stupid British Consulate almost turned us over to the Nazis when we escaped to Moscow."

She kept on pounding herself. "The bastards! Some of Chamberlain's gutless wonders are still around. Luckily, the American Embassy took us in. We worked from there. That's where we saw the photograph ..." Her voice faded. "So many dead." She hid her head in her hands. "The pit...that's where the nightmare's coming from...the picture of the mass grave. Now I understand."

"I'm glad you do because I'm totally confused," admitted Catherine.

Marla relaxed her tense pounding and became very quiet. "When we returned to London," she told Catherine, "only Sir Isaac believed us."

She stopped. "I drew some sketches of the scenes at the train stations. They can't be used as evidence, but maybe someday they'll have some significance."

"May I see them?"

"Sure." Marla's relief, once she started talking to Catherine, was lifting her mood. "I keep them in the closet." She slipped out of bed and went over to the closet where she rummaged around in the bottom and dragged out an old portable safe.

"That's your filing box!" Catherine laughed.

"You bet. No bomb is going to destroy all these years of work. I have a sketch for every assignment I've ever been on."

"I remember—*Some people take pictures, I draw*. Are the drawings of *Kristallnacht* here too?"

Marla nodded. "Everything." She opened the safe with a small key she took from her vanity drawer. "There," she said, as she lifted out an armful of files and sorted them on the floor. "Oh, goodness! Here's my folder on Guernica." She opened it and gazed at the picture inside. "It was so serene before all hell broke loose," she remembered.

"May I see it?" asked Catherine.

"Sure." Marla handed it to her.

Catherine looked it over and marvelled at the detail. "It's a beautiful drawing, Marla. You're really quite good."

Marla continued searching and then paused. She pulled out another folder and handed it to Catherine almost shyly. "Maybe this one will interest you."

Mystified, Catherine opened it and expressed surprise. "It's me! At the press recital."

Marla nodded. "I'm happy you recognize yourself."

"I've never seen myself in a drawing before." She studied it curiously. "It's definitely me," she decided.

Marla grinned. "Good."

"May I keep it?"

"I'd rather you didn't," Marla explained. "Drawing is something I do for me." She took Catherine's file back and handed her another. "I found them. There's five," she said.

Catherine opened up the folder and pulled out the sketches. Each line, contour and shading caught the despair and futility in the carriage of the bodies. Heads hung on necks that had lost their support. Vacant eyes stared into nothingness. Listless shoulders slumped. Spines folded into fetal humps. One portrait caught her eye. *It couldn't be.* "This picture," Catherine said, pointing to the old man. "He looks like Dr. Kantor."

"Do you mean the man who conducted you at the festival in Vienna?"

"Yes."

"Didn't you say he was Hungarian?" Catherine nodded. "A likeness maybe," said Marla, "but I doubt it."

"I know..." Catherine studied the sketch intently. "Nevertheless, the resemblance is uncanny. I think it's the quizzical eyebrows. You know," she said, holding it up to the light, "this drawing is magnificent. It shows so much, says so much. The deep set eyes. They express a strange compassion, almost as if he's passed into a life beyond and is looking back at us with pity. There's such love and forgiveness in those eyes, Marla. Not hate." Catherine lay the sketch on the bed. "The more I look at it, the more I see."

"His face haunted me. I had to draw it."

"I can see why. He is the uncorrupted soul in the midst of black evil. Where were the Nazis taking these people?"

"They were Jews and Poles, Catherine."

"How do you know they were all Jews and Poles, Marla?"

"In hiding, we heard the trucks and the loudspeakers ordering the Jews into the ghetto. Then later, days later, we saw them take truckloads of people out of the Jewish ghetto to the train station where there were freight cars already loaded with people. The Polish Underground told us the Nazis were not only rounding up Jews but

Polish intellectuals, political agitators, gypsies plus whoever they determined unfit or defective and were sending them to labor camps, to Treblinka and Majdanek. Tobin and I wanted to follow it up, but we had to get back to Sir Isaac with our information about the Russian plan to smuggle out German atomic scientists. It never occurred to us that the people we saw being loaded on those trains might be mass executed. I don't think we would have believed it anyway. It was just too monstrous to imagine."

"Mass extermination," Catherine protested weakly, remembering *Kristallnacht*. "Have the Nazis become that twisted?"

Marla nodded sadly. "In Moscow, Tobin and I saw the first evidence...a smuggled photograph showing a trainload of people being machine gunned over a massive pit we were told they were forced to dig for themselves. I've also seen smuggled documents that are even more frightening. Last year, in January, Hitler held a secret conference at Wannsee. There he issued instructions for the *Final Solution* of the Jewish problem. Hitler's words, not mine," she interjected. "A Lieutenant Colonel Adolf Eichmann of the SS was put in full charge of the administration—from organizing and co-ordinating transportation for the Jews captured from all over Nazi Europe to their final destination in Poland. *Resettlement* he called it."

"Maybe that's all it really is, Marla."

"Catherine, how can you be so damned naive? Sometimes you exhaust my patience!" Marla snapped. "I have read witnessed accounts by escapees. The *Final Solution* of the Jews means total extermination of the Jews. A cyanide gas known as Zylon B, a poison for rats, and carbon monoxide are dropped into gas chambers disguised as shower rooms. The SS proved it will work because the first ones they gassed at Auschwitz were Soviet prisoners of war and Poles. Auschwitz is the largest and most efficient camp, but even there, the odd escape occurs successfully. The intelligence reports I've seen says Auschwitz uses the faster and less messy Zyklon B because Eichmann doesn't want to see the Jews and the enemies of the Reich suffer needlessly. Can you believe the mentality? At Auschwitz, some reports have said an orchestra plays Tales of Hoffmann or The Merry Widow as prisoners are led to the gas chambers."

"Dear God!" Catherine grasped her throat in horror. "An orchestra?" She looked at the sketch of the old man again. "It can't be. It just can't be."

"No one's stopping those bastard barbarians. No one. Sir Isaac says the Jewish problem won't matter to any of us if the Nazis build the atomic bomb first." Marla mimicked Sir Isaac's Scottish accent. "Let us get on with the job at hand."

Marla bowed her head. Tears marbled the rims of her eyes. "My people are calling out to me in their pain and horror to account for them, and I'm bloody helpless. I can't do a damned thing. That's what's killing me!" Tears streamed down her face. "I want to do something, Catherine. God! How I want to do something!" She clenched her fists pounding her head. Her features contorted in terrible agony as she battled more sobs.

The phone jangled in the living room.

"I'll get it." Catherine jumped up and dashed from their bedroom. Marla could hear her pick up the receiver. From the delight in her voice, she guessed it must be

Nellie on the other end. “Oh no!” she heard Catherine suddenly gasp. “Isn’t she too early?”

Instantly Marla was alert. She grabbed her robe and wrapped it around her. By the time she reached Catherine, the receiver was back in its cradle, and Catherine was sitting silently on the sofa staring out the window.

“What’s happening?”

“Decency’s foaling.” A lone tear glistened on Catherine’s cheek. “I can’t be there for her. Sir Isaac’s giving a special briefing at 1000 hours.”

“I’m scheduled to attend that briefing too.” Marla sat quietly, thinking. “When was the last time you were out to Guild Oaks?”

“Six months ago.”

“We’re not getting enough R and R. I haven’t seen the children or the stable for a year.”

Catherine looked into Marla’s eyes, beginning to sense the direction of her thinking. “We can’t disobey orders. I’ll lose my chance to work on a special assignment.”

“If we can’t function because we haven’t had sufficient rest and recreation, would that make sense? Besides, regulations require us to take a furlough between assignments.”

“That’s true. But how often are they followed? This is war time.”

“So? That’s no reason to ignore regs. If Tobin’s back...” Marla became animated. “You call Nellie back and tell her we’ll be there as soon as we can while I plead our case to Sir Isaac. If Tobin’s just coming in from the field, I’ll bank he’s part of the same mission we’re on, and in all probability, Sir Isaac’s forgotten to rest him too. He needs us fresh and alert. He won't turn me down."

"We're on? Do you mean we're working together?"

Marla nodded. "Who do you think recommended you? The Chief of Field Training has some influence, you know."

They arrived at Guild Oaks just as Decency was in the last throes of delivery. The grand chestnut mare was lying on her side grunting when they reached her stall in time to see her expel a tremendous gush of water that flooded the bedding of straw. Immediately Catherine went over to her and began stroking her head. Under the mare's tail ballooned a white bag. Then one leg covered in a transparent sac, which to Marla was very much like parachute silk, eased out.

"Shouldn't the head come out first?" Marla asked alarmed.

"If the foal is in the right position, the front legs come out first, ahead of the head," explained George, who had been with Decency from the start of her labor.

"But there's only one leg showing."

"I think we'll see the other one after Decency's next push," he assured her.

Marla watched anxiously. Decency's back leg twitched, and she grunted again.

"Here we go," George said. "Push, girl. I can see the other leg." He was positioned behind her ready to pull the foal out if the mare needed help. "There it is. The head's next."

Marla watched fascinated. Still enclosed within the heavily veined amniotic sac, the foal's head emerged. George cut the sac at once and peeled it back from the foal's nostrils. As he continued to slip the bag off of its face, she could see its tongue extending from its mouth was blue and its eyes looked glued shut. Was it dead after all this?

George towelled its wet face, pulling a bluish-white mucus out of its nose and mouth. First, its eyes fluttered, then it uttered a soft mew-like sneeze. Its mouth opened, and its tongue, already amazingly pink, darted out between its lips. Decency grunted again. Now its shoulders, the largest and widest part of its body, were free of the birth canal. Blowing hard, Decency rested. The foal nickered. Decency tried to raise her head to see it struggling to break out of the sac with its forelegs jabbing at the membrane. Decency angrily snorted, bobbing her head back and forth. The foal lifted its head toward her and whinnied a strong protest.

"A cheeky little devil," George commented.

A whistle of air escaped as another contraction propelled the foal through the birth canal and its hind quarters and back legs cleared the passageway with a final slap of amniotic fluids as foal and sac landed on the straw bed. Its long umbilical cord pulsed, perfectly intact.

"Keep Decency's head down, Catherine. I don't want her to stand up while the cord is still beating. She could break it." George supported the foal beside the mother's back feet and gently held the cord with his free hand until the pulsation quit about a minute later. Then he let the foal kick away from Decency, and the cord ruptured itself.

Catherine let go of Decency's head, and the mare rolled awkwardly from her side to her stomach. Pawing with her front legs, she pushed herself up. Her back hoof hovered over the foal as if she might step on it.

Marla shivered and looked to Catherine and George for direction, but they patiently watched. *Geez!* she thought. Decency's hoof slid over the baby's struggling form until it cleared it before she shifted her weight and stepped around her foal.

"Wow!" Marla cried with relief as she watched the foal struggling to find its feet. It quivered and rocked until its gangly forelegs unfolded like a rusty card table, each leg awkwardly straightening as it tested its strength and balance. Unsteadily, it pulled itself up and, just as it looked as if it would make it, fell back down with a disgusted plop. All three of them broke out chuckling at the indignant expression on its face.

"Well, George, do we have a colt or a filly?" Catherine asked.

"Judging by its cheekiness, I'll wager it's a filly," he grinned.

"I'd challenge that," scoffed Marla.

"Me too," agreed Catherine.

The colt tried to co-ordinate his wobbly legs and push himself up on all fours at once. He collapsed in a heap on the straw. After several more tries, he stood up shaking, afraid to move in case he fell down again.

"Who's going to check it out?" asked Marla.

Catherine and George almost knocked heads as they bent down at the same time to see the foal's plumbing. Catherine stood up first with a satisfied smile. "You lose, George. Good thing we weren't wagering money." She helped support the colt while Decency walked over to sniff and lick his damp coat. He was a rich red with a black mane.

"He's so beautiful!" Marla's eyes filled with tenderness. "Is he a chestnut like Decency?"

"No," answered Catherine. "Even though he looks reddish in color, he's a blood bay. He'll be gorgeous when he grows up."

Swaying, the colt staggered, one foot in front of the other. Very carefully, he dragged his hind feet forward, one at a time. The next step was a little stronger. Then the next. Decency stood patiently waiting. He wavered. She nudged his rump, directing his nose to her full udder. "He's looking for milk, Marla." George instructed her, "Help steer him to his mom's underbelly."

Uncertain and awkward at first, Marla felt the colt's muscles tense until he trusted her support. She propped him up facing his mother's hindquarters. Wobbling forward he eagerly sniffed the droplets of colostrum leaking from her udder until he grasped one teat and began sucking. Decency snickered, well-pleased with her strapping son.

"Listen to the little pig slurp!" Marla exclaimed. She let him go and watched him nurse. In less than half an hour, she had seen a helpless newborn rise to its feet, walk and take his first drink. She had never experienced such a miracle of life before. A lovely serenity washed over her. "What will you call him, Catherine?" she asked curiously.

"He's not mine to name. He's yours."

"You're kidding!" Marla was feeling happier than she was willing to admit, as if by naming the colt, he belonged to her. "How do you figure that?"

"He's yours, Marla, because you're part of his first experience in this strange new world. You're part of the human family he's already learned to trust. He will always remember you."

"I'll always remember him too," Marla said. Her eyes misted. "A name. Well, let's see. It must be very special."

She looked at the colt with a new perception of life. For an instant, the world shrunk to just the two of them, and she talked to him as if he understood her. "With your mother's heart and your father's speed, I predict you're going to be a bold and fearless champion someday, little fella." Marla was quiet for a moment while she thought. Her eyes lit up. "I have it! We'll call him Intrepid."

"Intrepid..." Catherine repeated. She nodded. "Strong and brave. Our own Intrepid. I think it's perfect, Marla. Don't you George?"

"I do."

"Then Intrepid is his name."

Marla and Catherine touched shoulders as they continued to watch Intrepid nurse. Feeling part of Catherine's family filled Marla with overwhelming joy. Nodding at Intrepid, she declared, "This is what we're fighting for, Catherine. The right to be part of a family. The right to be born free. We can't let Hitler destroy everything that matters to us."

Chapter Thirteen

Wednesday, March 3rd, 1943

TOBIN WILL LEAD the tactical team," Sir Isaac explained to Marla, Catherine, Rorvig and Tobin, who sat grouped in front of him. He picked up a pointer from the blackboard ledge and continued.

"There are only two heavy water plants in the world. One's in Canada, at the Consolidated Mining and Smelting Plant in Trail, British Columbia. The other is controlled by the Germans in Norway." He rolled down the wall map of Europe.

This intelligence Marla knew well. Her mind drifted over to Christopher Tobin. The last time she had seen him was almost three years ago. Yet, this morning, when she saw him again, he had practically ignored her and Catherine except for a curt nod to them both. His snub burned her deeply. Despite his professional aloofness when they worked together through Germany, Poland and Russia, she had entrusted her soul to him. They had been as one mind and one spirit devoid of physical coupling, and in leaving him behind, she had left a part of herself with him. That part she expected to recover when they were reunited. Instead, his apparent indifference trapped her in limbo and tripped old feelings of abandonment. What had changed—no, she corrected herself, what had hardened him so? He'd become a finely honed guerrilla fighter, a killing instrument, she answered herself. Somewhere, during the depersonalizing process, he had lost the will to connect to his emotional nature.

The tapping of Sir Isaac's pointer drew her attention back to the map. Directing the pointer tip, he circled the Kjolen range of mountains near Rjukan in Norway. "Here," he said. "The Norsk Hydro Electric Plant." Then Sir Isaac turned to face them.

"Rorvig, as you know, has been inside here since 1938 as Norsk's chief engineer. When it's been necessary to frustrate the Germans' atomic research, he has performed little annoying sabotage tricks."

"Like what?" Marla, the ever curious journalist, jumped in without thinking.

Rorvig lifted an eyebrow to Sir Isaac for permission to speak. "By all means," he said, resigning himself to the interruption.

"Well, one of the things I've done is drop a cup of cod liver oil into an electrolytic tube. This jams up their whole process and makes the heavy water they ship to their experimental labs useless when the researchers try to restart it."

"You're kidding! Cod-liver oil?" Marla laughed. "What it loosens for humans it constipates for science. How ingenious!" She openly admired the strapping six-footer. He was a Norwegian-American engineer in his mid-thirties. They had met before, briefly, in Berlin, at Goring's Karinhall banquet. There she had passed a hidden message to him. A spark between them had caught fire then, but it was not the time nor the place to fan the flame, so they had let it fizzle. His peculiar contradiction of robust gentleness, rather like a Norse mythical god turned cowboy, was what originally drew Marla. Now his refreshing contrast from Tobin stirred her again. Sparse strands of sandy fluff sprouting from his shiny dome were just too sexy to resist. She engaged his eyes. His answering twinkle quickened her pulse.

Ulo Rorvig was one of Tobin's U.S. recruits. Because of his ethnic background, he could speak Norwegian fluently and was slipped into Norway before the German occupation so he could build up credentials as an electronics expert and a Nazi sympathizer at Norsk. When the Nazis took over the plant, they made him their chief engineer and unwittingly put in place one of *Project Amanita's* most strategic agents.

"...Scientists at the Kaiser Wilhelm Institute in Berlin have split the uranium atom, but they don't know how to control the resulting chain reaction. Dr. Holbak does." The mention of Dr. Holbak roused Marla from her thoughts.

"He is far ahead of the German scientists in his search to find a suitable moderator," Sir Isaac went on. "He's convinced it's deuterium oxide, in other words heavy water. We think he's right. It's got a double hydrogen nucleus that, in uranium fission, is a neutron slower. Rorvig tells us the Nazis plan to transport heavy water from Norsk to Holbak's lab in Copenhagen. We can't let that happen."

Marla stiffened and glanced at the others leaning forward in their seats.

"I want you to get used to addressing each other by

your code names," Sir Isaac began. "I am *Rufus*."

Self-conscious of his likeness to the cartoon character Rufus, a walrus with a big droopy mustache, Sir Isaac licked the shaggy tips of the red bush brushing his upper lip and decided to give in. "Churchill picks names he thinks fit the person." Everyone chuckled. He gestured to Marla to carry on.

"*Beryl*," she introduced herself.

"*Crystal*," Catherine said next.

"*Iceberg*."

"*Seagull*," said Tobin last.

"Iceberg and Seagull," Sir Isaac addressed the men first, "Beryl is your conducting officer. Through her you make all your arrangements—supplies, equipment, identity papers, transportation, personnel—whatever you need. Iceberg, your radio operator is Crystal. You two will practise transmitting to each other until you know the *fist* of the other intimately."

Catherine blushed slightly at Sir Isaac's use of the last word. Rorvig looked across at Marla, caught her little smirk, and winked.

By the end of an hour, Sir Isaac's objectives seemed more and more suicidal. Marla periodically glanced at Tobin, sick at heart. Once his gaze caught hers. Orbs of hammered steel peered back at her.

Observing Marla watching Tobin, Catherine saw the haunting pain return to Marla's eyes and suddenly grasped the root cause behind her recent confession: "I'm a sex machine. Turn me on, and I go wild. Men love it." Tobin was the man Marla's heart longed to be with while she sprinted from one man's bed to the next. She wasn't so much amoral as she was terribly deprived of love. Understanding the reason helped soothe Catherine's own struggle with Marla's promiscuity. She loved her friend and believed she had no right to judge her, but in truth her sexual indiscretions appalled her.

Rorvig was concentrating on the technical problems Sir Isaac was presenting and didn't notice the tension growing between Marla and Tobin.

"Do you all understand so far?" Sir Isaac questioned.

"No," Marla said, venting her frustration. "What's really bothering me is Holbak's relentless refusal to defect. He's as volatile as the research he's doing. He calls himself a pacifist, yet he keeps on experimenting with a power that could destroy the world under the protection of a mad man, who wouldn't hesitate to use it. He isolates himself in his damned lab and pays no attention to the atrocities happening around him. As far as I'm concerned, the worst kind of traitor is the one who fools himself. I think we would ultimately save more lives if we just executed the man."

Sir Isaac scowled. "You're out of line, lass. Way out of line."

"Marla, you don't know the whole picture," commented Tobin. His cool gaze steadied her, as it always did when she became upset on their assignments together. "We have a job to do. To do it well, we can't let sentiment stand in the way of our judgment or our action. Clear?"

Everyone's attention was riveted on her. She hesitated, still wrestling with her unresolved feelings, but then decided it was more pragmatic to comply. She nodded.

Sir Isaac accepted her decision. "We'll forget you made those remarks. Now, please, let's get back on track, shall we?"

"If I have it straight..." Tobin dribbled the tip of his pencil on the table while he organized his notes. "From Rorvig's architectural plan of the plant, our people are going to build us a scale model of Norsk. After Rorvig completes a crash course here on how to use our sabotage devices along with more field work training, he jumps back into Norway and returns to Norsk. He gathers the intelligence we need for our mission—deployment of guards, their schedule, inside security systems, access routes, whatever—and transmits this all back to *Amanita*. Rorvig's to operate out of a mountain village above Norsk. Because the region isn't policed, you say his radio won't be detected by SS watchers. Back here, you reconstruct the conditions he reports for me and my commando team to help us prepare. We parachute into Norway, into the mountains above Rorvig's village, meet up with him, and Rorvig escorts us inside Norsk. We deposit explosives in strategic locations, get out and detonate them. Norsk blows up. What could be simpler than that? Right, Rorvig?"

"It's suicide!" Marla protested again. "How can a handful of men be expected to get inside a concrete monster like that and effectively blow it up without killing themselves?"

"Marla," Rorvig reproached her, "we are talking about something far beyond individual survival. If the Germans learn the atom's secret before we do, we are allowing a colossal power to fall into the hands of the Nazis. Hitler will be able to hold the rest of the world hostage to his whims. That's not a world I want to live in. I accept responsibility for the risk we're taking. Besides, you're underestimating us, old girl. We can do the job the man wants. Scout's honor," he assured her.

"Good," Sir Isaac pronounced. "The code name for this operation is *Firebug*."

He gave them a moment to collect themselves before he lifted up a box to the desk and opened it. When he pulled the contents out, Catherine gasped. "It looks like horse manure!"

"Aye, lassie. It's meant to. Only this shit will blow you to kingdom come."

Marla hadn't been looking to be alone with Tobin, but it happened during their break in the galley kitchen. As she finished pouring herself a cup of black coffee, she looked up and found Tobin staring directly at her. He seemed to be measuring her but for what was beyond her. She dropped her eyes and mumbled, "I don't like the idea of Norwegians dying in this plan of Sir Isaac's."

"Neither does he," said Tobin.

"I missed you," she whispered. "How was it over there after I left?"

Tobin ignored her question and asked his own. "What about that radio show you and Catherine concocted for transmitting coded messages?"

"It's outlived its usefulness."

"Has Catherine given up all concert performances?"

Marla studied him. "You know she has... Let me come to you tonight."

He looked away. "No."

"Don't you want something more to remember than cold nights and gun butts?" she hissed at him just as Rorvig appeared in the doorway.

Tobin handed her his empty mess cup. "Take care of this, will you?"

"That's not part of my patriotic duty...*SIR!*"

He left before she could pitch the tin cup at his back. She slammed it down on the counter.

"I thought we were going to be one big happy family," said Rorvig.

"You thought wrong," she snapped. Rorvig looked down into her magnificent eyes that now smoldered with anger. *God!* he thought with despair. *She's beautiful!*

"Tell me," she said, switching subjects in a determined effort to bury Tobin and her past—he was not going to hurt her again, she deserved better treatment—"how did you manage to get away from Norsk without arousing suspicion?"

He grinned. "My family lives in the mountains, you see, and we have no phone. I've been struck with an illness that unfortunately takes a turn for the worse..."

"Something like walking pneumonia," added Marla, trying to pick up on the spirit of the ploy that was central to the success of their mission.

" ...And I have no way of getting a message to my boss except by hand delivery," he continued. "In a few days, he will receive a troubled note from my mother explaining how ill I am. She promises I will return to work as soon as I am well enough. Since I have always been a reliable worker, they will believe the note."

"Sent by the Underground, of course."

"Of course."

"After 11 days training with Tobin, you'll look the part."

"That bad," said Rorvig.

"Worse," Marla confirmed.

"Oh boy! Will you be attending training camp with us?"

"This *IS* training camp," said Marla.

Just then Catherine entered the galley kitchen. "Any chance you're serving tea?" she asked Marla.

"Nope. Just coffee."

"Ugh," Catherine grimaced after she looked into Marla's cup. "Look's too strong for me. Sir Isaac doesn't need me for the rest of the day, so I'll be on my way." She glanced at Rorvig. "Get lots of sleep tonight, Iceberg. I want you sharp for keyboard practise tomorrow."

Rorvig raised his eyebrows. "Keyboard practise?"

"Di-di-di-DA," sang Catherine.

"Oh, I get it. Crystal and ice. You're my receiver."

"Just think of me as your godmother," Catherine advised him and winked at Marla. "If it's a choice between the wind and the willow, I'd pick the willow."

A grin spread across her face as she left Marla to explain to Rorvig what she meant.

For the first time in her life, a man made Marla feel loved. Beginning that night until he left in the early morning 12 days later, Marla stayed with Ulo Rorvig every night in his cramped sleeping pod, in a section of sliver-like cells set aside as Amanita's sleeping quarters for transient agents. From the outset, she wanted to believe he was just another boy in the shelter of her bosom, someone she lusted to have, someone with whom she could indulge her fantasy of martyrdom in the endless self-depredation of her soul for her country fulfilling the physical needs of its secret saviors—she never thought any man she slept with could respond with anything more than simple gratitude.

Ulo was different. The impulse to trust, the hunger for special intimacy, the closeness that strips away all barriers guarding vulnerability—he had it, and she wanted it, all of it. His touch was like magic, throwing her back to a subconscious memory of security inside her mother's womb, to the caresses of the soothing embryonic waters washing over her, reminding her of warmth and snugness. The moment he took her into his arms and kissed her, she felt safe, as if she had come home.

And after the first rush of passion, their bonding began. Every waking moment they wcrc apart, she yearned for him. At night, when they were alone together, he explored her body with a tenderness she had never known: from pleasure to pleasure discovering, arousing, then relishing each swoon, a sweetness and an ecstasy purling through her that lifted him into her, and with a rising rhythm swept them into the universe beyond, groaning and writhing, peak upon peak, propelling them into the outer limits, his shaft thrusting deeper and deeper into the throes of her milky way, absorbing him into her deepest parts until every tingling nerve of their locked bodies flooded and burst with the immortal miracle of life forces fusing together their mind and body, heart and soul, into a single being, a completed entity from source to birth, until they lay and felt as one. As much pleasure as she could stand was unconditionally given to match and exceed the pleasure she desired to give.

On the night before he was scheduled to drop back into Norway, tears of joy spilled down her cheeks and wetted her hair.

Ulo felt the dampness. "Hey, why the tears? Did I hurt you?"

"No, you jerk. I'm happy."

"That's one helluva way to show it."

She choked up and nodded. He wrapped his arms around her and rocked her gently. "I've never felt like this before. Have you?"

When she didn't answer, he pulled back and tipped her head so he could see into her eyes. Fear filled them. She suddenly cupped his face with her hands. "Don't go," she pleaded. "Don't leave me."

"I have a job to do," he told her gently. "So do you. When it's all over, I'll come back."

She clutched him. "You promise?"

"You're the best thing that's ever happened to me. I want more." He hugged her and laughed. "The real question is...will you wait for me?"

"Oh yes," she breathed softly and caught another rising sob. She nestled her head against his chest. "I've waited my whole life for you. What's a little longer?"

"That's all I need to know," he said, gathering her close again.

In Ulo's arms, the fear fell away, and an expanding smile crept through her entire body, ending with a contented grin curling up her lips long after she had fallen asleep bundled up inside his arms.

As the sun crept up over the mountains the next day, Ulo Rorvig parachuted into Norway 16 miles above the Norsk hydro station. Within four days, he started sending signals back to *Amanita* according to the timetable he and Catherine had drawn up in advance. The first messages passed on the routine intelligence expected: WATCH CHANGES IN TWO SHIFTS INSIDE PLANT, 0800 AND 2000...DRAW BRIDGE GUARDED BY SENTRIES WITH DOGS ...GUARDSMEN GARRISONED BETWEEN ELECTROLYSIS PLANT AND ENGINE

HOUSE...ONLY ROADWAY INTO PLANT ELECTRONICALLY CONTROLLED...ALARM SIGNAL TRIGGERS FLOODLIGHTS...

The fifth transmission was signalled off the regular schedule alerting Catherine to its urgency: ENTIRE STOCK OF HEAVY WATER TO BE SHIPPED IN 15 DAYS...STOP... ESTIMATE SHIPMENT WILL SATISFY ALL CURRENT PRODUCTION DEMANDS... STOP...ADVISE ABORT FIREBUG...STOP...NEED SEAGULL BULLSHIT.

Almost simultaneously, Sir Isaac was reading a report from the Danish Resistance that had been contained in a microdot reduction brought back to *Amanita* by secret courier. It said: "Dr. Holbak refused our offer to arrange his escape. He says he feels responsible for the Jewish scientists still permitted to work on his project. If he goes, he fears he will be abandoning them to certain death. As yet, he claims he has discovered no practical way to test his theories and cannot offer London any immediate help with their atomic program. He warns the Germans are looking for more plutonium and heavy water to produce atomic bombs. He asks if you can do anything about this."

When they brought the two messages together, Tobin threw the pencil he was holding into the air and swore. Sir Isaac quoted Robbie Burns: *The best laid schemes o'mice an' men gang aft a-gley.* Marla mumbled to herself in disgust and worry: "The next person who says, *It never rains but it pours*, I will cheerfully kill." Catherine quietly asked, "What shall I radio *Iceberg*?"

Tobin took command. "Send him...BULLSHIT BAFFLES BRAINS...and sign it SEAGULL," he instructed. Sir Isaac nodded in agreement.

"What does it mean, Toby?" Marla asked.

"Rorvig wants me to bring in my commando team and plastic explosives disguised as horse manure. I've just told him we're on our way."

Chapter Fourteen

Friday, April 9th, 1943

THE JOURNEY began deep in the Kjolen range of Norway's mountains, near Rjukan, in a valley so deep and foreboding that in winter the sun could not reach its depths and the workers in the Norsk hydro complex had to be transported by cable car up to the top of the mountain for their daily requirement of sunlight. Over five thousand pounds of heavy water, the result of nearly six months of production, were loaded on a freight train that chugged through the Norwegian mountains down to the seaport where the railroad cars, carrying the secret cargo, were to be uncoupled on a barge and pulled across the sea by ferry to Copenhagen, Denmark.

Through the fiord country, tranquillity had ceased to exist. By nature, the Norwegians were peace loving and trusting, but after Hitler's bombing reprisals three years before—against the coastal towns and villages who helped King Haakon VII and members of his Norwegian government escape to England—the Nazi occupation had tapped primeval distrust and fretfulness in their Nordic cousins. Still, on this anniversary of the Nazis' April ninth invasion, the promise of spring sweetened the air.

Brooks bubbled playfully. Swollen rivers eagerly spilled over their banks and hurtled down slippery waterfalls, joyfully thundering on the rocks below. Against the distant sky, snowcrested mountains towered in every direction, like majestic sentinels patiently waiting for the tinkle of cowbells and the jingle of sheep bells to waken the fir-clad slopes. Where the Gulf Stream lapped their shores, bringing an unusually warm climate to this northern wonderland, the fiords feasted the eye with vibrant florals. Instead of expected spruce and pine scents filling the air, copper-beech, ash, lime and a host of other sub-tropical trees misted the firth with their delightful fragrances.

From a plateau overlooking a narrow inlet flanked by high banks, the sea was so smooth that the port of Kristiansand looked like an architect's model glued to tinted glass. Its sun-bleached buildings lay clustered in three groups that hooked together in a loop. Between them, a fleet of torpedo boats bobbed. It was the German naval base. Tobin carefully studied it through his binoculars.

For four days, Tobin and his men had hidden in the small mountain cabin behind him. Tiny tree shoots sprouted from its turf roof like eagle feathers on an Indian headdress. The isolation of the farmsteads dappling the hills protected them from discovery while they prepared for today's mission.

Out of sight of the clapboard hut, in front of the bank barn, the farmer hitched his prize Westland pony to the back of the hay wagon. Tears veined his weathered face as he stroked the beautiful cream-colored creature with the distinctive black stripe flashing down his mane and tail and the zebra markings along his legs. The pony gently nuzzled his master's cheek and neck and nibbled at his pant legs before his quivering nose undertook the playful search for the carrot sticking out of the farmer's hip pocket.

In winter, the farmers set their Westlands free on the highest slopes where they were known to be as nimble-footed as any goat, but in the early spring they would bring them back to work the regions too difficult for a tractor. The farmer lifted the pony's head by his halter to look squarely into his sensitive brown eyes. "You must prance with your head held high as I have taught you," he told him in Norwegian. "The Germans must feel as proud to have you as a gift as I have been to own you." He let go of the halter.

"I will miss you," he added with a heavy heart, gradually turning his back to allow the Westland to find the carrot dangling from his pocket. The pony tugged at the carrot greens and bit by bit pulled the whole thing out of its hiding place. He shook it with triumph. When the Westland started munching, the greens and the long fat carrot quickly vanished inside his mouth. Once gone, he furled his upper lip and whinnied for more.

"Good, eh?" The farmer patted the pony's thick muscled neck. "It was the largest and the sweetest I could find."

Tobin appeared on the shallow rise between the house and the barn. As if on cue, his three commandos emerged from the cabin's back door. One carried double bales of hay bundled together. He dumped them on top of the straw dripping over the sides of the wagon. Slung over his shoulder was a 9 mm. Browning FN rifle. The other two carried out three back packs, one Mark V.303 rifle, a Browning Automatic rifle and a portable transmission radio. Their pockets bulged with boxes of ammunition. Like the farmer, they were dressed in heavy winter gear.

He swung his attention back to the farmer. "The time has come."

The Norwegian nodded and strapped the 50-lb. pack, which he had dropped by his knees earlier while talking to his pony, to his back. He was responsible for guiding the special commando team across the mountains to Sweden, thus he carried their food rations and utensils. Tobin clasped the farmer's callused hands in his own.

"It's unfortunate that wars cause men to decide the fate of others, even of their loved ones."

"I understand." The farmer shifted the weight of his back pack more comfortably. "I have talked to the Westland. He will co-operate. Remember how I showed you to drive the wagon. The draught horse has a sensitive mouth. He needs little urging to do what you want. He knows his job."

"Better than I do." Tobin turned to his three men. "Good luck, men. Wish I were going with you. Stick close to your guide here. He knows the route as well as any mountain goat roaming these hills."

He swung his attention back to the farmer. "The SS will be looking for you, so I want you to fly out with my men. You can join a small band of Norwegians training in Scotland. I'm sure they will welcome your help."

The Norwegian nodded. "Go with God," he added with the simple faith of the country folk. His eyes teared as he drank in one last look around the farmstead, then he turned and started trudging toward the mountain trail. Each commando shook Tobin's hand and followed the farmer. The third one pulling up the rear didn't let go of his grip. "You shouldn't be going in alone, sir. One of us can stay back with you...in case you need a helping hand."

"If that happens, the mission is scrubbed anyway," Tobin reminded him. "One man alone is harmless. Two are a threat."

"Right you are, sir. We'll see you in England." He turned and followed the others trekking in tandem up the difficult slope.

Tobin watched until they were a good quarter mile away before he rushed up the porch steps and disappeared inside the deserted farmhouse. Raising the lid of his scuffed suitcase, he deftly adjusted the antenna lying across the miniaturized radio set contained within. Concealed inside the side pocket was a quartz crystal. He took it out and inserted it. The radio came alive. At once, he pulled on his headset and tapped out a short signal. Immediately Morse chattering buzzed in his ear. He sent his coded message and signed off, folded up the aerial and the ground wire, removed the quartz crystal and disconnected the headphones. Next he traced a very thin roll of plastic explosive under the bottom rim of the suitcase, all the way around, and affixed a friction-sensitive blasting cap to the grip's catch. Very gently he shut the lid and slowly, soundlessly, eased the spring bolt back into place, fastening the latch. The next person to open his suitcase would be blown to smithereens. He breathed in slowly and braced himself before he removed a crude single-shot pistol from his inside zipper pocket.

It was a special wartime design of .45 revolver the Office for Strategic Services used for assassinations. He carefully loaded the weapon nicknamed the Liberator and stuffed the gun into his sheepskin jacket pocket, yanked the farmer's forage cap low over his brow, gathered up a satchel of clothing along with the booby-trapped suitcase and headed out the door.

Outside, the draught horse harnessed to the hay wagon lazily chewed on his bit while the Westland pony hitched behind it swished his tail impatiently. Tobin lifted the suitcase onto the back of the wagon and meticulously cushioned the satchel under the loose hay, hiding them from casual inspection. Giving the pony a pat, he pleaded with the Westland, "Stick close." The cream pony's ears twitched forward, fully alert. Then he walked around to the front, eyed the huge draught horse, sighed, looked heavenward for help and climbed up into the driver's seat.

"It's now or never," he told himself. The nerves in his stomach steadied. "I'm ready."

He flicked the reins and yelled, "Giddy-up!"

They jogged through the main street of Kristiansand on their way to the German dockyards. Hearing the clip-clop of the horses' shoes against the cobblestone route, many Norwegians paused and pointed at the sturdy Westland proudly prancing behind the wagon and were visibly stirred. Steps that shuffled lightened. Heads that drooped lifted. Faded eyes brightened.

Tobin sensed rather than saw the shift in the spirit of the passersby and shared in their pride until the clack-clack of storm troopers goose-stepping up the street suddenly shattered that moment of private triumph.

Several platoons marched by. A cold sweat broke down Tobin's spine.

At the town square, he passed a giant rock covered by a bevy of noisy seagulls who remained unruffled by the mix of military and civilian traffic milling about. The smell of seawater drifted inland on the prevailing breezes fluttering the parade of Nazi flags raised in front of the town hall. Further west, he noticed cooing pigeons and shrilling seagulls cloistered like a nun's headband over the stone statue of a Norse sea god. Trotting past whitewashed houses with brightly painted flower boxes and quaint street lamps, they finally came to the bleak grey expanse of the German naval base.

"Whoa!" Tobin pulled up in front of the base gate. A serious young SS guard examined the waybill Tobin presented to him. It marked the paid delivery of a prize Westland pony to the Fuhrer's private estate in Bavaria and was stamped with Hitler's personal seal, a first-rate forgery produced by *Project Amanita*.

"Which horse?" demanded the gatehouse guard.

Tobin suppressed a twinkle. This pride of the SS was definitely not a country lad. He pointed to the cream-colored pony with the characteristic eel stripe streaking through his mane and tail and zebra-lined stockings. The German's icy features melted. "It is a rare animal, *Ja*?" he clucked.

Tobin nodded proudly. "*Ja. Ja.* Very special."

The SS guard opened the shipping orders attached to the sealed delivery paper and carefully read them before handing them back to Tobin. "The train ferry loads at Pier 16," he directed. "When you pass through the gates, go to your left, to the end of the boat sheds. The loading ramp for Pier 16 is there."

Tobin thanked him and snapped the reins. They had just passed the biggest hurdle to the mission and were safely inside the German base.

The unexpected sight of a horse-drawn wagon clip-clopping over the concrete dock aroused the interest of workmen inside the huge open sheds. The reek of tar, hot metal and primer paint cloyed the air. It was so heavy it made Tobin feel nauseous. Through the gaping half moons of light, he could see sparks from welding torches and hear jabbering riveters. Beyond, tied in clusters up to the quay, swayed the flotilla of S-Boats he had seen through his binoculars. These were the Kriegmarine's rugged torpedo boats. Tobin counted 15.

Armed with two single 21-inch torpedo tubes and twin 20mm. guns and outfitted with a Daimler-Benz lightweight diesel engine, they were fierce and fast warriors on the sea. During the Dunkirk evacuation, they sunk the British destroyer, *Wakeful*, and two French destroyers, *Jaguar* and *Sirocco*. In the southern North Sea, they were disrupting British convoys and had already sunk the destroyers *Exmoor, Eskdale, Penylan* and *Vortigern* along the east coast of England. These, Tobin surmised, were probably assigned to protect the Germans' supply line back and forth across the Skagerrak and in and out of the Kettegat south to Germany's Baltic ports. An imperceptible smile tugged at Tobin's lips. Not even these prize fighters could stop the surprise in store for the Germans. He'd make sure of it.

At Pier 16, the dock was on a man-made canal that met the junction of rail lines that ended at the town's bayshore. The long barge was already loaded with the flatcars carrying the sealed drums of heavy water. *Perfect*, Tobin noted to himself as he pulled up. Four crewmen from the barge were helping to tie it to the tugboat that would pull it across the sea to Denmark. They were Norwegians. Regret briefly needled Tobin's conscience. It was unfortunate, he rationalized to himself, but an unavoidable fact of war—innocent people die.

He produced his shipping orders to the Wehrmacht supply officer stationed at the gangplank. The officer's eyes bulged. "Where is this pony?" he demanded crossly.

Tobin pointed to the Westland.

"This is most unexpected. We have no livestock cars for this shipment."

Tobin's heart sank. To be defeated by a point of procedure was unthinkable. "We can easily cordon off an adequate stall with ropes braced to the rail and anchored to the deck. As you can see, the Fuhrer has placed some urgency on this delivery. It would not please him to have his prize gift detained," he suggested quietly.

A nerve spasmed in the supply officer's temple as he haughtily contemplated Tobin. His lips pursed. "Naturally. Vossana!" he called to one of the Norwegian crewmen. "Fix up a stall for this horse on the barge."

The Norwegian looked up in surprise. "A horse?" He came over to Tobin who showed him the shipping orders. "The Fuhrer wants a Westland from Norway." He went over to the pony and patted his neck. "No problem," he assured the German officer. "We can make a nice stall for Hitler's horse." He headed back toward the boat shed and returned with a portable cattle pen. "You see?" he grinned to Tobin. "No problem."

While Tobin waited for the Norwegian to install the compound, he whistled off key, a tuneless *tew...tew...tew...* Both horses listening to his whistling grew restless. Without warning, each one suddenly released his bladder. Their urge was trained to respond to that whistle, and their hard streams splattered on the concrete pier beneath. The Norwegian crewmen smirked and winked at Tobin.

The Wehrmacht supply officer shrieked in disgust. "You!" he shouted to a workman. "Get a hose and wash down this mess."

The angry tone of the officer made the draught horse nervous. He raised his tail and plopped a neat mound of mushy rank manure on the wharf. The German stood transfixed, staring at the dunghill as though it were a swelling pus boil of the bubonic plague. Red rage fired the skin above his collar and shot up from his neck to his ears to his cheeks to the translucent skin tightly stretched over the snarled veins threading his temples.

"It's your horse," he fumed to Tobin. "I won't have this shit on my dock. Clean it up," he hissed between clenched teeth.

Toying with the German's obsession for spotless order, he asked, "Do you have a shovel?"

"Bring this man a shovel!" bellowed the supply officer to the workman who was hooking up the hose to wash down the yellow rivers of horse urine already running across the dock. He looked at Tobin, shrugged, dropped the hose and scuttled back inside the boat shed to find a shovel.

As soon as the stall on the barge was ready, Toby unhitched the Westland pony and led him over the gangplank and into his makeshift quarters by the port rail. "Can I help you carry your straw?" one of the Norwegians asked him.

"That won't be necessary," Tobin quickly discouraged him. He went back to the wagon and filled his arms with straw treated with incendiaries.

As he passed the flatcars, some of the straw seemed to brush off against their sidings and left a sloppy trail behind him. Returning to the wagon for more straw, he made another trip. The same thing happened. When the supply officer saw the litter Tobin was dropping, he railed at him. Tobin apologized excessively for his clumsiness. The officer glowered as he filled the water bucket half full and carried it with one hand while he picked up the bundled double bales of hay with the other. The German's eagle eyes pinned Tobin's progress step-by-step. This time he managed to reach the pony's pen without dropping anything. The Nazi turned away to supervise the transfer of heavy equipment from the barge to the dock further aft.

In the stall, Tobin knelt down and untied the bundles of hay. Sandwiched between them appeared to be more horse manure. He gingerly laid it in the corner where the Westland had already deposited fresh dung. The piles matched, Tobin saw with satisfaction, and wondered if the Germans even remembered that this was the anniversary of their invasion of Norway.

Chapter Fifteen

MARLA had developed a habit of standing by Catherine's station around the time of Rorvig's expected transmissions. Catherine teased her. Ignoring her gentle jibes, Marla kept on talking. Her days were filled with thoughts of him, and her nights dreamed of his return. "We shared such joy and contentment," she confided to Catherine.

"Making love was so beautiful. Not emptying like usual. I didn't know it could be like that. I've always accepted ecstasy and emptiness as two faces of the same coin. I guess they still are when sex is purely physical, but..." A secret smile crossed her face. "The culmination of the spiritual joined together with the sexual ... well, there's no describing it. At long last I feel complete. Someday you'll know what I mean."

"Marla, that's wonderful! You've really fallen in love this time."

"Do you think so?"

"Yes, I do. Did you tell him?"

Marla shook her head. "No. I couldn't. I was too scared, but Ulo promised he would come back to me,

Catherine. How I want to believe it! I want him to come back to me so much."

"Then believe it and he will." Catherine's eyes shone.

"Nothing's ever that simple, Catherine. Nothing!"

"You mean because of Christopher Tobin."

Marla's eyes narrowed. "What do you mean?"

"I saw the way you were looking at him when Sir Isaac was briefing us for Operation Firebug."

"Watch that active imagination of yours. It could get you in trouble."

"Maybe. But I am right. You do love Tobin too, don't you?"

Marla stared down at her black oxford shoes as if she were intent on finding one scruffy spot to shine. "Maybe...*once*."

"What happened?" Catherine prompted.

Marla paused. "I don't know. We worked so closely together. I did things for him I wouldn't do for anyone else, but he always made me feel as if I weren't good enough. He said he had to keep our relationship strictly professional."

"That could be true."

"Yes, but something has happened to him since he's become a commando. He's colder, more detached. He lets nothing interfere with his objective. Sometimes he's so unfeeling."

"Don't you think that's what makes him such a good commando?"

"I suppose," Marla agreed. "We live side by side with death. Living with it the way we do, we come to fear it less, to see it less as an enemy and more as a fact of life, if for no other than reason than we can't deny it to ourselves. It's always with us. Sometimes it's even a merciful companion."

"Is that why you fell in love with Rorvig?"

Marla looked startled. "Because you can't count on your tomorrows?" She thought for a moment and shrugged. "I dunno. No. Definitely not," she decided. "Ulo showed me I'm not only desirable, but I'm also loveable. At last I know what it feels like to be loved by a man, unconditionally, and I have a chance to love him in return."

"Oh, Marla!" Catherine hugged her fiercely. "That's wonderful!"

ULO RORVIG climbed the steps of the *stabbur* in the mountains above the Norsk hydro plant. It was an old storehouse in which he had stashed his radio. In days gone by, the upper floor has been used as an extra guest room and was particularly grand as the villagers believed only the best was good enough for guests. The floating wooden staircase reached the finely carved balcony of the loft, ideal for a writer's or artist's hideaway. Robust smells of corn, apples and fermenting beer rose from the stored goods on the ground floor below.

Inside the charming guest room still comfortably furnished with classic antique furniture, Rorvig pulled out a battered suitcase from under the four poster bed and lifted it onto the side table. Then he opened the lid and expertly set up the antenna. He had complained of feeling sick to his assistant and left the heavy water plant to make this special transmission to London. At exactly 1500 hours he tapped out his call signal.

Catherine immediately answered. Beside her, Marla's

face flooded with relief. Listening to his dit-dit-da taps, she recognized her name in Morse code. "What's he saying?" she asked anxiously.

Catherine waved her to shush. As she scribbled out the message, she grinned and beckoned to Marla to look down at her code pad: BERYL GET HOME FIRE BURNING...STOP...JOB DONE...STOP. More static stuttering followed. Catherine continued to take down his rendezvous instructions for the sub.

In concentrating on his transmission, Rorvig missed the warning footfall on the bottom steps. The piercing creak of the balcony floor on the other side of the open door alerted him. Instinctively his free hand grabbed his semi-automatic pistol, a Colt .45, while he hastily signed off the emergency letter code, QUO, which stood for *I am forced to stop transmitting because of imminent danger*. A spray of bullets smashed his transmitting set. He rolled to the floor for cover.

Marla instantly recognized the QUO. Catherine glanced up at her face. The radiant joy that had been registered there one second before had dissolved into ashen horror. "*NOooo...*" Her protest came out in a squeaky mew. *"NOOO! Not him too!"* She backed away, shaking her head and repeating, "*NO... NO...*"

Catherine desperately signalled back to him, but the air waves were dead. He had been cut off. One of the older operators came over to comfort Marla. "Those signals are always scary, dearie. I had one earlier this week, but my laddie was back on the air yesterday. You mustn't give up hope. They depend on us for that, y'a know. To be here when they call us. Come. I'll make y'a a nice cup o' tea."

Marla, trembling, darting her eyes over her shoulder to her last tangible contact with Ulo Rorvig, let herself be led from the radio room. Her stricken face tore Catherine apart. With a heavy heart, she focused on the radio set, every field agent's umbilical link to home base. "Call, Iceberg," she pleaded softly, using his code name, which for her was more familiar. "For Marla's sake, call."

DROP YOUR GUN, ICEBERG," ordered a cold voice in accented English.

Rorvig raised his head. He had been called by his code name. His stomach lurched. Somewhere in the shattered mess on the table lay his cyanide pill. He had forgotten to insert it, the fatal flaw of the overconfident agent. Believing he was home free, he had dropped his guard. With resignation, he dropped his Colt .45 on the floor and pulled himself up to his full height, facing his captors.

Two figures in white Arctic coveralls stood astride the doorway with their MP40 sub-machine guns trained on him. The man who issued the command emerged through the door. Inside the loosened neck of his white ski suit peeked the twin lightning streaks of the secret police, the Gestapo. As he holstered his exquisite Polish Radom—a semi-automatic cavalry pistol German officers favored because of the Browning lock action which made it very rigorous—his eyes gleamed with self-satisfaction.

"So, Ulo Rorvig, you are the agent Iceberg we have been hunting!" His tight voice revealed a strained balancing act over the edge of sanity. Rorvig knew, if he made one wrong move, the commander of the SS security force at Norsk could slip out of control. The *Amanita* agent refused to give him the satisfaction of an answer and masked the fear seeping through every pore of his skin, greasing his arm pits, back and crotch. Gas blistered in his bowels. They stared icily at one another.

How much did the Gestapo really know? Rorvig wondered. Where the hell had he slipped up? He would give anything to know that. Taking in the Nazi's nostrils flaring with sadistic eagerness, he steeled himself for the worst. There would be no answers from this beast. Only questions.

"This time we got the heavy water out before your *Firebugs* could destroy it," the beast bragged. "*Ja*," he said, quickly detecting the slight widening of Rorvig's eyes. "We know all about your *Firebug* operation—your plan to plant explosives inside Norsk to blow up our heavy water supply. Isn't that a shame?" he sneered. "So much effort ... *Wasted*!"

There was a scurry of jackboots and jabbering of muffled voices on the ground floor. "What is it?" the Nazi barked down to the men below.

A few seconds later a SS captain in white coveralls charged up the stairs and entered the room. "We've just received word from the ferry base, Colonel Streicher. The heavy water cargo exploded at sea. None of it was salvaged," he reported.

Rorvig couldn't help enjoying the shock on Streicher's face and laughed triumphantly. "Tch...tch... Berlin won't be happy," he taunted.

Seething with hatred, Streicher turned on Rorvig. "Don't bask in your victory too long, Rorvig," he spat viciously. "We've both been betrayed...and by someone on your own team."

Disbelief flooded Rorvig's eyes. *Someone on his own team!*

"Hang him!" Streicher snarled at the SS captain and stomped out the door and down the storehouse steps.

The brutal order scarcely appeased Streicher's lust for revenge. Driven by his own demons, he snapped on his skis left standing in the drifts against the *stabbur* and pulled his black wool balaclava over his head. His eyes peering through the slits burned. He adjusted a pair of goggles snugly to his face, tightened the fur-lined hood around his head, dug his poles in, and jumped off, swooshing down the sheerest trail he could pick to the Norsk hydro station at the valley's bottom. Matching his skill against the treacherous terrain restored his self-esteem and determination to crush the faceless traitor who had humiliated him. Hanging Rorvig instead of interrogating him was Streicher's personal message to that traitor. He would not be thwarted again.

The SS ski squad dragged Rorvig outside and hauled him up to a barren tree at the side of the *stabbur*. About seven feet off the ground, the horny stub of a severed branch jutted out from its main trunk. The SS soldiers looped a noose of thin cord around Rorvig's neck and hoisted him up until the cord caught on the makeshift tree hook, then let him go. His body floundered in the open air. He bucked and kicked, resisting the noose that was choking him. The frigid cold frosted his last gasps of breath in ribbons of cloud that twined his head like a crown of thorns. As he continued to writhe, the cord gradually grew tighter and tighter until slowly, ever so slowly, in excruciating pain, Ulo Rorvig strangled to death. His last coherent thoughts were of Marla. He had promised her he would come back.

Chapter Sixteen

Friday, September 24th, 1944

PRIME MINISTER WINSTON CHURCHILL had requested an urgent meeting with *Project Amanita's* director, Sir Isaac Malcolm, and the chief co-ordinator of Allied Command Intelligence (ACI), Wendal Stevens, at his personal chamber in the "Hole in the Ground" as he called it, a labyrinth of tunnels converted into emergency war headquarters under Whitehall. Both men headed civilian intelligence groups, the one British, the other a joint Allied effort. He greeted them in bed.

Wendal Stevens slipped into the bedside chair leaving Sir Isaac to face Churchill from the other seat at the foot of his bed. The *former naval person* was in a thundering mood. "Am I given to understand that Dr. Holbak finally consented to smuggle out his journal to us and it's been lost at sea?"

"That's correct, Mr. Prime Minister." Sir Isaac braced himself for the brunt of Churchill's wrath.

"How much more insufferable stupidity must we endure?"

Churchill was on the edge of one of his tedious tantrums. Sir Isaac took the initiative. "In the confusion of the getaway," he explained, "Holbak's assistant dropped the manila envelope containing the journal into the ocean. He was very frightened at the time and clumsy. It's a regrettable accident, but one we are going to have to live with."

Churchill glowered. "If Holbak's papers, detailing all his experimental results in nuclear fission, wash up on shore and are handed over to German authorities, can they grasp the significance of these papers?"

Sir Isaac cleared his throat. The rim of his droopy mustache seemed to fold over his upper lip, and his mouth receded into a thin, grim line. "That's difficult to determine, sir. We can't project the condition of the recovered journal nor the inclination of the person or persons who may discover it."

"Where's Holbak now?" demanded Churchill.

Unconsciously, Sir Isaac steepled his finger tips together in prayerlike form. "In Copenhagen."

"*STILL!?*" roared Churchill. His chin retreated into jowls. "We have no choice," he said, as he pulled his afghan up more tightly to cover his chest. "The man has become a critical liability. With the Germans toughening up their policies in Denmark, it's clear he faces imminent arrest and interrogation. Under torture, who knows what he might tell."

"The Gestapo won't resort to torture. They'll use drugs," Sir Isaac pointed out.

Churchill's lips puckered in disapproval. "We've waited too long. Terminate him."

Sir Isaac glanced at Wendal Stevens for support. "I agree. His lab should be destroyed too."

"Why?" asked Stevens.

"The Americans are close to producing their own atomic bomb. Holbak's test results are no longer significant."

"The risk of atomic information falling into German hands has to be weighed against the danger of reprisals following the destruction of his lab," cautioned Stevens.

"The SS are liquidating entire communities anyway. We can't help that," countered Sir Isaac.

"We don't have to encourage it unnecessarily either," Stevens objected evenly.

"Granted," Sir Isaac almost smiled, "but we can take advantage of any counteractive retaliation the Nazis initiate against the Danes to galvanize the spirit of the resistance movement amongst local partisans. Without constant provocation, support for our secret armies will surely die."

Churchill nodded. "The tactic which brings an ally into the field is as serviceable as that which wins a great battle."

"I personally do not see the danger of reprisals as a strong enough deterrent to refrain from blowing up Holbak's lab," Sir Isaac flatly concluded.

Wendal Stevens leaned forward in his chair, convinced both men were toying with a strategical blunder. "Suppose Holbak's papers are never found," he argued. "If we blow up his lab, are we not signalling the German scientists that he's been on the right track all along?"

"True," Sir Isaac conceded.

Reaching for a cigar on his bedside table, Churchill deliberated as he slowly lit it. "Well, gentlemen, what do we do about this tricky situation? We don't want

Hitler speeding up his production," he said at length, sticking the loathsome thing between his lips. His bloated cheeks busily drew in and out like bellows. Puff balls of acrid smoke spewed into the air.

While Sir Isaac pulled out his pipe and packed it with tobacco from a pouch tucked in his jacket pocket, he used the guise to study Stevens unobtrusively. Other than he was a Canadian, he knew nothing about the ACI head. Lately, Churchill had been making his mysterious associate privy to all the subversive operations being run inside the Third Reich, and it irked Sir Isaac. He drew on his pipe as he lit it. Before he stuck his neck out, he wanted to hear what Stevens had in mind.

"I see it as a game of bluff," Stevens said. "If we first rescue Holbak and then leave his lab intact, we may fool Hitler's scientists into thinking his test results are worthless."

"To do that, we would have to countermand *Watchdog's* orders." Sir Isaac kept the pipe in his mouth.

"Who is *Watchdog*?"

"A plant inside Holbak's lab," replied Sir Isaac.

Stevens mentally sifted the information. "What are his orders?"

Sir Isaac smiled. "You're assuming *Watchdog* is a man."

He succeeded in raising a polite reaction from Stevens. "I'll rephrase the question: What are *Watchdog's* orders?"

"If the Germans decide to interrogate Dr. Holbak, our agent is to terminate him and destroy the lab."

"Aren't you assuming your agent will get prior notice of Holback's' arrest?"

"I'm not assuming anything," said Sir Isaac smugly.

"Prior notice is a surety."

"I see." A frown pinched Steven's forehead. "How do we contact *Watchdog*?"

"Our agent has operated with complete anonymity," said Sir Isaac. "He uses sleepers to run courier for him. He never sees nor talks directly to the ones he uses. This way no trail leads back to him. Neither can the sleeper decode the message he carries because he doesn't have the key."

Stevens noted Sir Isaac's territorial slip. The *Project Amanita* agent was male and probably very highly placed in the German High Command. "That explains how he contacts you, not how you contact him."

"We haven't."

This time Sir Isaac took Stevens by surprise. "You've never contacted *Watchdog* since you activated him?" he asked incredulously.

"Aye, that's right," said Sir Isaac. "Any information he has sent us has been based on our need to know. There's been no reason to jeapordize his cover by contacting him."

Wendal Stevens sat silently, sifting and balancing everything he had heard. He was medium-built, a faceless man with thinning salted hair who could fade into a crowd except for his emerald eyes. They probed, measured and digested, and then reconstructed what he saw on his inner screen, mixing and matching and splicing the images into little vignettes. Seeing a problem from different perceptions often inspired a daring new decision.

Churchill fidgeted restlessly. "Would you gentlemen care for a mulled wine? This living like a mole underground chills me to the bone."

Stevens nodded absent-mindedly. Sir Isaac agreed heartily. Churchill rang for his valet. When the attentive servant opened the private door of his chamber, Nelson, Churchill's black cat, darted inside and pounced on Churchill's bed. He padded up the thick outline of his master's body to sit on his portly stomach and looked expectantly into the prime minister's face.

"Cat, darling, have I been neglecting you?" Churchill stroked his silky ears and coat until the cat purred with contentment as he settled himself down in a half-circle ready to snooze. When the valet tried to shoosh him away, Churchill held up his hand. "Leave him," he ordered. "He's keeping me warm."

The chastized valet quickly withdrew, and Churchill returned his attention to the two men. "Well, gentlemen, what do we do? Rescue Holbak or terminate him? Demolish his lab or leave it to Providence?"

Stevens spoke quietly. "We have no choice. Rescue Holbak and forget his lab. The faster the better."

Churchill fastened his gaze on Sir Isaac. "Is that how you appraise the situation?"

He cleared his throat and nodded. "Aye, Wendal makes sense. Leaving Holbak's lab intact may put the Germans off long enough to give the Americans the lead in their production of the atomic bomb."

"Which brings us back to this *Watchdog* of yours. How do we contact him?" Churchill asked Sir Isaac.

He hesitated. Both Churchill and Stevens noticed.

"There is only one courier he would trust."

Churchill and Stevens leaned forward expectantly. Their postures demanded *WHO?*

"Lady Catherine Rushmore," said Sir Isaac.

"*No!*" Churchill's left eyebrow shot up in a lopsided

scowl. "You don't mean Lord James' daughter."

"I do."

"Good grief! Is there no one else you can send?" he grumbled. "She's the king's cousin for heaven's sake!"

"She's three full generations away from the throne," Stevens argued, eyeing Sir Isaac with growing respect. The man was willing to take risks.

"That's not the point," Churchill thundered. "If she's captured, the Nazis can hold her for ransom. Lord only knows what kind of trade-off they would use against us. Politically, I'd be ruined."

"Do we have any other choice?" Stevens asked Sir Isaac.

"Anyone else we send, *Watchdog* will suspect is a Gestapo plant."

To calm his agitation, Churchill unconsciously petted the back of his sleepy Nelson, evoking a loud steady purr from the cat curled up so peacefully on top of his broad belly.

"There's another factor," continued Sir Isaac. "She's one of the few people Dr. Holbak knows and respects. She gave a recital in Copenhagen in '37 at the Danish king's awards dinner for celebrities and scientists, and they set next to each other earnestly talking throughout the meal. She's also King Christian's cousin."

Sir Isaac summed it all up. "If Holbak has any last-minute misgivings about leaving Copenhagen, she can put them to rest. We must move quickly, and we must move now."

Churchill's jowls folded as his chin sank into his chest.

"May I suggest you familiarize King George with

the situation, Mr. Prime Minister, and find out his reactions before we proceed," Stevens urged.

Churchill's head shot up. Considering each man carefully, he pursed his lips and nodded his assent. At that point, the valet entered with a tray of mulled wine, and the three men downed its spicy warmth gratefully.

At midnight that same night, Churchill conveyed the king's prayers for the success of his cousin's mission to Stevens and Sir Isaac. Catherine would be sent to Copenhagen at the earliest dispatch.

Chapter Seventeen

Monday, September 27th, 1944

AFTER MANY SHIPYARD STRIKES, the sabotage of Copenhagen's rifle manufacturing plant in June and two five-day general strikes—one from June 30 to July 4 and the other between September 16 and 21 protesting against the Germans' mass deportations of Danes—Waffen-SS troops were storming Copenhagen, breaking into homes in the middle of the night and carrying off whole families to cattleships anchored in the harbor that were destined for Germany.

At Gestapo headquarters in the heart of Copenhagen, in a building that once served as the Shell Oil Company's main European office, SS Colonel Joachim von Daren read the arrest order for Dr. Sven Holbak and angrily flung it down on his desk. It was signed by the security commander for occupied Denmark, SS Colonel Friedrich Streicher.

Since the takeover of Denmark, the purebred officer with the title of Baron had used every ploy imaginable to entangle the nuclear scientist's reports in such a web of bureaucratic muddling that they either became lost or so bogged down they never reached the right analytical departments where the true progress of his daily experiments could be recognized. The Nazis' fastidious fascination with documenting everything had made them very tolerant of clogged paper channels. Nothing seemed amiss with more irregular tie-ups.

Hitler's own attitude towards academics served as Holbak's best protection. He hated teachers and especially theorems developed by Jewish scientists. Since Holbak's work evolved from Albert Einstein's *Theory of Relativity*, a Jew's physics rather than a German's, Hitler didn't take the doctor's findings as seriously as he might have. But, someone in the German High Command was growing impatient with Holbak, and Joachim suspected it was Streicher himself. It seemed the Gestapo intended to force him to speed up his trial runs with the heavy water cyclotron in his lab. He was trying to bridle the spontaneous energy released by nuclear fission, but he was taking too long fiddling with more variables in the experiments. Hitler needed monster weapons immediately—the atomic bomb, rockets with atomic warheads and jet fighters—to turn the tide of the war back in his favor. They were all on the drawing board, and the few prototype jet planes that had been produced were failing their initial tests dismally. Every scientist under the Third Reich, including the massive number employed at the top secret rocket base at Peenemunde 120 miles east of Copenhagen on the Baltic Sea, was assigned a personal SS monitor. This way the pressure to produce was sustained and leaks in information as well as sabotage efforts were discouraged. As Holbak's SS liaison officer, the arrest order on Joachim's desk questioned his loyalty and competence as much as the scientist's.

Joachim had come across Streicher in Berlin, when he was first assigned to the *Einsatzgruppen*, a formidable force of combined SS, SD, and Gestapo Special Action groups.

They were the official executioners, the Death Squads that slaughtered tens of thousands at a time in mass reprisals or secret "disinfections" ridding the Third Reich of its "subhumans." His reward for a job well done in Poland was to be made security commander of the Norsk hydro plant in Norway. Now, he had been transferred to Copenhagen to control the increasing activities of the resistance movement spreading through Denmark.

Joachim quickly considered. If Holbak were arrested and forced to talk, he would not be able to conceal that he already knew how to harness the atom's amazing mega force. With this information, Hitler could produce the elusive power to enslave the whole world. There was no doubt in Joachim's mind that Germany was equipped to build an atomic bomb faster than the Allies. The Nazis had the resources and the intensive labor necessary to achieve it. For them, it would be like assembling a toy. This had to be prevented at all costs, even if it meant the scientist must die.

In the meantime, he might be able to negotiate one more delay. His own chief, Brigadier General Schellenberg, headed the combined secret services. He had since the July plot, when Admiral Canaris of Military Intelligence had been arrested as a suspect in the assassination attempt on Hitler's life. The Admiral's active operations had been quickly absorbed by Schellenberg's SD. Everything else had been dismantled. Joachim was relying on his ability to persuade Schellenberg to postpone Holbak's arrest. It would give the scientist one last chance to escape.

He picked up the phone and asked the operator for a free line to Berlin. His fingers drummed impatiently on the desk while he waited for the connection. "*Herr General*?" He listened to the other end and muttered,

"*Iche verstehe. Danke.*"

Walther Schellenberg was the only cultured Nazi leader in Hitler's elite circle. He used stealth to ply the truth from unwilling minds—minds, like pockets, that did not feel they were "picked clean" until it was too late. He better than anyone understood Germany's desperate need to develop atomic energy. Next to Heinrich Himmler, who still controlled the whole SS organization, he held power over a dying monster. From the outset of the war, he had conspired to achieve a breakthrough and had assigned Joachim to watch Dr. Holbak for the duration of the scientist's research.

The refined voice of Walther Schellenberg came on the line. "*Herr General*," Joachim said, "it is *Standartenfuhrer von Daren* in Copenhagen."

"Ah, Joachim, it is good to hear from you. What news do you have for me?"

"I have good news, *Herr General*. From the gleam I see in Dr. Holbak's eyes, he cannot contain his excitement. He is very close to the end of his search, and being a man with such an inquiring mind, he cannot hide the final realization of his dream from me so easily."

"*Gut! Gut!* How much longer do you think he will take?"

"Days," Joachim assured him. "At most, no more than a few weeks. Since he received the requested supply of heavy water, he has made remarkable progress with his experiments." Joachim deliberately referred to the heavy water, reinforcing the Third Reich's failure to provide the necessary supply for the doctor to continue his work sooner rather than Holbak's failure to work faster. "That's why, sir, this arrest order seems rather untimely."

"What arrest order, Joachim? I know of no such order. Who authorized it?"

"It is signed by *Standartenfuhrer Friedrich Streicher*. He wants Dr. Holbak arrested immediately."

"Ah, I see. It is a mistake, I'm sure. He does not know Dr. Holbak is my own pet project. *Reichsfuhrer Himmler* has assigned him to direct the mass deportation of Jews and dissidents to Germany and to suppress the ground swell of resistance arising in Denmark," he explained. "Friedrich Streicher is a consummate man at his task. You will no doubt meet him shortly."

Joachim sincerely hoped not. The Gestapo officer had obviously remembered him from Catherine's recital in Berlin and suspected a connection between him and the British. "I look forward to meeting a fellow officer, *Herr General*," he lied, "especially one who comes so highly recommended. I will explain your purpose for intervening on this matter to him then."

"And I will forward your authorization by dispatch. It can only be a wise move to keep the shadow of our influence distant a while longer, since it is the scientist's own belief in the sun that makes his creative genius shine so brightly. It would be a pity to close the shades on his gentle soul just as he is so close to the end of his search. I would not like to see him withdraw into the darkness and harden against us, stubbornly holding back on what he would have willingly given us anyway."

"This was also my concern when I read the order, *mein General*. A humble genius quite often has an inflexible core, and like steel, will not break when it is pressured."

"There is no doubt in my mind, Joachim, that although the gentle soul of Dr. Holbak can sometimes seem a fool, he is never a coward. He would die before he would yield his own principles. We don't have time for a contest of wills, not if we expect to win our race with the Allies to produce the first atomic bomb."

"Another victory for the fatherland is close at hand." Joachim displayed suitable optimism. "And with it," he continued, "the glory which rightfully belongs to you, *mein General.*"

At the other end, a bland smile crossed Schellenberg's lips. "Without your patient reconnoitring all these years, Joachim, there would be no victory and therefore no glory to tap. We shall share the limelight in the event that monitoring the scientist bears fruit. In the meantime, the balance of the war may very well hang on how artfully you extract the information we want without alerting the good scientist to our ulterior purpose."

It was questionable whether Schellenberg would share praise, but it was clear that he would not share blame. Whatever Dr. Holbak did was Joachim's responsibility in the view of his superior. Ride or fall, Schellenberg was right about one thing: the balance of the war did depend on what Dr. Sven Holbak planned to do next.

Chapter Eighteen

Thursday, October 7th, 1944

I'M SORRY there's not more time to talk," Catherine said as she immediately began unbuttoning her coveralls and slipped them off. "Here. Put these on."

She handed the flight suit to the rather plump Swedish girl standing beside her. "I left the flight boots and the helmet in the plane," she told Inge Hasselholm. "Put them on as soon as you climb in. Close the hatch tightly and buckle up. You'll find an oxygen mask folded directly above you. The pilot will instruct you when and how to use it through the earphones in your helmet. He can talk to you, but you can't talk to him. If you have any questions, now is the time to ask them."

"I understand. Mme. Thirsted has already explained everything to me." The young girl began pulling the coveralls over her clothes. The thermal suit was still snugly warm from Catherine's body heat.

Mme. Thirsted removed a small suitcase and a canvas shopping bag from her car and brought them over to the plane. "Remember, Inge," she cautioned the young girl. "Answer no questions and stay in your room. Lady

Catherine's life is in your hands."

"I know. Don't worry, Mme. Thirsted," the girl reassured her as she dragged her suitcase up the ladder and climbed into the tandem cockpit behind the pilot. Inge's head disappeared while she fitted the flight boots on her feet and pulled on the helmet. Raising her head again, she almost bumped foreheads with Catherine, who had climbed up behind her with the bulging shopping bag.

"You'll kick yourself if you forget this," Catherine smiled at the young girl as she handed the bag over to her and pointed to the oxygen mask above her and to the seat belt. Catherine buckled her in firmly. "There's nothing to be afraid of," she told her. "Lizzie here can fly by herself if she has to."

"Lizzy?"

"That's what we call this old bird. She's the best," Catherine explained. "Remember now to close down the hatch and to secure it when I step down." She pointed to the latch.

Inge nodded. Catherine grasped her hand and shook it. "Thank you for letting me take your place. If all goes well, I will see you in a week, and you can carry on as you were before we involved you. If not," Catherine paused, "I'm afraid you'll have to sit out the rest of the war in London."

The young girl nodded again, this time regretfully, before she looked into Catherine's eyes and whispered, "Good luck."

Catherine grinned. "You too." Then she climbed back down the Lysander's ladder, jumped off the last few rungs, grasped one of the flashlights from Mme. Thirsted and gestured for them to stand back.

Lizzie's Bristol Perseus XII engines growled and roared. The Lysander, painted black, shook as it lined itself up along the axis of the airstrip and rolled forward. Almost instantly it was airborne and banked in a shallow turn to the north. Mme. Thirsted's impulsive wave was like a flapping flag. The moon plane hugged the tree tops, its black shape blending into the dark shades coloring the horizon and disappeared. Above the mountain peaks, a faint crown of pink began to rise gracefully, like a royal ballerina, bright and blazing, dancing on an orb of gold. As maroons diffused into mauves and blues, the crescent moon hung over the filtering streaks of gold beginning to shoot out from behind the distant treeline. They fanned into shimmering sheets of bronze over the grassy slopes.

A mixture of emotions played on Mme. Thirsted's face when she turned towards Catherine. "Of all people, why you?"

"Why not me?" Catherine greeted her concern with amusement.

"Why not indeed." The older woman grabbed Catherine and hugged her. "It's good to see you again. How's your mother?"

Catherine pulled back and looked into Mme. Thirsted's face. "Did no one tell you?" She could see by her face that she didn't know. "Mummy and daddy were killed in a bombing raid at the start of the war... September 11th, 1940."

The other woman's eyes filled with tears. She pulled Catherine to her again and wrapped her in a warm hug. Lilla Thirsted was Denmark's diva of opera. She and Princess Isabelle had studied music together in Paris, France. Princess Isabelle had married Lord James and given up a promising concert career while Lilla had gone on to become famous, but the two women had remained close friends. Before the war, Lilla had welcomed Catherine and her mother at King Christian's banquet dinner for celebrities and distinguished scientists where Catherine had also met Dr. Holbak. She was a big-boned but firm and handsome woman, whose face up close seemed perpetually uplifted in an expression of expectant joy, as if she were sniffing a rose. Most people remembered her for her hearty laugh as much as for her sonorous voice. These days, she didn't laugh often.

"Surely, King Christian must have known. Wouldn't he tell you?" Catherine asked with concern when they finally broke away.

"A break down in communication, no doubt, Catherine. We only receive intelligence directly related to our activities. Very few people in London realized your mother was related to King Christian."

"Yes, we use to joke about our being line bred and not too selectively. It is rather complicated. If I've got it right, King Christian's son, King Haakon of Norway, married the daughter of King Edward VII, who was Mummy's second cousin by marriage. Anyway, Mummy said all I had to remember was I was a distant cousin by marriage to all the royal families in Sweden, Norway and Denmark through King George's maternal side. Before I left England, I handed over the management of the Rushmore estates and holdings to King George. He'll see the horses are well looked after while I'm gone."

"Are you close to his two young princesses, Elizabeth and Margaret Rose?"

"No, Mummy and Daddy didn't want to be part of the royal circle. We've pretty well lived our lives the way we've wanted too."

"Your mother was very proud of you, Catherine. She believed you could have a brilliant concert career."

"Perhaps after the war. Right now, we have a very important job to do."

Mme. Thirsted nodded. "From this point on, we have to forget who you are. You are now Inge Hasselholm." As they walked toward the diva's car, she told Catherine, "I want everyone in Uppsala to see you with me. It will confirm for any questioning eyes that I have picked up Inge at the university dormitory and that we are enroute to Stockholm to see her family before carrying on to Malmo and Copenhagen this afternoon."

Catherine jumped into the front seat of the elegant two-door, canvas-topped Model J Duesenberg. "Vintage luxury," she remarked admiringly as Mme. Thirsted took her place behind the steering wheel.

"A diva's luxury," she corrected Catherine. Merriment danced in Mme. Thirsted's green eyes as she started the Duesenberg's engine and reversed the classic car back onto the dirt road running beside the landing field. But, the twinkle did not quite stretch down to her voice. Her tone was crisp. "A suitcase with all the clothes you'll need is packed and waiting for you at the Hasselholm's. They have been carefully briefed. It is wiser to play this mission assuming we are constantly under Gestapo surveillance."

By a stroke of uncanny luck, Goring really had invited Inge Hasselholm, whom Catherine was impersonating, to replace the Tivoli Orchestra's original pianist. He had been killed a year ago in April in a mysterious explosion at the Concert Hall. The resulting fire had shut down the Concert Hall, but by permitting the Danes to rebuild the hall so they could hold nightly concerts again, Goring hoped to win King Christian's collaboration.

"Some of Inge's clothes have been altered for you," Mme. Thirsted explained as they drove along. "Padding has been sewn inside to fill out your elegant figure." She gave her a sidelong glance. "The poor girl is really quite dumpy in shape." She went on. "The make of her shoes have been duplicated in your size. They are suitably scuffed and worn-looking. You already have spectacles exactly like hers and her actual passport with your picture pasted in instead of hers." She drove on, thinking. Abruptly she asked, "Do you speak any Swedish?"

"No, but my German is still fluent."

"Not good enough." Mme. Thirsted bit her lower lip. "I'm going to teach you a few key phrases. Around Germans, we must appear to be conversing in Swedish. It's well-known that I speak all the Scandinavian tongues, so it would be more natural to speak Swedish rather than German unless we have to. Now pay attention. If I raise my eyebrows, you just nod as if you agree with what I am saying. If I frown, you shake your head and wince. If I tug my right ear, you laugh. If I touch the tip of my nose as if I'm saying something very confidential, look sad. Go over these signals for me."

Catherine nodded, and repeated each cue with her correct response.

"What happens to your music program while you're over here?" Mme. Thirsted asked curiously.

"*Champagne Serenade* will go on as usual."

"That's impossible. You're here! How can you be two places at once?"

Catherine smiled. "That's exactly what we hope the Germans will think. But, it's not that difficult. We have such a backlog of submissions to *Ditties for Dotties* I could pre-record for a full year without anyone missing me."

In truth, Catherine had stopped making up silly limericks to disguise coded messages. Once she had become a radio telegraphist with her own set of field operators' transmissions to monitor, she could no longer host her *Champagne Serenade* program, so she and Marla had devised a way to hide her absence from the audience. They had prerecorded invited guests, usually a star entertainer, to make the introductions for the selections Catherine played each week. Next they had recorded Catherine playing her repertoire of classical and popular music and then rotated these selections with the prerecorded introductions. They still needed to send coded messages in the *Ditties For Dotties* segment, so they had catalogued all the backlogged submissions of limericks made up by their listeners and recorded Catherine reading them to tunes she appeared to be spontaneously composing as she spoke. On the air, it was impossible to distinguish a recording from a live performance. It meant any allied intelligence service, not just *Amanita*, could select a pre-recorded ditty to represent an operational code. Marla had nicknamed the process *Canned Codes*. Even if the enemy did intercept the show on the air, they could not break down what the message meant, to whom it was directed or where the receiver was located.

For the rest of the drive to Uppsala, they retreated

inside their own thoughts. Catherine dropped her head against the back of her seat and gazed out the car window. The sun's full blossom promised a delightful day ahead, but her mood did not match that promise. An inaudible sigh escaped. She needed to be quiet within herself, to still the nerves ripping at her stomach and heart, the same attack of jitters that gripped her before every concert performance. There could be no mistakes.

Suddenly, she thought of Marla, of the changes in her that saddened Catherine. But once she began training Catherine for this mission, understanding those changes came more easily. Every day, every minute really, Marla had to deal with dismal statistics and even starker realities. Her growing hardness was the survivor's stiff shell Catherine had yet to acquire.

The thought of possible capture tormented Catherine. How courageous was she? Was she tough enough to resist the sadistic viciousness of a Gestapo interrogation? How much pain could she endure? The fact that she was wrestling with this fear meant she had no choice. If she were captured, because of who she was, she would have to take her own life. Her capture would compromise both Winston Churchill and King George. Her whole being cried out against dying, against activating the awful cyanide pill. It contradicted every belief she held dear. She wanted to live.

In training, she had succeeded in squelching her original revulsion of the L-pill. Learning the art of survival to evade capture taught her the silent art of killing—from the lethal karate chop to slipping a sewing needle into the area of the neck that yielded instant death. She learned all the vulnerable parts of the body. She learned how to maintain her balance in a hand-to-hand attack on a man, to shove the heel of her hand upward to smash his jaw or to knee him in the groin. She learned the right way to explode a box of matches, blazing, into the eyes of a sneak attacker to blind him. She learned how to use ordinary objects a woman carries in her purse as weapons: a nail file, a pin, a fountain pen—actually a trick atomizer that sprayed poison gas, incendiary cigarettes set in a plain case with miniaturized dctonators that lookcd likc rcplaccmcnt wicks for thc lighter, and a marzipan bar that smelled like almonds but was really a plastic explosive camouflaged as a bar of chocolate. In less than a week, she crammed in a year's course of terrorist training.

Catherine momentarily closed her eyes. *I want to live...I want to live...* The same thought kept pounding over and over again through her head. Since the moon plane had taken off from a secret base somewhere in northern Scotland, wanting to live was all she thought about. Her tongue slid over the drilled tooth where the lethal L-pill had been inserted. She shivered.

Past the university in Uppsala and all the way on the cushioned drive to Stockholm in Mme. Thirsted's Duesenberg, the thought pestered...*I want to live...I want to live...*

Chapter Nineteen

Friday, October 8th, 1944

SINCE ULO RORVIG'S DEATH had been confirmed over a year ago, a vital part of Marla had died. She functioned, yet she did not feel. But, as her heart withered in grief, her mind excelled, the same as the taking of one sense strengthens another. There were no more sexual involvements with men. Her passing fulfillment of love had finally resolved that restless search for acceptance she yearned, committing her more to Ulo in death than in life.

Professionally, she hardened, driving agents to develop wired instincts, testing their endurance and stamina to their outer limits, pushing them to block out all interference except for a focus on their objective and their determination to survive.

She told them: "When your gut screams at you, listen to it. *Obey it.* Your subconscious can absorb more than you consciously can. *Let it. Trust it. Believe in it.* A highly developed sixth sense is your guardian angel. Then she warned, "If you relax, even for one second, you become vulnerable. Thinking you are safe betrays more agents than any other single thing. You are *never safe* as long as you are on occupied soil."

Ironically, Ulo's death had transformed her into the inscrutable machine she had accused Tobin of becoming. Her impulse to react to everything had been stilled. Instead, she had learned how to pull back to the realm of abstract detachment, to that level of cold-blooded decision making that could zero in on a single objective with special tunnel vision. In her mind's eye, she saw a blown up teletype message in neon lights blinking in the darkest region of remaining sanity: *destroy Hitler*, it repeated.

Her rationale charged Hitler's evil power with Ulo Rorvig's murder. He bombed children in the name of victory, leaving most of them maimed and mutilated. He took loved ones away, tortured them and butchered them, without mercy, without remorse. He alone was responsible for this cruel war, for turning ordinary people into terrorists and killers. There could be no peace, no satisfaction, until Adolf Hitler was utterly squashed and squished into the ground, like the disgusting worm he was. He had crawled out of a foxhole and left his squalid secretions all over the land, mixing and turning them over in the good earth, spreading a rot from his bowels that infected the new crops and ravaged them wholly.

Marla could not, would not, let Ulo's death pass in vain. He symbolized all the death and destruction, pain and suffering she had helplessly witnessed since the Spanish Civil War. Every agent she prepared now was a human weapon, a faithful hunter supremely engineered to persevere to the very end against Hitler's concerted madness. She consumed no further energy in resenting the human sacrifices necessary to the process. Marla targeted solely on the success of each mission, on the effectiveness of the task to be done. Each one chalked up another square tag on the wall map above her desk, white tabs that sprinkled the black areas of Nazi-occupied territories.

When Sir Isaac briefed her about sending Catherine into Denmark to convince Dr. Holbak to escape and to carry counter orders to the double agent called *Watchdog*, she accepted the decision without protest. Sir Isaac found this change from her usual protectiveness of Catherine disconcerting. He realized then that he wished she would fight him, if only to relieve his guilt.

From the time Marla had discussed her recurring nightmare with Catherine, it had not bothered her. But, on the same night Catherine departed for Sweden, her first rendezvous before entering Copenhagen, Marla bolted awake in terror. It was back.

Gripping the covers wildly, she trembled under the sheets. Her white knuckles and white face broke the night like pale beams drawing a path to their ghostly fright. Beads of sweat popped out over her brow. Their wet shininess reflected a haunting glow. The vividness of the nightmare still seized her like a stuck record playing over and over again, refusing to push away the sea of open mouths she mentally saw screaming.

Their voices were silent. Lips chewed and churned. Bubbles boiled everywhere, spitting up the mouths jawing in disgust. The gurgling waves sunk deeper and deeper...out of sight into the endless pit. In a daze, Marla peered over the rim. The bottom was sucked dry. Below her lay a massive grave piled end to end with skeletal bodies lined standing up side by side. Hollow-eyed skulls rattled, bobbing back and forth on eroded spines as if dancing on invisible strings. Their staring sockets and gangrenous tongues lolling out of their wide open mouths accused her.

Every senseless grotesque detail magnified itself in Marla's dream. Then, she awoke.

Please leave me alone, she begged the dream, and rolled over on the bed, face down. She plopped the pillow on top of her head, hoping to smother the relentless images invading her mind. They persisted. Wearily, she gave in and sat up. After turning on the bedside lamp, she hugged her knees and rocked herself.

God, what a dream! What can it mean? Is Catherine in some kind of danger? She rocked faster and faster as she reviewed every detail of Catherine's mission. She had tried to be more than usually thorough, leaving no angle to chance.

"The first thing you have to learn and to live with is your cover story," she had told Catherine. "I have prepared two. Read both and pick the one you're most comfortable with. Memorize it."

Catherine had seen nothing odd in being offered a choice and had quietly scanned the pair of synopses Marla extended to her. "I can do Inge Hasselholm, I think. The role of the accompanist for the Tivoli Symphony Orchestra is closer to me."

"Fine," Marla said. "Then I am placing the other scenario—the one we are *not* using—in your official dossier. This one," and she pointed to the stapled sheets Catherine held, "is going in my personal filing box."

"Do you mean the strong box at home?"

Marla nodded. Catherine looked dumbstruck. "*WHY*?"

Marla calmly explained. "Because something very strange has been going on for some time. Our turnover of radio operators in the field has shot up alarmingly. What's even more disturbing is the pattern I see building. In each network, the *pianist* is the last to be caught. The Gestapo arrests our agents, and their units of resistance fighters, right after the damage is done—not before the completion of the mission."

"A coincidence, surely."

"I don't believe in coincidence, Marla. The pattern began with Ulo's mission. He was apprehended when his usefulness was over."

She was so matter-of-fact Catherine became concerned. She checked Marla's eyes. They were unwavering.

"And it keeps happening," Marla went on. "My gut tells me there is a traitor inside *Project Amanita*, and I don't want you to be that cad's next victim."

Catherine's jaw dropped. "I can't imagine it."

"We can't dismiss the possibility. This decoy story we're planting in your file will buy you more time, maybe even your life, Catherine." Her solemn tone convinced Catherine that the reality of betrayal was suddenly quite possible.

"Before you begin training, I want you to understand the risk you are taking. Statistically, everything is going against you. Going in, you have three chances in 100 of being disabled before you even see action; three chances in 100 of being captured, and *one chance in three* that, if captured, you will be tortured by the Gestapo." Marla handed Catherine a capsule. "This is cyanide. The L-pill."

Catherine recoiled. Marla would never forget her

look of wretched contempt, but she pressed on. "It will be imbedded in one of your back molars. Should you be caught, bite down on it. The capsule coating will break, and you will die within seconds."

"What if I don't choose to die?"

"Most people when tortured eventually talk. You know too much. We can't risk your talking. Do you understand?"

"You're saying dying is better than being torturcd."

"Probably, but the real issue is whether you are willing to sacrifice your life to save a greater number."

"*If not now, WHEN?*" had been Catherine's reply.

Was this at the root of her dreadful dream? The fear that she was sending Catherine to her death? She shuddered. *Damn the dream!* She needed her rest. She had to be absolutely alert and sensitive to every subtle change in the field that might affect Catherine. Only the strong-willed could train people to meet probable death the way she did. Deep down, in the furthest recesses of her inner self, she admitted she still suffered. She still bled. For every agent. And now there was Catherine to worry about.

Marla picked up Catherine's folded note on the night table and reread it: "If anything happens to me, don't blame yourself for doing your job. It's not your fault Ulo died. It's not your fault I'm the only one von Daren will trust. God is with you and with me. Remember that. We're never alone. You've been the most wonderful friend, and I thank you for that. Be good to yourself, and look after everyone at Guild Oaks for me. Love, Catherine."

Marla dropped her head. The tears she had rigidly held back flowed, until they fell dripping off the end of her nose to wet the letter. *Shit! I'm going in circles!* she sniffed angrily. *This is crazy. Maybe if I sketch what I saw in the dream I can exorcise this damned thing and get it out of my system.*

That was a good idea. She would chase the nightmare away on paper.

She rummaged in her night table for a soft lead pencil and pulled out her sketching pad. She worked meticulously, feeling each desolate stroke that gave life to the pitiful picture. Marla guessed it was the subconscious assimilation of all the intelligence she had read and heard and of all the things, either real or imagined, she had experienced working their way out. For two hours she sketched.

By then, the dismal drip of another London drizzle pitter-pattered across the roof of the Rushmore coach house, gently tinging in rhythm with the first morning rustle. Marla crawled out of bed and went over to the closet to drag out her old portable safe. As she grabbed the padlock, it snapped off in her hand. She stared stupidly at the broken lock. "*How the blazes...*?!" Fear gripped her heart.

She threw open the lid and pulled out her picture box. Catherine's secret dossier—her portrait was filed with it! Frantically Marla fingered through the "C" folders. It was not there! In panic, she checked again. It was definitely not filed under "C". She pulled out every folder and systematically searched through every paper. *Nothing!* Catherine's dossier and portrait were missing! Someone had broken into her private safe and stolen her secret file.

"Oh, Catherine," she blurted out in despair, "whoever has done this knows your real cover story."

She struggled to think. Sir Isaac! She would have to tell Sir Isaac. Maybe he would figure out a way to warn Catherine that her cover was compromised. Marla checked her watch. It was 0600 hours. Catherine was expected to transmit back to *Project Amanita* tomorrow night at 1900 hours. If the traitor held true to his pattern, the Gestapo would not arrest her until after she had contacted Holbak and *Watchdog*. That gave her less than 37 hours to rescue Catherine.

Marla dashed out to the living room and phoned Sir Isaac. "It's urgent, sir," she told him as soon as he lifted his receiver. "Meet me in Communications in 15 minutes."

Exactly 15 minutes later they faced each other in Sir Isaac's command office in underground Amanita. "Catherine's file is missing," she informed him. "I've checked with records. Someone has forged my signature and signed out her dossier."

"Bloody damn!"

"That's not the worst of it, sir."

"What do you mean?" he asked sharply. Just then, the phone on his desk jangled. He picked it up. "Yes?" He listened. "We'll be right there." He turned to Marla as he replaced the receiver. "It's PUFFIN'S *godmother*. There's trouble. He's transmitting to her off schedule. Let's go."

Marla followed Sir Isaac down the aisle of radio stations. Only one set was active. PUFFIN's stuttering transmission was suddenly interrupted with the dreaded code letters, QUO. "Oh no!" Marla cried out in alarm. Her hands flew to cover her face. "Oh no! It's a trap!" Tears streamed down her cheeks.

Sir Isaac put a comforting hand on her shoulder.

"Get a grip on yourself, lassie. PUFFIN's not Catherine's call station. SKYLARK is."

"That's where you're wrong," Marla corrected him miserably. "PUFFIN is. I put a decoy story in her file to fool a possible traitor. No one else was to know Catherine's real cover story except her and me. It should have worked, but somehow the traitor has found out. I don't understand. I just don't understand."

"Let me understand," Sir Isaac thundered. "On your own initiative, without consulting Stevens or me, you arranged a substitute secret cover for the one we authorized."

"Yes, sir."

"For god's sake, woman, you can't do that! You don't know the whole picture. I've warned you repeatedly..." He stopped mid-tantrum. "Hold on. The story in her file is the decoy you *planted.* Maybe it has worked out for the best this time."

"No, sir, it hasn't." Marla almost choked on the words. Feeling wretched guilt, she confessed, "I kept her secret file in a private safe I keep back at the coach house, in my bedroom closet. It's where I keep all my sketches from my news assignments."

"Sketches?" Sir Isaac asked incredulously.

"I don't take photographs, sir. I draw my subjects. That's beside the point. What I'm trying to tell you is her secret file is missing too. I found the padlock to my safe broken. Someone has stolen Catherine's secret file and my drawing of her!"

"Of all the stupid..." Sir Isaac sputtered.

"I don't understand," went on Marla bleakly. "It's not a random robbery either. Nothing else was taken. Just her file and picture."

"Marla," Sir Isaac roared, "sometimes you're so damned naive! If you had discussed your idea with Stevens and me, we could have safeguarded its secrecy. The proper procedure in the switch you pulled is to destroy the dossier you're actually using. *To destroy it!*" he repeated angrily. "You can't trace what doesn't exist! By keeping that damned file, you've condemned Catherine."

Stricken, Marla backed away from him. "No," she denied, "I couldn't have. It was strictly between Catherine and me. We couldn't trust anyone but ourselves. There's a traitor here...inside *Amanita*. Somehow...someone...has found out what we are doing."

"Marla," Sir Isaac addressed her more civilly, "have you inspected your apartment for hidden microphones?"

"Microphones! At home?"

"Aye."

"No! It never occurred to me to check for such a thing in the privacy of our own apartment."

"Well, that's the first possibility we'll have to investigate. How old is that girl now?" he asked gruffly.

"Twenty-four."

"Humph! What a shame! You did issue her with an L-Pill, I hope," he checked suspiciously, expecting another unwelcome surprise.

"Yes, sir. The dentist inserted it in her back molar. Bottom left side to be precise."

"Pray her sacrifice isn't in vain then," he growled. "I'll have to report this to Stevens, Churchill and the king." He groaned. "We're in a helluva lot of trouble. I don't know why I am surprised. I warned Churchill you were too close to Catherine...that you might try some stupid stunt like this. I told him to run the operation from SOE's headquarters at Bletchley, but he insisted."

He turned away to look for an ash tray on the table behind him. "You take things upon yourself you have no right to do. We have a system here. You have upset the system," he blustered.

He pulled out his pipe from his jacket pocket and proceeded to light it. "You could be courtmartialled, you know," he said, dousing his match and depositing it into the ash tray. He puffed hard on his pipe.

When he turned back to confront Marla, she was gone. "That infernal woman!" he exploded. "Now where the hell has she gone? Marla?" he called after her. "*MARLA?!*" But she had disappeared.

Chapter Twenty

Saturday, October 9th, 1944

SS COLONEL VON DAREN enjoyed his daily stroll through the Tivoli Gardens in downtown Copenhagen. It reminded him of Berlin's Tiergarten in the days before it was overrun with Nazi culture. Here, in the midst of century-old garden terraces, tree-shaded paths, gentle ponds and playful waterfalls, he could still find peace. There were no erratic tantrums to appease, no unreasonable expectations to meet, no talk of war, no despairing statistics, no sneaky hypocrites, no unnerving head games, no frustrations...no, correction...there was one frustration that plagued him no matter where he was or what he did. Dr. Sven Holbak.

As if to punctuate his bafflement, a duck from one of the forever present fleet peddling across the ponds suddenly floundered midway. Like a broken reel, it turned in aimless circles, quacking and quacking. As Joachim watched the frenzied duck's widening circles, he wondered for the umpteenth time, *Why won't the old fool leave his lab? What's holding him here?*

He picked up a pebble and angrily skipped it across the water's surface at the duck so inexplicably out of control. Frantically flapping their wings and fretting noisily, the rest of the flock lifted off the pond to escape the path of the spinning missile. They hovered above until the splashes settled and the stone sunk from sight; then they abandoned the lone duck to his crazy circles and flew off to a safer shore.

Joachim's mouth set in a grim line. The atomic physicist was engineering his own doom, leaving Joachim with no choice. He would have to blow up the scientist inside his own lab. Joachim clenched a fist, then flexed it and moved further along, to the storybook carousel, and watched the apple-cheeked children ride the fanciful elephants and capricious horses. Their delighted squeals lifted his spirits. Pausing to read the Tivoli's motto, as he did on every walk through the gardens, he quoted aloud: *Always the same, always new.*

Outside the concert hall, he stopped to study the renovations. Last year, when the pianist, who was alone at the time, tried to open a suitcase left on his piano stool, it blew up, killing him and setting off a fire that gutted the grand hall. Amongst the ruins, the investigators found the remains of a booby-trapped portable transmitter. The Germans had then blamed the explosion on the Danes, and they, in turn, blamed the Germans.

Whoever planted the bomb attacked the heart of Denmark's culture, and the tragic blow helped to galvanize the Danes' determination to resist the Nazis terrorizing their country. The Underground's illegal presses cranked out massive strike calls that shut down the city for days at a time. These relentless work stoppages bewildered the Nazis, and eventually, over 300,000 Wehrmacht and Waffen-SS troops were rushed into Copenhagen to control the rising sabotage and guerrilla-style ambushes of the people.

The Danes were paying dearly for their organized resistance with middle-of-the-night arrests, torture, large-scale deportations, arbitrary executions and random shootings. Even so, the Danes persisted, and after September's general strike protesting the newest mass expulsions, the Germans abruptly changed their tactics. Hoping to restore a more co-operative spirit between the Danish government and its Nazi administrators, they offered the people some minor concessions, one of which was the reopening of the Tivoli's concert hall.

Joachim could hear piano music. He began walking away and stopped short. Something about the playing reminded him of...*NO! Surely not!*...The sparkling passages, the singing ripple of the keys—only one person played like that. Lady Catherine. *No!* It must be his imagination. After all these years, his memory of her was still so fresh. But, the rousing strains of Beethoven's *Ninth Symphony* filled him. He had to know who was playing this marvellous music. He turned on his heel and followed the workmen's path to the side entrance of the building. The door was off its hinges. He entered eagerly and sprinted up the metal stairs leading to the wings. He peeked around the fire curtain.

At center stage sat a plain-looking girl bent over the keys of the grand piano. She was totally wrapped up in her music. Straight, almost colorless hair hung over her bowed head. Rimless glasses saddled her nose. He could not see her face, but from where he stood, she seemed heavy-bodied. He sighed in relief. Though this girl was magnificently talented, she was definitely not his English angel.

As he listened further, however, he became enchanted with her similarity to Catherine's touch and awesome conformance to musical structure. He watched her quietly. Beside him was an old upright piano. Drawn to it, he yearned to play again. On top lay the orchestral score. He thumbed through it until he came to the passage she was playing. Smoothing out the music sheets in front of him, he sat down on the stool and followed closely along. At the lead-in to the chorus, he impulsively began playing with her.

So in tune with the invisible carillon ringing within her mind, Catherine did not immediately react to the richer sounds filling the hall. They seemed more like natural partners on a stirring inward journey, to a lyrical and glorious time when her mother practised with her. Everything but Princess Isabelle's precious smile faded from view. Once again, they faced each other from across their baby grands. Her fingers rippled over the keys in joyous song. Her spirit reached out to the monumental harmonies the two pianos consummated to the very end.

"Bravo! Bravo!" Joachim clapped from his perch on the piano stool when they finished the Beethoven work. He rose and walked towards the girl. "It is a gift to play such marvellous music," he told her in German.

Startled, Catherine looked up. She was stunned to realize that she had lost herself in her music, leaving herself vulnerable to this advancing enemy. But, to her utter relief, she instantly recognized the SS officer. Coming towards her was *Watchdog*. Catherine lit up.

"My goodness, Colonel, the unexpected pleasure of

your playing a duet with me has taken my breath away," she said in German. "You are a fine pianist. Perhaps you would join me in another duet? I have a number of..." At the expression on his face, her nervous chatter trailed off.

Joachim stared at her incredulously. The voice. The sea-blue eyes peering up at him. His heart skipped a beat. There was no disguising that shy indwelling beauty shining out from her eyes. Every detail of that lovely face had dwelled with him for years. At once, he was both distressed and excited. Why was Catherine here?

"As much as I would enjoy that, *Fraulein*, *now* is not the best time," he warned her carefully.

"*If not now, WHEN*?" She feigned an injured pout.

He grinned despite his concern. It was definitely Catherine. She was replaying their first face-to-face meeting at the Press Club in Berlin. "Later," he said. "I'm off duty at 1500 Hours. I can make the rest of the weekend yours."

"I'm afraid I am going to be too busy." She looked genuinely distressed.

"Too busy to eat?"

"I hope not."

He glanced at his watch. "If you have the time, we could have lunch together *now.* I'm not expected back at headquarters for at least another hour."

"Where is that...your headquarters?"

"We've taken over the old Shell building."

Alarm widened her eyes. "I believe that's a Gestapo building."

"Yes, it is," he said, quietly emphasizing each word to give her time to control her nervousness. "We could picnic in the gardens," he suggested.

"That would be very nice," she said. "Please give

me a moment to pack up my music, and we can go."

He helped her gather up the orchestral scores and music sheets, which she slid into her valise. "You'll need your coat," he reminded her and reached for her trench coat. "It's a bit cool outside," he said, helping her slip into it.

She quickly tied a scarf around her hair and knotted it behind at the nape of her neck before she picked up the valise and her shoulder bag. The innocent clearness of her eyes caused a lump to rise in this throat.

"Do you realize I don't know your name, *Fraulein*?"

"I don't know yours either," she returned, carrying on with the pretense.

"I'm Colonel Joachim von Daren," he said and clicked his heels.

A faint blush crept into her cheeks. She offered her hand. "I'm Inge Hasselholm."

They shook hands shyly. It was the first time they had touched each other. As they walked along, side by side, he asked, "Are you Swedish?"

"Did my German give me away?" she asked.

He chuckled, "Your German is very good."

Then she delved into her cover story. He listened intently, with his head cocked to one side. Concentration puckered his wide brow and squinted the corners of his blue eyes, which to Catherine seemed weathered and tired. In the years since she had last seen him, his face had changed. His dimples, once boyishly cute, had cracked and sunk into craggy rivers that ran into his jawline and around his squared chin. Maturity had taken youth's perfect features and made them rugged and lean. Walking beside him, Catherine became painfully aware of how homely and clumsy she must look in her disguise.

He stopped at one of the outdoor cafés to pick up a basket of smorrebrod and two Fadols, the Danes' draft beer, and borrowed a small checkered tablecloth for their picnic. Carrying their lunch, he led her across a footbridge onto a tiny island.

"We have the world to ourselves here," he said, switching to English. "Let's set up over there." He pointed his head in the direction of a weeping willow tree. They settled down on its burrowing trunk. Catherine laid out their food and drinks on top of the fresh tablecloth that Joachim fluttered open on the grass.

"You'll have to get used to smorrebrod while you're here. The Danes eat it for every meal," he told her as he handed her a plate, knife and fork. "Don't eat it with your fingers though. That's a foreigner's dead giveaway."

"Yes, I know," she said, reaching out for one of the open-faced sandwiches. "I must always use a knife and fork. Mme. Thirsted already told me. Are we being watched by the Gestapo?"

"I don't think so, but you can never be sure." He removed his SS cap and laid it beside him. Sunny peepholes opened up through the cloudy overcast. White beams of light streaming through the overhanging boughs dripped like shredded silk and tipped his golden hair with silver specks. He stared at her with a deep longing. Then his jaw clenched. "Why are you here?" he asked huskily.

"Sir Isaac sent me. He doesn't want you to detonate Dr. Holbak's lab."

"Why?"

"It's a bluff. By leaving Dr. Holbak's lab intact, he wants the Nazis to think the Allies don't consider his experiments valuable enough to destroy. Churchill's hoping the ploy will sidetrack Hitler from discovering how close Dr. Holbak really is to building an atomic bomb."

"And where is the good doctor through this big... bluff?"

"We're taking him out today."

Joachim smiled bitterly. "The Gestapo have already issued a warrant for his arrest. I've been stalling that arrest order for nearly two weeks."

"Can you give us another 12 hours?"

"You have until Streicher returns Monday morning."

"Who's he?"

"A thoroughly disagreeable man. If I don't deliver Holbak then, we'll both be arrested."

"What happens to you when Dr. Holbak disappears?"

"I arrange a fatal accident for myself."

"*NO! You can't!!*" she cried out in horror.

"I don't intend to die." A little smile teased his lips at her reaction. "I just want the Gestapo to think I'm dead."

"Oh," she said, feeling somewhat foolish, "I'm glad to hear that." She hesitated. "How did you know I was here?"

"I didn't. I was taking my usual stroll through the Tivoli..." He hesitated, noting her surprise. "Didn't you position yourself where I could hear you and make contact?"

"No, I didn't. At least not deliberately." She frowned. Mme. Thirsted had arranged for her rehearsal this morning at the concert hall. Was it just a crazy coincidence she should meet Joachim like this? Marla, she remembered, didn't believe in coincidences. The eerie feeling that a master hand was fitting together a million separate pieces into an intricate puzzle gripped her.

“”What’s wrong?” he asked.

“My stomach twisted.”

He understood. A tennis ball was lobbying in his own stomach. His jaw tensed. “I still don’t understand why London sent you.”

“Sir Isaac feared you wouldn’t believe Churchill changed your orders. Anyone else he sent except me you might suspect is a Gestapo plant and carry out your original order.”

“Sir Isaac is the one who worked out prearranged emergency codes British Intelligence could use to contact me without jeapordizing my identity. Sending you in needlessly risks us both. It doesn’t make sense.”

“What kind of codes are you talking about?”

“I have perfect pitch. I can pick out the exact note any instrument plays. We decided to use this talent by communicating through music.”

Knowing how she transmitted codes on her broadcast program, Catherine was fascinated. “How?”

“By altering the inner harmonies and rhythms of selected pieces based on Hitler’s approved list of music. We decided to use the last note of each bar in the alto line for our code. Because there are only seven notes, A through G become symbols for a series of letters or numbers. Let’s say A sharp is played twice followed by a rest in the fourth bar. The sharp means convert the following letters into their corresponding numbers. That would be one-one...11. Do you see?”

“Yes, I do. The rest is used in place of STOP. So the message now is 11...STOP.”

“Right. My key for codes in music is *Mein Kampf*. How’s that for poetic justice?”

Catherine smiled with him.

"The first number represents the page number in the book. The rest of the series refers to the word count on that page. Eleven, rest...five, rest...nine, rest...would mean page 11, word five, word nine, and so on. If a flat is struck instead of a sharp, then the letter for the note, not its number, represents a key phrase from a prearranged list."

"The way our QUO stands for *I'm in imminent danger of capture*."

"Precisely. The method is impossible to detect. Even if a Gestapo cryptographer detects the pattern, he doesn't have the key. An arranger alters the music. Sir Isaac's orchestra makes a recording of the new arrangement and delivers it to Dr. Holbak at his lab. As his security officer, any gift sent to him has to be inspected by me first. Naturally, I would play the recording before I would hand it over to Dr. Holbak."

She frowned. "Churchill's order could have been transmitted and delivered much faster than it has taken to train me to bring it to you personally. It doesn't make sense, does it?"

"No, it doesn't."

Catherine shifted into a more comfortable position on the grass. She inclined her head shyly. "I've often wondered where you were, if you were safe..." Her voice trailed off, and her eyes sought his. "I'm glad you're all right. I prayed you would be."

"You've been in my thoughts from the first time I saw you," he admitted hoarsely. "What happened after I saw you in Berlin?"

"I worked as a nurse's aid. Then my parents were killed in a bombing raid, and I became a radio operator at *Project Amanita*. Playing the piano was great training for transmitting."

The innocence in her brilliant blue eyes tore into his heart. Seven endless years of mutual longing and secret devotion crammed through the sieve of the moment. Theirs was a love born of the spirit, and they sat silently, feeling and enjoying the sight of the other.

"How are you involved with Dr. Holbak?" Joachim eventually asked as he picked up the last smorrebrod.

"Sir Isaac thinks I am the only one who can convince him to flcc to England."

"That nut should have been taken out a year ago!" he suddenly exploded. "After your people scuttled the Germans' heavy water supply, do you know what a nightmare it has been keeping him out of Gestapo hands?"

"We've lost a lot of good agents protecting Dr. Holbak," Catherine admitted.

"Let's make sure you're not another one. When do you go back to England?"

"As soon as I radio back to Amanita that Dr. Holbak's lab has been neutralized."

"Do you have a transmitter?"

"No." She shook her head. "I'm to deliver my message to the safe house at *Palae 1254v*—our PUFFIN station."

"That's in the Nyhaven District!" he protested. "You can't go there alone. It's crawling with drunken sailors. How do you contact Dr. Holbak?"

"Mme. Thirsted has arranged for us to meet him at a café near the university this afternoon. At 1400 hours actually."

"Then what?"

"I was to find you?"

"How?"

"Now you'll never know," she teased.

"Too bad," he twinkled. "When is your rendezvous at the safe house?"

"1900 hours."

"Isn't that cutting it close to concert time?"

"I'm not required on stage until after the intermission."

"How are you getting there?"

"Cycle."

Joachim ripped out a blade of grass and chewed on the tip thoughtfully. "Where does Mme. Thirsted live?"

"3 Hindegade."

"I'll pick you up at 1700 hours," he said decisively. "Be dressed for walking." Then he quickly rose to his feet and brushed himself off. "You're not going alone." His tone discouraged any argument.

"I'm glad Fate gave us a chance to meet again," Catherine told him.

"If it really was Fate," he said dubiously while scooping up his SS cap and adjusting it to his head. "I have to get back now, Catherine. Be very careful contacting Dr. Holbak. He *IS* being watched," he warned her and crisply walked away, leaving her to clean up the luncheon leftovers.

Chapter Twenty One

BOISTEROUS LAUGHTER tripped out of the Sailor's Inn in Copenhagen's old waterfront district. The cheerful tunes of the accordion playing softly in the background mixed with the rowdy voices of old sea dogs and their salty mates trading tale for tale and drink for drink in the crowded tavern, their drunken revelry never more than a beer away from sobriety, a conditioning triggered by unpredictable German raids on the dockside life of the Nyhaven Canal.

Two swaggering merchant seamen stumbled out of *Tattoo Jack's*. Their raucous titters and bold shouts invited German sailors lounging outside the next café to inspect the needleman's handiwork on their chests. They lifted up their tunics to reveal the torso of a stripper with gigantic balloon-shaped boobs. Under each tattoo was the name Rosa. The sailors stared in fascinated wonder while the two drunks flexed their chest muscles to make Rosa's boobs jiggle up and down. Behind them, over 5,000 different designs hung in the tattoo parlor's window.

Further down the cobbled street, the giant hands of an astronomical clock towering over a shabby bar approached 7 P.M. Next to it, in chipped paint, was *Palae 1254v*. A red and yellow awning, striped and shaped like a puffin's bill—the resemblance to the bird had inspired the call station's name—covered the entranceway into the quaint bistro. Its long narrow windows overlooked the quay. It was a comfortable view of sturdy fishing boats and whalers bobbing in their beds along the canal. Somewhere, out in the harbor, a ship's siren hooted like a night owl with whooping cough.

Everything was carrying on normally as far as the couple inspecting the junk shop across from the bistro could tell. Seemingly intrigued with the transformation other people's castoffs took to become the beautiful artefacts now cluttering the storefront, they watched the shopkeeper heap forlorn-looking rejects from a horsedrawn cart onto the sidewalk. Once the pile threatened to topple over, he began picking up the items, one by one, and carrying them into his store, forcing the man and woman to move inside the doorway out of his way. While he shuffled back and forth with his loads, the old grey mare in front stood sleepily flicking her tail. The rakish straw hat plunked between her donkeylike ears distracted attention away from the couple loitering inside the window.

Catherine clutched Joachim's hand. The closer they had drawn to PUFFIN, the more jittery she had become. Despite the natural rhythm of the nightlife along Nyhaven, a feeling of foreboding—an icy patch between her shoulder blades and hairs prickling at the nape of her neck—warned her something was terribly wrong.

But what was it?

After Joachim arrived at precisely 1700 hours, she had not let herself slip into English until they were well out of earshot of Mme. Thirsted's apartment and on their way through the oldest part of Copenhagen. The diva suspected the Gestapo were listening through her walls. As Catherine described her meeting with Dr. Holbak, Joachim walked beside her, engrossed in her every word. Feeling as distraught as she was, she failed to notice that, out of uniform, in his grey flannel slacks and Herringbone double-breasted jacket, Joachim's Nordic features and sun-bleached hair, like spun silk dipped in gold, had lost their rigid control. A fleecy forelock fell boyishly over his right brow and invited touching. All at once she became aware of his unguarded vulnerability and slipped her hand through his arm.

"Something's wrong, Joachim," she said. "I didn't have to convince Dr. Holbak to go. He wanted to go. In fact, he accused British Intelligence of exposing him to unnecessary risk leaving him here so long. He said he had run out of ways to make his experiments fail. He even knew you've been protecting him."

"He said that?"

She nodded.

"He's never given me the slightest hint. Has he also realized I was ready to kill him rather than let him be arrested?"

"He didn't say and I didn't ask."

Catherine glanced off into space and back to the 300-year-old street, struggling with the premonition that pecked like a humming bird jack-hammering up and down her spine. She felt as out of touch with the present as these baroque gas lamps and tiny orange-painted houses with their dwarf-sized doors.

"Everything went like clockwork," she went on. "He got on his bicycle and peddled down to the Havnegade docks. That's where Mme. Thirsted told him fishermen working for the Resistance would be waiting to smuggle him out to Lanskrona in Sweden. By now, he should be safely on his way to England. I should feel relieved, shouldn't I? Instead of feeling so scared."

"Easy," Joachim cautioned her, patting her hand resting on the crook of his arm. The warmth of his hand covering hers sent sharp tingles charging through her body. Now conscious of his strength, she felt an urge to be held. Sensing it, he pulled her more tightly against him, locking her arm over his. Her hip touched his thigh, and with instinctive rhythm, their strides became welded into one effortless gait, like dancers flowing together.

Once they reached King's Square, Joachim took Catherine to a cellar café that dated back to 1723. It was the favorite haunt of Copenhagen's great rhetoric thinkers before German occupation, he told her while their main course was being served...

The rattle of a car slowly inching its way over cobblestones outside the junk shop jarred Catherine out of her thoughts. Joachim poked her and signalled her to stand still. The shopkeeper, stacking shelves in the front of the store, eyed them nervously. He had heard the smothered clatter as well. Across the street, a black Mercedes pulled up in front of the bistro's door. The old grey mare and the junk cart blocked Joachim's view.

"*Gestapo!*" he suddenly hissed and grabbed Catherine in a crushing embrace, burying her face in his chest as he angled himself for a better look at what was happening.

A man in a slouch hat and a dark trench coat emerged from the *Palae 1254v.* Two SD officers followed dragging a woman between them. The three Germans and the woman stood briefly under the red and yellow awning. Something vaguely familiar about the slim blonde woman struck Joachim.

Catherine! She looks like Catherine! My God! It was a trap! They think they've arrested Catherine. But they had arrested this woman instead. Who was she? Why was she pretending to be Catherine? Question after question buzzed through Joachim's mind. He unconsciously pressed Catherine's face more deeply into his chest, almost smothering her.

One of the secret policeman pushed the woman into the back seat of the black sedan. The two uniformed officers then climbed in the back with her, while the plainclothes one got in front, and the Mercedes gunned its engine as it swiftly made a U-turn heading back towards them. When the car swerved out to avoid the old grey mare and the cart, Catherine twisted her head in time to see what Joachim was watching. Instantly she saw the blonde woman sitting between the two SD officers in the back seat, and when the Mercedes wheeled back close to the curb, she could clearly see her face. Catherine's world exploded.

"*MARLA*!!" The scream tore from her throat as she impulsively reached out to grab her.

Joachim quickly muffled her second cry and held her struggling against him. With growing distress, the shopkeeper watched them.

When the black Mercedes safely passed out of sight, Joachim released Catherine. "Who did you say?" he asked.

"Marla." Tears streamed down her face. "Marla Franklin."

Joachim was taken aback. "I didn't recognize her. What's she doing here?"

"She's my conducting officer." Catherine shook with soundless sobs. *"Marla...Marla... Why Marla? Why?"*

"Obviously you've been betrayed," Joachim muttered harshly. "Somehow Marla found out in time and sacrificed herself to give you a chance to escape."

"*Oh no!*" Catherine shook her head, too shocked to think coherently.

Joachim's mind was racing. "How much does the Gestapo know, I wonder?"

"They must know everything." The painful realization gripped her. "The call station in my official file was a decoy. PUFFIN was a last-minute switch we made ourselves. No one knew about it except Marla and me."

"Someone found out."

"Mme. Thirsted!" Catherine moaned in despair as the impact of what exposing her cover fully meant. She grabbed Joachim's lapels. "Mme. Thirsted! She's in danger too. We've got to warn her."

Joachim turned to the merchant watching them suspiciously from behind his shelves. "Do you have a phone?" Joachim asked him. The shopkeeper hesitated.

"Mme. Thirsted!" Catherine added anxiously. She remembered how much the Danes love their diva. "She's in danger. Do you understand? The Gestapo..." Fear choked her. Barely above a whisper the words came. "Please let us warn her." Her sorrowing eyes begged him.

He bit his lip and nodded and showed them to his storage room at the back of the shop. Mounted behind the door was an old-fashioned wall phone. Joachim frantically cranked it and rushed through a line of instructions to the operator. He waited while she rang Mme. Thirsted's dressing room at the concert hall. The phone rang and rang.

"Please!" Catherine prayed. "Oh please answer it."

Nine. Ten rings. Finally, there was a click at the other end. "Hello. This is Mme. Thirsted's room."

Immediately Joachim slammed down the receiver. He knew that voice. The Gestapo was already there. Who tipped the bastards off?

THE AUDIENCE rustled as Mme. Thirsted unexpectedly stepped across the stage. They all rose and clapped as one tumultuous body. Graciously, she bowed and smiled before she whispered to the conductor. His bushy eyebrows puckered in concern. Their eyes locked in silent communion. Briefly, he rested his hand on her shoulder in a gesture of comfort. After this touching exchange, he tapped his baton on the music stand for the orchestra's attention.

"There's been a change in program," he announced in a hushed voice. "We're opening with our national anthem," and he looked sadly at the empty piano seat. A tight hum passed from lip to lip amongst the musicians. When they were settled with their instruments ready, Mme. Thirsted gestured for the chorus to file on stage. They split into two wings that jutted out from either side of the orchestra.

She had managed to persuade the smug SS captain and the Gestapo agent to permit her the dignity of one last performance before they spirited her away to the Gestapo dungeons at Aarhus. She had reminded them that the concert had been sponsored by Goring himself. Did they really want to risk embarrassing the Reichsmarshall by arresting the concert's top star?

She stepped up on the podium beside the grand piano and turned to gaze down at the sea of adoring faces. Her people. She believed in them. She loved them. For a moment, she clung to the great love she felt pouring back from them. It strengthened her. Two spotlights, one beaming down on the empty piano bench and the other on her, bathed her white sequinned gown in a wash of glittering sprinkles. The long funnel of light illuminated her radiant face. She lifted her head proudly and sniffed an imaginary rose. The conductor flicked his baton, and the Danes' beautiful stirring anthem began.

Below the stage, inside the prompter's box, a lone stagehand in black coveralls pulled a black wool hood over his head, covering his russet hair. When he turned around, only his eyes peered out of the two holes in his face mask. Quietly he opened his tool box. At the bottom of the kit lay a crude single shot .45-inch pistol. The Liberator. He adjusted a silencer to its muzzle and patiently waited for the finale.

A part of him grieved. He had hoped it would not come to this, but he had promised Lilla Thirsted a long time ago—subsequent to the Spanish Civil War, when she had first joined the Red Brigade after the League of Nations failed to send in an Allied fighting force to support the Republicans against Franco and Hitler and to punish Hitler for contravening the Non-intervention Pact—he had promised that she would never be taken by the Gestapo. Neither did she want to commit suicide in some unknown cell, her death another forgotten incident in the ugly business of war. If she must die, she wanted her death to have meaning in a way her people could recognize and understand, in a way that would solidify their support for the Resistance, in a way that would give them tenacity and heart.

The music peaked. Her voice trilled. The masked man raised the gun and aimed the Liberator directly at Mme. Thirsted's heart. He fired. Simultaneously, a red spot marked her white dress. She clutched her left breast, hiding the ruby splotch that was spreading. Except for a slight catch in her voice when the bullet hit, she miraculously held on to the last note of the anthem until, with voice trembling and rapidly fading, she lifted up her arms in jubilant victory. For a split second, time froze. Then, like a grand swan folding its majestic wings, she finally collapsed, falling down the podium steps to end up lying spread-eagled at the feet of the horror-stricken conductor. The uplifted expression of perpetual expectation still graced her face.

Chapter Twenty Two

Monday, October 11th, 1944

SOUNDS BROKE the endless hours of isolation … the clack-clack of jackboots on a terrazzo floor, clanging clicks and the whirr of an electronic door sliding back and forth…the changing of the guard. Occasionally, metal on metal noises vibrated through the old stone walls…a toilet flushed, a tap squealed and a pipe banged…the habitual sounds of life going on.

To Marla's parched lips and dried mouth, the sounds meant water…waters flushing, waters swirling and gurgling around and around and down the toilet bowl, out of sight and filling again…running tap water…cool, refreshing, quenching…images that tortured the relentless thirst clawing at her raw throat.

She tried to lick her lips, but her rough tongue rubbed over the sore cracks like an emery board. Even her saliva had dried up. Desperately, she strained against the handcuffs that bound her wrists to an iron ring pounded into the masonry, forcing her to sit in a fetal position on the cold concrete floor.

She had been stripped naked and left manacled in

this locked room so that all her toiletries had to be attended to by a male guard. The more pressing her miseries grew, the less her humiliation mattered. Thus, caring more about survival than weakening valuable energies resisting, she submitted to the urgings of her bladder. The longer she could hold out against the devastating cold and the tortuous thirst, which was even worse than the hunger, the more time she was giving Catherine to escape. Time…just a little more time, she reminded herself.

The pain gripping her head like an orange being hammered to pulp never let go. If only she could stretch her stiffened joints and cramped muscles, but when agonizing spasms seized her legs, her lower back and her crooked neck, she dreaded moving for fear of losing the little heat her body had taken ages to warm against the icy stone wall and cement floor. To shift position, even slightly, risked touching those cold surfaces with her bare skin, starting off perishing shakes all over again. She breathed in and out very slowly, forcing as much oxygen into her lungs as she could inhale, but without water, every living cell in her body was shrivelling up and slowly dying.

Between the exhausting bouts of perpetual pain and teeth-chattering chills, when she was not drifting in and out of consciousness, lucid moments did take hold. During times like these, she swivelled her head…left, right, left, right…and arched her neck…up, down, up, down…she repeated the exercises over and over until she usually dropped off and disconnected memories tormented her.

She was in a clearheaded state now. After she turned her head from side to side and stretched her neck a couple of times, she let her head drop backwards, resting it on her spine, and closed her eyes while breathing heavily through her nostrils. A suffocating dryness tightened like a rubber band around her chest. All at once, a brightness—a white veil swirling around and around beyond her eyelids—bathed her face with a delicate warmth. Her lids flashed open.

High above her, almost touching the ceiling on the opposite wall, was a window, small, round and recessed back about six inches. Through it, the first rays of sunshine Marla had seen since her internment streamed into the tiny barren room.

"Oh God but that's beautiful!"

Startled, she drew in a quick breath. That pitiful voice croaking between her cracked lips could not be hers. Hacking coughs ripped from her throat like branding irons fireballed from the burning pit within her chest.

"*Oh God!*" she rasped in despair. It seemed as if the choking would never stop, as if her guts would turn inside out before the blood vessels in her head burst. She was going to expire in a convulsive fit of petrified spit.

The sunlight spilling down from the overhead window gently kissed her skin. With a shaky sigh, she again looked up at the captured loop of light, drawn by its eerie radiance so like a luminous pearl, and then she knew she was not alone. Ulo was with her. The bleak room seemed to fill with his spirit. She wanted to melt into the comfort of his arms.

Oh, Ulo, hold me. Please hold me!

Suddenly he was there, gathering her up into his arms and cradling her against his cheek. Where once happy tears shed in his embrace, only dried grit burned her tear wells now, and she couldn't weep.

Soon, my darling. Soon we'll be together again, she promised him, beginning to feel a lovely euphoria falling over her.

The tip of her suddy tongue reached for the L-pill lodged in her back molar. It was still there. She jiggled it. Her wracking coughs had not jarred it loose. Unless she bit down on it and crushed the rubber seal, it would pass through her body harmlessly. The idea that she controlled her death sustained a sense of ironic justice. The Gestapo could do nothing to her that she did not allow. It was her private joke. If it had not hurt so, she would have broken into riotous gales of laughter.

Suddenly, her mother's voice echoed from a forgotten past. A voice, deep and lyrical and soothing, saying words she liked to hear because it was her voice: "You don't face death. You face life! Remember that. Life at best is a challenging journey, never death, so there's nothing to fear. Death's but a light snapping off."

After all the bitterness Marla harbored against her mother, it felt strange finding comfort and wisdom in what she said. It was, as if in linking minds with her, that resentment was dissolving. In this period before death, she was seeing many things differently.

Her head lolled, and a silly smile twitched at her lips. A drowsy blackness was sucking her into a swirling tunnel and bashing her against the remnants of her own nightmares mirrored on its walls...a hooded form vaguely suggesting a child, a young boy hidden deep in the shadows, browns upon browns, brown mouths, brown mouths in voiceless screams, brown flies swarming over frothy dribbles running down brown lips, brown mushrooms, giant amanita exploding in her face, splintering, dismembered arms and legs flying off in all directions, brown faces bobbing in the midst of dancing mists and then fading, buried in an avalanche of falling brown mortar—the endless cavern of mouths wide-open and silent, layers and layers of skeletons stacked upright in brown pits, dangling, rattling... images gyrating from one mirror to another, in a maddening blur twirling deeper and deeper.

She was a little girl again, playing with her Alice-in-Wonderland doll...golden ringlets and an angel's face... she lovingly cradled her doll...it mustn't cry...*Hush little baby, don't you cry*...she sang the way her mother sang to her when she was sad...the doll's eyes blinked open... Catherine's lovely eyes...pearldrop tears trickled down her face.

"There, there... Shhhhh..." Marla comforted her doll. "You mustn't be sad."

"Don't go away!" wailed her doll.

"I must, sweet Catherine. Don't you see? I've told my truth, and no one listened." She rocked her doll. "Someday you'll understand. We were betrayed."

The distant peel of steeple bells ringing out the noon-day hour roused Marla from her confusing dream. Her head jerked in frightened flutters. The residue meaning of the dream filled her with a sudden sense of remorse. She stared up at the lone high window, thinking of her mother.

Mother, mother, mother. Her spirit ached. *I've wasted so much precious time hating you.*

Her heartsick pain was as cruel as any torture, for she would never have a chance to mend the stupid useless years absorbed in anger and hate. She was thirty-two-years old and finally ready to forgive her mother for her long ago desertion. But then, childhood reflections became confused with memories of miserable loneliness and rejection, and she hated her again.

Like a neon light, Catherine flashed to mind...the only person who loved her for herself, demanding nothing in return…the only one who listened with her heart and reached out to Marla's inner loneliness…*sisters-in-spirit* Catherine called them. It was more than that. Their bond transcended time and space. It was something quite extraordinary, and she drew strength from thinking about her. They had embraced good-bye beside the Lysander moments before Catherine flew off into the dark cover of night to Sweden.

"If anything happens to me," Marla recalled her last words, "notify King George. As my closest living relative, he must take over my estate to ensure the special conditions applied to *Project Amanita* are carried on."

Marla had stuffed the piece of paper Catherine had given her in her pocket. Then Catherine had hugged her and whispered, "I love you. Remember that always." Marla had stiffened, struggling to control the well of emotion threatening to abort Catherine's mission on the spot. Catherine understood that battle with her feelings, and as she was about to climb up the Lysander's ladder, she said one final thing Marla would never forget.

"I'll make you proud of me. I'm not scared any more. I feel very calm inside, and protected. We're never alone, Marla. God's with us. I believe that. Perhaps someday you will too."

Before the "cheerio" had passed her lips, Catherine had clambered up the ladder and was in the moon plane's cockpit.

Later, after Marla had discovered their betrayal and run from Sir Isaac, she had called the private number Catherine had given her for Buckingham Palace. The king was her only hope, and he agreed to see her immediately. While he read Catherine's will and personal directions in private, she waited in the royal drawing room, dazzled by the richness and historic splendor displayed there. When the king re-entered the room, he was sadly grim-faced.

"You are quite correct," he said. "We must not let her be captured by the Gestapo. Something very strange is going on at *Project Amanita*, and I fear Catherine, in all her innocence, has been victimized by a very sinister plot."

He had paused then and gazed very solemnly into her eyes. "I am going to arrange for you to meet Wendal Stevens at the Whitehall bunker. Tell him everything you have told me and trust him. Whatever you two decide to do, do it with a clear conscience, my dear. Lady Catherine accepted all the risks when she accepted her mission. You cannot hold yourself responsible for the madness of war and the unfortunate luck it brings to some. That is a burden we all must share. Now, go with God. Mr. Stevens will keep me informed."

The king had graciously ushered Marla to the door where his personal secretary met her and escorted her to the underground bunker at Whitehall.

Despite the urgency, Wendal Stevens managed to relax her. Even his unnerving habit of concentrating on her eyes at the same time as he watched her lips did not bother her. With someone else, she might have felt violated except his eyes—eyes that saw through everything—weren't threatening. Instead, his eyes listened, they absorbed and they analyzed, and when she had finished talking, they studied her and quietly approved her plan.

Few words passed between them, yet she experienced the eerie sense that they thoroughly knew each other. When it was time for her to board the moon plane for Denmark, he jammed his hands in his pockets rather than shake her hand and mumbled, "God speed."

At take-off, he was still standing there, a forlorn figure in the grey mist watching after her, as if willing her courage from the shadow of her tormented dream. Clinging to that life force binding her to Stevens, she had stared back at his image long after he was out of sight.

Once she had settled back, she spent the rest of the flight reviewing her plan. As Marla had told Stevens, she had a personal interest vested in stopping Hitler's monstrous insanity from devouring the whole world.

The time to pay the piper had come for her. She could not stand aside and let Catherine die a needless death. Too many had already been sacrificed for reasons they did not understand, innocents like Catherine, and in the manipulation of events, Marla had played a part. She had sent many agents to certain death. But not this time. The sacrifice was not Catherine's to make. It was hers. Catherine was not going to pay with her life for a mistake Marla made underestimating *Project Amanita's* traitor.

Now Marla's nightmare was no longer a figment of her imagination. She was living it. If she were to feel absolved of guilt, being arrested by the Gestapo in Catherine's place was something she had to do. For Catherine was not much more than a child herself, with her humble faith and simple belief in hope, in life, in the very goodness of people. She believed in God and country and had done her duty, but if the war ended tomorrow, she could pick up her life where it last left off and continue as if it had never been interrupted.

The same was not true for Marla. She would miss the intrigue, the sudden boost of adrenaline shooting through her veins, the risk of danger and death. She was part of a ripple feeding on itself, growing in wider and wider circles, like a tumbleweed rolling on forever, faster and faster. She was addicted to war, as shameful as that was. In saving Catherine's life, she was saving herself; and in saving herself, she was saving many. One small act, repeated over and over again, multiplies until it forms one great tidal wave, and she was part of the tidal wave sweeping Europe. Eventually, the Resistance would grow so great it would swamp the Nazi vermin and drown them in their own blood. She swelled with pride knowing she was part of the wave that would win the war. From this sense of vindication sprang her joy and absolution.

It was with this insight that she suddenly recognized how much alike she and her mother were. They belonged to those they wrote about. Their words spoke for those who could not speak for themselves. Their words immortalized those who would otherwise be forgotten. Their words nurtured, cared and revealed. They belonged to their words. They were creations conceived and delivered with love. Their words were their children.

The voiceless screams of her nightmares were today's and tomorrow's generations helplessly trapped in a world gone berserk. They were her unborn children, the words never written. In dying, she could bring them peace, and with that thought, she made peace with herself.

THE ELECTRICAL WHIRR as the door slid open…the clump of jackboots…the murmur of guttural voices...the soft bang as the door slid closed again. The shutter over the window panel rattled when it was drawn back, and two pair of eyes looked into Marla's cell. She had mercifully slipped into unconsciousness again. Her chin had fallen forward on her chest, and lacelike strands of bleached hair trickled down the front of her, daintily capping her exposed nipples. Quick anger sparked in the one pair of sky blue eyes.

"Is she dead?" he demanded in German.

The other pair of hard blue eyes blinked. "No, my colonel. She has fainted."

"How can you be sure?" he barked. "Release this woman from those damned bonds and find her some clothes. *At once!*"

The sound of the electric door sliding open again drew both pairs of eyes away from the pitiful sight of Marla.

"Countermanding my orders, Colonel?" The most recent arrival coldly glared at them from a piercing blackness under his hooded lids.

The sky blue eyes of Joachim von Daren deadened. "Begging your pardon, Colonel Streicher, I was not aware this woman was your prisoner. She was delivered into my custody," he informed him as he produced orders from his breast pocket.

"How convenient!" Streicher's sinister voice dripped with sarcasm. He took the orders Joachim handed him and gave him a hard look. Joachim stood at stiff attention while Streicher read through the papers. An evil smirk curled his lips when he looked up again.

"These orders are useless, Colonel von Daren. Your General Schellenberg has been relieved of his command. You serve Reichsfuhrer Himmler now, and you take your orders from me."

Joachim's shock was genuine. For Catherine's sake, he had been willing to take the extra risk to try and rescue Marla, but Streicher's sudden appearance and this news jeapordized everything. Once Streicher recognized Marla wasn't Catherine, he would realize, of anyone, von Daren not only should have known the prisoner was an impostor but who she really was. Joachim fished for time.

"Since Lady Catherine is a cousin of England's King George, my concern is that the British and the Allies may want to negotiate for her safe return. If she dies, we've lost our bargaining power."

Streicher's black pair of eyes darkened and narrowed. "Colonel von Daren, have you no finesse? We don't want Lady Catherine to die. We just want to show her who her real friends are."

The Gestapo officer flicked his gloves at the other SD officer beside Joachim, directing him to open the door into Marla's cell. The heavy metal door scraped against the concrete floor as Streicher gestured with another flick of his gloves to Joachim to precede him into the cell. Following him into the cold dank room, Streicher remarked, "Precise and meticulous timing, Colonel, is of the essence."

Inside, he strode over to Marla's slumped body. His piercing black eyes devoured her disgrace before he shoved Marla's hair back from her forehead and lifted her face up by her chin for his inspection. Instant fury stained his eyesockets with an inky red.

"I've been cheated again!" he thundered and cruelly dug his fingers into her cheeks. "Wake up, you whore!" He screamed. "*Wake up!*"

Marla groaned. The zigzagging pain darting through her jaws stabbed the comfortable darkness. She gagged and coughed. That awful smell of garlic sausage...she had smelled it before at Catherine's press recital...*in Berlin!* Her eyes flashed open. Above her loomed the hateful face of the SS officer she had challenged on *Kristallnacht*. She flicked her tongue inside her back tooth and tried to loosen the imbedded L-pill.

"*Oh no, YOU DON'T!*" he roared. His fist slammed into her mouth and jammed it open. She bit into his flesh struggling to crush the poison capsule. He howled and swore and, with his fist still jammed up against the roof of her mouth, knocked her head against the wall.

"You can't bite it," he hissed. "Now swallow it, you slut! The whole pill!"

She couldn't breathe and began choking. Instinctively she swallowed. The pill slipped down her throat unharmed.

A cruel triumphant smile lit up the blackness of his eyes. "So, we meet again, Marla Franklin," he sneered.

"Marla Franklin!" gasped Joachim, feigning shock. "Let me see her."

Streicher stood aside. "Am I to believe this is the first time you've seen your prisoner?" he snarled.

"*Jawohl,*" Joachim lied. "I only received orders this morning to take over Lady Catherine's interrogation. I was not the arresting officer. Major Richter here was."

Joachim looked down at Marla. "She is indeed the journalist, but her hair and coloring are different. Her likeness to Lady Catherine is astounding."

"*It's more than astounding!!* Her appearance is a perfect duplicate of the drawing London sent us." In a rage, Streicher slapped his black leather gloves against the concrete wall. "We've been tricked."

Colonel Streicher suddenly turned on Joachim.

"Berlin. *Ja*. I remember how fascinated you were with the pianist…with Lady Catherine."

"I was," Joachim admitted. "She's beautiful, and she's a magnificent musician. I could not believe she is also a spy. That is why, as soon as I received these orders, I came to see her."

"But instead of a royal prize, we are delivered this impostor." Streicher clamped Marla's face between fingers that looked like squared gills. Renewed rage reddened his cheeks. "The *swine!*" he cursed. "I want that traitor. *I want him!*"

"Who? What traitor?" Joachim demanded.

"The Abwehr," Streicher impatiently explained. "Admiral Canaris himself set up a double agent in London…a plant inside British Intelligence. Only he's not working for us *or* them. Moscow runs him." The idea triggered a mean laugh.

"He makes the British look like such fools. The Americans can't trust them. Divide and conquer. A typical Stalin trick. And this woman…" he said, suddenly pointing at Marla, "works with the traitor. She is a *Red agent, a Red whore*."

Stunned with horror, Marla stared into his mad black eyes and, seeing the reflection of her nakedness there, cringed. Joachim likewise absorbed Streicher's assumption with concealed dismay, but it confirmed Amanita agents were being betrayed and why. He looked on Marla with even graver pity and wished, as he resigned himself to her sacrifice, he could free her from Streicher's inevitable torture. Now, however, it was more important he survive to get back to London as quickly as possible.

Marla's reaction to Streicher's accusation was

playing into his obsession. "Ah, my Red whore. You are afraid," he smirked. "That is good. Very very good. You and I have a lot to talk about. It would be easier if you co-operated. Easier and shorter."

The meaning of his words toyed with the darkness of his eyes, their pools upon pools growing and growing into wider and wider circles of sinister ripples. Suddenly, Streicher pulled out a switch blade from his polished jackboot and released the blade.

Joachim watched dry-mouthed. Marla's eyes widened with expectation, and when she glanced at Joachim, the shock of recognizing him magnified her fear. Streicher then walked in front of her, blocking Joachim's view. With the tip of the cold steel knife, he drew an imaginary line from her throat down to the cleavage of her breast. Marla shivered.

"No doubt you have other duties to attend to Colonel von Meyer," he said. "See to them at once and forget this treachery. I will get at the truth."

Staring at Streicher's back, Joachim swallowed and squared his shoulders. "Of course." Then he abruptly swung about and left Marla's cell, forgetting to salute Hitler. His oversight did not escape Streicher's notice.

Once von Daren was gone, Streicher folded up the switch blade and slipped the knife back into his boot. He motioned to the SD officer standing in the hallway. "Unlock her," he ordered.

As the other officer moved to do his bidding, Streicher paced the floor of the cell. "Von Daren is not one of us," he told him. "Have him watched day and night." Then he paused. "Major Richter?"

"Yes, Colonel Streicher."

Streicher's evil black eyes bore into the other man.

"What do you think of whores?"

"I hate them."

Streicher nodded. "I thought I remembered that correctly about you. You have not served me long, Major Richter, but I am going to leave this Red whore in your capable hands until I return."

Turning his attention back to Marla, his eyes hardened with hate. "How I long to direct your interrogation myself, dear lady, but alas," he affected a long deep sigh, "I have been transferred to Poland. It's only a temporary assignment, you understand. I shall come back, Miss Franklin, and I trust that when we next meet you will be more agreeable."

Smiling with self-satisfaction, he turned away from her, back to Major Richter. His face darkened. The smirk died. "I don't care what you do to her. Understand?"

"Indeed, Colonel Streicher."

"Just make her talk," he said and tromped out of Marla's prison cell.

Chapter Twenty Three

Wednesday, October 13th, 1944

JOACHIM WELCOMED the pregnant rainclouds looming over the deserted stone cottage with its thatched roof and windbattered sign squeaking on rusty hinges in rhythm with the howling night. The inscription, *HAVNEHUS*, could still be made out of the letters peeling off the sign's wooden plaque.

Once a tourist tea house, the owner had abandoned it soon after the occupation forces overran the northern outskirts of Copenhagen and had escaped to England with some merchant marines. Behind it, neglected terraces and wild lawns stretched down the lap of the forest clearing to the sea. In daylight, the Oresund reflected a breathtaking blue, and the Swedish coastline was clearly visible across the narrow waterway connecting the Baltic Sea to the North Sea.

Tonight, all was in syrupy darkness. The wind stirred treacherously, and the air smelled of rain. The coming downpour would wash away his tire tracks, Joachim thought with relief, as he cautiously opened the garage door of the forgotten country tea house. Inside, covered by a tarpaulin, was his car, a 1938 Mercedes-Benz convertible. It was part of his getaway plan.

Returning to the pick-up truck outside, he unloaded the long bulky bedroll clumsily wrapped in oilcloth and sail twine and hoisted it over his shoulder. Under the rigid deadweight, he lurched as he hauled it inside and dumped it one the running board of his car. Squatting, he propped up the bundled truss against the car door, but no sooner did he let it go than it slid down and fell on the cement floor. He thought about lifting it back up again, then decided against it and reached over the front seat of the open convertible to yank up the rear seat cushion. Under it, he found the duffel bag exactly where he had stashed it. Lugging it out, he loosened the draw string and, turning it upside down, shook the contents on the ground: his SS boots, black and silver uniform, cap and waterproof pouch with all his identification papers tucked inside. From it, he removed his family ring and his wrist watch. It was a few minutes after midnight.

Slipping a penknife out of his pant pocket, he took the tied-up bundle and cut the cords holding it together. The oilcloth slackened, and Joachim unrolled it. A corpse, about his own age and size with thick blonde hair, tumbled free. The sudden release of the body's wretched odor overwhelmed him, and he gagged. Coughing and spitting, he groped in his hip pocket for his scarf and hurriedly tied it over his nose and around his face. This done, he set himself to dressing the corpse in his uniform.

The jackboots were a struggle. He tugged and cursed. There was no give. He started to sweat. Impatiently, he jammed the boots on as far as they would fit and opened the driver's door. Locking his arms around the dead man's chest, he dragged him up onto the seat and pushed and shoved...and pushed and shoved...until he had him facing the steering wheel. But rigor mortis had set in so he could not fold him into the seat. He pushed and shoved some more, but the cadaver would not bend. It was literally standing on the gas pedal.

"*What the hell...!*" Joachim groaned in disgust. "I asked for a stiff, but this is ridiculous. They should have drugged the bastard instead of killing him."

After a moment's rest, he decided to lay the corpse down across the front seat. Next, he checked his pouch. All of his papers were there. For a second he held them, reflecting. He was about to snuff out his whole existence with one tap of his finger. Reluctantly, he straightened his shoulders and inserted the pouch inside the dead man's breast pocket. He fingered his ring, his mother's *Uradel* seal, before he slipped it on the fourth finger of the dead man's right hand. It fit as if it belonged there. He felt no remorse. The man delivered to Joachim deserved to die. He was a Nazi collaborator the Resistance gladly executed to save the life of a secret allied agent.

At this moment, Joachim thought of Catherine. She was his life now. He loved her with all his heart. For the time being, he had safely hidden her with the nuns in the convent across the street from Gestapo headquarters. There was a certain irony to the proximity of the enemy that tickled his sense of comic relief. The abbess of St. Joan's was one of the *sleepers* he recruited for his secret network before the war. He avoided using her, but protecting Catherine altered his gallant intent not to involve the nun in his subversive activities. Until he could determine who had betrayed Catherine, there was no one else he could trust except God's own angel of mercy.

After he hung up the phone at the shopkeeper's store,

the jumpy merchant's reaction to the news that the Gestapo were already at Mme. Thirsted's to arrest her had utterly awed him. The man's face had paled, then stilled, a granite monument to transmuted courage—steady eyes and bold chin. Without a word, he found them a complete change of clothing.

Catherine discarded her padded outfit, and, when she reappeared from behind a wall of shelves, looked like a young boy, lean and hard, in a fisherman's sweater and duffel coat. Her hair was pulled up under a wool toque. Oil smudges over her forehead, nose and chin toughened her finer feminine features. Joachim emerged a burly seaman, fully bearded with thick dark whiskers and a bushy mustache, courtesy of an old stage make-up kit left open on one of the junk shelves in the back. He had yanked a toque down over his face to hide his blonde hair underneath.

The shopkeeper found them two bicycles in good riding condition, and they left him feeling very grateful for the disguises and transportation he had provided.

Later, they understood the significance of that help, of the adoration and magnificent respect Mme. Thirsted commanded from the Danish people. She was their grand dame of opera, their symbolic voice of freedom, the bountiful earth mother of all Denmark. The shot that silenced her golden voice stunned the Danes, but once the shock wore off, anger replaced the numbness. A public will of steel stiffened the country's spine. There was no gift greater than the gift of life Lilla Thirsted gave for her beloved people. All Denmark rallied to resist the Nazi assassins terrorizing their sacred land.

Joachim gritted his teeth and picked up his watch. Ten minutes had passed. He was taking far too long. He eased the watch onto the dead man's wrist and hurried outside again to the pick-up truck. This time he went to the cab and retrieved a small tackle box from under the front seat. He brought it to his car. Placing the box on the convertible's chassis, he opened it wide, exposing a Gammon grenade filled with enough plastic explosive to mutilate the corpse beyond recognition without destroying the planted identification papers. He inserted a delayed-reaction detonating fuse and scrambled back to the truck.

The truck grunted and sputtered as he turned over the engine. "Come on! This is no time to flood the bloody thing!" he reproached himself and gave the engine a little more choke. At once the truck growled and fired. Joachim immediately shifted into reverse and catapulted the truck backwards onto the roadway. Braking hard, he turned the wheels in the direction of Copenhagen and shot forward. The squeal of his tires stung the sudden calm.

With foot to the floor, Joachim raced the old pickup down the country road. Thunder clapped. Lightning zigzagged over the rolling horizon. Sharp cracks split the air. The raging storm above handily masked the booming thunder of the sudden explosion behind him. He slowed down to look back.

More than anything Joachim mourned for his car. It was the only thing left he could call his own. Hitler had confiscated his beautiful farm and his champion trotters as the Allies cut through France on their advance to Germany. He had pampered his Mercedes, relieved to have something on which to shower all his penned-up affections. Blowing up the car felt as if he had betrayed a friend.

Slowly, he untied the scarf still wrapped around his face and, with his free hand, smoothed and folded it on his knee, again and again until it was no bigger than the width of a pfennig. Finally, he took the tight little ball and pocketed it.

Huge drops of rain splattered across the truck's windshield. Blackness consumed the fertile flat lands and the tall leafy forests. *Good*, he thought to himself. *There will be no patrols in this weather. It will be hours before my pitiful remains are discovered. Even if Streicher does suspect I let Holbak escape and was fleeing to Sweden, he won't have time to prove it. The SS report will read that I was ambushed and murdered by the Resistance.* He smiled ruefully. *Who says God isn't on our side?*

Torrents of rain whipped the truck and rattled its roof. He battled the wind, steering against its angry gusts. As he sliced through the thundersquall, he risked turning on his headlights on his way back to the outskirts of Copenhagen and to the Brothers of the Good Shepherd, a Basilian order of monks. The last *sleeper* in his network dwelled there.

Joachim would give him Catherine's message to carry to the Resistance and let them radio Churchill: CHARGES NEUTRALIZED...STOP...WATCHDOG. For now, it was not safe to inform London that Catherine was safely hidden or that Marla had been captured in Catherine's place. As long as the traitor, this triple agent if Streicher were correct, believed the Gestapo had Catherine, he might make a mistake. Joachim was counting on that.

Chapter Twenty Four

Monday, October 18th, 1944

KNOWING THE CONDITIONS on the Eastern Front, Major Waldemar Richter of the *Sicherheitsdienst*—the Nazi Party's security service or SD as it was called—did not expect Streicher to return to Copenhagen and immediately moved Lady Catherine's beautiful impostor into his own quarters as his concubine. He provided her with a basic wardrobe. Making her talk was not his pressing purpose. She was to become his private experiment, and while he was out, he chained her to his bed so she could not escape.

Each night, when he returned from Gestapo Headquarters at Shell House, he brought her a day's supply of sandwiches and ersatz coffee. He made no effort to question her and no attempt to touch her. At night—for six, long, silent nights—he lay on the bed beside her and slept.

Not sure what to make out of this treatment, Marla eventually decided to take advantage of it and welcomed the relief, if only to regain her strength from the ordeal suffered during the first days of her imprisonment.

In his early, maybe middle thirties, Richter seemed a very remote man. He had chiselled features like a Roman centurion and an Aquarian dimple in his chin. The way his locks of short flaxen waves flopped over his smooth brow reminded Marla of dried wheat fringing his forehead. A broad delta ran between his hard blue eyes and down his square-tipped nose. Across his face, his straight mouth formed an upside down T-square to his short nose. He never smiled. Marla sensed a sadness beneath the hardness.

On this night, as soon as he walked in the door, she knew something had changed. He carried no food with him. Instead, he stood at the foot of the bed and deliberately undressed, revealing his firm, well-muscled frame. Emotions she could not identify twirled and twisted in the depths of his eyes like rocky shadows eddying in layers under their steel-smooth surface. Without a word, he bent down and began massaging her feet, then he stroked her legs.

She closed her eyes and bit her lips. *Oh no, dear God! No! Help me!* she fervently prayed. In anticipation, long forgotten sensations began to overtake her body. *NO! NO! NO!* she cried out against herself. *I must not feel. Dear God! Please don't let me feel anything!*

When she opened her eyes, the sharp blade of a trench knife glinted above her. In horror, she gasped, expecting the stinging stab of death. He slipped the pointed tip under the neckline of her flannelette nightgown and slashed upwards, tearing the material. Slowly, very slowly, he ripped it all the way down the front of her and parted it open, like filleting a fish, exposing her nude body beneath. The rush of cool air against her flesh raised goose bumps, and darts of pleasure shot through her. He felt her stiffen in resistance and smiled for the first time—a dreamy smile.

He twiddled her nipples and watched them harden. "Ready and willing, aren't you? All I have to do is play the right notes, and your body will sing the whole damned chorus."

She cowered from her body's betrayal.

"Oh, this is just the beginning, whore," he crowed. His pale lips curled back over model-perfect teeth. "Hitler has his little Eva, and I have a sex doll. Who is luckier, *ja*?"

His smile shrunk. "Before I am done with you, you will want me as you have never wanted any man. You will be my slave, eager to please me. I promise you," he said, and then buried his head between her clenched legs.

Chapter Twenty Five

Wednesday, January 10th, 1945

NO ONE QUESTIONED a Nazi security or intelligence officer keeping a woman prisoner in his personal quarters for his sexual slave. The SS and the SD were always selecting the prettiest and the sexiest internees as their choice concubines. No one cared what they did to them, and those women who were picked quickly accepted that the prostitution of their body was the price they paid to survive, so they learned to please their masters. Some were treated better than others. Marla discovered she was one of the luckier ones.

In the beginning, SD Major Waldemar Richter behaved with obsessed delight chaining her to his bed, subjecting her to his sexual fantasies. Marla accepted this enslavement as her deserving punishment as she succumbed to his imaginative techniques—which seemed less perverted and more exploitative of her pleasures—with a wild abandon that shamed her. Her body seemed beyond her control, hungering for a gratification disassociated from her soul yet wholly physical.

As time passed however, Marla observed changes in her Nazi captor. A tenderness entered into their strange relationship. At first, hesitantly, in monosyllables, testing each other. They talked because their need to talk to someone broke down the remaining barriers. With their increasing closeness came an emotional vulnerability that tore open the old wound of Ulo's death. The grief she had denied herself now consumed her.

When she was alone, chained to Richter's bed so she couldn't escape, she thought of Ulo, of how wonderful their love could have been. And she ached for his touch, his arms, his voice, his laugh, for what was happening between her and Richter was not love. It was a desperate act of survival, for both of them. She recognized the difference and felt only relief and gratefulness to Richter because Streicher's alternative for her was torture and death.

Richter was convinced Streicher was obsessed, insanely seeing a Communist plot in everything that happened, but his accusing words, *She's a Red agent*, kept bothering her. True, she was not a Red agent, but some of what Streicher said made sense. His belief that there was a triple agent operating in London, who was betraying both the Germans and the British, made sense. If *Project Amanita* could be made to look incompetent, the Americans, in spite of their formal nuclear agreement with Britain, would not trust the British. That could well be the traitor's motive: to support the destruction of the Nazis' capabilities to produce their own atomic bomb while causing dissension between Britain and the United States.

But how could turning the western allies against themselves help Stalin's objectives? Catherine had to be the key. Sir Isaac had said if the Gestapo captured her they were all in trouble. *They*. Who was *they*? Didn't he really mean Churchill?

She could imagine the blazing headlines: HITLER HOLDS KING'S COUSIN FOR RANSOM. What a field day the Nazis would have with that propaganda! Politically, they could discredit Churchill. Churchill. That was the key. He was the target. He had been opposing Stalin's demands for a second front, despite Stalin's threat to make a separate peace with Hitler if the Allies would not join him in a squeeze play. He wanted to split the power of the Third Reich on two fronts, to divide their forces and to drain their resources. His position made sense except Churchill feared a western frontal attack would fail without the full co-operation and mobilization of the secret armies and civilian resistance groups within Europe. In his opinion, Stalin's strategy was premature, so he continued to oppose him.

The Russian bear already blamed the Allies for mismanaging the events leading up to the outbreak of war and for Russia's suffering the worst under Hitler's invasions. No doubt Stalin was looking to the future, to the end of the war when Hitler's conquered lands would be divided up amongst the victors. If the Allies ended up bickering amongst themselves, Russia definitely gained more control of the negotiations. That had to be it! Churchill would be a formidable opponent at the bargaining table. Stalin needed him out of the way.

That explained a triple Red agent's motive, but she still could not fathom who the traitor could be. Mulling over the possibilities drew her away from the sink hole of sorrow and despair during the long hours when

Richter left her alone.

As the weeks turned into months, Marla's sympathy for Richter grew. His world was gradually collapsing. By the 10th of January, 1945, the U.S. Third Army under General Patton was at Germany's door. Having taken Bouzonville on the River Nied and Metz, he along with the U.S. First Army was moving on Bastogne. At the same time, in the Ardennes Battle, the British XXX Corps were fighting German troops near Laroche. The Allies were steadily gaining. For Marla, the news was hopeful. For Richter, it was demoralizing.

She encouraged him to talk, not only for the information he gave her but also for his own sake, and she listened with sensitive ears.

"Why do you hate women so?"

"I don't. I hate you. You are the enemy."

"Is that why you drive me crazy with so much pleasure when you could torture me instead?"

"Is pleasure not a form of torture? Do you not beg me to stop what I do to you because you can't endure any more?"

Marla only looked at him, patiently waiting.

Richter's eyes dropped. "If I can turn my enemy into my sexual slave, then I will know how to bond any woman I choose to me. She will never want to betray me for another man." He rolled over on his back and lay staring at the ceiling. They were both covered in sweat from another prolonged exercise in ecstasy.

"So you've been jilted. Hasn't everyone?" Marla asked.

He turned over and glared at her fiercely. It was Marla's turn to drop her eyes. How could she hate someone who needed approval so badly?

He rolled back and resumed his preoccupation with the ceiling. This woman by his side, whom he had originally hated, had become strangely close to him. Physically, he knew everything about her. He knew how to exploit her every weakness, but in her defenselessness to him, he discovered he was feeling protective of her. Since she was completely dependent on him for her survival, he enjoyed her needing him. This was an emotional element to the bonding process he had not considered when he launched his sexual experiment. She knew what pleased him, and what pleased him most was her personal interest in him. When he talked, she genuinely listened. She didn't patronize him the way everyone else did. The understanding was in her magnificent eyes, the way she looked at him. She understood what he was saying, what he was feeling. He expected her resentment. Instead, she was giving him back a part of himself he thought he had lost, a part he liked. He no longer felt like an outcast. In the privacy of his own room, he had comfort now. This woman, his prisoner, was giving it to him.

"There was a girl once...," he admitted. Richter's voice trailed off with his memories. Suddenly, he wanted to talk, to vent the hurt. "When I was in the Hitler Youth," he began, "she belonged to the League of German Girls. Everything was so simple then."

He smiled sadly. "And happy. Everyone was happy. We met at the Nuremberg Rally in '34. As it happened, we both came from Munich. We had been selected by our local chapters to represent our districts. It was a great honor, you know. I was graduating from Hitler School at the top of my class and looking forward to joining the SS. We were 18."

So he was younger than she had guessed, Marla thought.

"Ingrid had a flawless background. Everything was perfect for us. The festival... Ah, the festival! How can I describe it to you?"

He paused. "Every September, hundreds...no, thousands of Nazi Party members along with the labor corps and regiments of Brown Shirts and stormtroops gathered in Nuremberg. We came to hear the Fuhrer speak and to celebrate the rebirth of our Fatherland." His eyes shone remembering.

"It was an exhilarating experience. I was so proud to be a part of it. Through the packed streets, the crowds cheered us as we marched by. When you looked up, all you could see were our swastika bloodflags draped over every building. The sight filled me with power. We were invincible I thought. At night, we swarmed around Hitler's hotel shouting, *We want our Fuhrer! We want our Fuhrer!* And then, when he finally appeared and waved to us, I felt he was waving to me. I was so overcome with joy. I can't describe that joy. He made me proud to be a German. I wanted only to please him, to serve him well." He fell silent, lost in his memories, reliving the moment.

"Each day," he went on with his story, "through the festival, there were grand pageants and torchlight parades. Ingrid and I bumped into each other at the Old Congress Hall in the Luitpoldhain. There were so many people we let ourselves be pushed to our seats. We were both so excited. I have never seen anything like it. Flags everywhere. The platform was dressed like a Gothic cathedral. Giant klieg lights lit the stage. An orchestra played Beethoven's *Egmont Overture*. When the music stopped, Rudolf Hess read out the roll call of Brownshirts killed during street fighting for the Nazi cause. It was a solemn memorial. This was the night Hitler promised us the Third Reich would last 1,000 years. We cheered and clapped. We felt as one body, strong and indivisible. Ingrid and I were both affected. All of us were. Couples conjugated in the heat of joyous fervor, as if in anti-climax to Hitler's speech."

"During the rally?" Marla asked incredulously.

Richter looked startled at her question. "No, of course not. Afterwards...after the sing songs around the campfires...under the stars and the cloak of night, we joined our hearts and souls in physical unions... thousands of us...it was truly beautiful."

"My God!" exclaimed Marla. "A national orgy!"

He stiffened. "It was our patriotic duty!" he protested. "We were chosen to be the fountainhead of the new Germany. It was an honor. Many married after the Nuremberg rallies."

"Did you and Ingrid get married?"

"No," he said huskily and hung his head. "Shortly afterward, my mother caught my father working secretly for the Communists. She was a loyal party member. She turned him in, and I was disgraced. She believed the Fuhrer," he defended her, "when he said that, if war comes to Europe, the Communists would be to blame. She believed she was saving Germany from war when she informed on him to the Gestapo."

Marla imagined how this betrayal must have devastated him. "How did you feel about your father working for the Communists?"

"I hated him," he said simply. "I couldn't enter the SS then, and Ingrid married someone else the SS approved."

They lay silently beside each other. He with his memories. She with the tragic impact of his story. She broke their silence first. "What did you feel about your mother?"

"Nothing."

"But Waldemar, if she had kept her mouth shut and protected your father, you might have been accepted into the SS, and then you would have been able to marry your Ingrid. Surely your mother is as much to blame for your disgrace as your father."

Richter scowled, agitated. He shook his head. "No. She was my mother. She did her duty. She was a good woman."

Marla sighed. "Where is your mother now?"

"Dead. Killed in a bombing raid on Munich."

"I'm sorry."

"I'm not. She still believed in Hitler. What do the rest of us have to believe in now?" he asked bitterly.

"Yourselves."

"*Ourselves?*"

"Yes," she affirmed. "You've put all your faith in one man, in his dream, instead of believing in yourselves. Hitler obviously believes in himself, or he couldn't have achieved what he has. But now Germany is collapsing. His dream is not working because, to deify himself, he robbed you of your faith in yourself. Once you lose the freedom to make your own choices, all is lost."

Her candid talk made Richter feel awkward. His mouth pursed in a grim line. She was saying things he didn't want to hear. Marla, observing his discomfort, switched the direction of their conversation. "How did you get in the SD?"

"Through the Abwehr." Her quizzical expression

prompted him to explain. "Counterintelligence. Admiral Wilhelm Canaris."

She still couldn't make the connection. "When I couldn't get into the SS," he explained further, "I joined the Navy. When Admiral Canaris wanted an aide with a photographic memory, he searched military records for a candidate and picked me. I have this ability. He then had me transferred to the Abwehr where he reassigned me to his personal staff. After the Gestapo arrested Canaris for treason, Schellenberg absorbed the Abwehr into his Combined Secret Services. The Gestapo interrogated those of us who served the Admiral directly. Their reasoning was that, if he was a traitor, we must be traitors too. But, for some reason I still don't understand, Schellenberg reassigned me to Copenhagen to serve under Colonel Streicher."

"You really don't know what it is like to live as a free man, do you?" observed Marla.

A sudden commotion downstairs interrupted his reply. Marla immediately covered herself with the bedspread. Richter jumped out of bed, rushed to the window and cautiously pulled the curtain back. "*Hell!*" he exclaimed incredulously and bolted to the closet for his uniform. Dressing frantically, he told Marla, "It's *Streicher!*"

Jackboots hammered up the bottom flight of stairs. Richter nervously knotted his tie.

"Waldemar!" The plea escaped from Marla's frightened lips. "You should have arrested Lady Catherine, not me. I replaced her when I found out she had been betrayed. Who turned her in? I must know."

"An unsigned message was delivered to me," he answered breathlessly. "And a sketch that looked like you."

A sketch? It must have been the one stolen from her file. "The double agent Streicher said Canaris planted in British Intelligence," she persisted. "Do you know who it is? A code name? Anything?"

He looked stricken. "I know nothing." Loud knocks banged on his door. "Marla," he said, rushing his words, "no matter what happens, hang on! Do you understand? Save yourself. For God's sake, tell him anything. He's mad!"

A shot shattered the end of his sentence as a Waffen-SS trooper kicked in his door. Three more troopers burst into the tiny bedroom and aimed MP40 submachine guns at Marla and Richter as Colonel Streicher strode in. "So this is your little love nest, Major Richter," he immediately commented. He looked around and sneered, "Surely you could do better than this!"

From under his hooded lids, Streicher's piercing black eyes fell on Marla clutching the bedspread protectively up to her neck. A catlike satisfaction narrowed his frightening eyes and thin lips. He sniffed. Marla trembled as he bent over her. His breath reeked of Polish sausage.

"The smell of hot steamy sex fills the room." From his mouth, the words sounded sick and sordid. "It seems we missed quite the show, boys," Streicher remarked as he straightened himself up and turned to his troopers. "Isn't that too bad!"

He seemed crestfallen. "Ah, but I have an idea." His expression lifted. "Bring in our toy," he instructed the soldiers.

Two of them left and wheeled in a gurney through the door to the edge of her bed. "Don't forget my cameras," Streicher directed.

Next, lights and camera equipment were dragged into the small room. Marla stared in amazement. Richter stood rigidly at attention, not trusting himself to look at Marla. He had a good idea what Streicher had in mind for them.

Ignoring Richter, Streicher turned his full attention on Marla. "Did you know I was a famous movie-maker before the war?"

She shook her head.

"*NO!*" He looked insulted. "Over a million prints of my movies were sent to every part of the world. They were distributed for private showings."

Marla stiffened. Cold chills scurried down her spine. She was beginning to understand what was in store for her and Waldemar too.

"You chose to ignore my orders, Major Richter. You took this *Red whore—this SPY—* for your personal enjoyment. I've known about it for months, of course, but I didn't want to spoil your fun until I could return. It has been fun, hasn't it?"

Richter remained silent. Streicher walked over to him and gripped his face between his square finger tips. "I asked you, has it been fun?"

Richter spat in his face. His hostile resistance took Streicher by surprise. He stepped back and grimaced as he wiped the spit from his face. Then he smiled, a slow evil smile. "Good, Richter, good. This is going to be better than I planned. Fury heightens passion."

Richter nervously glanced at Marla. Streicher noticed his quick look and sniggered, "Has this whore infected you with her venom, Richter? Do you suppose yourself in love with her? With this *Red* whore?" he screeched and pointed to Marla. Then he turned his head back to Richter, and his voice dropped to a hiss.

"The sins of the father are visited upon the son. You are a traitor, Richter," he said. "A damned traitor just like your father. And you are going to pay in full." He turned away. "Are my cameras and lights ready?"

"Yes, Herr Colonel," one of the troopers replied.

Streicher took his position behind the mounted movie camera and focused the lens. He swivelled the camera through 180 degrees. "Perfect," he declared. "When I say *action*, two of you grab and hold him while the other one strips his uniform off. Remember he is in disgrace. Have no mercy. Understand?"

He looked up at the three soldiers. They each nodded. Streicher's head again disappeared behind the camera. "Ready?" he called. "*ACTION!*"

Marla watched with sick horror as they degraded and mutilated every part of Richter's beautiful body except his penis. "That we are keeping for you, whore," Streicher jeered from behind the camera.

Richter endured Streicher's depraved directions and abuses with the occasional grunt and moan. Those few signals of surrender to his suffering spurred Streicher's evil imagination. On and on went his torture.

"Enough!" Streicher suddenly yelled. "I want enough of him left for our final act with the whore." He came out from behind the camera and stood over Marla. She cringed. His eyes gleamed as he tore the bedspread away from her clutches. She tried to cover her breasts.

"Chain her wrists to the bed posts," he instructed. One soldier came forward and wrenched her arms away from her body. Another one locked the chains dangling from the bed posts around her wrists.

Streicher stood expressionless as he studied her

body. Marla lay petrified imaging what terrible things he intended to do to her. He savored her fear and fed it with touches to her face, hair, nipples and crotch. Her legs tightened at his invasive liberties. "You are a better specimen than I usually get," he pronounced.

She trembled uncontrollably as he went to adjust the lights and his camera angles. Richter's guards supported his poor racked body, forcing him to watch.

"Now, Richter," Streicher told him. "Show us what you have learned from your Red whore. Do everything you would do if we weren't here. If you refuse to co-operate," Streicher added menacingly, "we will shoot her, and you can fuck her dead body. Understand?"

Reluctantly, Richter nodded.

"I didn't hear you, Richter. Speak up," demanded Streicher.

"Yes," he croaked between his swollen lips.

"Good. When I call *ready*, you come out of the shadows and start staggering towards the whore on the bed. There you explore her body with all your special techniques and bring her to an agonizing pitch of passion. At this peak, troopers, I want you to unchain her from the bed and lift her unto the gurney. Strap her down. Now, Richter, you will bring her to fever pitch ecstasy again, and as you do, I want to shoot close-up the reactions of every part of her body. Then you will empty all your manhood into the whore. Understand, Richter?"

"Yes," he croaked again.

"*Ready...*"

Richter stepped out of the shadows. He looked miserably at Marla. Her tragic frightened eyes forgave him.

"*ACTION!*"

And then the bizarre ordeal began. Marla resented

the stirring lust that betrayed her in this degrading episode. After awhile she became so lost to the sensations washing over her she became transcended by the things Richter did to her. She knew that in front of these demented pigs, he was making love to her.

At one point, she vaguely sensed their freeing her wrists and lifting her up onto the gurney. A cold shaft of air sent shivers through her before the fire began travelling through her body again. It raged until explosions burst within her. A shot rang out. She opened her eyes. Above her loomed Richter's poor bruised and battered face. His eyes stared into hers as he fell with crushing weight upon her. As she felt the warm blood pour from the gaping hole in his forehead down her breast, she never knew the terrible scream tearing from her throat was her own.

THE VIEW from St. Joan's bell tower overlooked Gestapo Headquarters across the city square. Crouching on the top step of the tower, Catherine clung to the shadows and cautiously scanned the square from there. All was strangely quiet. As usual, her gaze settled on the converted office building directly across from the convent. The Danes still called it *Shell House.* If asked, she would probably concede it was a trick of her imagination but to her, the snow-packed square seemed soaked in translucent red, a mirrored image of the massive Nazi blood flag draping the front of the building. The Gestapo had marked Shell House boldly, mocking the Allies in the belief that if British squadrons bombed Copenhagen, they would not target their headquarters so close to a convent filled with a cloistered order of nuns and Danish schoolgirls.

Beside her, a cold wind jingled the chapel bell's clapper. The tinglings clanged out a Morse code of their own. Catherine shivered and huddled more tightly beneath her nun's robe.

Day after day, she made this sojourn to the tower alone, where she prayed and meditated in the brisk wintry air, for as much as she knew Marla had chosen to sacrifice herself, she could find no relief from the lonely guilt and loss she suffered. Dear Mme. Thirsted was dead, and Marla was in the clutches of the Gestapo or dead. Catherine did not know what to pray for. If she prayed for Marla to be alive, would Marla alive be praying for death to free her from her tormentors? Marla had emphasized the duty of an agent to protect the mission, and if the situation were reversed, if the Gestapo had captured Catherine, she would expect Catherine to swallow the cyanide capsule lodged in her back molar. Catherine's heart could not accept what her mind knew was true. Marla must be dead.

Neither had she heard from Joachim. What if he had been captured too? Dreadful thoughts gnawed at her, chipping at her faith, the fortress of her own survival. She felt abandoned and bewildered. As the days passed into months, nothing made any sense, and she was filled with despair.

The squish of tires crossing the snowy square and the hiss of brakes in front of Gestapo Headquarters snapped Catherine out of her gloomy thoughts. She peered curiously at the black car that had just pulled up. A blackcoated SS officer and a woman emerged. For a moment they paused. The woman turned as if she were trying to catch her bearings. She glanced up at the sky, and in that instant, her full face came into Catherine's view. Catherine sucked in her breath. *Dear God, it can't be!* The woman's face held a fraction longer. Then the SS officer yanked her arm and steered her up the entrance steps. The woman carried herself proudly as she disappeared inside.

With joyous disbelief, Catherine scrambled down the tower steps, tripping on her habit skirt as her feet flew out from under her. Racing out of the bell tower, she forgot to lock the door and had to dash back. In her hurry, she fumbled the key, losing more valuable seconds. About to run again, the memory of the Mother Superior's instructions suddenly contained her: *A nun never runs and never walks too quickly.* Resisting the urge to break the rule, she folded her hands inside her habit and forced herself to walk sedately along the cloisters into the abbey while silently singing a hymn of praise. Inside, she found Mother Superior on her way to morning chapel. With barely noticeable hand movements, she signalled her urgent need to talk.

The abbess merely smiled and ignored her plea. "Sister Angelique, I'm so glad I've found you. One of the Basilian brothers is in the vestry. Please go there at once. He is very anxious to see the crypt."

When Catherine's eyes voiced her frustrated objection, she added, "I will see you after morning vespers. You must learn to trust God, my dear." And with great dignity, she proceeded down the arched corridor to the chapel.

Bowing her head in expected obedience, Catherine masked her frustration and meekly followed the Mother Superior down the hall to the chapel, but instead of entering the chapel with her, she slipped around the corner and headed for the vestry.

Of all times for a Basilian monk to choose to see the crypt, she fumed silently. *Marla's still alive. I have to find some way to contact the Underground. God only knows what will happen to her in Shell House, and He's not talking!* Catherine had heard one of the sisters call Shell House "the Gestapo's chamber of horrors."

In the vestry, a hooded monk stood in the shadows of the library shelves, waiting for her. She gestured for him to move aside and deftly reached behind the canonical books searching for a hidden lever recessed into the side of the fourth shelf. Finding it, she pressed down. A soft click released the wooden shelves. As she pulled the secret door open, it creaked—a loud crack it seemed to her—and she eased it open more slowly until there was enough space for each of them to squeeze through soundlessly. Beyond descended flagstone steps that led into an underground passageway lined with burial niches. She signalled the monk to follow her.

Dim torch lights set in cast iron wall brackets illuminated their way. Several times she paused and pointed to abandoned excavation tools. He nodded and motioned for her to keep going. Finally they came to a crypt that had been built under the chapel's original foundation 300 years before. Cobwebs clung inside the doorway. Catherine swept them aside as they stepped into the burial chamber. When she found the small petroleum lamp stored on one of the cubbyhole shelves, she took a matchstick out of the box kept beside it, lit the lantern and hung it from a rusty hook. Turning to speak to the monk, she found he had slipped his hood back from his face.

"Joachim!" she cried. "Oh my God, I don't believe it! Am I dreaming? First Marla. Now you!"

"What are you talking about?"

She went on with rambling excitement. "Joachim, Marla's still alive! I just saw her. An SS officer took her into Shell House."

"I told you not to go outside. Someone might recognize you."

"I didn't leave the convent. I was in the bell tower. I saw them from there."

She suddenly fell silent, struck with his actual presence and the joy of their reunion. "Oh Joachim!" she cried softly, and melted into his arms. "You're alive." Tears of relief streamed down her face. "I've been so worried."

He hugged her tightly, squeezing the breath out of her. "At long last I can hold you," he whispered and drew her even closer. They stood pressed together for a long time. When he eventually stood back and looked longingly into her radiant face, he murmured, "Let me feel your hair."

She gazed up at him with shining adoration, raised her hands and began unpinning her nun's veil. He slid his fingers under the edge and helped it fall to the ground. Never letting her eyes leave his, she then slipped the nun's tight wimple up over her head and let it drop to the ground. He shook her blonde hair free and tenderly held her face between his hands. "You are more beautiful than ever," he said and gently brushed her lips with his.

"Oh Joachim, I love you!" she cried and flung her arms around his neck. "There's nothing to hold us back any more."

He covered her face and hair with rapturous kisses. "My darling, my darling," he repeated. "I love you, I love you, I love you." His mouth closed over hers, and with years of longing, kissed her deeply and completely.

She swayed in his arms. "How much time do we

have?" she asked breathlessly when he released her.

"Four days."

"Four days!"

"Four, wonderful, enchanting days," he confirmed.

"But we must use this time to free Marla," she protested.

"A plan is already in the making," he assured her and playfully tweaked her nose. "This is to be our time, Catherine. Yours and mine." He wrapped her tightly in his arms again. "Let us not waste one precious moment," and dreamily hummed the Viennese Waltz in her ear. "May I have this dance, dear lady?" His hand slipped down her back.

"It would be my pleasure, sire."

Softly their voices hummed the lilting dance tune together as their bodies gracefully swayed and stepped to the waltz rhythm. Like dolls on top of a music box, they swirled and swirled, and when they finally stopped, Catherine looked shyly into Joachim's face. "Come with me. I have something to show you."

She led him to a lowered recess behind the tomb's shrine and tugged on an iron ring. A short metal door swung in. She bent down and passed inside. Joachim ducked and followed her. As his eyes adjusted to the dimness, he made out the bare outlines of a cot and a sidetable in the tiny storage chamber.

"The Mother Superior prepared it for me in case the Gestapo ever searched the convent. It's our room for as long as you stay with me," she told him softly.

He took her hand. "Are you sure this is what you want?"

"I've been sure since the first time we met. There's been no one else."

"Oh Catherine, my lovely Catherine," he whispered and drew her to him. "The war has cheated us of enough time."

"No matter what happens now, we will be a part of each other forever."

A single tear trickled down one side of his face as he took her in his arms. "You have no idea how often I dreamed of this. I want it to be beautiful for you," he said gently as he freed her from her robe.

The soft slant of the petroleum lamp from the main chamber fell on the spot where they stood. As their garments slipped down, piece by piece, their flesh gleamed in the surrounding darkness like gothic statues—perfect, beautiful works of art. Joachim lifted Catherine up and carried her to the cot. Their forms melted into the shadows, and there they made love with all the freedom of joyful lovers. When they were content to relax, Catherine snuggled in Joachim's arms.

"It can't be wrong to feel this happy," she said.

"It's never wrong to feel this happy."

"But something is wrong, Joachim. While we're safe in each other's arms, Marla is suffering God knows what horrors at the hands of the Gestapo."

Joachim sighed. "I know."

"You said you have a plan," she persisted.

"London has a plan," he corrected her with a heavy sadness and held her tighter.

"Are you going to tell me what it is?"

He gave in. "Sit up, Catherine." He pulled the blanket around them in Indian fashion. They rested their backs against the stone wall as he began talking.

"By the time I reached London and reported directly to Churchill, it was mid-November. Churchill and Stevens…"

"Who's Stevens?"

He paused, surprised. "You've never met the Chief of Allied Intelligence?"

"No. Amanita's section head is Sir Isaac."

"Indeed. Well, after I returned, Churchill turned me over to Stevens. They had already received an urgent message by courier from King Christian." He paused again. "Forty of Denmark's secret army chiefs have been captured by the Gestapo. They're detained in Shell House. Now that we know Marla is there for sure, and alive, the problem is even more serious. They all know the significance of Holbak's documents if the Nazis should accidentally recover them. Since none of the leaders were issued suicide pills, and Marla was tricked from using hers…"

"How do you know that?"

"I tried to rescue her before I left, but I was too late. Do you remember Col. Streicher?"

"No. Should I?"

"Probably not. He was at your recital in Berlin. At the time of Marla's arrest, he had just been appointed the commander of the SS in Copenhagen. He came to her cell while I was there and recognized her. When she came to, she remembered him as well and tried to bite down on the capsule, but he held her throat so she couldn't bite it and was forced to swallow it harmlessly."

Catherine curled up more tightly in his arms. She had long since thrown away her L-pill. "Churchill's naturally concerned that someone will break down under torture and reveal that Holbak's papers were lost at sea with the formulas that could build an atomic bomb."

"Right. There's more," he continued. "The chiefs also know the Underground's secret plans to keep German forces in Denmark policing General Workers' Strikes and sabotage actions. Stevens has come up with a scheme to rescue the chiefs that will now include Marla. It's very risky," he said flatly.

His arms tightened around Catherine again. "The plan is to use a low-level bombing raid to rupture the foundations of Shell House. The prisoners being held on the top floors will be able to escape while the Gestapo files in the bottom part of the building will be destroyed. If the records are not destroyed, the entire Danish Resistance may be wiped out, freeing 200,000 German troops stationed here to fight the allied armies closing in on Germany instead. Churchill has given the project to the RAF's Specialized Air Arm under Steven's command. He sent me back here to take photographs of the target from the sea. He needs them to solve the navigational problems for the air strike."

"Won't everybody be killed?"

"In theory, no." He fell quiet. "In reality..." He tried to shake free of the morbid thoughts gripping him. "In reality, the tactic is based on the same principle the Dam Busters used—making low level runs at high speed skipping eleven-second-delay bombs up the Nyhaven Canal to the base of Shell House. The building is made of reinforced concrete. By blasting the support pillars simultaneously, we can explode it so it will collapse like a deck of cards, from its base. The walls will break apart as the structure tumbles down. The main Gestapo garrison and their files on the ground floor will be buried under the rubble while the prisoners on the top six floors will simply walk out between the cracks in the walls."

"It sounds too easy."

"It's not foolproof," Joachim admitted. "What grieves me most is that we have to put you and the convent at risk. You're too close to the target."

"If you warn me of the attack in advance, I can evacuate the nuns and the girls to the crypt."

He shook his head. "That won't guarantee them safety from the bombs. What's worse, someone noticing the disappearance of the nuns and girls could alert the Gestapo. No. There can be no warning. If, for any reason, the Gestapo suspect an attack, the strike will be useless."

"We practise for bombing raids all the time. Why is this strike different?"

"There's too much at stake. The Germans still have time to build an atomic bomb if Holbak's papers are recovered, and reinforcements from Denmark along the German defense lines could turn the tide of war against us."

"I see," Catherine said. She had become quietly composed. "Then it must be done, Joachim. Marla's sacrifice for me must not be in vain. The lives of all those who have been sacrificed in an effort to prevent Hitler from building this terrible bomb must not be in vain. May God have mercy on us all."

And they continued to hold each other in solemn silence until desire stirred again, and they made love, slowly and wholly consummate.

Chapter Twenty Six

Friday, March 16th, 1945

MARLA SHIVERED. In the chilled air of Shell House's unheated attic floor, her teeth chattered endlessly. With her wrists handcuffed to the head of the cot and her ankles manacled to the foot, she could barely roll or flex her muscles to keep her blood circulating. Left chained like this, and naked, she fell into trembling fits of demented consciousness.

Feeling herself slipping under once more, she struggled and strained against the grinning skulls swarming, like cockroaches, all over her. They chanted and moaned with eerie howls. Between them, like a jack-in-a-box, Ulo's face bobbed up and down or, like a balloon, drifted in and out, all the while grinning madly, a gargoyle's mad grin painted on a gold mask.

"They're losers, Marla. All losers!"

His voice jeered. Crazy laughter followed as he would whisk the horrible mask away to reveal his pleading face underneath. "Who betrayed me, baby? Who set me up?"

She writhed and screamed. "For God's sake, let me go! Please let me die!"

His laughing face swam back. "They're losers, Marla. All losers!" Then his pleading face. "Who betrayed me, baby? Who set me up?"

"I dunno… I dunno… " She cried pitifully.

The laughing mask again. "They're losers, Marla. All losers!" The pleading face. "Who betrayed me, baby? Who set me up?"

A specter of death heads chanting sailed in and out of her murky consciousness where she floundered in burning pain and sulfurous smells that suffocated her. Sharp insistent raps broke through...a distant thumping ...hammering...pecking...a woodpecker in Shell House?! No, it was a woodpecker chipping away at her head. Clear consciousness wavered. Her eyes flickered open.

MORSE CODE! Someone was trying to tap out a message in Morse code. She struggled to concentrate on the staccato signals. *HOLD ON...RESCUE NEAR* ...There was a long pause before the tapping began again. *HOLD ON...RESCUE NEAR...*

Hope summoned her spirit, then distrust shoved it down. *It could be a Gestapo trick,* she told herself, *to make me feel hopeful...and safe...to get me to drop my guard. A trick...yes, it must be a trick...but if it's true...*

She resisted the urge to void. The scratchy blanket covering the mattress under her already stank of her urine and runny feces.

A key turned in the door lock. Her nerves screamed. Sweat squeezed out her palms. Her heart hammered her throat, and her stomach lurched and quivered. The heavy door squeaked. Lutz, her keeper, entered with her food tray and toiletries.

Tears leapfrogged down Marla's face. Her pressing bladder spasmed and emptied, saturating the towel under her. The sudden flood of urine soaking the rash of raw sores covering her bum caused her to cry out.

When Streicher tired of torturing her, he allowed Lutz to attend her once a day. This guard, who resembled a brutish-looking escapee from a prehistoric zoo, was the one respite from her misery she could look forward to.

He laid the tray on the floor beside her cot and sat down beside her. Surprisingly gentle, he lifted her head and spooned a little of the thin potato soup into her. She gagged and spat it out. Watery gruel dribbled down her chin. Lutz quickly wiped it away before he broke off a piece of stale hard bread and tried to feed it to her. The rock-sharp crust ripped at the ulcerated roof of her mouth, stinging her. She clamped her mouth shut and turned her head away from the food.

Lutz clucked. "*Essen sie.*" He wanted her to eat.

Marla stubbornly shook her head.

"*Bitte*," he begged.

She lay withdrawn. He dunked the piece of dry hard bread into the grey gruel and repeated gently, "*Bitte. Essen sie.*"

She turned her head back to look into the caring eyes of the big flat-headed German. He dipped the bread again and held it to her mouth. She belligerently tightened her lips. Patiently, he waited. When she tired, he gently eased the spongy bread into her sore mouth. She sucked out the juice and gratefully gulped it down. Eventually she chewed the mushy bit of bread and swallowed it down. He gave her the rest of the soup and bread the same way.

Afterwards, Lutz crooned to her while he tenderly

sponged her skin and gingerly cleansed the lesions inflicted during Streicher's interrogations. As if she were a baby, he also changed her makeshift diaper of thick towelling.

Just as he finished, the key turned in the lock again, and the door flung wide open. Streicher loomed in the doorway. Immediately, the room reeked of his garlic breath.

Marla stared at him in sick horror. Everything within her cried out. "*No more...no more...no more...*"

He stormed up to her cot and glared down on her humiliating nakedness. "While the Third Reich fights for its life, you lie here sneering!"

Her head shook spastically. "*NOoo...nooo...*," she whimpered.

"You think I don't know who sent you!" he raged. Every day he had been growing more and more obsessed with who sent her to replace Catherine. "You think I don't know why you are here!" He smirked and began his ritualistic pacing.

"That traitor in London takes me for a fool. A fool! He dangles caviar and sends me worms. You are another of his rotten worms. An impostor. Holbak's gone, and I am left with a *Red whore*!"

He stopped and approached her again. "You hid Dr. Holbak's notes…his blueprints for the atomic bomb, didn't you? I know you were sent to hide them before you were delivered to me. What did you do with them? Where did you hide them? *Tell* me!"

"*NOOooo...*," she mewed. Her cringing denial spurred him on.

"With Holbak's formula, Germany can rise again. It's not too late. It's not! We shall find his blueprints and make the atomic bomb. We will stop the Allies from taking Berlin. Our time is not yet over! We will reign one thousand years!"

Abruptly, Streicher's mood shifted. He calmed down. "I have sent men to dismantle Holbak's lab and to search his house."

Good luck! Marla mentally mocked him. The panic that had tightened her chest was gradually giving way to an inner core of steel.

"We shall find his notes whether you talk or not." Streicher licked his words like a panther finishing his feast. "I suggest you co-operate and make it easier for yourself. For you, the war is over."

Over? The ghostly image of Ulo flashed in front of her. Standing strong and tall with his arms outstretched, he was reaching out to her, welcoming her. She rose up. They came together laughing, laughing hysterically at the vain Nazi. Stripping down the doctor's lab and house was he! *Dig, you bastard, dig*! They wildly applauded him.

Streicher's leering face zoomed in on their private joke. The mad desire to laugh gurgled in Marla's throat. This demon towering over her was no joke. He threatened all life, not just hers. *Ask, you bastard! Go ahead and ask. Ask! ASK! ASK!*

She knew what he wanted to know, but he could not get inside her thoughts. No one could. If she did not want to tell him, he had one great big goose egg. *NOTHING. Absolutely nothing!* She was not going to let him in on her and Ulo's private joke. *The doctor's papers are lost. Somewhere out on the sea, they are drifting, drifting, drifting, along to some unknown shore. Isn't that funny, you bastard? The joke's on you.*

Her spirit soared with sudden jubilation. Silence was her finest weapon. It would pass with her into Ulo's safe arms on the other side of hell.

Streicher saw Marla's resolve to resist brighten the whites of her eyes. He cursed and ordered Lutz to bring in the gurney. Like a whipped slave, Lutz did his bidding. When he had wheeled in the stretcher, he unbound Marla from the cot and lifted her shaking body onto it, then he strapped her feet into the steel-cold stirrups. She lay submissively while Lutz wrapped a clean white sheet snugly around her. Its thin warmth enshrouded her. Hungrily, she drank in its lingering clean scent, a fresh sweetness like a fleeting reprieve from the sourness of her soiled blanket.

Streicher instructed Lutz to wheel her up and down the hall outside. The scratchy squeak and rattle of the gurney's unoiled wheels played on the nerves of the prisoners confined in other cells on the top floor of Shell House.

At seven o'clock that night, the BBC blared over the loudspeaker through the dimly lit corridor. Suddenly, Marla was listening to Catherine's easy chatter on the air. Homesick tears stung her eyes. Catherine's voice reached out and touched her, as if she were there beside her, soothing her and stroking her with every word, carrying her away from the torment of her ceaseless nightmare.

Remembering their kidding while they prerecorded the ridiculous ditty now on the air, Marla smiled. From behind her, Streicher said softly, " Amusing is it? Is it also amusing that secret codes are hidden in every *Ditties For Dotties* dear Catherine broadcasts."

Marla's smile died.

"Someone here knows what the message in this ditty means," he said. "By morning, I will know too."

At her stunned surprise, he broke into diabolical laughter. She had no idea what the code meant. But the resistance fighter, who had been deliberately betrayed to get him inside Shell House to warn the others of the planned breakout, did. It was the *GO* signal to the Danish Underground.

In the hallway, Streicher relentlessly questioned Marla. Every prisoner on the top floor could hear her interrogation. Her silent responses drummed on their nerves. They feared for her sanity and were thankful for her resilience. Impatient with her tenacious refusal to talk, Streicher finally lit up one cigarette after another and began grinding the burning butts into Marla's cheeks to punish her each time she resisted. All night long the other prisoners were subjected to her pathetic screams until their own endurance threatened to give way.

When morning came and she still had not talked, Streicher pronounced, "The witch's allure to control men's fate was in your beautiful face. Now all men will look upon you with revulsion."

Chapter Twenty Seven

Monday, March 19th, 1945

THE STREET VENDOR, barely glancing at the young German soldier standing outside the convent gate, shuffled his cart over the cobblestones, but the nerve-chilling tingles running up and down his spine proved he was aware of every movement the Waffen-SS troops were making in and out of the Shell House square. He was monitoring any unusual activity in the Gestapo block. His deceptive apathy was the result of rigid discipline over the hate he felt for the enemy who had occupied his land and terrorized his people. The time for revenge would come. He only needed to be patient. *All things come to those who wait. Patience*, the vendor reminded himself as he continued down the old back street and out of the soldier's view, but his tightly controlled hate electrified the distance growing between them.

The young German ignored the slow plodding Dane. Beautiful organ music drifting out between the beech trees behind the convent gate distracted him. He stood spellbound as a forgotten yearning triggered memories of a time when his parents took him to their parish church in the Saar Valley, to the heady smell of incense and aromatic altar flowers, to the glorious choral music, to the *rainbow ring of light*, that awesome shaft of sunlight beaming down from the stained glass window arched over the altar.

As a little boy, he believed the *rainbow ring of light* was a ladder dropped from heaven. For, at every service he attended, it seemed to beam down just as the priest was about to start his sermon. The warm light would wrap the priest in a cloak of gold. Likc magic, it bronzed his face and expressive hands. That's what he thought "to be blessed" meant—to be bronzed by the *rainbow ring of light*. This wondrous effect prompted his deep down longing to see the face of God. What did *He* really look like?

One Sunday, when he could no longer withstand the urge to climb up the magical ladder the way Jack had climbed the beanstalk, he slipped out of the family pew and ran up the center aisle. But when he reached the chancel steps, the *rainbow ring of light* disappeared. Around and around he spun, searching upwards for the heaven-sent ladder until, utterly dizzy and flustered, his little arms sprung upward and he cried, "God, are You up there?" His father then scooped him up and rushed him out of the church.

No one ever explained to him what he had done that was so wrong. Once he knew he could not climb the magical ladder, however, the *rainbow ring of light* ceased to enchant him. Through his years in the Hitler Youth, he had forgotten his original fascination with God until this moment, when he heard the organ music coming from the convent chapel.

Impulsively, he slid through the unlocked iron gates of the convent and crept along the cloistered corridor leading to the chapel. He entered unnoticed and tiptoed up the side aisle, keeping well hidden within the pillars' shadows as he went. From the steeple tower, diffused rays of sunshine spilled down upon a group of schoolgirls ringed around a lovely nun playing the organ. Their clear sweet voices stirred that long ago yearning to see the face of God.

As he leaned closer to absorb the lilting music, his rifle butt clanged against the stone buttress. Instantly, the music stopped, and all eyes converged on him. The older girls, recognizing he was a soldier, stared at him, frightened, while the younger ones studied him curiously. One cherub with bright brown eyes and fawn-colored curls piped up, "What are you doing here? This is God's house." She spoke in flawless German.

Feeling foolish, he stammered, "I…I don't mean to intrude. It's the music. It's beautiful." He turned to the nun. "Please don't stop playing, Sister."

The nun masked her alarm with a shy smile. The cherub spoke out again. "Sister Angelique has taken the Vow of Silence. She cannot speak to you."

"A Vow of Silence? You mean she can never talk?" He stepped up closer to the circle of students who quietly tightened their ring around the nun.

The little one with tousled curls nodded very solemnly. "She can never talk because she is listening for the Voice of God. He dwells inside her. If she talks, she will not hear Him."

Catherine, dressed in this nun's habit, marvelled at the seriousness of the little girl's answer. Her heart quickened. She didn't want anything to happen to these precious children because they were protecting her.

"The Sister plays the organ while you sing. Will not the sound of your music hide the Lord's voice?"

All at once a bell shrilled. The German soldier's

question hung unanswered in the excitement of dismal. An impish twinkle filled his eyes as the girls rushed to form a line and waited expectantly for the nun's nod. He could remember how he eagerly looked to the end of the school day so he could play outside with his friends. At her gracious signal, they quickly filed out, leaving him and the nun alone.

Catherine gave silent thanks for the dismissal bell. A more persistent soldier would have pursued the flaw in the little girl's story. Fleecy fuzz beginning to sprout over his upper lip made her regret that she wasn't the nun he believed she was.

He grinned sheepishly. "Sister Angelique…Oh!"

He stopped himself. The child had said she took a Vow of Silence. He couldn't imagine anyone choosing not to talk. "Sister Angelique," he said instead, "I wish you could talk." Despair pursed his brow. "There are so many things I need to understand."

Catherine reached out and touched his arm. With her other hand, she pointed to the waterfall of light spilling over the altar.

He stared. It was the *rainbow ring of light.*

Catherine saw an expression of awe wash over his face, softening his boyish features even more. Above him, hanging on the wall, was an icon of Jesus. Glancing up at it and then at him, Catherine was caught up in the gentle innocence reflected in the young German soldier's face under the Lord's picture. She carried on playing the organ and watched him as he listened to the music. He seemed lost in another time, in another world. His vulnerability touched Catherine's heart.

This soldier was not her enemy. When she looked into his eyes, she saw a boy chasing a butterfly, trying to capture it in a bottle, so he could keep it with him always. But, once trapped inside his bottle, it fluttered and died. He did not understand what he had done wrong. What is free cannot be kept under glass and survive. Love is like that butterfly, she thought. It needs the freedom of an open heart to thrive.

A final silence trailed after the last lingering note of the music died. Tears glistened in the young soldier's eyes. For a moment, he was too moved to speak. He turned to her in gratitude.

Catherine gently smiled at him. Her glowing face was filled with such all-embracing love that he felt warmed and cherished by it, as if she had wrapped him in the *rainbow ring of light* itself. Many times, through the dark days of humiliation and recrimination to come, he would look back on this moment when he saw the clear love of God shining in the face of the woman he believed to be a nun and be comforted.

The squeak of the chancel door startled him. The abbess emerged. He nervously bowed his head and hastily withdrew. When he was safely out of sight, the Mother Superior softly approached Catherine. "Is Hitler so desperate for men he must recruit boys?" she asked. "What did he want?"

"To listen to our music."

"Is that all?"

"Yes," Catherine said. "That is all."

"How can you be sure?"

Catherine looked away, first at the altar and then above it, to the funnel of shimmering sunlight streaming down from the chancel's stained glass window. The light was so alive with magical colors that it danced and swirled in a prism of spinning glory.

"I'm sure," she said. "He was only a homesick boy."

"I hope you're right."

Sad doubt in the voice of the abbess brought Catherine's full attention back to her. "Something is troubling you, Mother Superior. What is it?"

The abbess resolutely stiffened. "Catherine, I wasn't planning on worrying you, but that soldier's visit today has changed my mind. The Gestapo is circulating a poster with a drawing of you. Many of the girls here know you are the British agent in the picture."

"Oh no!" cried out Catherine in alarm. "My presence endangers everyone. I must leave at once. If I am caught here, who knows what terrible reprisals there may be against you and the convent!"

The abbess shook her head. "I didn't tell you this to make you leave. Quite the contrary. Our girls are Danes, and as Danes they will not betray you. It's crucial you stay here, but you must be more careful. Chance meetings like this one with the soldier are too risky. If he sees the poster, he may recognize you and turn you in."

"I understand, Mother Superior. I shall be most careful."

But once again, the specter of pearly sunbeams twirling over the altar caught her eye, and she felt protected as she watched the interchanging rays, in their own celebration of life, become a divine ring of light.

Chapter Twenty Eight

Wednesday, March 21st, 1945

SHORTLY BEFORE DAWN, three flights of De Havilland Mosquitoes lifted off from Norfolk and headed across to the English coastline and on out to the North Sea. Flying these long range fighter-bombers were 21 select pilots from the 2nd Tactical Air Command.

For the strike on Gestapo Headquarters at Shell House, Air Chief Marshall Smith had chosen B.MK XVI models because of their superior versatility. At high speeds, their controls did not *harden*. They could dive and turn in evasive actions very easily, but like royally bred race horses, they needed the handling of highly trained, very competent air jockeys to guide them through the critically timed attack on Shell House. Their two supercharged Rolls-Royce Merlin engines generated maximum speeds of up to 410 miles per hour and, if necessary, with their pressurized cabins, the Mosquitoes could climb up to 38,000 feet on their way home to escape Luftwaffe fighters, which Smith expected would descend on them like angry hornets after the raid.

Over the North Sea, a half gale squalled making navigation difficult. Sea salt clung to the Mosquitoes' wind screens, blocking their navigators' views of the necessary visual checks to keep them on course as they flew, rocking and buffeting barely over the wave tops. Despite the frightening risk of turbulent and unpredictable winds throwing their aircraft loaded with fire bombs and skipping bombs into the grasping sea, no one wanted to turn back. And so, they powered on, trusting their compasses and their adjusted calculations on the wind factor to keep them on course.

ON THE TOP FLOOR OF SHELL HOUSE, in one of the smaller interrogation rooms, Streicher badgered Marla with questions. At one o'clock in the morning, he had ordered Lutz to drag her out of her cell for another all-night session. For the past three hours, she had stood on her feet, refusing to answer him. Some inner resilience held her together, enduring the fatigue and the pain of standing continually straight until she had grown numb and immune to her own discomfort.

Suddenly changing the direction of his questions, Streicher snarled. "Do you know how we recognize Jews?"

The sunken hollows above her cheeks fixed on him curiously. Her fear had long since died. What more could he do to her than he had already done? She felt like a shell of a being abandoned on a desert where only the occasional tumbleweed whisked up dried-out feelings. She watched him draw out an envelope from his desk and open it. He pulled out an enlarged photograph and wordlessly handed it to her. She took it, and immediately, when she looked at it, her hands began shaking.

Shrewdly, like a fox snaring a hound, Streicher

observed her reaction and congratulated himself. He had found a weakness. He could break through her defenses.

In the picture, naked Jews stood in a pit. Though the lighting was poor, their skeletal shapes and bleak faces were distinguishable, like ghastly masks, each one cut with two black holes staring emptily into the eye of the camera and an open canyon resembling lips contorted in soundless and endless screams. The silence of their mass horror shattered her ears. They were calling to her again. The ghosts of her nightmare.

Streicher shook his head contemptuously. "Such pitiful disbelief caught in the midst of an execution! A sheer work of art, don't you think?"

He gloated and, like the director he believed he was, went on to describe the scene from behind his camera.

"The wretches dig and dig…down down down into the bowels of the earth until their graves are dug…I raise my camera…the rim of guards separate…and the machine guns appear over the top. The miserable cowards look up and see them. At precisely the same instant as the machine guns fire, I click my camera and PRESTO! This moment of time is locked in history. The Great Reich's *Final Solution* to its Jewish problem." His upper lip curled in a sneer.

The startling similarity to her nightmare ripped open Marla's dulled sanity. She stared and tottered. The picture fell from her numb fingers onto the floor, and animal-like mews gurgled from her throat.

Satisfied he was pressing her mind to the brink, Streicher sadistically toyed with her, savoring her delicate edge of invading madness. He steadily tapped on the top of his desk trying to drive Marla to a primal scream of pure desperation.

"Precise and meticulous timing," he droned on in a flat voice. His square-shaped fingers continued their relentless drumming. With barely a break in the rhythm, he pointed to a silver frame sitting face down on his desk. "Pick it up," he ordered her.

She blinked, unresponsive. She watched his pupils distend, and blue veins bulge in nasty ridges across the oily planes of his shark-like features. His frustration awakened her to the carefully chained Jekyll within him straining to break loose, and she regained a sense of control.

"Pick it up," he growled more viciously.

She stared ahead, passively defying him. His drumming fingers stopped. Dead sound stretched between them. In it, Marla heard the pounding of her own heart thumping inside her chest. The beat echoed like a war cry within her head, rallying her spirit. Streicher's silence was more menacing than his tantrums. She stiffened in readiness.

Grabbing up the silver frame from his desk, he leaned across to her unyielding body and jabbed it into her midriff with a force so hard that it knocked the breath out of her. She grunted. At the same time as he thrust it into her outstretched hands, a reflex action jerked her arms upward. She grasped for the silver frame before she could control her automatic response.

"Precise and meticulous timing," he hissed.

She opened her hands. The crash of the metallic frame hitting the marble floor and the sound of the mirror splintering exploded between them.

"Precise and meticulous timing," Marla repeated evenly.

The rage behind his eyes swelled with scorn, then abruptly, his expression resumed a placid set. Rocking back on his heels, he contemplated her coldly. He moved slowly around the desk, never taking his eyes off of her, and carefully picked up one of the largest shards from the floor.

"It's bad luck to break a mirror, you know. Seven years bad luck," Streicher said very quietly, standing and facing her directly. His repulsive garlic breath overpowered her, and despite her resolve to keep rigid control of herself, she grimaced with disgust and drew back from him.

The sniff of another small triumph spread into Streicher's hooded eyes. They gleamed with fanatic fire as he reached around behind her head and yanked her hair without warning. With a murderous grip, he pulled on her hair roots until their nerve ends shrieked in protest.

"Do you know what a Jew looks like?" he rasped savagely. "*Do you?*" He roughly shoved the jagged fragment of mirror in front of her eyes and jeered. "*LIKE THIS!*"

She stared at herself in horror. Shrunken dark hollows stared back at her from the reflection. What Marla saw belonged to a wasted creature. Lifeless strangles of bleached hair fell from a scaly scalp down the sides of a sickly grey mask made of dried parchment stretched over a bony mold. Festering scabs pitted gaunt cheeks. There was no mouth, only a dried crack that shivered like an earthquake about to split open the orb fastened to a skeleton. He was trying to trick her again! This was not the face of a Jew. This was not the face of anyone human!

As Marla's eyes grew in horrified recognition, they rounded into bleaker and deeper holes until the walls protecting her sanity collapsed and the similarity between her and the wretches in the photograph became one and the same image in her mind. The mouth in the mirror shook.

"*NOOooooo....!*" Marla whimpered. "*NOooo... nooo... no.* That's *not* me!" she denied desperately over and over again.

It was as if she were standing on the edge of a tremendous cliff, looking down into the *Pit of Hell*, exactly as it had been in her dream. Only then she awoke, and the tortured souls with the faceless and voiceless mouths disappeared. Now, in Streicher's mirror, they claimed her as their own. Her silent wails matched theirs as she fainted into their bottomless pit of obscurity. Above her slumped form, Streicher's satanic laughter peeled loose.

THE MOSQUITOES were flying over their first checkpoint on the west coast of Denmark's Jutland, Esbjerg. Below them, fishing smacks rolled on the foamy sea. The storm clouds had lifted, and the rising sun was like a blazing cannon firing copper flames across their wing tips. They flew so low weaving between the tree tops and over the power lines, even a pimple could be seen on the face of the cheering Danes waving to them along their flight path. As they drew closer to the east coast and Kolding, their second checkpoint, they skimmed over acres of farmers' fields and lacy woods.

Spread out in single-file formation so that each of the pilots could see the other's hand signals, the extremely agile, lightning fast fighter-bombers dipped under the enemy's radar and avoided detection. The surprise of their bold morning attack depended on absolute radio silence.

In the lead plane, the navigator quickly calculated on his knee pad and touched the shoulder of his commander. "We're exactly on time, sir," he reported.

The commander nodded and grinned.

STREICHER eased Marla's dead weight into a straight back chair leaning against the wall and squirted some water on her face. When she groaned, he raised a glass of water to her lips. Feeling the coolness, she opened her mouth and licked the refreshing wetness. A sudden thirst demanded to be satisfied. Even though her mind had slipped into the depths of hopeless despair, her heart insisted she endure, and she gulped for more water. Slobbering rivulets trickled down her chin as she slurped for each mouthful. When her thirst was quenched, she waved her hand to signal *no more* and slumped back into the chair, fully conscious now.

The memory of her face in the mirror flooded her mind, and she hung her head. She was the ugliest sight she had ever seen. This crazy insistence on living was stupid! For what? Streicher had ruined her looks and her body. She wasn't a woman any more. She was a freak! A freak who refused to die! She winced in disgust. Every reason to live had been taken from her. Ulo. Her self-respect. Her self-image. And Waldemar too. What began in decadence and self-depredation grew into something beautifully intimate between them. In the end, he loved her as much as Ulo had, and Streicher had savagely executed him. *Why doesn't he kill me and be done with it? Lord, I'd welcome death. Why do I keep hanging on?*

Uncharacteristically quiet, Streicher sat the water glass down on the desk where she could reach it and returned to his own side. He seemed to drag the swish of his tail over his seat, like a shark settling down to spawn, before he sank down into the deep cushion and squirmed himself into the shape of his chair.

He snorted. "I've broken you, but I've never made you talk." His shoulders slumped, and he heaved a defeated sigh. "Who is the victor and who is the victim, *ja*?" He shrugged. "Oh well, what does it matter? For us the game is over."

He lapsed into sullen silence. In his lap, his gill-like fingers zipped together like a row of fish hooks while his thumbs idly rotated around each other like boat propellers. He carried on talking as if he had forgotten she was there.

"I'm going to escape to Argentina, but before I melt into the dark corners of South America, I am going to find that son-of-a-bitch traitor in London who made a fool of me. Because of him, I lost face with my Fuhrer. Because of him, I was sent to those filthy death camps in Poland. Twice Himmler transferred me back here. Twice Eichmann ordered my return to establish more efficient procedures for trafficking the trainloads of miserable, smelly Jews in and out of the camps. We needed those trains to transport our troops…to bring reinforcements to the two fronts… but the Jews kept pouring in and pouring in from all over Europe…trainload after trainload of stinking Jews. I did not think there could be so many…"

His voice trailed off. "We had the world at our feet. We should be the victors. Not you, with your pitiful cow's eyes."

His jaw twitched. "I should have recognized you were a Jew at once. All Jews have the same cow's eyes. They shuffle to their deaths as if they don't know what is happening…except for their cow's eyes staring back...never accusing...accepting...silently...like stupid cows lining up for the slaughter."

He casually arched his back and stretched. "Tell me, are you all cowards? Why would you not try to save yourselves when you had the chance?"

Marla stared at him blankly.

"Ah, *ja*. I had forgotten. No one else wanted our filthy Jews when we tried to deport them. So, while we rid the world of its Jewish problem, we cannot supply our troops with reinforcements. So, for the sake of the Jews, we lose the war again. Ironic, *ja*? And yet, the Fuhrer seems to think we can stop the Allies. He still believes he can win the war. Without the atomic bomb, how can he? Funny, *ja*?"

His face grew grim and hard set. "Funny? *Nein*! One man stopped us from producing the atomic bomb. *One man*!" His fingers drummed the top of his desk again. "*RUFUS!*"

Marla stared. Shock charged her root hairs.

"With some difficulty, I have finally learned the British code name of Canaris' double agent. *RUFUS*. But I couldn't track down his personal records to help me identify him. No doubt the Abwehr destroyed them before the SD took over Military Intelligence. So, it is more difficult to find him. But not impossible."

He paused, then spat out the words: "*I want that bastard!* Tell me. Do you know who this *RUFUS* could be?"

Marla mind whirled. *RUFUS* was Sir Isaac's code name.

"Did you know he sent me our contact codes in those crazy *Ditties For Dotties* the real Lady Catherine produces on her show?" He read the startled look in

Marla's eyes. Then it hit him. "You didn't know, did you?"

Streicher softly cackled. "That bastard's been stringing you along at the same time as he's been betraying me, hasn't he?"

Clearly confused, a pain more searing than physical torture surged through Marla's mind. Sir Isaac. Could he really have betrayed them? A double agent for German Military Intelligence and a triple agent for Moscow? The idea was ludicrous! Yet, he was the one to convince Churchill and Stevens to send Catherine to Denmark to contact *Watchdog* and to persuade Dr. Holbak to flee to England. He engineered the operational details of Tobin's and Ulo's caper when they blew up the Germans' heavy water in the North Sea. Did he betray Ulo? Why? Why destroy *Project Amanita*? It was his baby from the start. He picked the scientists and recruited the agents. He was Churchill's confidant.

"Tell me who *RUFUS* is, Marla," Streicher urged. "Let me avenge us both."

For a fleeting second, he thought he saw a flicker, but in the next instant, he was not sure what he had seen. The invisible veil that dulled her eyes had dropped over them again.

"I want him, Marla. I want *RUFUS*. He robbed the Third Reich of its thousand years of golden rule, and when I find him after the war, I am going to kill him. When he thinks he is safe, when he believes he has fooled everyone, that is the precise moment when I shall kill him." His eyes flared with anticipation.

"I shall relish watching him die…slowly…with the agony he deserves."

Marla kept her silence, but inside she raged. *RUFUS* was Sir Isaac. For Ulo, for Catherine, for herself, for every agent betrayed, she ached to confront him, to let him see what Streicher had done to her. She had as much right to be his judge and executioner as Streicher did, but she would obviously not live to see such a day. Streicher was finished with her.

It would be easy to tell Streicher what he wanted to know, she admitted to herself, to tell him *RUFUS* is Sir Isaac Malcolm, SOE's Director of *Project Amanita*. Certainly the traitor deserved a slow death, slow and torturous, one that was branded with Streicher's style of savagery, yet she could not tell him. A deeper integrity, an abiding belief in the "innocent-until-proven-guilty" overrode the bitter and vindictive hate she felt and held her back from saying the words that would condemn Sir Isaac to death. Grimly she gritted her teeth.

The rims of Streicher's hooded eyelids perceptibly narrowed. His jaw clenched, and his veins, like little moles burrowing under his taunt temples, twisted and knotted. His chilling gaze locked on Marla. In a silent struggle of wills, they stubbornly stared each other down. He waited. Eventually he heaved a great embattled sigh and gave in.

"Have it your way…stupid though it is. You could save yourself. I no longer have any quarrel with you. We're on the same side."

Marla's expression remained inscrutable.

"Well, then," he said, "you leave me no choice." He rose to his feet.

"I will issue your execution order for tomorrow morning at dawn."

Marla listened to her sentence with apparent indifference.

"In a way, I regret that our relationship must end

like this. You have been a worthy adversary, Marla Franklin…even for a Jew."

The hint of a derisive twinkle flashed in the sunken hollows over her cheeks. Streicher caught it, and with unexpected misgivings, added, "I promise you, Marla, I will find the London traitor. I don't know why you are protecting him, but he has never been worth the price you are paying."

He rang for thc guard outside the door to the interrogation room. "Lutz can prepare you" were his last words to her.

Chapter Twenty Nine

BY NOW, THE THREE WAVES OF MOSQUITOES along with their fighter cover of 30 Mustangs were hedge-hopping their way across the island of Funen over the Great Belt to Zealand and were closing on their target. They had just passed their third checkpoint—Odense, the island's capital and the original home of the 19th Century master of fairy tales, Hans Christian Andersen. A simple cobbler's son, he would have been dismayed to know the armada flying overhead, on the last leg of its journey, was destined to drop fiery death on his beloved Copenhagen.

Disguised as fishermen, Joachim von Daren and Christopher Tobin rested their bicycles against the stone wall fence of St. Joan's. Through the back streets leading into the square between Shell House and the convent straggled other men. Some dragged vegetable carts or market wagons while others shuffled along carrying lunch pails, pretending to be workers on their way to the docks. A baker's truck stuttered…coughed…and died, blocking the roadway to the loading ramp behind the Gestapo building.

A young German soldier, seeming distracted in thought, saw nothing strange in the congregation of local Danes gathering as he crossed the square. The closer he came to the front steps of Gestapo Headquarters, the slower he walked until he reached the foot of the stairs and stopped. He drew a folded piece of paper from his pant pocket and smoothed it open with his hands. It was the poster of Catherine.

Just then, Streicher opened the main door and strode out on the landing. The German soldier looked up at the imposing SS officer and back to the poster. It said the woman was an escaped British agent. If anyone recognized her they were to report to the Gestapo at once. The features that seemed so familiar in the drawing suddenly blurred and transformed into the serene face of the nun he had found in the chapel. The memory of her all-embracing love wrapped him up again in the warmth of her smile. She couldn't be the enemy, he thought. She just couldn't.

"Damn!" swore Tobin by the convent wall, as he pulled his cap lower over his face.

"What's wrong?" Joachim asked warily, scrutinizing the square for trouble.

"Would you look at the front steps? Blast! Why couldn't he wait another 10 minutes?"

Joachim focused on the Gestapo entrance and spotted Streicher. He raised an eyebrow in surprise. How could Tobin know Streicher? Suddenly he remembered Catherine's recital at the Berlin Press Club. Tobin had been there, with Marla Franklin. So had Streicher. No doubt, in pre-war Germany, the journalist and Berlin's head of security had crossed paths many times.

As Streicher began descending the steps, the young German soldier looked up into his hard cold eyes and nervously toyed with the poster he held. The closer Streicher drew to him, the more he fingered the paper until Streicher's menacing shape towered above him. In that instant he hurriedly crunched the paper up into a ball and stuffed it back into his hip pocket before he snapped to attention and saluted, *Heil Hitler*.

Streicher regarded the young soldier with less than his usual arrogance. "Are you lost, soldier?"

"*Nein... ja, mein Standartenfuhrer*," he changed his mind sheepishly. "I'm looking for my unit."

Streicher peered at him more closely. "How old are you?" he demanded.

"Fourteen."

"*Mein Gott!*" Streicher said, taken aback. "Now children defend the fatherland." He shook his head in disbelief and brushed past the young soldier as if he didn't exist.

Joachim, anxiously watching this exchange from across the square, bent over his bicycle as if he were checking the air in the tires. "What's he doing now?" he asked Tobin.

"Staring at us," Tobin said without moving his lips and squatted down to help him examine the tire. "Everyone's in position."

"I know. I saw them."

Tobin covertly watched Streicher. "Shit! He's walking right toward us!"

"That bastard has the nose of a vulture," Joachim said, tensing for action. "We can't take him without giving everything away."

"Hang on. He's changing direction. God, no! He's checking the gate of the convent. The gate's open. He's going inside!"

Catherine! Joachim silently cried. With a sick heart, he helplessly watched the gate swing shut behind the disappearing figure of Streicher.

COLONEL STREICHER could not explain why he found himself walking through the grounds of the Catholic convent. He wanted something, but he didn't know what. Weeks of intensely questioning Marla had unsettled him as interrogating no other prisoner had. No matter what he did, the whore never broke. He still believed she was the key to Holbak's papers. What she knew could have restored glory to Germany. He was sure of it. Just as he was equally sure she could tell him who *RUFUS* was. All he had was this code name of the London informant from Canaris' records, but the woman had recognized it. For a fleeting second, he had discerned a deep inner hatred flash in those haunted eyes. It was so fleeting he could almost believe he was mistaken, except for that brief reaction, which had been enough to renew her will against him.

He stopped and looked around. Frustrated misery filled him, and he sighed, a deep heavy sigh. Just as he thought he had won, he had lost. To the very end, the whore was holding out in silence. Begrudgingly, he had to respect her. She had beaten him and executing her tomorrow morning ended their game of wills. He would miss it, he mused. The challenge of testing the human threshold for pain consumed him. Some people cracked so easily. Others, like Marla, endured. He had yet to understand why, and not understanding it further depressed him. He strolled aimlessly under the beech trees, feeling more and more disturbed. The serenity of the spiritual sanctuary irked him. It was *too* quiet. The demons within him shrank from its hallowed seclusion and hounded him to flee back to the vexing noises of his confusing world, to the stimulation of disruption and disharmony. He wheeled around and quickened his pace back the way he had come. Whatever he had hoped to find was not here.

Suddenly, in the midst of his retreat, the laughing voices of children halted him. He peeked through the shrubs. A group of little girls were playing nursery games in the garden. In the center of their circle was a nun, a very beautiful nun. Fascinated, he moved out of his hiding place and drew closer and closer, until he was so close one little girl spotted him and screeched in terror. The girls broke up their game and scurried to the shelter of the nun's habit, grasping for bits of her robe to cling to as they stared up at him with enormous eyes of fright.

He noticed none of this. He saw only the nun and the purity of her Aryan beauty. He was spellbound. Her calm eyes challenged him. He knew that look of serenity. He searched back through his memory. If he had seen her before, he would recall it. She stood before him, so poised. Her composure triggered a memory. He mentally watched himself open a folder. Inside there was a newspaper clipping…a blurred photo. He focused on the heading underneath…LADY CATHERINE DAZZLES BERLIN. In his mind's eye, he also saw a sketch of the pianist sent anonymously to Richter before he arrested the woman he thought was her.

Streicher caught his breath. Had the London

informant been telling the truth? Had Lady Catherine been under his nose the whole time? Damn the British! How deviously cunning! He bitterly raged to himself. What stroke of luck delivered her to him now of all times? He reached out and grabbed her.

At the same time, the little girls pointed behind him and screamed. "*Sister Angelique! The planes come! The planes come!*"

Streicher glanced behind him and gazed aghast at the belly of a Mosquito fighter bomber peeling off over the trees bordering the chapel. Its Merlin engines whined as the earth shook beneath them. "*NO!*" he gasped in disbelief.

Catherine tried to wrench herself free of his grip. He clamped down harder, with vicious strength, and started dragging her toward the convent gate. "Let me go!" she cried and kicked.

Mosquito after Mosquito swooped over the convent. Cowering under the ear splitting noise, the little girls seemed rooted in the garden watching the awesome sight. Thud after thud rained, then a terrible thundering and the ground quaked with aftershocks from the bombings. Belches of fire and smoke puffed above the centurion trees guarding the convent.

Catherine desperately struggled with Streicher. "The children! The children! I have to get the children!"

He muffled her mouth and yanked her around to face him. "*Never!*" he spat. Hypnotic hate galvanized his actions, but as he raised his fist to strike her, there was a crack second when his chin was vulnerable. Instinctively, Catherine responded to her conditioned training and rammed the heel of her free hand upward to smash his jaw. Caught off guard, he reeled backwards.

His grip loosened. She broke free and ran towards the children in the garden. He staggered after her. Flashing a quick glance over her shoulder to see if he were following, she was horrified to see a plane chasing her with its starboard wing clipped like a broken bird.

She yelled at the girls. "*TAKE COVER!*" When they didn't react, she hoisted her habit and, bursting into manic speed, raced to reach them. Her black robes billowed behind her. Overhead the busted bird screeched and nosed directly toward the convent.

"*NOOOooo......! NOT the children!*" she screamed.

Her agonized cry fell on deafened silence as the wounded Mosquito plowed into its midst. A moment of stillness preceded the monstrous explosion that ripped the morning sky.

In the garden, the blast whipped Catherine and the girls up like rag dolls in a whirlwind and, when the force was spent, threw their bodies over the courtyard like freshly scattered seeds. Their last vision of the convent was a brilliant flash of light before darkness consumed them.

As Streicher dashed to escape the impact, he tripped and fell. The tumble saved his life. The blast that uprooted the tree nearest him hurled it across his path. As it came crashing down, one of its snapped-off twigs snagged his Death Head's cap. In the flurry of forces battering the land, his cap waved playfully back and forth. He watched it stupidly.

INSIDE SHELL HOUSE, Marla was reclining on her cot escaping thoughts of her execution by making up silly ditties, senseless verses that subconsciously rose up from her relentless core of survival that refused to give in. Earlier, when she was standing before her tormentor, she had prayed for death. Now she wanted to live.

*RUFUS...RUFUS...RUFUS...*she repeated over and over again, training her mind on the sheer idiocy of words she could shape into something that rhymed, no matter how inane their meaning.

Rufus...Rufus...Rufus...
Is an imbecile and a poop is.
He cuts off your leg and says,
"What a bag!"
Rufus
The poop is
A gag.

"There, that's more like it," she decided, when the building mysteriously shook, and an ear-splitting *SWOOSH* swept over the roof top. Fully alert, she raised herself up on one elbow.

THUD...SWOOSH! Marla counted 10 seconds until the next one. *THUD...SWOOSH!*

"We're being bombed!" she cried and broke into an incredible grin. The coded message tapped on her wall was true! She hooted and hollered. "Yippy! Go to it, guys! Roast the bastards!"

All at once the floor tilted and heaved. The walls shook, and tiny cracks zigzagged across the concrete. Outside the only window too high to reach, she saw trails of black smoke trickling upward. Then greater puffs spurted into the sky. Grey wisps began seeping under her door just as the acrid smell of smoke clogged her nose and throat, and a raging heat invaded her cell. She gagged. Suddenly she realized she was going to be trapped inside this blistering oven. Being eaten alive by the spreading fire before the Black Death could overcome her filled her with terror. She scrambled to her feet and desperately banged on her locked door. As more smoke filled the small room, she choked and shrieked hysterically.

Another *THUD*, and the room listed to one side, as if it were a sinking ship in the last throes of death. Her bed skidded across the stone floor, pinning her against the door. Suddenly the door flung open, and Lutz filled the doorway. His face was bruised, and his lips were chewed to raw meet. He lurched and grabbed her. One more terrific *BANG* and the walls of her room began to crumble. Marla latched on to the big German guard and wildly clung to him.

THUD…THUD…THUD… One after the other. A giant groan leapt up through the floors followed by a great trembling, before the zigzag crack in the wall split wide open. The floor heaved. She screamed as the entire room shifted crazily and sagged. With superhuman strength, Lutz braced his great hulk inside the door frame and sheltered her between the door jambs. Angry fingers of black smoke licked the ceiling. While watching its progress, little beads of sweat studded Lutz's brow. Marla seized up with fits of coughing and desperately smothered them against his chest. More black smoke curled up the hallways. He shoved her down into a crouching position and squatted beside her, taking a tight hold of her as she shook in his arms. In the midst of hell, he stroked her hair and crooned.

Immediately the superstructure gave way. Tremendous thunderings like stampeding buffalo rumbling over the crumbling walls roared in their ears. As if in suspended motion, the top floors collapsed and tumbled downward, crushing the bottom floors and burying them under a cloudburst of suffocating plaster, cement and sand.

Miraculously, when the rubble settled, the prisoners who were still alive sprang out of the ruins. While the Danish Resistance were able to rescue 30 of the 40 secret army chiefs from their breached cells, Gestapo files on Denmark's anti-Nazi movement lay smothered in flames, never to be retrieved again. Smith's raid was a monumental success.

Across the square from Shell House, however, the convent also burned, another victim of human error in a war filled with human error. Confused by the black columns of smoke streaming upwards from the target site and by the fires below, some of the third wave of Mosquitoes dropped their incendiary bombs on St. Joan's instead of on Gestapo Headquarters. Within one minute, both buildings were blazing infernos.

Chapter Thirty

JOACHIM AND TOBIN desperately searched the smoking ruins of the convent for Catherine. Sirens wailed and bells clanged as fire trucks and ambulances converged on the bombed out area. With their bare hands, the men frantically pulled away fallen debris and dug through the burnt mess of broken concrete and splintered wood until their hands were bloody from cuts and scratches and their faces were black with soot. They called out Catherine's name and then listened for her voice, for any human voice that answered.

In St. Joan's churchyard, Joachim found a little girl trapped under a heavy wooden beam. The beam had freakishly blown out from the chapel and landed on her, crushing her leg. At first Joachim thought she was dead as he gently brushed away the clay caking her eyes and nose. But, at his touch, her eyelids fluttered open, and she looked up at him, dazed.

"Everything went black," she told him. "The planes came and everything went black."

"Did it? I'm so sorry," he said, choking on tears caught in his throat. He did not want to upset the child, for she was only one of scores of mutilated victims he was seeing in the wake of the bombing. Around him, the Danes stoically gathered up their dead and wounded, wholly convinced that the air raid was necessary to prevent worse tragedies in the reprisals the Gestapo had planned against their people. But for Joachim, terrible guilt tore at his heart, especially for the children. They were so young to be sacrificed for the mistakes of war. His guilt was also dampening any hope he had of finding his lovely Catherine alive.

He knelt over the little girl with the big brown eyes and fawn-colored curls peeping out between patches of grey ash. "You're going to be fine," he tried to assure her.

"Can you smell it?" she whispered eagerly.

"Smell what?"

"The smell of spring."

He stared at her in amazement. She looked at him so expectantly that he sniffed the air to please her. To his astonishment, it was true. Penetrating the smells of gasoline, smoke and death was the fresh scent of new foliage budding on the beech and linden trees.

"Do you smell it?" she asked again.

He nodded. The little girl smiled and groped for his hand. "Sister Angelique said it was the first day of spring. She took us to the garden to smell..."

"Do you mean you were outside in the garden with Sister Angelique when the planes came?" he interrupted her. Hope gripped him again.

"Yes," the little girl said. Suddenly she grew anxious. "Why did everything go black?"

Joachim didn't know what to tell her. A woman near

them sobbed. The sound of her crying made the little girl aware of other people's voices. They frightened her. "Why is everyone crying and praying?"

She tried to move. "My leg!" she cried out. "Oh, it hurts so much. I want my mummy." Big tears rolled down her cheeks.

"Please, please, you must not try to move again," Joachim warned her.

"I hurt!" she sobbed.

"I know. I know," he said sadly. "But please stay still. You may hurt yourself more." He tried to soothe her. "Someone is coming to get you out. Can you be very brave for me?"

Her little lips quivered in a pout. "I don't know."

"I've found you." He briefly turned away and yelled. "*Help! Over here!*" Then he went on quietly to explain to her, "There are many nuns and children who need help. I'm looking for Sister Angelique. I must find her too. Can you be brave? Can you keep still until someone frees you while I go look for Sister Angelique?"

He stroked her forehead as she looked up at him with complete trust. "I can try," she said.

"That's a good girl. Thank you," he said, playfully ruffling the fawn-colored curls bobbing above her forehead. "Sister Angelique will be very proud of you."

That pleased her and her eyes followed him as he crawled off the pile of rubble and hurriedly dashed to check every bloodied body lying on the abbey grounds.

He found Streicher curled up in a heap by an uprooted birch tree. Joachim rolled him over. A ragged rust splotch stamped the Gestapo colonel's temple. He looked dead. Joachim didn't take time to feel his pulse. Instead, he hollered for Tobin and kept on searching for

Catherine through the scattered injured. A stifled groan caught his ear. He paused and listened. A louder moan, coming from inside the shattered grove of trees.

Crashing through the underbrush looking for the source of the moans, he whisked aside mangled twigs and broken branches. Suddenly he saw her. Her black frock entangled her face and arms, pinning her under a fallen tree that was crushing her pelvis. She was on her side and bareheaded. Next to her lay the nun's wimple, twisted and forgotten.

With tearful thankfulness, he sank down beside her. "Catherine," he whispered hoarsely.

He bent his ear down to her mouth. He thought he heard her say his name. Her lips slightly parted.

"I'm here, darling. You must hold on for me," he begged. "I'm going to get you to Sweden. We are going to make it. Do you hear me? We are going to make it!" A desperate sob choked him. "You must hold on. Please hold on. For me. For us. Oh God, I love you so much!" He broke down.

"*Joachim...*" It was the barest whisper, then Catherine's head went limp against the earth under her.

"*NO!*" he screamed. "*CATHERINE!*" Panic ripped him apart until he realized she had only fainted. He tried to remove the tree laying on top of her. His struggling didn't budge it.

"We'll get this damned thing off of you if it's the last thing I do," he grunted.

Crouching to take the weight off his back, he breathed in slowly several times with tremendous concentration and, when he felt ready, strained to lift the fallen tree. Gradually, with every muscle powered by a sudden surge in his adrenaline, he succeeded in raising the dead weight and heaved it away from Catherine's body. He could see that she was badly hurt and quickly knelt to tuck in the edges of her habit around her body to keep her warm.

"I'm going for help, darling. I'll be right back." And he raced back through the trees to find a stretcher bearer.

In the meantime, Resistance workers had enlisted Tobin to help them look for surviving prisoners buried under the crumbled Gestapo building before Wehrmacht rescue teams arrived. Scurrying over the mounds of fallen mortar, they took advantage of the confusion to pull Danish victims still alive out of the rubble. A bloodied hand waving helplessly between two chunks of concrete wedged together caught Tobin's eye. Scrambling towards it, he hollered, "Over here!" He tried to jar the collapsed masonry loose. Soon other hands joined his. They freed a hole and looked down inside.

Between the remaining section of a door frame huddled the bulky shape of a German guard, barely conscious. The hand he had been waving slipped down from between the cracks and fell listlessly to his side. Sheltered by his body was another body. Tobin shimmied down into the hole for a closer look. Dried blood caked the German's mouth. Barely breathing, he was dying from internal injuries, yet as Tobin passed over him to look at the body he was hiding, the dying man gripped his wrist with amazing strength. For a second they stared at each other. Spit gurgled from the guard's mouth, then his eyes stared into nothingness.

Tobin wrenched his wrist free of the dead man's hold to push his body off of the stooped figure it shielded underneath. When Tobin touched the other body, it trembled. As he gathered his arms around its midsection to hoist it out from under the guard's dead hulk, he realized he was holding a woman.

"Holy shit!" he exclaimed. Without thinking, he told her in English, "I don't know if you can understand me, but you've got to trust me. We have to get you out of here before we can help you. Now, at the count of three, we're going to move slow and easy. Ready?"

Tobin's voicc reached down into Marla's depths. She latched on to the familiar sound. "*Toby...*" Her cracked lips stammered his name in disbelief.

At the pathetic sound of his name, Tobin's heart lurched. "Marla?" he responded incredibly.

She managed a relieved *yes*.

Unshed tears built up through the whole war welled in his eyes. "What are you doing here? What have they done to you?"

"Toby," she managed to whisper. "Get me out of here, but..." she faltered, "promise you won't look at me...*please*."

"Marla, I don't care what you look like. All that matters is you are alive."

Very tenderly he dragged her towards him, and when she was free of the German's body, he gathered her up in his arms and cradled her against his chest. She hid her face in his jacket and clung.

"Oh God," he cried, "I don't understand what you are doing here. Marla, Marla. My dear Marla. I never wanted you to be hurt. Never." Tears shredded the dust and dirt caking his face.

She was so painfully thin he worried about bruising her when he lifted her out of the hole and handed her to one of the men waiting to pull them out. "Be very gentle," he instructed. "We don't know how badly hurt she is."

Marla folded her arms over her face to prevent anyone from looking at her. Once in the sunshine, she buried her face in the stranger's shoulder, not only because she was ashamed to show her tortured face but because her eyes could not immediately adjust to the brightness of the sunlight.

As Tobin followed, the Resistance worker carried her to an ambulance in a nearby back street. Tobin climbed inside first and reached out to receive Marla in his arms. He delicately lowered her onto the stretcher. She continued to hide her face from him.

Her pathetic condition thoroughly shook him. He was unsure of what he could say to help her feel…he stopped himself…to help her feel *what? What do you say to someone who has suffered things you've never experienced?* He hunched down beside her and very gently covered her hand with his. Silently, he tried to give her his strength.

The Resistance workers were anxious to leave. "We're not going without von Daren," Tobin stubbornly insisted. After a few more jumpy moments, Joachim appeared, breathing hard from running.

"I've found Catherine."

"Catherine?" Marla cried out. Forgetting herself, she turned to Joachim's voice. "She's still here?" she croaked.

Joachim nodded, relieved to see Marla had also been rescued. He gulped to catch his breath. "She's badly hurt. We'll have to lay her stretcher across the laps of the people who are sitting."

"No, you won't," Marla said. And then as she sat

up, Joachim, Tobin and the Resistance workers saw her face. She saw the shock mirrored in their eyes and quickly turned away from their pitiful reaction. "I'm not hurt. Use this stretcher," she said as clearly as she could and crawled to the back corner where she sat, deep in the shadows, folded up in a fetal position on the jump seat.

Joachim recovered first. "I'll get Catherine."

Tobin grabbed his arm. "Did you know Marla was a prisoner here before Stevens ordered the raid?"

Joachim looked at him squarely. "I knew."

Tobin's grip hardened and his eyes turned to steel. "When we get back to England, you and I have a score to settle."

"First we have to get back," Joachim said evenly. "Now let me go."

Streicher, who had regained consciousness and was trying to escape, had taken refuge in one of the bombed out buildings bordering the square when he heard English voices heading for the ambulance. Hiding behind a doorway he was able to watch Tobin and von Daren load Marla into the ambulance and overhear their conversation. Von Daren's resurrection from the dead only proved to Streicher that the Baron had always been what he suspected he was, a traitor, but the presence of Christopher Tobin, Marla's former bureau chief—that was unexpected and puzzling. Why didn't he know Marla was a prisoner? If he had known, it didn't sound as if he agreed with the air strike. Both men seemed to have key positions in British Intelligence. He mused, only the Special Operations Executive risked high ranking experienced officers on dangerous field missions. He must let Berlin know. There was still time to capture them. Streicher slunk back into the shadows as von Daren dashed down the alley. Once he passed his hiding place, Streicher waited until Joachim's running footsteps faded before he slipped out and followed him to a parallel street filled with dazed pedestrians aimlessly rushing back and forth. Tossing his SS jacket to the ground, he kicked it out of sight and moved to blend in with the confused survivors.

THE NEXT EVENING, the room in Churchill's London Bunker was unlit save for the stark film being shown. Frozen on screen was an aerial shot of the Gestapo building and the convent burning in the Copenhagen air raid. The quiet voice of Wendal Stevens reported the full implications of the still picture.

"The Gestapo files on Denmark's anti-Nazi movement were totally destroyed. Unfortunately, the price for our success was heavy: 10 allied airmen, 87 children and 27 nuns. In addition to these fatalities, there were scores of injured."

"And the prisoners?" Churchill's gravely voice demanded.

"Thirty of the 40 Danish leaders survived."

"Thirty! I never believed anyone could survive that fool plan," explained Churchill.

"You can always give God the credit," Stevens said dryly.

"What about Lady Catherine and that Franklin woman?"

"They're safe, sir, in Malmo, Sweden."

"Another miracle, Wendal?"

"I believe so, sir."

"When can the king expect to see Lady Catherine?"

"Not for some time. Lady Catherine has suffered crippling injuries."

"Will she walk again."

"The prognosis is guarded at present."

"I see," grunted Churchill. "And Marla Franklin. What's the story on her?"

"She was tortured—ruthlessly, particularly her face—and raped, with the result she's pregnant, sir."

"Good gricf! Do thc woman a favor and get rid of it."

"Very risky, sir. According to Swedish doctors, she's too far along."

"If Sweden won't do it, no country will."

Wendal let the significance of what he had told Churchill sink in before he suggested, "I'd like permission to send Marla to a sanatorium in Switzerland as soon as the hospital in Malmo agrees to release her. Lady Catherine has already been flown back to a special rehabilitation hospital in Scotland."

"Of course. Make sure they both get the best of care. It's the least we can do."

Churchill fell into thoughtful silence. When he spoke again, his voice was barely audible. "Eighty-seven children, 27 nuns and 10 allied airmen, you say."

"That's correct."

He sighed. "Our gratitude seems so little when they have paid so much."

Chapter Thirty One

Thursday, August 9th, 1945

WENDAL STEVENS personally flew over to debrief Marla in Sweden, in the Roman Catholic hospital that sheltered her until the end of the war in Europe. For some reason, she could not bring herself to tell him about Streicher's revelation that his London contact had been code-named *RUFUS*. Before she could condemn him, she needed to hear the truth from his lips herself. Stevens suspected she was not telling him everything but assumed it was the unspeakable tortures she was leaving out.

Christopher Tobin never left her side, particularly after the doctors told her she was carrying a baby. To his surprise, she never asked for an abortion. He read that as a hopeful sign and immediately formed plans to marry her. After so many years of living on the edge of danger, he was unprepared for the rush of feelings he felt toward her. He wanted to give her and her baby a home, to protect her from prying busy-bodies, to shower her with gifts with anything she wanted and to be a father to her baby, to have a family, their family—for him suddenly finding a state of normalcy mattered.

Yet, she not only resisted his comfort, she withdrew from everyone. Once she heard Catherine would survive and was being flown back to Scotland, she seemed to give up.

The tenacity that had sustained Tobin through the war now carried him through her prolonged period of self-pity. Close to her due date, however, his patience began running thin. She didn't seem to understand how much he needed her to need him. He decided to draw her out of the shadowed corner of her private room where she persisted in staying whenever he visited.

"The war is over, Marla. You're going to have a baby soon. You have to think of the little life inside you." He hoisted himself up on her bed while he talked to her dim shape in the dark corner. Ever since she had revealed her face in the ambulance to him, she had refused to expose herself again. Frequently, she sat in the corner for long hours rocking in silence, completely unresponsive, no matter what he talked about. He wondered if this was going to be another one-sided session.

"It's time to move on," he ventured. "I want to take care of you, you and your baby, if you'll let me."

Silence blanketed the corner where she sat. He waited, letting her think about what he had said. The rocker scraped against the terrazzo floor, but he couldn't see whether she had stood up or was beginning her rocking.

"By some miracle," came her disembodied voice, "we survived the bombing of Guernica together…you and I. Remember how I babbled on?"

He couldn't make out if she were talking to him or

the wall behind her, but he nodded, hoping she was looking at him. It was the first encouraging effort she had made.

"I had never opened up to anyone like that before. I was so thankful we were alive, so thankful to find someone who understood how much my mother had shamed me. That's when I knew I loved you, but when I tried to show you my love, you turned away."

Tobin bowed his head in regret. "Things are different now. I want to take care of you and your baby."

"Instead you recruited me," she droned on as if he had never spoken. "The bodies of the children…It was so easy, wasn't it? I wanted to please you, and I hated Hitler."

"We were at war. I had no choice. Neither did you."

"I became a whore. Your whore. The only way I could live with myself was to believe that someday you would love me."

His heart quickened. "If there had been any other way... "

"And at *Amanita*," she continued, "it was business as usual. You still could not show me any love. Do you know how dirty that made me feel?"

"I explained... "

She plunged on, not listening to him. "Except for Ulo. For one brief wonderful time, he took away the emptiness."

Tobin squirmed and clenched his jaw. He didn't like the direction she was taking but at least she was talking.

"I could dream about a normal life and feel loved, honestly loved. If this baby were his, how happy I would be!"

He heard the scraping sound again.

"Ulo Rorvig. I'm going to find the place where the SS executed him and put up a memorial. If he has any family, I'm going to find them too."

"I'll help you," Tobin said.

"*NO!*" Marla spat out the word. Her anger startled him. "I don't want your help. And I sure as hell don't want your pity!"

"I tried to protect you, Marla. You have to believe that."

She laughed, a coarse dry outburst. "I survived being what you trained me to be. A whore. That's protection to be proud of."

"You survived, didn't you?"

"Oh yeah, I survived." An ugly bitterness crept into her tone. "And d'ya know what? Streicher didn't rape me. He filled his emptiness with me. And I lived for it. I was his sexual slave."

It was a lie. Only she knew Streicher had ravaged her with his torture but never raped her. But she told no one about Waldemar Richter. Their time together was their secret, and it would die with her. If Streicher had not seized them and shot Richter, she would have happily stayed Richter's captive without being chained for the duration of the war. It was easier than thinking, easier than longing for Ulo, easier than hurting and dying. Not until Streicher shot him did she realize Richter loved her in his strange way as much as Ulo had.

Tobin steeled himself against her spite and emphasized, "You survived. That's all that matters."

"No, Toby, that's not all that matters. He filled my emptiness too. In his mad way, he claimed me. That's why he destroyed my looks. So no other man could want me."

"Marla, I don't care how you look!" Tobin cried out in anguish. "I love you."

"Do you?" she said shuffling forward from the shadows, taunting him. "Look at me and tell me you love me."

He stared at her and swallowed. Her face was covered in hideous bumps of flesh. One eye sagged. Raw blisters that refused to heal lined her brows where her eyebrows used to be. She cupped her enlarged belly with her hands and stepped closer to him.

When she saw his deep down revulsion and pain, she pitied him and knew she could not live with his oppressive sense of debt. More than anything she wanted to tackle life on her own terms. Honestly and equally. She needed someone like Ulo, whom she knew could have accepted her imperfection no matter what it was. He loved the person, not the face, and not the body.

"Go, Tobin. Go. I don't need you," she said and retreated back into the shadows of the corner. He could hear the sound of the rocker scraping the floor and the creaking as she settled her swollen body into the seat, then her rocking began—slow and steady, like an incantation that numbed his senses.

"There *is* one thing you could do, Toby. For Catherine and me. And Ulo. Find out if Sir Isaac betrayed *Project Amanita*."

"Sir Isaac?" A fire flickered in the blacks of his eyes. "Whatever are you talking about?"

"Colonel Streicher found out the code name of the London traitor from the Abwehr's files. *RUFUS*. He said it was *RUFUS*."

"That's the information you've been keeping from Stevens?"

"Yes. I wanted to interrogate Sir Isaac myself. I wanted him to look in my face and tell me the truth, but I'm not going back to London. Stevens is sending me to a sanatorium in Switzerland. Will you do it?"

It was his turn to remain silent.

From the corner's shadowy protection that obscured her face and figure, her voice sounded faraway, beyond the realm of the here and now, yet her hate penetrated. "If he betrayed us, terminate him, Toby. I want him dead. Can you do that for us?"

"I can. If what you say is true, he's a dead man," he said. Tobin stared at her in the darkness and felt nothing. She didn't want him. There was no reason to stay. "Well Marla, I guess this is the end of the road for us."

"I guess it is."

"I wish you well."

"And I you, Toby." She added nothing further, so he slipped off her bed and quietly left the room. She watched him leave with tears streaming down her face. She was so tired of feeling alone. Except for Richter's life inside her, she would have gladly given up with one bullet to the brain.

Chapter Thirty Two

Wednesday, August 15th, 1945

A SUMMER BREEZE offering the first relief in two days of clammy weather rustled the swag curtains draping the open French doors of the bedroom filled with priceless but opulent antiques. Through the opening, moonlight shed a wide path across an imperial Brussels carpet, caught the foot of a four-poster mahogany bed at the other end of the room and lit up a prismatic pool on top of red satin sheets. Their iridescent surface shimmied over the molded shape of bodies spooning underneath. As they rolled and bunched up in mounts that rose and fell, their muffled groans and sighs scaled the sticky night air, heavy with the scent of lavender and English woodland primrose.

When their tossing and turning eventually stilled, Sir Isaac's Scottish accent clearly declared, "You're my most exciting lover."

The red satin sheets were folded back from the edge of the bed as a man's pair of legs slipped out. He planted his feet on the rich carpet and began moving towards an antique chair opposite the bed where he picked up a satin lounging robe and wrapped it around himself. Tying the cord, he turned toward the open French doors to savor the refreshing breeze. The reflections of the moon illuminated his face.

He walked over to an elaborate well-stocked bar and looked over the bottles. Finally he chose Regal scotch and opened it.

"Can I pour you one?"

Sir Isaac's head slid out from under the lustrous sheets as he raised himself into a sitting position and settled himself against a luxurious backrest of satin pillows. His chest was bare. "Aye," he answered.

With his back to Sir Isaac, his lover poured the scotch three fingers high into two brandy glasses.

"Have you ever loved anyone, Tobin?" Sir Isaac asked him.

"Yes," Tobin admitted while inconspicuously slipping a cyanide capsule out from the breast pocket of his robe. He broke the capsule's contents into Sir Isaac's drink before carefully stirring it. "A woman."

"A woman! That's difficult to believe. Was it as good with her as it's been with me?"

"I can't answer that. We've never slept together." Tobin dropped two ice cubes into each drink and stirred them again.

Sir Isaac considered him with renewed interest. "Why not? It would look better in your records if you were married…and protect us."

Tobin smiled as he slowly turned around carrying both glasses in his hands and started towards Sir Isaac. "I agree. I've already proposed."

"Well laddie, congratulations."

"You're a little premature. She turned me down."

Sir Isaac was genuinely surprised. He considered Tobin a prize catch. "Go on."

"More to the point, she doesn't trust me. She doesn't trust any man. And I can't convince her I would make a good father for her baby."

"Good grief!" Sir Isaac exclaimed. "You can't mean Marla! You would marry her and father that Nazi bastard she's carrying?"

"If she would let me—yes." As Tobin passed Sir Isaac's drink over to him, he asked, "Tell me...I've wondered for some time...how did you get the code name *RUFUS*?"

"Churchill picked it. I reminded him of a cartoon character he enjoyed. A walrus."

"And you named me *SEAGULL*. Why?"

Sir Isaac's eyes narrowed, then he smiled slyly. "A seagull is a scavenger. Isn't that what you are?"

"I see. A play on words." Locking eyes with him, Tobin held up his glass and said, "Here's to you."

"Come on, laddie. You can do better than that. How long have we been working together?"

"Ten years."

"Aye, ten years. Let's see. How about this old Scotch toast?

Here's to you, as good as you are,
And here's to me, as bad as I am;
But as good as you are,
And as bad as I am,
I am as good as you are,
As bad as I am."

Tobin nodded. "I'll drink to that." He watched Sir Isaac take a swig of his scotch as he sipped his own.

"With the war over," Tobin said crossing over to

the easy chair beside the bed and comfortably sitting himself down, "our civilian intelligence agencies are being disbanded and the old boys' network is back smelling old closets. I think it's time we cleaned ours."

Sir Isaac took a bigger swig of his scotch. "Now laddie, you've got nothing to worry about."

Tobin smiled. "I know. I pulled your blackmail file on me years ago."

"What do you mean?" Sir Isaac demanded in surprise while trying to massage his throat, which was beginning to burn. He belted down the rest of the scotch and extended the empty glass to Tobin. "How about another..."

Suddenly his fingers let go and the glass fell to the carpet. He grabbed his throat. Horrible rattling sprang from it. His eyes bulged in disbelief.

Tobin sat unmoved, watching him. "You thought you recruited me, but it was I who recruited you. We knew what you were. And you have served us well. Better than I intended."

He savored a mouthful of his drink. "A fine scotch. Very fine." He went on. "Marla says Streicher told her *RUFUS* betrayed both sides to the Reds. She thinks that's you."

Sir Isaac, aware he was dying, weakly shook his head in final denial. Tobin rose from the chair and stood over him. "I promised Marla I would take care of you." He leaned down and whispered in Sir Isaac's face, "*And I am.*"

Then he stood upright again and laughed cynically. "So many fools played into my hands. Especially Holbak." He indulged in some more self-satisfaction. "After you got him out, did you know he sent all his secret notes to an associate, a physicist, in Moscow? He has probably helped advance Russian atomic research 10 years."

Sir Isaac gagged on his spit.

Ignoring him, Tobin answered his own question. "Of course you didn't. We were too clever for you." He looked down on Sir Isaac, whose eyes stared up into his, into nothingness. His mouth gaped open. Froth leaked out one side. Tobin raised his glass in a toast. "To victory!" he cried.

Having slipped out of rigid control, he let the smug smile loose, then a tinkle of laughter bubbled from his lips before he burst into a flood of mad laughter.

Hidden in the bushes outside the French doors, Streicher used this moment to sneak away. He had spotted Tobin in London and followed him to Sir Isaac's expecting he would lead him to his prey. He had, but the traitor had not been Sir Isaac. It had been Tobin. He could have executed him immediately. The Luger in his hand had a silencer. No one would have heard. It would have been easy for him to make a clean break and escape to Argentina as he originally planned. His secret account in Switzerland made him a very rich man. There was poetic justice in that, but it wasn't enough, he decided. The police would treat Tobin's death, and Sir Isaac's, as a bizarre murder while the only one who knew Tobin was actually a traitor was Streicher. He wanted Tobin's treachery exposed, especially to Marla. He owed her that much, so he had to find another way to reveal his betrayal and kill him. For now, he had the advantage: Tobin didn't know he had been uncovered. Beyond that, Streicher understood madness. He and Tobin were an even match.

Chapter Thirty Three

April 1946

SHE FELT ABANDONED to the damned. The nightmare was always the same, before the sudden flash of bright light awoke her. Marla instinctively pulled the covers up over her bandaged face. "What do you think you're doing?" she raged from under the sheets. "Get those damned shades down."

Her baby started crying. "Take her away. She hates me. I can't stand the crying."

A strange woman's voice ignored her outburst. "It's morning, young lady. Time to get up. Your baby's hungry."

"You feed her," Marla ordered petulantly from under the sheets.

"That's it," said this new voice. "Your self-pity party has gone on long enough."

"What do you know?"

The woman yanked the covers off Marla. "You haven't even given this wee tyke a fair chance. Now sit up."

Marla blinked at the light and, with difficulty,

focused on this person who dared defy her. "Who are you?"

"Your nanny."

"My what?"

The blurry image cleared. A little bit of a woman with steel grey hair and flashing green eyes stood before her. "You heard me," she said.

"I never asked for a nanny."

"Wendal Stevens did. You have exhausted the staff at the sanatorium with your mean moods, but now I'm here. I will be nursing you through your recovery and looking after your baby."

She plumped the pillows behind Marla's head. "Now sit up so you can feed her."

"When you pull the shades down."

"That's not negotiable. If you don't want to know the difference between day and night, your baby has to learn the difference or she'll never sleep through the night."

"Why should she have it any better than me?"

The nanny glared. Marla realized she was acting childish but a hatefulness within her didn't want to give it up. The baby's cry turned into an angry wailing. "Okay. Okay. Anything to stop her bloody crying."

The nanny lifted the baby from her carriage and settled her into Marla's arms. She talked soothingly to the baby while she brushed her lips with the nipple of the bottle. Her little arms and legs stopped flailing as she grabbed on. "She's settled," she told Marla and gestured for Marla to hold the bottle. Marla took it, and the room filled with the sound of the baby sucking.

"She's a beautiful little girl. What's her name?" the nanny asked.

"Caitlin."

"How lovely. That's Gaelic for Catherine I believe."

"Yes."

Marla didn't ask the woman her name. She didn't want to know it. And she ignored the nanny's efforts for a friendly chat.

No one cared how the war was won or what was lost to win it. What did Gertie's hang nail or the price of butter have to do with what she suffered? Why would anyone think that washing diapers and preparing baby formulas would heal her scars and erase her nightmares? No one understood. No one wanted to understand. She was abandoned to the damned.

Voiceless screams struggled for release. She felt old, too old, as if her soul had travelled a million years through the galaxy, lost and afraid, and was finally too weary of the journey and the things she had seen to keep on going from one empty hope to another. She did not fit in anywhere. There was too much to absorb, too much to resolve, too much hate, too much disillusionment, and too much recrimination. What was normal for other people was not normal for her. She had come back from hell only to find a different hell awaiting her.

After Tobin left her in Sweden, she had begged Wendal Stevens to secret her away to some place where no one could find her. He moved her to Switzerland, to a remote sanatorium in the Alps. At Meiringen, she underwent plastic surgery to smooth out the grotesque pits ground into her cheeks by Streicher's cigarette butts. Little could be done for the less visible mutilations to her feet and body.

Stevens had hoped the peaceful scenery surrounding the sanatorium and the birth of her baby would heal her spirit. For a time, she savored her secret: Richter had not violated her body, and she had no desire to destroy the decent part of Richter she carried inside her. Her body amazed her. Through all the horror, it had clung to that little fetus. She was proud of that. Richter in death had granted her the last chance to experience the greatest sexual miracle of womanhood—the birth of a baby.

But, when the time came for delivery, her mind could not bear even joyous pain. Being strapped into the stirrups brought back all the terror. Each contraction became a cruel torture revisited. Mercifully, the doctors performed a caesarean section. Once the umbilical cord was cut, however, her bond to motherhood seemed severed. When she awoke, she felt no flood of motherly love spilling over to the baby she bore.

Instead, she saw a tiny creature screaming, a stranger demanding the subjection of her will to it. Her newborn's cries convinced Marla it was her disfigured face that terrified the infant. Each wail reinforced her mistaken belief that the baby was rejecting her. It never occurred to her that the baby was miserable with colic. Out of this frustrated motherhood spawned a new resentment, which festered into more self-hatred, dark and uncommunicative. The doctors feared she would withdraw so far into herself that she could never be saved from the impregnable black hole of madness.

And so the middle-of-the-night visitations from hell, the wandering in and out of Streicher's fiendish face in her dreams, of his demonic voice hissing forth from the gaping jaws of death, which grew and multiplied into chanting hooded sunken-eyed masks of satanic laughter, the confusion of haunting echoes tearing at her, reminding her of her own fragile immortality—they all congealed with the infant's real-life wails until she could not tell them apart. The scars that scourged her soul robbed her baby of a natural mother. She had nothing left with which to nurture this little one born of her body. Only an inner will to survive prevailed.

As she was burping Caitlin, Stevens walked in. "Well, if it isn't my two favorite girls," he said cheerfully.

Through her bandages, Marla glared at him. "Get rid of this woman. I don't want her."

The nanny and he exchanged silent messages. He bent over and lifted Caitlin up. She gave him a delighted grin. "Well thank-you. At least you're glad to see me." He played with her for a moment before he handed her over to the nanny and suggested she return with Caitlin to the nursery.

He put his arm around Marla. "Come over to the rocker, Marla. We have to talk."

"We certainly do," she agreed.

He lead her to the rocking chair. She shuddered as he helped her into it. "Please pull down the shades."

"I have some papers with me I want you to read. You need the light."

"This isn't working, Wendal," she cried. "Before I conceived the baby I felt empty. Now that she's here, I feel trapped. I can't breathe. I can't think. I can't sleep. Maybe this is what I did to my mother. Maybe this is why she gave me up."

"When are you going to face you need professional help?"

"No, I need to go back to work."

"And when you have to interview someone face-to-face, how will you feel?"

"The doctors say this last operation completely restored my face."

"But not your mind. What about Caitlin?"

She was silent. He changed the subject. "I have news."

"About Catherine?"

"Her too."

"Tell me about Catherine first."

"The operations were successful. She will walk normally, eventually, but she will never have children."

Marla winced. "It's not fair, is it?"

"I told her you had refused to see anyone, but she told me to tell you that she and Joachim want you and the baby to join them when Intrepid races in the Epsom Derby."

"Intrepid?" Her voice lifted, then it dropped. "That's rotten blackmail."

"Your face should be completely healed by then. After the race, they will be leaving for Canada. It's your last chance to see them before they go into hiding," Stevens reminded her.

"Hiding?"

"Yes. Remember Joachim and Catherine have been declared dead. The Official Secrets Act prevents us from revealing their activities for British Intelligence during the war, so it makes greater sense to give them new identities and a new location."

"But Catherine loves Guild Oaks and her horses." A thought struck her. "Has she lost her inheritance because she has been declared dead?"

"No. We've sold most of her father's art treasures and Rushmore House for a handsome sum. That's being laundered back to her through an investment foundation funded by her estate, Guild Oaks and the stables she specifically left to King George."

Marla looked down at her hands. "Wendal, now I know what I have to do."

He knew what she was going to say next. He had seen it coming for months.

"Caitlin needs the love of parents who really want her. She belongs with Catherine and Joachim. They will give her what I never can. Family roots. I'm a tumbleweed. Ruined goods. Don't you see?" she pleaded.

"I can't give Caitlin the normal life she deserves. I belong to a world that has no place in it for her. I need to be absorbed in work again…to be with other agents who have known the hell of war and survived…to feel the rush of adrenaline through my veins…to have challenging problems to solve and exciting ideas to explore. To write again.

"I know. I'm doing to Caitlin what my mother did to me. I guess we weren't cut out for motherhood. I feel badly about that, and I have tried, Wendal. For months, I've tried. Gawd! How I've tried! But it's not working."

"You're right," Stevens said. "It's not working."

A sigh of relief engulfed Marla. At least Wendal understood.

"We do it your way on one condition," he said. "You have to hand over the baby to Catherine yourself."

She fidgeted. He and Catherine were really forcing her out of hiding. For Caitlin, she could do it. She no longer had any choice. "Agreed." But she couldn't face making specific arrangements right now. "You said you had other news."

"Sir Isaac's dead. He died last August."

"He's dead?" She was astonished. "Why didn't you tell me when it happened?"

"You weren't in any shape to handle it."

"How did it happen?"

"An apparent suicide. He took an L-pill." Instead of a dreadful sadness, Stevens was shocked to see sudden excitement fill Marla's eyes.

Toby, she was thinking. *He did it!* "Wendal, I want to go outside. Can we sit on the terrace?"

How long had he been trying to get her to go outside? What had happened here? Her switch in behavior totally baffled Stevens but his professional curiosity followed her bidding.

There was no one on the terrace, and Marla rushed to the rail and breathed in the sweet fresh air. The blooming Edelweiss in the terrace garden caught her attention. She focused on its puffy parasols so like the plump amanita she had once wanted to pick in Spain. Each flower was like a cluster of frothy toadstools or cauliflower buttons erupting out of plants with large pointed leaves. They looked good enough to eat—delightful, delectable, deceptive and deadly. Wild poisonous mushrooms. The amanita fungi. Her jaw flinched. *Damn Sir Isaac*!

Wendal noticed her sudden tension. "Do you want to tell me about it?"

"The amanita," she said in a faraway voice.

"Sir Isaac's project?"

"No, the poisonous mushroom. How deceptive and very deadly it is. How very deadly... " she said with low-pitched venom.

Observing this sudden shift in mood, Stevens decided to treat her very carefully. "Let's sit down and talk."

He waited. Slips of bright sunshine dappled his fine grey hair and the ridge of his nose, splashing his pale skin with the first blushes of alpine color. She moved slowly, as if in a trance. He directed her to the lounge seat while he took the arm chair fashioned from local wood.

"He betrayed Catherine," Marla blurted out suddenly. "Sir Isaac betrayed us all," she said with bitter disgust. "I'm glad he's dead. I wanted to see his face for myself, then I would havc known for sure if he was the traitor."

The thrust of her revelation startled Stevens. "You think Sir Isaac was *Project Amanita's* traitor! Why, for goodness sake?"

"He was the Abwehr's contact. Streicher admitted it when he decided to execute me. NO," she checked herself. "He didn't admit it. He *revealed* it. *RUFUS* was the Germans' London contact. That was Sir Isaac's code name, you know. *RUFUS*!" She spat it out.

"*RUFUS, RUFUS, RUFUS.*" The crazy ditty she had made up in prison while waiting to be executed came spilling out in a rush of anguish. "*RUFUS...RUFUS... RUFUS... is an imbecile and a poop is...he cuts off your leg and says, `What a bag!' RUFUS, the poop, is a gag.*" Her shoulders sagged. "I wanted to kill him myself," she moaned.

"Marla, is this what you held back in your debriefing?"

She nodded miserably.

"Good God!" Stevens shook his head in disbelief. "Marla, why didn't you tell me? I could have saved you so much..." His eyes bled. "Marla," he said quietly and evenly, "Sir Isaac was never the traitor. He was framed."

"Streicher said..."

"I know what Streicher said," he interrupted. "I'm sure *RUFUS* was the name of the Germans' London contact precisely to point the finger at him. Think for a moment. If you were Sir Isaac, could you destroy the very thing that you gave your life to build?"

Confusion entered Marla's voice. "I asked myself that..." She sat upright. "But if it wasn't Sir Isaac, then who betrayed us? Who betrayed *Project Amanita*?"

"Most likely the same person who murdered Sir Isaac," Stevens replied.

"You said it was suicide. He took an L-pill."

"I said apparent suicide. I'm convinced he was murdered."

Marla's heart throbbed wildly. She had told Toby. She gripped her head in her hands and began rocking.

"We've been investigating the betrayal of *Amanita* agents since *ICEBERG's* death. We've come across one piece of evidence that helps isolate the traitor."

"What's that?"

"We have tracked down the prisoners from the SS unit who hanged *ICEBERG*. Streicher was their commander. The radio man said he received a coded message giving *ICEBERG's* exact position."

"Colonel Streicher? *He killed Ulo!*" The impact of Wendal's information ripped open an old wound like the jagged edge of a tin can tearing away flesh from bone.

"Yes," he confirmed. "The same man who tortured you. I then went back over all our debriefing files with surviving *Amanita* agents and resistance groups that worked with them. Something of interest popped up in the Denmark file. Mme. Thirsted sponsored a group of Spanish Civil War veterans before the war. I pursued that and tracked down some of the underground leaders who knew her. Understand she's a national martyr. I had to be very careful with my questioning, but I unearthed something quite unexpected."

"What?" Wendal had her total attention.

"Mme. Thirsted was the leader of a secret cell of Communist Resistance Fighters known as the *Red Orchestra*. They were mainly formed from a band of Spanish Civil War vets."

"Frankly, Wendal, out of this whole damned mess, that makes the most sense."

Wendal squinted. "I don't understand."

"Were you there—in Spain, I mean?"

"No, I wasn't."

"Well, I was."

"I know."

"But you don't know what it was like. Toby and I gave the League of Nations evidence that Hitler and Mussolini were providing Franco and his Fascist rebels with military advisors, trained reinforcements, air cover and their best arms technology and equipment. Yet we, and the Spanish people's plea for help, were ignored. It was a bitter pill to swallow, let me tell you. The only real help I saw the fighting Republicans get was from the Communists. Though the weapons Russia sent were antiquated issue and far too few to be effective, it was the Communist leaders who recruited and trained the International Brigade. They taught the Republicans how to use what they had to fight with ably. They taught how to harass Hitler's hordes with guerrilla terrorism. Yes, Spanish Civil War vets joining the *Red Orchestra* bunch to resist Nazis invading their homeland makes a lot of sense to me. Hell, if I hadn't been so damned American, I might have been tempted to turn Communist myself."

"Is that how Tobin felt?"

"Toby...?" Marla thought back and shrugged. "Who

knows?" Then she slowly nodded. "Maybe—maybe. We had hard evidence. We could prove Nazi Germany was breaking the Nonintervention Pact in Spain. The League of Nations knew the truth, yet they still continued to do nothing to discipline Hitler. How do you accept something like that? We felt betrayed—just as the Spanish people felt betrayed."

She scoffed. "Where were their good neighbors when they really needed them? Double talk does not save the man choking to death, you know," she added with a dry laugh.

Now Stevens wished he had sent Marla a carbon copy of his report to Churchill. "Well, there's no point thinking Stalin was a hero in that civil fight," he told her. "The Madrid government emptied its gold treasury and secretly delivered it to Moscow to pay for all those outdated and useless weapons you praised Russia for sending to Spain. Who betrayed whom, eh? Believe me, the Communists were not the Republicans' benefactors either."

Marla gripped her stomach. She suddenly felt sick. "Is nothing we believe in sacred?"

Wendal ignored the question and went on. "No doubt Mme. Thirsted was disillusioned with the Allies for precisely that reason," he admitted. "The point is, however, she was killed deliberately, and the Underground leaders I talked to believe the *Red Orchestra* assassinated her solely to make her the public martyr she became. Her final act drew the Underground and the Danish people into one giant fist of resistance against the Nazi occupation forces."

He paused. "Did you know, after *Iceberg* was hung, Sir Isaac asked me to help him track down the traitor?"

Marla shook her head.

Wendal went on. "By this time, he was sure the traitor was a triple agent, for the political and diplomatic damage was extensive. The Americans had lost confidence in *Amanita's* capabilities. They were refusing to co-operate with the British team of refugee scientists. Eventually, Churchill persuaded Roosevelt at the Quebec Conference in Canada to sign a formal agreement assuring both powers that they would not use atomic weapons against each other, that they would not use atomic weaponry without the other's consent, and that they would not give their shared knowledge on nuclear development to a third party, which obviously meant the Soviet Union. When the string of arrests and breakdowns in *Amanita's* espionage networks continued, the Americans—in spite of this formal agreement—did not trust the British. In reality, the ones who most benefited from this bickering were the Russians."

"How?" Marla asked.

"The Americans' distrust of the British strengthened Stalin's bargaining position at Yalta. He got the part of conquered Europe he wanted from the Allies. Roosevelt didn't rely on Churchill's warning that Josef Stalin was treacherous because he had lost faith in British Intelligence. Now we're plunged into a cold war with the Soviet Union exactly as Churchill predicted we would be."

"And if the intelligence networks of the two western super powers remain suspicious of each other, Stalin benefits again," Marla interjected.

"I'm afraid so."

"What about Catherine?" Marla asked.

"There is no doubt in my mind that Stalin wanted

Churchill out of the picture. Catherine's capture would have ruined him politically." Wendal stopped to clear his throat.

"That was my conclusion too," Marla commented dryly, "once Streicher made me realize the traitor had to be a triple agent working for Moscow."

"It has to be," Wendal agreed. "Since Roosevelt wanted Stalin's help to fight the Japanese, he could be duped into an agreeable bargain, but Churchill—*NEVAH!* What better way to throw out his influence at the negotiating table than to discredit him? The possibility that our traitor is a deep-cover Red agent makes perfect sense."

"But how does all this tie in to Sir Isaac's death?"

"I think there's a connection between Mme. Thirstead's death, *Iceberg's* execution and Sir Isaac's murder."

Marla looked doubtful.

"Sir Isaac's death creates more hostility between British and American Intelligence," Wendal argued. "It could be the traitor's intent to prevent these two formidable organizations from joining forces in an international program of post-war intelligence."

"Does the Special Operations Executive blame the Americans for Sir Isaac's death?"

"No, of course not. But, that's immaterial because SOE and my own unit of Allied Command Intelligence are being dismantled. We amateurs are being moved out and the original establishment brought back in, along with their petty pre-war rivalries and power struggles."

"I see," said Marla. "They didn't mind the volunteer organizations assuming all the risk in the heat of war—we were convenient scapegoats for operations that went sour—but now that the war is over, they want both their power back and the glory of *our* accomplishments."

"That's the way it looks."

"How nice!" she said sarcastically. "And what is the British Secret Service doing about Sir Isaac's murder?"

"The obvious," said Wendal. "Nothing. *Project Amanita's* failure is an embarrassment to them. Sir Isaac's death conveniently closes the chapter on that perplexing problem. He can't point the finger at anyone, and he can't answer any questions. His murder becomes an unsolved mystery that teases but does not reveal uncomfortable secrets."

"So it is up to us."

"You've got it. Now think back. Who knew *Iceberg's* position on the mountain, Marla?"

"Sir Isaac, Tobin and, of course, Catherine and me."

"Sir Isaac is dead. That leaves three possibilities. Who knew you kept your own special file of drawings?"

Marla stopped rocking and lifted her head. "Other than Catherine, Toby was the only one. When we worked together in Spain, I drew a picture of him. *He knew.*"

Suddenly she buried her head in her hands and began weeping. "I killed Sir Isaac."

Stevens shook his head. "Marla…"

She cut him off. "You don't understand. I told Tobin. I told him Sir Isaac was the traitor, and I asked him to terminate him because I wouldn't be going back to London to do it myself."

Now everything fits, thought Stevens.

He rose up from the chair and gathered Marla up in his arms. "You didn't kill Sir Isaac. From the very beginning Tobin sat him up for execution if he succeeded with his mission. We've all been pawns in his game plan."

All at once Marla gripped Stevens' sleeve. "*Streicher!*" she cried. "Did the Resistance ever find his body after the raid?"

"Von Daren saw him when he was looking for Catherine. He thought he was dead, but the Resistance never found his body."

"He said he would get revenge. He vowed to *kill RUFUS* when he found him."

"Well now, maybe we have two suspects." Stevens stroked her hair.

The thrum of a humming bird hovering over the floral bed twanged in the quiet like a violinist tuning his strings. "Marla," he said softly, "I have an idea that might trap them both. Are you game?"

Marla looked past him to the mountain peaks beyond. In the vivid blue sky, an eagle soared, free and alone, sailing above the pistachio slopes. For a fleeting moment she envied the eagle, so majestic in his natural habitat. She looked across the valley's tablespread of lush green peppered with gingerbread chalets and flowered gardens that sprayed the air with their alpine perfumes.

This was the sanctuary I longed for, she mused. *And I didn't even know it.* Now she would have to leave it.

Chapter Thirty Four

June 1946

A SCENT OF ROSES filled her nostrils. It was a hot June day, and the air over Epsom Downs was melting like warm wax. Looking through it, Marla became dazzled with the shimmering green turf beyond which hazy images of hedges and ponds seemed to float with dreamy grace. Over the fairgrounds poured a human sea, and above it, like a ship's pennants, fluttered gaily colored flags. As far as her eye could see, cluttered assortments of rainbow cones arched skyward while below, refreshment stands—mainly selling cockles and mussels—and bookies' booths waved between the bulk of tents and stalls offering palm reading and fortune telling.

Crowds, waiting to see the spectacle of the Royal Cavalcade and the Epsom Derby Race, picnicked for free on the common land beside the finishing stretch. The track for the three-year-old thoroughbreds competing on the mile-and-a-half course started with a climb, which rose 150 feet in the first half before gradually turning at Tottenham Corner into a downhill stretch to the straightaway and then finished on a considerable rise to the winning post. It was demanding of any champion, a test for the greatest heart.

Marla drew her eyes back to the serene face of her one true friend. She hadn't expected this likeness, as if she were seeing into the past and confronting herself. She focused on Catherine's flawless skin and glowing English complexion and resisted the need to finger her own cheeks, just newly healed—a habit she had developed when the scars pitted her face.

Catherine's eyes, as clear as the blue sky above, peered back at her. Marla could see her concern. She knew the subtle cosmetic changes were only meant to disguise the famous pianist's features, not to mimic her own. But, it was the switch from flaxen to dark hair and her pencilled brows, not the blunt cut, that created the astonishing likeness, she decided. Catherine's ethereal beauty had been transformed into a sensual vulnerability that reached out and touched her with such familiarity that she longed to run from it.

Catherine's hip injury had required two operations, and after the last one she had lapsed into a lingering coma. Periodic flashes of the convent exploding penetrated the blackness. "*Not the children!*" she cried out over and over again.

Joachim von Daren grieved with her, ashamed that his homeland was the instrument of war that caused such suffering and human loss. Eventually their love consoled them, and the healing process began. For the duration of Catherine's recuperation, they stayed at a secret hospital base north of Edinburgh in Scotland. When she and Joachim were married at the base in a quiet civil ceremony, Wendal Stevens was their only attendant.

Marla's absence disappointed them, but Wendal explained she was still suffering through her own hell and couldn't cope with public exposure. Shortly afterward, the couple took on new identities and made plans to settle in Canada where they would breed their own world class trotters to race in North America. They developed simple disguises to modify their appearances, believing that a look-alike suggestion to their former selves was easier to explain and less suspicious than undergoing drastic plastic surgery.

But when the cosmetician and hair stylist introduced Catherine to herself in the mirror, she stared, numb with shock. The face staring back at her was Marla's, not hers. In awe, she traced her finger around the image she saw in the reflection. Smooth and unflawed. The likeness hurt. Marla's face would never be creamy smooth like this again. She gazed deeply into the sad eyes fixed on her own. Since their lives were moving in separate directions, was this strange resemblance to Marla Fate's cruel joke?

Even without planning what they would wear in advance, their outfits, magnificent picture hats angled to hide their faces along with the traditional white gloves made a harmonious fashion statement. Marla was dressed in a silk suit of heather lavender, while Catherine had picked a pale green tailored dress.

The silence between them spread. Marla couldn't find the words. Stevens shouldn't have insisted on their seeing each other even if it was their last chance to be together. It was just too difficult. A letter would have been fine, a letter along with her special gift.

Marla's daughter stirred in her arms. Catherine's gaze fell to the sweet smelling baby Marla held. She was dressed in a pretty pink smock and wrapped in a crocheted white blanket. Marla had gathered her wispy fleece of blonde hair and brushed it into one big curl on top of her head.

"From the ashes of sin, the seed of innocence," Catherine observed in a barely audible voice, yet her words cut into Marla like a stonemason's chisel, perfectly clean and straight, exposing the truth without understanding it.

Catherine dissolved in delight as the baby's tiny fingers explored her hand. The ache for a baby of her own stretched and pushed, like a birth contraction expelling empty air, disappointing yet crushing in its futile effort. "May I hold her?" she asked wistfully.

Marla nodded, not trusting her voice, and handed the yawning baby over to Catherine who instinctively cradled her against her breast and gently rocked her in her arms.

"She's so beautiful. What is she now...nine months?"

"Ten. She was born September 4th."

"The 4th! Why your birthday is on the 4th too! April 4th."

"So it is."

Envy niggled Marla. This woman, for whom everything—including mothering—came so easily, was picking up her life as if the war had never happened while the war had left a black ugly scar across Marla's soul. Every time she looked into a mirror she was bitterly reminded of its deception. She slept with the war. She woke with the war. It was difficult to tell when, or if, the war would ever end for her. But Catherine seemed spared from her torment. She embraced peace and was ready to move on. The difference between them also made it easier for Marla to carry out her decision. She wasted no words and no sentiment.

"I want you to have my baby, Catherine."

She spoke so matter-of-factly, Catherine wasn't sure she had heard her correctly. "What did you say?"

"She'll be safe with you."

Catherine's eyes widened. "What are you talking about? No one is going to harm your baby."

Marla enunciated her words more pointedly. "I want you to keep my baby, Catherine."

"No, no, you don't, Marla." The mirrored vision of herself pleaded. "You're hurt and angry. If you would just hand over your hate to God and let Him carry it, you would have the peace of mind you so desperately seek. He suffers with you. Let Him comfort you."

Marla sighed with exasperation. "I know that's what you believe, Catherine, but I don't. I can't. We were betrayed. I have to find the traitor, and I can't take my baby with me."

"I'll look after her then, until you come for her."

"It won't work. She needs roots and two parents who want her and will love her, like you and Joachim. If you take her, we can't stay in touch. It's too risky. There are those obsessed with retribution, and you are bound by the Secrecy Act to hide what really happened."

"I don't want to lose you again." A tear loomed in the corner of Catherine's eye.

Marla didn't want to deal with the nostalgia rising within her but compassion prompted her. "You won't," she said softly. "You'll have my baby. She can take the place of all the babies you'll never have."

"Oh God!" moaned Catherine. "You've sacrificed

so much for me. I can't take any more. It's not fair."

"What's not fair?" asked a tall man coming between them. His rugged lean face bore little resemblance to the golden SS boy Marla had first seen in Berlin. Concern puckered Joachim's wide brows and squinted the corners of his very blue eyes. A handlebar mustache, newly grown in and surprisingly reddish in contrast to his dyed brown hair, captured the air of a proud ex-Highlander rather than a man hiding his Germanic roots. He was dressed in the traditional black top hat and tails for the Epsom Derby race.

"The war," she answered him. "No war is fair."

Joachim's jaw tightened, and his brow twitched. She sensed his nightmare was the same as hers. She waited. He said nothing, but his eyes locked on hers, searching through her muteness to the things unsaid. He saw her hate. His pupils flinched, acknowledging her torment and what she had to do. His silent approval gave Marla courage.

He bent over the bundle in his wife's arms and crooked his little finger inside the curl of the baby's chubby fist. She gripped it and yawned again. For a moment, intensely curious violet eyes stared up at him.

"How golden her hair is!" he marvelled, lightly stroking it.

"I named her Caitlin," Marla said.

"That's Gaelic for Catherine," Catherine explained to Joachim.

Catherine, watching Joachim pretend to play a tug of war with his finger in the baby's grasp, was filled with an overwhelming love for Marla. Out of evil's torment, the lonely tumbleweed had left behind her a tiny root that preserved their immortality and forever bound their kindred spirits together. Marla and Caitlin and Joachim…they were all that was left of her world now. Her eyes brimmed, and tears choked her voice. "She will always be Caitlin to us too, Marla."

Joachim glanced up and gently pulled his finger out of the Caitlin's grip. "I can hear the band. The race will be starting soon. Let's move up to the front and see what's going on."

Below the grandstand, the dignitaries' boxes overlooked the track. Wendal had reserved one allotted to VIPs for Marla's and Catherine's reunion at Intrepid's race in the Epsom Derby. Joachim guided both women over to their railside box seats.

"Well, little one, you can't go to sleep for your first horse race," Catherine whispered to the yawning bundle in her arms. Joachim tweaked Caitlin's chubby cheeks. The baby rewarded him with a delighted smile. Marla moved slightly away, separating herself from the little happy family, and anxiously scanned the crowds for some sight of Wendal. He was late, and that was worrying her.

As Catherine watched the royal procession coming down the track, a moment of guilt nudged her. King George had taken charge of the management of Guild Oaks—the stable and the orphanage. Under the king's colors, her father's horses would continue to breed and race with the best under old George's training,. and Nellie would carry on running the orphanage for abandoned refugee children. These responsibilities were rightfully hers, but King George had insisted it was the least he could do for the service she had rendered her country and him. Her parents would want her to be happy, and if beginning a new life with Joachim provided her with that happiness, then she was to do it with his blessing and never look back. She would liked to have said good-bye to Nellie and old George, but since they had already mourned for her when she was reported captured and presumed dead, it would be cruel to put them through it again. Otherwise, there was no one else who would be really affected by her survival except... she felt a stab of regret... Decency's colt, Intrepid. He was racing for his majesty today, not for her. Nonetheless, she could still feel proud that it was her choice of breeding that had produced Decency's champion line.

A red-coated band of Welsh Guardsmen in great bearskin hats led the royal carriage with the king and queen and two princesses inside into the center circle of the arena. Strains of the martial band playing *Men of Harlech* and *The Ash Grove* lifted Catherine into breathless memories, carrying her back to Decency's triumphant race for the Breeder's Cup. As the royal party stepped onto center stage, a cluster of dignitaries swarmed forward, engulfing the king, his elegant queen and precious daughters in a wave of official greetings. The tide swept back, and the royal party settled into their seats.

"Catherine, would you mind terribly if I went over to the walking ring to watch Intrepid parade in front of the fans?"

Marla's question drew Catherine's attention away from the royal gathering. "That's a splendid idea," she said. "We'll go with you."

Joachim frowned. "No, we won't, Catherine. From what you've told me about this horse, your hats won't fool him. He'll know your smells. He could get excited and that will bring attention to us. Marla, I suggest you stay here too."

Catherine glanced at him and back at Marla. A silent message passed between the two women. "Sorry, Joachim," said Marla. "I don't expect you to understand, but Intrepid will race better if he knows Catherine and I are here."

Joachim firmly objected. "We promised Stevens we would stay as inconspicuous as possible. You're asking us to break his orders."

His warning tone told Marla Wendal had included Joachim in his plan to bait Tobin and Streicher. "What orders? I don't see Stevens here," she countered. "Do you see him?"

Her snippy remark revealed to Joachim how worried she was about Stevens. He suddenly understood her true intent, but before he could reverse his position, she went on. "When Catherine's Decency foaled Intrepid, I was there. Catherine let me name him. He's the last connection we have to the only family I've ever known. I at least have to see him. Right, Catherine?"

Catherine nodded in agreement. "Let her go, Joachim."

He groaned. "This doesn't feel right."

"For me."

He looked into his wife's resolute eyes and sighed. "I surrender. Go, Marla, but be careful," he warned.

"Count on it," she promised. As she was about to melt into the crowd outside their VIP box, she turned back to Catherine, "I'll tell Intrepid you're watching him too."

If Marla hadn't spotted old George leading Intrepid out of the paddock to the walking ring where the horses parade in front of the fans before they are led to the starting gate, she suddenly realized she couldn't identify Intrepid. He was one of four blood bays racing in the Derby, and they all looked exceedingly handsome.

"Intrepid," she called softly.

The bay's ears perked straight up. He pressed his whole weight against the trainer, trying to force him to turn. The jockey quickly tightened his grip on the reins, and Intrepid stiffened his body ready to rear. Old George searched the faces lining the rail, looking for the voice he and Intrepid knew.

A lady in a lilac dress and huge picture hat motioned to him. Old George peered at the striking woman. "Marla? Marla Franklin? Is that you?" He felt the horse trembling with excitement beside him.

She nodded.

"Well, come here, lassie, and give me a hug."

She rushed into his arms. He rocked her in a bear hold and almost knocked her hat off. "I didn't know whether I would ever see you again. Nellie and I miss Catherine terribly."

Marla nodded. "I know. How have you both been keeping?"

"Oh, we're fine. The children and the horses don't give us a chance to get old." He pulled away and looked at her intently. "Big hat. You hiding from someone, lassie."

"It's the fashion."

"Aye. And I'm King George. No matter. Can you go back with us to Guild Oaks after the race?"

"I wish I could, but I've got another assignment."

"Well then, you'd better calm this colt down, or we can kiss the race good-bye."

"Now that would never do," she laughed. "Do you remember me, fella?" she asked Intrepid when George handed her the horse's lead.

The magnificent thoroughbred nuzzled her as she petted the velvet softness of his nose. He playfully tried to grab her sleeve.

Marla laughed. "You rascal! You *do* remember." She patted his neck. "You must behave…for Catherine and me."

His finely cut ears twitched listening to her.

"Yes," she pulled his head down to whisper in his ear so George wouldn't hear her. "Catherine's here too. We're both here to watch you race. You must win, Intrepid. Do you hear me? You must win, just like your mom did."

The bay's luminous brown eyes seemed to soak Marla up. She rested her face against his nose in complete trust and stroked the sides of his sleek head. His muscles rippled and melted as her scent filled his flared nostrils. They stood quietly clasped, letting the past meld with the present. When Marla stepped back, Intrepid was so settled down, he seemed almost sedated. He bowed his head inviting her to rub the diamond plane on his high forehead between his brows.

She stroked the spot in a gentle circular motion. "We love you, Intrepid. Race your best for us. Now go with George and meet your fans."

She stood back, and the beautiful bay raised his head. His expressive eyes fixed on her. She sensed he understood it was good-bye.

"Good luck, you guys." She handed the lead back to George.

"You take care of yourself, Marla, and any time

you want to visit us, you know you're always welcome."

"I know. Give my love to Nellie."

"I will." George lightly yanked the lead to turn the horse around. Intrepid followed him, but his tail plumed and swished, missing Marla but brushing the man who had silently inched up beside her. The brisk lashing toppled the man's hat. He bent down to pick it up.

"I think you just got flicked by the Epsom winner," Marla chuckled.

"He better be because I just wagered a fortune on him."

The man's voice froze her heart.

Tobin adjusted his top hat and faced Marla. "I took a chance you would come to the race. Is Catherine here too?"

"Yes." Marla could see no point in lying.

His eyes drifted over her face. "You look marvellous."

"I was lucky. The cosmetic surgery worked."

"And your baby?"

"I don't know. I gave her up for adoption." She told part lie and part truth.

Tobin looked genuinely pained. "Did you really have to do that? I was hoping you had overcome your bitterness. I still believe we could make a very happy family together."

Marla steeled the fury that gripped her, but she couldn't quite mask the coldness from her reply. "Not in this world."

Tobin stood with his hands in his pockets and watched George hand over Intrepid to his jockey as horse and rider joined the parade to the starting gate. "You never drew Intrepid. I've often wondered why."

"How would you know what I've drawn?" she asked quietly.

Too late he realized his slip.

"Only someone who has been through my private files would know what sketches I've done," she pressed. "You stole my drawing of Catherine, didn't you, Toby? You're the traitor. It was never Sir Isaac, was it?"

"Brilliant, Marla. I'm proud of you."

Marla shuddered involuntarily. The voice from her nightmares suddenly showed himself and moved out from behind shrubbery bordering the paddock to face Tobin. A sports jacket draped his arm, concealing the semi-automatic cavalry pistol he held, but the snout of the Polish Radom, which was covered with a silencer, was clearly visible to Marla. Streicher was pointing the gun directly at Tobin's heart.

Tobin stiffened with the wariness of a trapped animal.

"Take your hands out of your pockets, Tobin... slowly, one at a time," Streicher ordered. He watched Tobin clear his hands. "Now walk up to me and turn around," he commanded.

Tobin followed his instruction with deliberate indolence.

"I followed him to Sir Isaac's estate because I thought he was leading me to the traitor," Streicher told her as he frisked Tobin for a weapon. He pulled out a Liberator .45 from a holster slung under Tobin's jacket. "An assassinator's favorite firearm," he observed, pocketing it, and went on as if he hadn't paused.

"The French doors were open. I heard them."

Tobin's jaw clenched.

"He killed Sir Isaac, poisoned him actually, and

while he was dying, Tobin admitted everything. I missed an opportunity for some good pornography footage. They were lovers, you know."

That news stunned Marla. She couldn't picture it, but it did explain why Tobin had persistently brushed her off. To learn that his rejection was based on his own sexual orientation meant it had nothing to do with her and everything to do with him. An invisible smile burst between her shoulder blades. *The truth will set you free.*

"Don't do anything foolish, Tobin. Or you either, Streicher," commanded Stevens, who unexpectedly appeared to Marla's right. He was positioned so that one bullet from his gun would pass through the heads of both men at the same time. "Marla, go back to the box. The race is about to start."

Marla glanced around. The walking ring was cleared of horses. People were heading to the grandstand, ignoring the drama by the paddock. Stevens' men, dressed as stewards, were converging on the trapped pair.

Tobin grunted. Marla turned back at the sound. His eyes glazed and his knees buckled. Streicher grabbed him and swerved, hoisting him up like a shield, to face Stevens and the men surrounding him. Blood dribbled out the corner of Tobin's slack mouth.

"Don't come any closer or Marla gets it next," he warned Stevens. He pointed his pistol at Marla's head.

"Remove your hat," Streicher ordered her.

In the background, Marla could hear the bugle calling the Epsom Derby race. She stood rooted to the ground.

"*Now!*" he roared.

Invisible arms held her back.

The veins on Streicher's forehead bulged. "I've done what I came to do. We were betrayed. I am the executioner," he said, pointing the gun menacingly at her from behind Tobin's body.

Stevens inclined his head signalling Marla to follow his wishes. She slowly removed the large picture hat that hid her features and raised her face to Streicher proudly. He stared, incredulously. "They've restored your beauty."

In that moment of unguarded wonder, it was impossible to read what went through his demented mind, but he suddenly turned the gun on himself and fired. Marla screamed, but no sound cleared her mouth. Her hands sprang to her throat, plucking at the horror strangling her voice. She watched in dazed silence as Streicher and Tobin slumped to the ground together. Their pools of blood merged.

From the grandstand, the loudspeaker blared. *The horses are at the gate. The 1946 Derby Race is about to begin.*

Stevens motioned to his men while hastily issuing instructions. He rushed up to Marla and wrapped her in his arms. "It's all over, Marla. You're safe now."

"*Safe?*" she repeated in an incredulous whisper against his chest.

"Safe," he affirmed.

She nestled into the haven of his arms and lost herself to the wonderful sense of coming home. She finally felt safe. Wendal Stevens made her feel safe.

And they're off! Aloha, Sea Nymph and La Pomme d'Amour get away first. Razor's Edge is on the inside. Intrepid is far back in the pack.

The announcer's voice broke into her cozy refuge. *Intrepid!* She drew away from Wendal's comfortable embrace. "We've forgotten Catherine and Joachim. We've got to get back to them!"

"Of course. Come on." He gripped her hand, and they made a mad dash for the grandstand. When they breathlessly reached their private box, the horses were just rounding the first turn. Marla rushed up to Catherine. "How's Intrepid doing?"

She pointed. "He's lost his cover. He's falling back."

"Oh no!" Marla shouted at the top of her lungs, "Come on, Intrepid! You can do it! Dig in! Go, boy, go!"

Startled by Marla's voice, Caitlin raised her head from Catherine's shoulder and looked nervously about.

"Oh, I'm sorry, Caitlin, but this is a horse race. See!" Marla pointed down to the track for her. "See the horse down there. Cheer for Intrepid, Caitlin. We want him to win."

Caitlin bounced in Catherine's arms, sensing everyone's excitement. Fully alert now, she became intrigued with all the sights below and the horses streaking around the track.

"What took you so long?" Catherine asked. "And where's your hat?"

Marla touched her hair and face and laughed. "I lost it."

Joachim looked over her shoulder to Stevens and silently raised one brow in question.

Stevens mouthed, "We got them."

Joachim breathed a sigh of relief.

As they pass in front of the stands, Sea Nymph is in front. Battling her for the lead is Razor's Edge. They are neck and neck.

Catherine's voice rose in excitement. "Come on!" she urged Intrepid. "Change gears, boy. You can take the field from the outside the same as your mother did."

As if tuned into her voice, Intrepid's ears pricked forward, and he strode out. Little by little he gained ground around the backstretch. Marla's eyes stayed glued to the greased horse flying past the half, the momentum of her mind racing with him, faster and faster, reeling information around and around chasing an idea. She tugged Wendal's sleeve.

"I remember you said you had to isolate Dr. Holbak at the Manhattan Project after we got him out."

"That's right. After all the lives sacrificed to protect him and his knowledge, the silly old fool mailed a full report of his findings to a Russian associate in Moscow. Those damned notes probably helped the Reds advance their atomic research by 10 years."

"Didn't anyone try to quarantine him at *Amanita*?"

Wendal's eyes widened. "Shit, no!"

Intrepid's coming up on the outside! Now seventh. Now sixth. Now fifth. Now fourth. He's winging up with amazing speed!

Catherine turned Caitlin around and cushioned her with her arms, one braced underneath like a bench and the other slung around her waist. "Go, boy, go!" she chanted in the baby's ear.

Caitlin's enormous eyes ogled with excitement. She patted Catherine's arm and squealed. Catherine laughed joyfully. "Watch the horses, Caitlin. Out there!" She pointed to them again. "See? Say *GO… GO… GO…!*" Caitlin clapped her hands in glee.

Marla grabbed Wendal's arm. "Do you see what I'm getting at? They didn't have to race us because they were already learning everything our atomic scientists were doing from Tobin!"

Marla's chest suddenly caved in. She coughed a dry short spurt. Then, without warning, she burst into hysterical laughter. "Oh God! It's too funny. A real RED joke!"

Her breath came too rapidly and she choked, sputtering through her teeth. "Damn it! Damn it! Damn it! Does it ever end?"

Wendal gripped her shoulder and drew her to him in the tight shelter of his arms.

What a race we are seeing here! Muscle and motion in perfect harmony.

Glancing over, Catherine saw them together and gratefully smiled. The idea of Wendal and Marla together relieved her nagging guilt.

"Marla," Wendal spoke softly in her ear, "this isn't the time to tell you, but I don't know when I'll have another chance. The Americans have asked me to head up a special investigations team for the Allied Tribunal at the Nuremberg Trials. I leave tonight."

She stared at him. Catherine, Caitlin and Joachim were leaving tonight. Wendal was leaving. She was going to be *alone*! The race, the excitement disintegrated before her eyes and she was filled with a terrible emptiness.

"I want you to be part of my team, Marla. Do you feel ready to go with me?"

"Ready? *READY?*" She rested her forehead against his chest and nodded so he wouldn't see the crazy tears flooding her eyes.

"Good," he said massaging her shoulders.

Intrepid is refusing to quit.

Catherine jabbed Marla with her elbow. Her eyes danced.

"Isn't he magnificent?" Her voice trembled with pride.

Marla impulsively hugged her. "He certainly has his mother's heart and his father's speed."

This horse holds nothing back. Intrepid's inching up to the front. Now he's nip and tuck with Razor's Edge. Sea Nymph can't keep up. She's falling back.

They're coming to the finish.Intrepid is lunging for the lead. Can he do it? He's getting up! YES!! He's IN FRONT!! He's done it! He's beaten Razor's Edge. INTREPID HAS WON!!!

In the railside box, their cheers ripped the air. Marla turned to Catherine and her baby daughter still clapping in Catherine's arms and gathered them up in a tight embrace. Suddenly, through the veil of tears streaming down her face, Marla smiled. A joyous smile. For that one glorious moment, nothing separated them.

About the Author

Bonnie Toews is an award-winning business journalist whose articles have appeared in Canadian magazines and newspapers. This is her first novel.